Lilly looked do
guilty in the sand, as realization hit her.

"Oh my God, Que! Are you okay?"

She examined Que's head and neck checking for injuries, with rapid authority. A small goose egg already formed just above her right temple. A tiny cut opened in her eyebrow, from her broken sunglasses now laying in the sand, causing a small bead of blood to well up.

Used to the recklessness of her son and his friends regarding the sport, Lilly turned, gearing up for an impressive tongue lashing to teenagers.

"What in the hell…" she bellowed, turning around and smacking her face into the sweaty muscular chest of a massive redhead. Refusing to let the fourteen-inch height difference and the hundred and sixty pounds of additional weight intimidate her, Lilly balled her small fists on her hips, shifted her gaze up, and narrowed her eyes.

"What in the hell is the matter with you? You're on a crowded beach with a bunch of young children and families. You're a grown-ass man. Can't you catch a football?" When he stared down at her in fascinated disbelief, she continued. "There is a wide-open park just over there," she said, stabbing her finger in the general vicinity. "Maybe you and your little friends"—she looked over at all the massive men in his group, but continued undaunted—"should go over there and pull your heads out of your asses."

Praise for Jeny Heckman and...

THE SEA ARCHER, winner of the "Best in Category" Chanticleer International Book Awards:

"The plot [of *THE SEA ARCHER*] is realistic and the romance is strong in this suspenseful fantasy romance."
~*InD'Tale Magazine*

~

"The mythology and fantasy combined [in *THE SEA ARCHER*] were extraordinarily woven together with the present, the past, the suspense, romance and the thrill of a mystery."

~*Quirky K., Netgalley*

~*~

Books by Jeny Heckman
published by The Wild Rose Press, Inc.
THE SEA ARCHER
THE WARRIOR'S PROGENY
DANCING THROUGH TEARS

The Warrior's Progeny

by

Jeny Heckman

The Heaven & Earth Series, Book 2

The Warrior's Progeny

Cover Art by *Debbie Taylor*

The Wild Rose Press, Inc.
PO Box 708
Adams Basin, NY 14410-0708
Visit us at www.thewildrosepress.com

Publishing History
First Fantasy Rose Edition, 2020
Trade Paperback ISBN 978-1-5092-3219-2
Digital ISBN 978-1-5092-3220-8

The Heaven & Earth Series, Book 2
Published in the United States of America

Dedication

For my children, Paisley and Charlie:
my amazing warriors,
and the two biggest chambers of my heart

Please Note:

There is a Glossary on page 407 for names and terms you may find unfamiliar.

Prologue

Zeus's eyes shimmered as he stumbled to a narrow stone bench, drained by an unknown force. He stood unblinking as he scanned the sky and the small window closing in on the mortal, modern world. The ocean spray, once his brother, Poseidon, floated downward and into oblivion. Only his salty scent lingered now. Placing an elbow on his knee, he supported his head with a broad hand and let his thoughts turn toward Apollo, who now joined his uncle in the Elysium. His beautiful angel-haired boy, instruments now unmoving, beautiful voice now still. The ruler closed his eyes and could still hear his music, the essence of his son.

Guttural screams bellowed from the depths below as something stripped the two descending gods of their remaining power. A hideous light and energy erupted from the bowels of Tartarus, suffusing pain into the center of Zeus's chest, punching the breath from him, and causing him to gasp. He looked down at Apollo and Poseidon's combined residual power sizzling through the veins in his arms, like the robust thunderbolts he wielded. When the final force permeated through him, he realized his brother and son now lay mortal. Zeus opened his eyes doubting the impossible reality, but the suspended drops of light and water still burned their truth into his mind, taunting him like a bully.

The mighty ruler gazed out over the vista. Summer blossomed all around him. The first two gods had sacrificed, so the prophecy of a dark age, and the return of his father Cronus to power, could be forestalled. A peacock walked by him in haughty reproach, feathers fanned in a rich display. The animal stopped to ponder the giant lilies spread open near his head, with derision. Walking to the next flower, the bird sparked an idea in Zeus's mind of what the prophecy required next of the ruler.

The lily flower and peacock, sacred to his wife, Hera, fit her persona with pinpoint precision. Proud, adorned, and beautiful, Hera even had the glorious explosion of color and temperament. The goddess also had the uncanny ability to be remarkable in seduction, then fantastic in her jealous fury and indifference.

Zeus stood and paced, muttering his conclusions to the empty garden, in front of the cave he used as his temporary dwelling.

"We've built the foundation with Poseidon and Apollo. Thus, we begin the destruction of this damned prophecy and its claim of death to the Olympians. We must support that sacrifice with a fiery devotion to me and to the family. Yes, Hera, should be next to provide stability to our fractured kingdom, but who to send with her? We need strategy, but also power—someone who will fight with determination."

Ares came to mind, but he tried to shake the notion loose. However, when the vision of his son returned, he let it develop. Ares, Violent and Untamed War, full of righteous ire, fighting for his mother, and his family. Once more the ruler of Olympus gazed across Earth but only saw Ares, holding up the small victory god, Nike, like a trophy.

"Yes, he bears it often enough," Zeus said with bitterness of the young god's bravado and resumed his seat. "However, Fear, Terror, and Discord also ride in his chariot."

"That's because they provide me comfort. That's more than you could claim, Father."

Zeus turned to examine the newcomer, oblivious to the fact that through his thoughts he summoned both Ares and his wife to the small garden.

"What happened?" Hera demanded without preamble, nor did she wait for a reply before continuing. "Are you very weak? Are you hurt?"

"On the contrary. All is well," he replied in sad resignation and moved to stand, as she clutched at his arm.

"You must not stay here, Zeus, the Okapnose will discover you," Hera darted a glance to the underbrush, fearing the black serpentine bonds lurked nearby waiting to fulfill the prophecy by capturing and dragging them all into the darkness of Tartarus.

In dismissal, Zeus showed her his back and turned to Ares. "We require strength now and resolve within our family to be victorious. You must be next." He raised a hand for his son to clasp with grandiosity.

"And you," he nodded toward Hera, "will also go. For Ares is strength, and you, my majestic, are the family nucleus. You will now play your part through your descendants in fulfilling the prophecy to save us all."

"But it is too soon?" she stated with confusion, then eyed her husband with suspicion, perhaps wondering if he only tried to flatter her to get rid of her.

"Who will help you?"

"What happened with Poseidon and Apollo?" Ares asked, speaking over his mother.

"They were victorious." Zeus replied to his son and ignored his wife. "The challenge is in the mortal descendants. In their time, the population is plentiful, and are reluctant to believe. Much slower than I foresaw."

"Are they fools?" Ares asked with agitation, before accusing his ruler, "or did you not send warning?"

"Of course he sent warning," Themis, the Oracle of Delphi responded as she suddenly appeared in the clearing, with Athena. "The mortals are not of our golden age—they put little significance on dreams, discounting them as figments of their imagination."

"They resist seeing beyond their own emotions," Athena confirmed.

"How can we combat their ignorance?" Hera spat, appearing threatened by the all-knowing prophetess and Zeus's daughter.

"Poseidon could communicate with his spawn, but the time was brief and for the man, Finn, and his woman, Raven, enlightenment did not come as much as we hoped," Themis responded. "We'll only be able to do that twice more, with Hades and Zeus." The ruler paced in agitation.

"Perhaps if Athena goes…" Hera suggested. Zeus knew his wife wished to rid herself of his preferred child, rather than using strategy toward their predicament.

"Strategy," Zeus murmured to himself, considering. "No, for now, we need overwhelming strength." He looked at Athena with affection, causing Hera's jaw to tighten. His daughter picked up where the ruler left off.

"Father's right. Poseidon and Apollo sacrificed themselves to establish the infrastructure of our stand and our fight against the threat of Cronus. He waits for our power to weaken. The mortals require strength in the family, belief and trust in their potential soul mates. That is Marriage." Athena looked at Hera. "They also need belief in one another to accept each of their fates, and our own."

"Athena will remain for decisive counsel," Zeus stated again with finality, before glancing at his son.

Ares bristled. He shared the burden of war with his sister. Zeus knew that the brazen god understood Athena was the favored, and why not, for she came birthed from his own head, in full battle regalia. Ares, known for his physical and untamed nature, was too impulsive. The mortals heralded Athena for her strategic mind, and calm, measured demeanor. Where the warrior desired violence at any provocation, the strategist only fought for honor and cause. Athena, the virgin and virtuous, and Ares, the passionate, ruthless, adulterer. However, no one could deny his bravery, and daring devotion, to his family, regardless of how misguided it could sometimes be. Zeus knew his son must understand he had reason to choose him now.

"Go forth in haste. We've exposed ourselves too long, and the Okapnose will soon discover us, bind us, and cast us into Tartarus." He divided his remarks to each of them. "If Cronus captures just one of our number, we are all vanquished." He turned to Themis and gave a nod.

"Feral ire and violence to tame," the Oracle eyed Ares, her voice a powerful monotone. "For only then can we remain." She looked to Hera. "Quell your covetousness that causes one to demand too much of another. If you prevail, you may save another."

Themis walked to the sheer wall of the cliff. A filmy material pooled in her eyes then spilled across her temples until it formed into a band tied around her skull. She lowered her hand and cracked a rib bone from her body that sharpened into a sword of ruthless virtuosity and directed it to the sky, chanting the prophecy.

Those that now rule will rue a day; When those they command refuse to pray.

An old, most powerful foe will find a way; To escape the bonds of yesterday.

Continuing to chant out the prophecy, she dipped her head toward the ground where Poseidon and Apollo lay deep beneath its surface, then raised it to Zeus. Even with her eyes bound, the ruler felt the weight of her unyielding stare, as she continued.

There they will remain for as long as time rules; Until the last bead of their blood is collected and cooled.

The outcome they fear, fate could yet reject; If the children of tomorrow's lives intersect.

And in their quest, three discoveries must be found; Or the deities will face the Moirai and be cut to the underground.

First, god and mortal alike, there's a weakness to conquer; And only from there, a key the next children may conjure.

Second, something gods have naught to know; Selflessness, devotion and love-eternal the hardest to sow.

The final discovery for this quest to take place; Is when all the children are in the same time and same space.

She continued to chant as the clouds parted and a beam of sunlight illuminated mother and son, like a beacon. Athena's head swiveled as she scanned for danger. Themis chanted louder, as she spoke the final words of the prophecy.

And though their time of rule may end; Full assimilation of immortal blood, this Oracle will send.

For even if one pure drop remains; Ascending the steps, Olympians may again reign.

Silence reverberated off the nearby cliffs, and when Zeus looked again, mother and son, Oracle and daughter, had vanished, and once more he stood alone.

****

The ground above Cronus's head trembled, as electricity and sparks flew across the room, and black power exploded into his body. He convulsed, his arms and legs flailing out. His chest heaved forward, and light permeated from it. Where Zeus felt the agonizing pain of his brother and son's separation from immortal life, Cronus savored it with a rich indulgence.

"So, Poseidon is gone, forevermore," his deep graveled baritone announced to the tense room. Echoes of residual power continued to snap off the walls.

He moved his foot with absentmindedness, and the Okapnose that incarcerated him pooled at his feet, swirled around in a thick, acrid fog, then vanished. Perplexed, his eyes traveled up his body to his hands. One by one, the black bonds of his captivity released him—albeit still in the bowels of Hell, but no longer shackled.

7

"How can this be?"

A whisper scurried across the stone and up his form until it breathed with seduction in his ear. "Desire grew within you in its purest form. It breeds with Retribution, eager to mate with Victory and with this new enlightenment, a key unlocked to guide you. For I am Deep Abyss and I am the key."

"Mighty Tartarus?" Cronus dropped to his knees. "Will you aid me in this endeavor and tell me what I need to know."

"You are a Titan god, son of my nephew. You stand on Deep Abyss. It is here you sought to exact your revenge, so here, you must also seek your answers."

The whisper circled Cronus, who spun in the room, no longer able to contain him. "Tartarus…I implore your aid." Excited, Cronus tried to collect his thoughts. "What is this new power?"

"The Oracle, Themis, intercepted the prophecy before its completion and altered its conclusion. It means the prophecy and its conclusion has yet to set. She has empowered the descendants of your children and their children's children. If their descendants are successful in their quest, they will destroy the prophecy which you created."

"What can I do?"

"You conjured Fates to do your bidding, did you not?"

"Yes, through Retribution and Misery."

"You also conjured others and laid them in the Moirai mask when you manipulated The One and sent them all to the modern world. You brought Death to the sea creature and Doubt, Insecurity, and Pride to Apollo and Poseidon's spawn. Those gods, now mortal, rest in the Elysium. However, they set the foundation for defeat of your prophecy. The Elysium does not allow their omnipotent power within its realm. So, upon their arrival, it transferred—split between the mighty Zeus and the old Titan king."

"I have their power? Can I now leave you, Tartarus?"

"You contain a measure of their power, as does Zeus. Though your bonds are no more, you must find your way from the Abyss to Daylight. In the labyrinths of the Underworld, who let no man pass once the end of days has begun, your journey will be difficult."

"Then what good is this power?"

"Each god will transition to the Elysium where only you and Zeus will gain their endowment. If their spawn succeed, they will thwart you. If any quest is not complete, you will control the fate of all. As your power grows, so will your knowledge to solve this labyrinth."

The Okapnose once more circled Cronus, and he eyed them with suspicion. "I dreamed of this raven smoke, these bands. What is it that held me captive?"

"The Okapnose holds you captive no more. They also lie in the Fates' mask, created that insidious eve of the prophecy. They are conjured from your mind and seek to do your bidding—to destroy as you do. It is *the* deadliest plague left, but not the only. It can control aspects of weakness, of which the mortals and gods alike have many. It entraps not only the body, but the mind as well. You now have limited access to it, without being aware you've been making use of it, and even now, it searches for the Olympians on your behalf."

"If it finds them?"

"On this plane, you will hold Victory. On the other? You will capture and control the weak mind."

"If I find my way to the light of Day," Cronus said, grinning, "will it reinstate my personal power?"

"Yes, in measure, with time."

"And Zeus will grow weaker with each effort?" the old king decided, then asked, "And what of these descendants? How can I stop them?"

"Zeus's power will grow as your own until the last," Tartarus corrected. "You may use the Primordials, the essences you laid within the Moirai's mask, but I warn you their strength, like yours, is weak and new in that world. As you strengthen, so may they, yet only in measure, with time."

"I can send Primordials to weaken their resolve. Does Zeus know of this?"

"You may, yet only those conjured within purest Desire. Again, I caution you, Zeus may do the same. He learns this only now, from Themis," Tartarus stated.

"I can affect the modern world," Cronus said with conviction to the room, then turned. "Whom did Zeus send next?"

"His lady Hera, and the warrior Ares, to set strength within the unions of the mortal seekers, now that the foundation is set. You have until the Immaculate Conjunction, when all affiliated planets intersect, beginning with your Saturn to Zeus's Jupiter."

And with that, Cronus stood alone, standing in disbelief a moment, before a slow smile feathered across his ancient face. He analyzed Tartarus's words. Freed. However, he would need to find his way from the Abyss. No small feat. Hera would cross next, the jealous Libra, and Ares, the hardheaded Ram.

"Jealousy! Envy! Rage, Pride, and Arrogance, come! For I have a vocation for you."

Chapter One

"Well, shit."

Colton Stone dropped his tattered leather satchel onto the cool marble entryway of his new home. He scanned the space and doorways to adjoining rooms. The hours and expense did not escape his attention. The complete grandeur the interior designer had created left the comfortable and modest home he grew up in deep in the dust. Soon, she'd be arriving to explain things, twitch, and hang on him, so he toed off his shoes, and stepped over his luggage toward the expansive kitchen.

As in the manner of most men, he opened the refrigerator and peered inside. A six-pack of his favorite IPA winked out at him. Being a football hero *did* have its perks sometimes. The invasive and ridiculous questions about his favorite this or that resulted in the inviting, frosty bottles lined up in a row in front of him. He snatched two of the beers and cantilevering one cap against the other, popped off a bottle cap before replacing the unopened bottle back into the refrigerator. Taking a long thirst-quenching swallow, he sighed over the long afternoon of dozens of sports journalists asking him how he felt about leaving Texas, the fans seeking autographs, and the long, dismal flight to Seattle. Large French patio doors to his left looked encouraging, so Colt padded the distance, eager to see the view and feel the night's cool embrace.

As he neared the threshold, he glanced to the right and considered the two heavy, ancient looking spears crossed at their centers, and the great Trojan helmet protruding from the wall. The weapons, given to him by his late grandfather, illustrated his gladiator roots. Pausing long enough to look at them, he experienced the familiar tingle throughout his body. Colt glanced around the rest of the room and discovered the interior designer had taken his warrior theme to heart. The displays, cold and ruthless, gleamed under the spotlights. With heightened expectation, he turned to open the double doors and stepped out onto the veranda, and the beautiful view of glossy Lake Sammamish.

Someone had mowed the lawn, and the aroma of fresh cut grass permeated his nostrils. Colt tipped the bottle to his mouth and smirked. Well, if he had to trade his home, life, and career from the dusty heat of Houston, Texas, he could do worse than this serene landscape of deep blues and greens.

An extensive, lagoon style swimming pool, filled with inviting aquamarine water, consumed the center of his new backyard. A fountain, composed on a rock formation, babbled into it. Golden-light appeared from somewhere in the granite-tiled depths of the pool, and on its surface, the true black of night devoured the deep purple and cobalt sky.

An impressive chime echoed from somewhere in the house, announcing the interior designer. Colt sighed in resignation to the task ahead and strode back through the living area. He kicked his bag out of the way before jerking open the heavy leaded-glass door.

A stylish woman somewhere in her fifties stood before him, beaming in an immaculate pearl suit and matching six-inch stiletto heels. She extended fingers to him that he didn't know if he should shake or kiss. Drawing his brows together in irritation, he shook her hand, and instantly regretted it, as her fingers felt like large, al dente, rigatoni noodles.

"Mr. Stone? Angela Stanford. It's fabulous to meet you, at last. Of course, Mr. Iverson has told me so much about you. Sam, that is. Sam Iverson," she clarified, in case he didn't remember the name of his agent and manager. "And of course, I've seen you play. Naturally, I hoped to arrive before you, but of course, you just whisked right through the airport." She transformed her fingers into running legs, her sleek silver and black bob swaying with each gesture. "Have you looked around any? Are you happy with everything?"

"Of course." Colt smiled and let his eyes dance off the lights at her.

She must have realized her nervous faux pas, and grinned, pointing one long, rose enamel-tipped finger.

"Oh, you," she beamed at him, and they dropped into a heavy, awkward silence.

"Well, please, come in," he said, and stepped back to allow her entry. Once inside, Angela looked around the dwelling with obvious anxiety. He assumed to check it out and make sure they had placed everything in its correct location. Angela returned her gaze to him with a nervous smile and tittered.

"I'm so sorry." She blushed. "I'm sure you get this all the time, but I'm an enormous football fan, and designing the interior of your home has been my true honor. Thank you for entrusting it to me."

"Not a problem at all." He laid a hand at the small of her back to keep the momentum moving forward down the hall. "I just got here myself. So, let's see what you came up with?"

When she just continued to stand rigid in the foyer, star-struck, he took a deep breath and turned away from her. Rolling his eyes, he strode down the hall and heard her sigh. Glancing into a hallway mirror, he caught her gaze fused on his ass.

"How tall are you, Mr. Stone?" Angela asked, as she finally scurried to follow him. Colt turned, and she blushed, as if in disbelief she'd said the words out loud, adding, "That is, if you don't mind me asking?"

"Six-seven, two hundred and sixty-five pounds," he replied, expecting her next question. He ran long fingers through his thick, copper hair, hating the mindlessness of idle chit-chat. Inspired, his eyes, the color of expensive cognac, found hers. "Maybe I should try out for football. What do you think?"

When she blushed yet again and dipped her head, while laughing so hard he worried she might burst the large blue blood vessel revealed just under her makeup, at her temple.

As the couple moved through each room, Colton admired the expensive, dark furnishings Angela chose for most rooms. Deep burgundy walls, with worn, black leather sofas so supple he thought he might just crawl in one and sleep there that night.

"I decided on burgundy because red incites passion and anger, and I thought to myself, 'Angela, he probably has enough of that on the field.' " The woman gave a high girlish giggle and slid her fingers down a damask drape.

"You can never have too much passion, can ya?"

"No." She giggled again. "Not in my book."

Looking around at all the furnishings that he now claimed as his, Colt reveled in the newness of it all. He'd left almost everything back in Texas, when the wealthy oil tycoon wanted the football hero's furnishings, along with his estate. After fourteen years of playing professional football, he indulged a whim and purchased the seventy-two hundred square-foot home in Bellevue. Colt would live out the rest of his life, career or not, in Washington state. He wanted his relocation days over and desperately needed a fresh start.

By the time they completed the house tour, he wanted—no, craved—quiet from the endless stream of babbling, another beer, and bed. Angela had been none too subtle in laying out a jersey for him to autograph in his man cave. Next to it lay a binder full of information on his new home, complete with passwords and appliance instructions. She left with the signed jersey, a smile, and an enviable commission.

Gaining a second wind, Colt took his time and walked through his new domain again. Six bedrooms, seven bathrooms, and a commercial kitchen, though he didn't even cook. He had a closet the size of a bedroom, a rec room that would make grown men cry, and dining inside and on the outside balcony. A wine cellar, steam room, pool house, and a private pier jutting out into the water rounded out the opulence.

Now, he stood alone on the patio again, bewildered and not a little overwhelmed. What in the hell would he do in this enormous house all by himself? Colt made multi-millions on his contracts over his career. Though his earlier years were a bit reckless with toys, women, and parties, the last decade was spent saving, for no other reason than he had everything he needed, and in darker moments, wondered if he'd need the money for medical issues, once his career was over. The cellphone in his back pocket began to ring. He withdrew it, and proceeded to the refrigerator to retrieve that final beer for the evening.

"Yeah?" he barked with impatience.

"Hey bud, you all moved in?" Sam Iverson's soft melodic voice washed over him like a cool, refreshing wave in the heat of summer. "What do you think of it?"

"It's big, I'll tell ya that."

The tall, glass window beckoned, so he moved to it and stared out into the darkness. He could smell the deep hops of his IPA and tilted it back for another swallow.

"All right! Well, I'm sure you're tired from everything today, so I'll make this as brief as possible."

"Appreciate it."

"Okay, so I talked with Bill Mitchell," he said, speaking of Colt's new head coach. "He wants you to come over to the athletic training center tomorrow morning at ten. That doable?"

"Yeah, I can make that work. He say why?"

"Just wants you to get all your passcodes and the final paperwork complete. Then, I guess he wants Derek…"

"Watson?" Colt asked, referring to the teams' quarterback.

"Yeah. He'll show you around the ATC a little and then the stadium, to tell you what's what."

"Really rolling out the red carpet, huh?"

"You bet your ass they are," Sam said with confidence and pride. "This should be a good fit for you. Don't you think?"

"We'll see."

"We will at that." His agent laughed. "Okay, well, get some sleep, and welcome to your new home, Colt."

"Thanks, man. We'll talk soon."

"You got it. Oh, hey, have you heard from your old man?"

"No, he's still pissed at me. Why?"

"He keeps calling, asking if you're in Seattle yet. I told him I wasn't sure, which he took for a yes. So, I'm sure he'll be calling you soon."

And with that Colt's cellphone beeped. Looking at the caller ID, he grimaced.

"Well, speak of Satan himself. I got him calling in right now."

"Good luck." Sam chuckled and disconnected the call.

"Hey, been awhile."

"And why do you think that is?" Andrew Stone retorted, then continued, not requiring his son's answer. "You talk to your coach yet?"

"Iverson just told me he wants to see me tomorrow to get things straightened out."

"What he wants is to hear straight from the horse's mouth that you won't fuck with his team dynamic."

"I won't fuck with the team dynamic. He just wants to…"

"Keep your head in the game," his father continued, as if Colt hadn't spoken, "not in your pants!"

Colt exhaled, exasperated. "Look, I told you before I didn't sleep with Carlson's wife. He told people that to…"

"Whatever. You're there to play football, Colton."

"I know why I'm here, Dad!" Colt snapped. A furious flush ran up his neck.

"Watch it," his father threatened. "You're there to be the best."

"I am the best, or haven't you been paying attention?"

"Still got that guy from San Francisco on your heels though, don't ya?" Andrew retorted. "Execution, excellence, focus, and fury."

"Focus and fury," Colt said the last part with his father. "Yeah, you might have said that a few million times over the years."

"Damn it, stop being a smart ass and listen for once. The only one of those you got down is fury. Your fucking temper."

"Yeah, well, wonder where I got that from."

"Oh no, you brought this shit storm down on yourself with that mouth of yours."

"So, what you're saying is you want me to be a team player?" Colt said with a patronizing edge to his voice. "That it?"

"Fuck the team. Be better than the team," Andrew spat. "Stop conforming to the lowest common denominator and dominate! Enough with the problems in the locker room! Enough with taunting the reporters! Enough with alienating the coaching staff! And for Christ's sake, keep your damn dick in your pants! Offloaded like a common rookie."

"The trade was about the cap, as much as anything else," Colt retorted, indicating the salary cap the football league had to adhere to, rather than accept his old man's victory of being correct.

"Oh, bullshit." The elder Stone heaved out a sigh of impatience. "That isn't the only reason, and you know it."

"And how would you know?" Colt retorted. "As far as I remember, you only played high school ball, didn't ya?"

"What the hell did you say to me?" his father railed.

"Laid out Senior year, as I recall."

"The only reason I didn't play was because those God damn kids blew out my fucking knee and broke my leg," his father spat. Colt rolled his eyes, in a face of red-hot fury. "If that hadn't happened, I'd still be running circles around you, little piece of shit. I've worked too hard and spent a damn fortune to make you the best. I won't accept anything less from you, Colton. Do you understand me? Your mother would be so damned disappointed in you right now. I'm glad she's not here to witness all this shit."

That pierced Colt's heart and threw a bucket of ice water on his temper. The old bastard always knew how to cut the deepest.

"I let you down that much?" Colt asked in a deadly quiet voice.

"Daily," the older man boomed and disconnected the call.

Colt drank from his beer, then rubbed the cold bottle along his forehead, irritated at the same conversation he'd experienced his entire life. Be the best. Work harder. Get disciplined. From the moment he picked up the football and showed a talent for the game, his father had been the drill sergeant bellowing both in and out of his head. When he did well, Andrew would proclaim him the 'chosen' one, even if only for a few 'chosen' moments. When he failed, his father would withdraw his love in its entirety, until the next game, when Colt would need to seek redemption once more. One day it would just have to stop.

Chapter Two

"So, have you spent any real time here before?"

Known for his philanthropic nature every bit as much as his one-hundred-two-point-eight QB rating, Derek Watson personified the all-American, golden boy his image boasted. At six-two, clear blue eyes, and hair the color of rich caramel, he could be a model rather than the modern-day gladiator he chose for his profession. Long, strong fingers shifted the gears of his sleek red sports car, before he glanced over at Colt.

"No, not really. I had an interesting night with one of your cheerleaders a few years ago though."

"Oh, yeah?" Derek laughed. "Which one? I should get her fired for fraternizing with the enemy."

"Oh, hell no, she's still here and I might want to tap that again."

Derek frowned at the crassness before turning into the VIP lot at SeaCrest Football Stadium, and waited for the guard to lift the gate. The quarterback gave a friendly wave as he drove through.

"So, usually we meet over at the ATC three hours before game time and all come over on the bus," he explained. "Afterwards, we have about two hours to shower, clean up, and do the press junket, before getting back on the bus, and back to the ATC, before we can go home."

"We have to come back and forth like that or can we just park somewhere over here?"

"Well, Mitchell likes us to ride over together as much as possible. So, going to the game with the team is mandatory. But"—Derek maneuvered into the parking garage and drove down the circular ramp—"he also recognizes afterwards might be a different story. If you tell him ahead of time, he's cool about whatever you want to do. Just as long as you stay through debrief and media."

"All of us getting in the zone together?"

"Well," he clarified, "it's that, but also, to make sure no one's late. If you can believe it, that used to be a problem. After the game, it's so we can address any issues that arise from situations on the field. Again, home games are different. He's a lot more lenient. The debrief might be a little longer, so we can deal with those issues, but he knows everyone wants to get home. Away games we ride together."

"All right. Is media mandatory here?"

"Yeah, if you're called by the network," Derek said. "And guys come in the locker room. Most of the time it's Mitchell and me and then anyone they ask for. Gotta be the same for the Thoroughbreds?"

"Yeah."

"If I were you, I'd expect it for a little while. You're big news for the team, and this town will want to get to know you as one of theirs." Derek drove off the winding ramp and onto the player's floor. "I don't know if you did this in Texas, but we have themed days for each practice day of the week."

"Themed days?" Colt asked, a slight mocking tone in his voice.

"Yeah. Wednesday, Thursday, and Friday are the most physical."

Derek pulled into a parking space, turned off the car, and both men unfolded themselves from their seats. As they walked toward the entrance, Derek pressed his key fob and the chirp of the alarm system signaled the car's security.

"'Mindful Mondays,' are where we watch film, talk about what went right or wrong during the game, work out problems with conduct, and come up with a specific plan for the next opponent."

"'Kay."

"That's also our light day. We're encouraged to spend it out in the public, through charities or appearances, something that promotes the machine. We workout or work on specific stuff with trainers or coaches."

"You have a shit ton of those, right?"

"What?" Derek asked, puzzled.

"Charities?"

"Oh, yeah. I have nine."

"That's a lot, isn't it?"

"Well, I guess for me I see this position as a gift. There're very few people that get to do what we do. The fame, and everything that goes with it, is work, but also a privilege. That's how I see it, anyway."

"So, it's charity…"

"No, more like giving back."

Colt gave a nod of his head, but didn't see the difference. In all the years of playing, he'd only done his part for the team charities, or guest spots for friends, not any he supported himself. However, he was there to make a fresh start. They walked down the large, wide hall in the stadium's underbelly. Derek acknowledged workers and employees, who stopped for a look at their star and the newest player, as they walked by.

"See, I wasn't a number one draft pick like you," Derek said with modest admission. "And I always told myself if I made it onto a professional team I would give back and be a role model. We've just got such a small window to make a significant difference, ya know."

"Not being a number one DP hasn't hurt you. Wasn't Cincinnati and Oakland first and second that year?" acknowledging the two top teams of the year that wound up having lackluster performances from their acquired players.

"Yeah," Derek acknowledged, with a broad grin. "That *is* true."

"So, they can suck it," Colt said with significant snark.

Derek laughed and gave a nod of gratitude to his new teammate. They walked in silence for a while, before Colt spoke again.

"How did you decide which ones to do?"

"What?"

"Charities. Don't they take up a lot of time?"

"Sometimes they can, but I love kids. And my wife, Katherine—Katie—and I have six-year-old fraternal twin boys, Dillon and Daniel. Daniel had this thing called hydrocephalus when he was born. It's a little extra fluid that causes pressure on the brain. He had to have a small shunt placed to drain it."

"Oh, shit, man."

"No, it's all good. It was a onetime thing, and no harm done. He's perfect. Anyway, the Seattle

Children's Hospital Medical Center took amazing care of him, so I made neurosurgery one of my charities. My boys even help with it."

"Oh, that's cool then," Colt said, even though he knew it wasn't as simple as the quarterback made it out to be.

"One of our offensive tackles, Aulelei…"

"Tua?"

"Yep." Derek grinned. "He works with pediatric oncology, so we partner up sometimes. We also partner with cardiology too, which is another heavy hitter."

They walked through a set of double doors, and the QB showed Colt everything from the locker room set up, medical suite, and coaching staff offices, to the tunnel they'd sprint through on game days, and the massive field and stadium seats. As they drove back to the ATC, Derek reached up to his dash and handed the tight end a manila envelope.

"Okay, so that's about it. You'll find a spreadsheet in there with everyone's cellphone numbers on it. The rest is like a packet all the players put together for new guys. I know you aren't new, but you're new to the team. It's the basic gist of how we do things here and how to be a cohesive team member. If you have any questions or need anything, don't hesitate to call." Derek paused, glancing over at his passenger. "Look, I know this all happened pretty quick. One minute you're in a hundred plus degree heat, with a bunch of guys you know and are comfortable with, and the next it's mid-seventies, raining, and you don't know anyone. I asked Mitchell to let me do this today because Katie and I are having a barbeque tonight for some of the guys on the team, and we wanted you to come too. Most of the offense will be there, and it would be a great time for you to meet everyone. We try and connect as often as possible to keep things tight."

"Oh, thanks but I…"

"No. No but's. Seriously, man, dive in with both feet." Before Colt could say anything, Derek continued, "We also have a trip coming up in a couple of weeks that a few of us do every year. It'll be our last one before training starts. We go over to Hawai'i and just chill for a week."

"Yeah. Well, I just got here and…" Colt evaded, removing his seatbelt.

"Colt," Derek shifted his car into park, before turning to face him. "Look, I'm just going to say it."

Colt leaned back in his seat and placed his hands on his thighs, before staring straight ahead out the window. He told himself not to react to what he believed would be a character condemnation.

"I'm listening."

"You're coming here with a reputation, and whether it's fair, there's a predetermined idea about who you are. I'm not saying it's right or even accurate." He glanced over and noticed the redhead's ruddy face deepen in color. "I'm just saying it's there. You and I know a lot of this stuff's mental. We've got to have a solid connection and go that extra mile with each other to work, and you're a huge part of that now. So, I'm asking for your help here as one old timer to another. You going to be up for that?"

"Mitchell tell you to say all that?"

"I'm sure he suspects I'll say it, but no, I have to be the leader for this team. It's my job to create a unified offense which flows into a dedicated defense. I'm excited you're here. Hell, everyone's excited you're here. So, what d'ya say? You in?" He extended a hand.

Colt looked at his quarterback's face. The man seemed genuine, and he reminded himself, he wanted to make a fresh start, so raised a hand of goodwill.

"Yeah," Colt said after a moment and shook his new QB's hand. "I'm in."

"Great, so let's go eat."

****

"Hey babe," Derek greeted his wife and lingered a kiss on her mouth before she turned to introduce herself.

"Hi Colt, I'm Katie." She extended a hand to his. "I've heard so much about you. It's great to finally meet you."

"You too." He grasped her hand with caution, unsure of what he'd get back in a handshake. When she shook it with surprising firmness, he smiled. The exotic looking woman appraised him with piercing, deep hazel eyes, and a freckle that winked near the pupil in her iris. "You've got a great place here," he commented.

"Thanks. We like it." Katie rubbed a hand on her husband's back before returning her eyes to Colt's. "I understand you're just down the street?"

"Ah, yeah, 'bout three or four blocks over."

"That's great. Aulelei lives over here too. Actually, a lot of the players do, so, hopefully we'll see each other. Derek, honey, some guys are already here."

"I'll get the grill started," he said, collecting condiments. "Babe, can you grab Colt a beer and we'll go out?"

After she retrieved Colt's refreshment, Katie opened the patio doors to an enormous lawn, and began the introductions of the TE to his new teammates.

****

"Hey man, I'm just glad your twelves are my twelves now," Colt said, hours later. "It'll be nice being in the stadium when they're cheering for me instead of screaming at me."

"They're our secret weapon, baby," said Trevor Bryant, one of the Warrior's wide receivers.

"Hey, Colt."

A large meaty hand slapped the redhead's back. The impact had Colt fighting not to step forward. Turning, he considered the warm, dark eyes of a six-six, three-hundred and fifteen-pound Polynesian. The man grinned and held up his other hand, which Colt grasped with a grin, as they bumped shoulders.

"Aulelei." Colt smiled. He'd always liked the look of the large offensive tackle.

"Naw, brother, we're on the same side now." Aulelei slapped a hand onto his own chest. "It's Tua," he almost sang, elongating the vowels.

"Aulelei, you're supposed to use your first name when you become friends, not your last," Katie replied, laughing.

"Not in football," all the men in the circle retorted in unison. Shaking her head and still chuckling, Katie turned her attention to a group of friends that called out for her to join them.

"So, what's good? All moved in?" Tua asked, turning back to Colt, after Katie's exit.

"Yeah, it was great. I didn't have to do a damn thing."

"Fuckin' awesome being us, ain't it?" Trevor quipped, spreading his arms wide.

"You coming to Hawai'i with us?" Tua asked, with a wide, ivory-tooth grin.

"Yeah," Derek chirped, "you coming?"

Much to his surprise, Colt realized he'd been enjoying his time. He hadn't met everyone, but the ones he had seemed to accept him. Sipping his beer, he decided to heed Derek's earlier advice.

"What the hell. Yeah, I'm in. When and where?"

"We leave in a week. We rented a few houses that are all together right off the beach. There's plenty of…"

"Well, if it isn't the King Player himself." A voice reverberated through the throng. The small group turned, and Colt noticed Derek tense as a long, lanky man with wide-set eyes the color of dark chocolate, approached glaring. "What d'ya say asshole?"

"Eli…" Derek warned. "Come on, we've got kids running around."

"Sorry, QB," the cornerback snapped, shifting his weight from foot to foot. "But I've got a problem with him, and need to make my sentiments known."

"You got problems period, Williams," Colt quipped. "Always have."

"Aw, see there, you *are* suited up and ready to play," Eli hissed. "We have business, Stone."

"None that I know of," Colt remarked with cool detachment.

"Carlson's my boy."

"Yeah, well, Carlson's a fuckin' liar."

Eli straightened, puffed out his chest, flung out his hands, and pushed Colt back a step. Stone's cognac eyes fired, and he lunged at Williams in a tackle. Two of Eli's friends restrained Colt as Tua and Derek stood between them. The party stopped, and some children ran frightened to their mothers. Eli sprang to his feet, and seeing Colt restrained, punched him in the stomach. As the tight end doubled over, Eli sought his advantage by kneeing him in the head. Colt's head snapped back. He saw stars, then a crimson rage seized every part of him. He jerked his arms free and cracked a fist against Williams's jaw, before four players held off the furious redhead. The host yelled at Eli and his friends to leave, as Katie approached Colt but upon seeing his face, didn't get too close. With blood in his eye, Colt struggled against his captors once more and Tua made the most of his large frame by filling the angry man's view.

"Dude, you must chill," he warned. Eli drew breath to say something, and Tua turned to stare him down. "Eli, get the fuck out of here, man."

Ready to attack again, the cornerback seemed to notice the angry faces surrounding him, and mothers trying to calm down their kids. He turned to leave, but not before muttering, "Welcome to Seattle, King Shit. I'm gonna make sure your life's hell here."

Chapter Three

Raven Hunter flipped her long, golden hair over her shoulder, while she finished pouring the table out a second cup of coffee. Her fiancé slid a hand around her waist and pulled her onto his lap to kiss her soundly on the mouth.

"Finn! I almost spilled the coffee on you," Raven squeaked, gazing into his eyes.

Finn Taylor's eyes shone spectacular. Blue graphite, with almost sea-green starbursts in the center and dark charcoal rims. They appeared from an unworldly realm. She fell in love with those eyes, and the man, after arriving on Kaua'i less than a year prior.

Her lengthy divorce became final from her ultra-successful husband and manager, Donovan Fortner, after discovering his affair with one of her backup singers. Though twenty years her senior, and his primary interest in her money and career, Raven took the breakup as *her* failure. She needed to remove herself from him and the business, to gain a new perspective on how to begin again. Though always confident and powerful onstage, as a worldwide singing and musical sensation, offstage, her shy and unsure demeanor captured the heart of the marine biologist.

Now, she smiled at him with serene contentment, then looked over at his grandmother, Dee, as she placed a plate of steaming hot waffles on the table with one hand. In her other hand, she held a large crystal pitcher of guava juice. Raven hopped off her inamorato's lap to help.

"Dee, sit down," she pleaded, taking the pitcher from her grip.

"Oh, thank you, dear," the old woman replied, setting the plate onto the table and grinning at her handsome grandson. "I hope you're hungry. Oh, wait"—she turned and started back toward the stove—"there's bacon."

"I'll get it. You sit and get started." Raven removed the bacon from the oil, drained it, then placed it on a plate, as Finn called out for chocolate chips. She turned and gave him a blank stare. "Chocolate chips? For what?"

"To melt on the waffles."

"You want to put chocolate chips on your waffles?" she asked, checking to make sure she'd heard him correctly.

"Yeah." He looked at his grandmother's cherubic face as if to say, *duh.*

Dee giggled and straightened her sunhat, which today held a spicy fragrant garland of red ginger encircling its brim. A peacock feather, with its large green and blue eye, stuck off to the side, like a swashbuckling pirate. If her grandson's eyes originated from another realm, Dee's whole persona transcended another universe entirely.

"He melts them on the top." The older lady chuckled. "Has ever since he was little."

Raven looked at them as if they said purple dots made up the sun. "That's disgusting," she retorted, but reached into the freezer which, lo and behold, contained a large bag of chocolate chips.

"So, when is everyone arriving today?" Dee asked as Raven returned to the table and handed the sweets to Finn.

"Well, Wyatt, Que, and Abby come in at eight this morning." She checked the clock. "Oh, wow, an hour," she replied, then watched Finn place each chocolate dollop in the indentations all over his waffle. "And Lilly and the kids come in around noon."

"Why didn't they come in together?"

"Lilly took two weeks off, and they already spent the first one in California."

Dee nodded in understanding and sipped her fresh guava juice. "God love her."

"So then," Finn said after several minutes of eating, "let's bring this meeting to order." He reached for his coffee and drank. "So, how are we going to approach all of this?"

The three looked at each other, all hoping someone else would start. It had been a year since Dee witnessed the strange waterspout in the ocean, with the beam of light shooting through it, as if igniting its power. Raven knew every aspect of the story now too.

Something propelled Dee to her bedroom, where an old chest lay high on a shelf in her closet. Handed down several generations, the box unsealed when she touched it, and power sizzled through her, causing her to spasm and connect to a sphere, made of pure energy, residing within its depths. Paralyzed to speak, Dee closed her eyes in concentration, and when she opened them again her face and body contained the soft curves of youth. A misty form had become clear, and soon she beheld a woman.

Hair fell around the being's shoulders like liquid gold, and it blew gently across a gauzy thong that blinded her eyes. Her arms stretched outward with what appeared to be luminescence rather than skin, and sheer robes blew in an unseen wind. Knowledge seemed to physically emit from her, yet Dee had shaken her head in disbelief that knowledge could be seen at all.

"I am Themis." The name came from nowhere, yet everywhere, causing the older woman to cower as the being took the shape of extraordinary beauty and omnificence. "Daughter of the goddess Demeter, it has begun. The first two of this prophecy, sharing the same time and same space, endeavor to join."

"Prophecy?" Dee croaked.

"Son of the mighty Poseidon and daughter of Apollo, for it begins with them. I may come to you now, with whom I have an affinity, mothers of those connected with new life and reluctant death. Our life, our death, our world."

"Our world?" Terrified, the old woman didn't know what to say or do. "I—I don't understand..." she looked around, gesticulating "...this. Who are you?"

"Builders of Troy reunite to build the foundation of our last stand."

"Last stand? Is it... Just... What the hell is going on!" Dee shouted in angry bewilderment. The orb flashed with impatience.

"Silence must prevail, for time grows short. Hold strong to what you know, what you see, and what you dream. Beware, for there are shadows among you that will attempt to hinder your path. Our strength fades, and there must be a new beginning at each end."

"Each end?"

"Twelve in all, the descendants must unite, for Cronus grows stronger with every passing sun."

"Cronus? Who in the hell is…?"

"The gods of the past will descend into Tartarus, and Cronus's power will grow unchecked. His power already sings in some who serve. The implications have extended not only to my time, but your time as well." The image started to fade. *"My time grows short; your questions now ask."*

"Um, o-okay." Dee searched for inspiration, but her mind went blank. She shook her head as if to clear it. *"Ah, son of Poseidon. Apollo. That's mythology, right?"* Dee looked around helplessly at the beautiful being growing more translucent. *"Wait, where's this prophecy thing?"*

In a last effort, the bottom of the chest gleamed, and Dee turned it over. The light had settled onto a carving that hadn't been there before. She looked back up, but the lady disappeared. A flood of heaviness and pain brought her up breathless, as arthritis once more seeped into her bones and joints. Her vision blurred, and her hands once again threaded with age. Dee sat, cramped and uncomfortable, as thoughts rushed in like a tsunami washing away what she had always known to be real.

Dee reached a hand to her jack-hammering heart, then head and wondered if she'd had some kind of stroke. Taking an internal inventory, she realized that on a psychological level, the sensations felt incredible. In fact, better than she had in years, full of optimism, and an innate curiosity about recent events. She took a deep breath, and with violently-shaking hands turned *the box over. It re-sealed itself to once again mock her, as Dee read aloud the words of the prophecy etched into the wood that forever changed their world.*

Time passed, bringing Finn and Raven together, and though confused, they ultimately accepted their genealogy, the prophecy, and their destiny within it. Now, the trio had to find ten strangers and convince them to take part in the quest too. Ten people just as non-believing, where the suggestion of being a real descendant from mythical Greek gods would have them, at best, running to the police requesting restraining orders or at worst, demanding psychiatrists place them in strait jackets. However, they knew the truth now, and understood that knowledge brought responsibility. The need to do everything in their power to thwart Cronus and convince the others to take part sizzled in their very blood.

"Well, maybe we should..." Dee started, then trailed off at a loss.

"Um. I guess..." Raven tried, but also stopped.

"How in the hell are we going to do this?" Finn asked, agitated, confirming what they all seemed to be thinking. "I mean, at least with us, there was already a level of trust that's been there my whole life." Dee smiled back at him as he continued. "I might have thought you were crazy, but you were my crazy lady."

"Okay," Dee started. "Well, how confident are we that it's Lilly?" She reached behind her to the shelf in a nook and grabbed a stack of loose papers. "I've been looking at all the research Finn has done on Hera and then tried to think about what you've said about Lilly." She glanced up at her soon-to-be granddaughter. "I mean, you know her better than we do, Raven. Finn's only met her a few times, and I've only just heard you talk about her. I gotta say though, she sure doesn't sound much like Hera."

Finn glanced down at the papers too and sifted through them. Finding the one he wanted, read aloud.

"Hera, goddess of marriage, childbirth and family. Not very agreeable. Very jealous, vindictive, and obstinate. She was hell bent on getting revenge on the women that slept with Zeus, but not so much on the ruler himself. Sometimes she'd lose her temper, just to lose it."

"But," Raven interjected, "she was also super intelligent and had a commanding presence. She protected children and married women and had large open eyes."

Finn widened his own eyes at her with dramatic flair, causing her to chuckle.

"But how does all of that correlate to a widowed, pediatric heart surgeon, with two children?" Dee asked. "Is it because she has children?"

"Look, I don't know what it is," Raven admitted, a little weary. "I just know I'm right on this. Lilly's commanding at what she does. She's got a very regal quality about her I can't describe. I don't know if she's a very jealous person, but if she is, I've never seen it. I think she could be fierce about not only her kids, but all kids. She heals them, thereby healing the family unit." She looked around the table and drew her brows together as she retrieved a thread of connection to something.

"What?' Dee asked.

"I don't know. Something about marriage." Raven tried to solidify her thoughts. "Hera was all about marriage and was jealous of all of Zeus's conquests. She wanted her marriage to be perfect and never got that. Lilly's marriage, by the small snippets I've heard her tell, was perfect. You'd think the man was a saint to hear her talk about him. A devoted man to her and their kids, then he died. That's another kind of betrayal, right? I mean, obviously not one of his choosing, but he left her all the same." She looked out the window toward the water. "I'm right about her. I just know I am."

"Okay, so who's the guy then?" Finn asked. "Themis said Ares the Warrior and Hera the mother were next, right? Que said Lilly isn't interested in *anyone* right now. And even though she went out with Wyatt once, there's no way he's Ares." Raven thought of her twin brother. No, Wyatt wasn't Ares. Artemis maybe, but not the god of violent war. She looked down and scanned the sheets of paper on the table, as Finn read aloud. "Ares had an insatiable need for battle, destruction and man-slaughter." He looked up. "Nice. This should be fun."

"It doesn't mean he *is* those things. It just means he might have those tendencies, or maybe some of those abstract elements lay there dormant, or something."

"I don't think I want that coming uncorked around my wife and grandmother either."

"Finn, you don't have all of Poseidon's characteristics, thank God." Raven eyed him.

"I still can't believe this is our life now," Finn retorted, running two broad hands through his shoulder length mane. As if just realizing he hadn't put it up in a bun yet, he reached over to the counter and grabbed a rubber band to secure it. "If someone told me a year ago that I'd believe all this shit, I'd have laughed my ass off. It still sounds stupid when you say it out loud."

"Yeah, well, try keeping your cool when you tell someone the truth and they want to have you committed," Dee replied, with a little snark.

"I'm sorry about that. It was before the fish man splashed around in the living room with her tow-headed, harp-strumming forebearer." He jerked a thumb at his affianced. "Not to mention Vapor Chick, sparking this whole thing off in the first place."

Dee rolled her eyes as she took the paper from Finn and looked at the picture of Ares.

"He was very handsome," Dee noted. "Very muscular and strong."

"So, maybe he's in the military," Raven added, "like special ops or something. Maybe a boxer or a fighter." They all stopped to consider this and frowned in unison at all the possibilities.

"How in the *hell* are we going to do this?" Finn said again, sitting back in frustration and slapping his hands on his hips.

"The other problem is we're so far away," Raven commented. "How are we supposed to do all this from Hawai'i?"

"We need to find some help," Dee suggested. "Someone that knows a little more about this. Maybe someone in, I don't know, Greece, that could shed some light on everything. I've been reading about the festivals and events that still honor the gods over there."

"That's a great idea. Maybe even a professor at a university that specializes in Greek mythology." Raven looked at Finn. "There have to be people like that, right?"

"I guess. We also need to know about this conjunction thing. What was it? The Immaculate Conjunction," Finn said, shuffling through a stack of papers, containing all their notes. A couple papers fell on the floor. Finn picked them up with a curse and shoved them back into the pile.

"Maybe we should start an organized journal to keep everything straight," Raven observed.

"That's a good idea," Finn said.

"Maybe have it contain what works and doesn't work too," Dee supplied. "We could show it to people. Be a little more legit."

"Okay, back to the conjunction thing," Finn said. "Maybe we should try an astronomer or astrophysicist or someone like that."

"Well," Dee said deciding, "I don't think I'm the right person to work on Lilly and her prospective beau. You guys have gone through it and know a helluva lot more what you need to hear to be convinced." The couple looked at each other dubiously, but decided not to retort, as the older woman continued, "I think I'll focus on the research part, and get someone to help us."

Dee looked at the couple with a worried expression.

"Now listen," she said, standing up and grabbing dishes. "You guys need to shelve all of this right now. You've only got a few more days to finish up all the wedding details. You've got your friends and family coming in less than an hour, and this should be a happy time." She placed the dishes in the sink, then sat back down and clasped each of their hands. "You both deserve to enjoy this and just love each other. Go have some fun, and we'll regroup later, when we have more time to focus."

"Dee, we aren't leaving all of this up to you," Raven said with quiet resolution. "We've talked about it a lot and decided to wait on the honeymoon. Just for a while." She continued quicker, when the older woman's face expressed disappointment. "Dee, Themis said there isn't a lot of time, and we may need to travel somewhere later or take time off."

"Besides," Finn retorted, gazing at his two women, "we live in paradise. Where do you go from here?"

"Well, I can't argue that." Dee chuckled. "But I *do* want this to be a happy time for you two. And this"— she gestured at the papers—"is stressful. So, I want you to set it aside for at least a week. Deal?"

Raven stood and walked behind the older woman, wrapping arms around her thin shoulders.

"Deal," Raven confirmed. "Nothing more until after the wedding." Her eyes lifted to Finn, and he winked at her, resolute that after the wedding the real work would begin.

Chapter Four

"Mommy, Mommy, look at me!"

Chelsea Morgan pulled down on the arm of her mother, which was laden with backpacks, juice boxes, and a small box of color crayons. The waxy cylinders fell and broke on the aggregate floor because the little girl hadn't secured the top of the cardboard flap. Her mother's dark hair stuck on her face, damp with exertion. Lilly tried to blow it out of her mossy green eyes, but it remained glued there in stubborn refusal. Her son, Travis, shoved past them and ran toward the open air and freedom of the sunshine and outdoors, after the lengthy and exhaustive flight. Lilly dropped the gear, stumbling over it, as she reached a hand out to restrain him.

"Travis," Lilly called with exasperation when he eluded her grasp. He ran in circles, so she injected some anger into her next command. "Travis David! Come back here...now!"

Chastened by his mother's tone, the boy returned, eyes lowered and shoulders slumped. A miserable expression stretched across his face.

"Mom," he whined. "Why can't we go out there where it's sunny?" He gestured toward the baggage claim gate. "We were on that stupid plane for forever. I've got nervous energy to burn off."

Lilly laughed at her own words spoken through her eight-year-old's mouth.

"I know." She sighed and knelt to his eye level, placing hands on his shoulders with gentle affection. "Believe me, I want to get out of here too, but before we can, we have to get our stuff, get the car, and drive to the house. The sooner you help me do that, the sooner we can get into the ocean. Yes, darling." She smiled with strained indulgence as Chelsea shoved the Plumeria lei, placed around her neck, into her mothers' face. "It's very beautiful, just like a princess. Now, come on, let's get our bags."

The mother peered around the small baggage claim of the Lihue Airport with optimism, yet the two carousels remained defiant and unmoving. Bored within minutes, Travis ran around the carousel they waited at, causing Chelsea to imitate his actions with enthusiastic determination.

Lilly stared up toward heaven for inspiration and patience, before dumping the lot of her burden again and grabbing each of her offspring by a bicep. Kneeling, she turned a gimlet eye on the duo.

"Now look. Mama is losing her patience. There's only one of me and two of you, plus the luggage. We *have* to be the three musketeers, okay?" She looked at her son, then her daughter. "I need your help for just a little while more. I promise, the very first thing we'll do, when we get to the house, is hop in the ocean, okay? Before we even unpack."

"Okay, Mama." Chelsea raised her small fist to her heart. "I am the Hawai'ian Princess Mohanna." Travis rolled his eyes, as Lilly laughed.

"Thank you." She turned to her son. "You are the

44

young man of the family," she stated. "Can you please help me?" The boy swirled with pride, as he straightened, grinned, and nodded.

"Well, I'm not sure if I've ever seen a more suspicious group of characters." The trio looked up and discovered Finn striding over toward them. Relief flooded Lilly's face as she leaned into his embrace and kissed his cheek.

"What're you doing here?" she asked. "I thought we were meeting up later. You've got to be crazy busy with all the last minute stuff you gotta do."

"Nah, I told Rave she's in charge, just tell me when and where to show up."

"Ah, so we have a typical man on matrimony."

"Yep," he replied without apology. "Besides, I thought you might need some help." He looked back at her and perhaps seeing the truth there, winked. Looking over at Travis, who eyed Finn's bicep with wide eyed wonder, he said, "Come on Trav, this is man's work."

The young boy scrambled after him and before she knew it, they followed his motorcycle along the Kaumuali'i Highway toward Po'ipū.

Lilly smiled as she scanned the rich foliage followed by the crystal blue water of the ocean. It had been a year since she, a pediatric cardiothoracic surgeon, responded to a summons for a consult on a small seven-year-old girl named Abby in her ER. The girl collapsed on a basketball court with undiagnosed Obstructive Hypertrophic Cardiomyopathy. Though rare in children her age, it had the severity of requiring surgery. Lilly's wittiness and confident personality comforted Abby's mom, Que, also a single mother, and the two made a connection. Once Que's surrogate siblings, Wyatt and Raven Hunter arrived, the small group created a wonderful friendship. Now, Raven would marry Finn in three days' time on the Hanalei Pier after a crazy whirlwind romance.

"I'm getting a motorcycle," Travis announced.

"No, you are not," Lilly retorted.

"How come? Finn gets to have one."

"Because he's an adult and a crazy man."

"I wanna be crazy when I get old like him, too."

"Me too!" cried Chelsea.

"Girls can't ride motorcycles. They're for boys!"

"Of course they aren't just for boys," Lilly responded, then rolled her eyes at the idea she defended the motorcycle. Changing the subject, she said, "What's been everyone's favorite thing we've done so far?"

Never taking a proper holiday in the four years since her husband David's death, Lilly threw caution to the wind, taking her children on a two-week-long adventure. The first week they spent at a theme park, and the overstimulation had taken its toll on each of them. She wanted...no needed, to relax and see some romance. As the kids rattled off all their favorite parts of their vacation, her excitement to watch her new friends get married grew, as she took in the landscape's lushness.

Thirty minutes later, the family arrived at a large airy bungalow rented for them by the bride-to-be. As Lilly turned off the engine and looked at the cozy house, an adorable girl with corkscrew curls pointing out in haphazard senselessness sat in obvious boredom on the steps. Elbows on her knees and hands supporting her chin, she bobbed her head to a rhythm heard only within the confines of her own imagination. Upon seeing their friend, the Morgan children threw open the doors and sprang out of the car, running for her. Abby's face brightened, and she met them halfway. The trio looked like three people dying of thirst, who glimpsed a glass of water for the first time. They started to jump and speak over one another animatedly, in a way only excited children could. Finn dismounted and smiled at the sight before looking over at Lilly.

"Go in. I've got this."

"No, I…"

"Lil, go on in. They're waiting for you and I'm sure you could use a drink."

"Thanks," she replied with a sheepish grin, and grabbed the carry-on's before walking toward the steps. Que, Raven, and Wyatt stepped out onto the front porch to investigate the commotion and noticed her. She looked at the trio, appraising each one.

"Well, it's about time ya got here," Que remarked, her own corkscrew curls springing out with a mind of their own. Clad in a peasant skirt and a tank top of deep oranges and rusts, the effects of which proved striking against her lovely cocoa skin, Que seemed to study the new arrivals with anticipation.

"You made it!" Raven radiated a glowing hue all around her. Her cornflower blue eyes sparkled, and long caramel locks fell in a fluid cascade down her back. Her sun-kissed body seemed to vibrate with joy.

"Finn, here let me help you," Wyatt called. Hunky Wyatt. Where his sister had fair hair, Wyatt's was darker. His eyes, unpredictable as they shifted from brown to green, in the way of hazel eyes, crinkled at her as he ran by to help with their luggage. Lilly's gaze followed, and she gave a thorough appreciative scan of the way he filled out his board shorts.

The women ran down to join her and exchanged hugs before Que danced back into the house, proclaiming the time.

"It's happy hour!"

"Are they okay out there?" Lilly queried and gestured in the general direction of the fleeing children as she followed her friend.

"Yeah," Que called out. "Ab knows better than to leave the yard, and the beach gate's locked."

The rented bungalow, only a few lots from Finn and his grandmother's house, appeared inviting. As Lilly entered the living room, she smiled at the spaciousness and warmth of it. It was decorated in shades of neutrals with gauzy drapes billowing in the wind. A huge veranda wrapped around the back of the house, with the optimal vantage point for ocean-gazing and sunbathing. A large, rectangular-shaped swimming pool consumed the backyard, and Lilly could see Travis gravitating toward it.

"Hey, Trav, why don't you guys come in and get your swimsuits on?" Lilly called over the sound of the blender.

"All right!" he squealed and ran past the girls, who scrambled to catch up to his long legs.

"Here ya go." Que beamed at Lilly and poured out a frosty glass full of blended margarita. A broad, genuine grin ignited on the mother's face as she reached out for the cocktail. Raven handed beers to Finn and Wyatt, who dumped their burdens to the floor before raising their glasses.

"To Raven and Finn," Que said, raising a glass that everyone clinked, before adding with a smirk, "there's still enough of time for either of you to bolt."

"Bite your tongue," Raven chortled, bumping her friend's shoulder. She walked to her groom and flung an arm around his shoulder to kiss him. "He is so stuck with me now." She gazed up at Finn, who smiled back nodding, unabashed love in his eyes, and kissed her again.

"Ugh, gag," Wyatt groaned.

Lilly experienced an unexpected jab to her gut, followed by a quick jolt of anger squeeze tightly around her heart. Confused, she put a hand to her stomach as her mouth opened in surprise. *What the hell was that?* Lilly peered around to see if anyone else had seen her reaction. Realizing no one had, a tremulous smile plastered on her face. She bit her bottom lip, then took another drink of her margarita.

The kids ran back into the kitchen, jumping and pleading to go into the pool, and the strange feeling evaporated. Without warning, Wyatt grabbed Travis under one arm and Abby under the other. Chelsea didn't understand she had put on her swimsuit bottoms backwards and struggled in a circle, like a puppy chasing its tail. Finn kissed his affianced on the temple, then walked over to help straighten them out. He swung the little girl onto his shoulders, and she giggled, clasping her small hands under his chin, as they disappeared out the back door.

"Come on"—Raven gestured—"let's go outside where we can watch them from the deck."

"Oh." Lilly looked over at the pile of suitcases with consternation. "Wait. Just let me get all that crap out of the living room first."

"Please, there's plenty of time for that," Que

coaxed. "Let's go relax and have some fun."

Settling onto a plush sectional that overlooked the pool and laughing at the men and children, the ladies soaked up the delicious sun. Lilly glanced over at Raven, who couldn't stop beaming at her intended. She supposed she couldn't blame her, taking in Finn too. The man could put the Greek gods to shame. His shoulder-length hair and short beard glistened with the color of summer wheat. Golden curls whorled across his chest and abdomen. Turning, he threw Travis into the cool water. Inked on his back was the most magnificent, almost regal tattoo of an elaborate trident. The staff started in the small of his back, to center between the bottom of his scapulae. The arms splayed across the planes of muscle in his back and onto his shoulders. Razor sharp points capped each prong, and the result looked both beautiful and ruthless at the same time. He glanced up and locked eyes with Raven.

A fierce pain stabbed at Lilly's heart again, and what felt like snakes tried to wiggle in her belly. To her horror, she identified it as jealousy. Lilly had known love before. The kind where one look promised the friendship and security of a future together. She missed that connection and promise but felt anger at herself for projecting it onto the sweet purity of her friends' relationship. She clenched her jaw. Typically, she wasn't a jealous woman, and thought it a very corrosive way to think. The unfamiliar emotion didn't sit well with the good doctor and again she tried to push it out of her mind.

"Cannon ball!" Travis screamed and ran off the side of the pool, but he couldn't squish into a ball quick enough before landing in the slap of a belly flop. A sympathetic groan emanated from the assembled crowd, but the young boy came up grinning and waved at his mother with love. Lilly leaned back and sipped her cold beverage, bright understanding on her face. She illuminated the entire universe to the two pieces of her late husband's immortality and that should be more than enough.

****

"Anyone up for a run?" Lilly sang as she entered the kitchen early the next morning.

Raven grunted from behind her cup of coffee and Que glared at her through bloodshot eyes, with attitude.

"Lil, how can you be so...awake, at six in the morning? You weren't as tipsy as I was last night but stayed up just as late," Que accused, but with little conviction.

"I don't know. I guess it has something to do with spending the past decade on call. That and a lot of water."

She glanced at the ladies, then smiled at Finn as he walked around the corner, bedhead falling in sexy waves around his shoulders. A shirtless Wyatt followed him. *Christ,* Lilly mused, eyes widening, *maybe I do need a man.* She blanched before correcting herself with indignation. *No, I absolutely do not!*

"Would you guys mind if I ran then? Chels and Travis won't be up for at least an hour. I'll be back before then."

Que rolled her eyes and blew out an exasperated breath. "Are you going to give me shit later, if I ask you to watch Ab?"

"What? No. Of course not." Lilly laughed. "Do you need to go somewhere? I can wait to run."

"Ugh, stop pissing me off. The kids won't even know you're gone. Go waste time, get a coffee, be irresponsible. We're all good here."

By the time Lilly returned, showered, and dressed, an older woman had joined the party and stood at the stove top cooking up flapjacks with supreme merriment. One of the oddest apparitions Lilly had ever seen in the flesh, she wore a muumuu of deep magenta and lime green, with bright blue hibiscus flowers splayed across each breast, like pasties. Her wide brimmed floppy hat contained a circlet of the same flowers in bright reds, oranges and yellows. And, *was that an actual lime stuck in there?* Lilly grinned, knowing she'd like this woman before she even opened her mouth.

When she did, she sang one of Raven's songs. Bright bluebell eyes twinkled as she laid a tan, papery hand on the singer's arm. Raven beamed and started to sing along with her. It always shocked Lilly to realize her friendship with a global celebrity. Some people held a more favorable position with a higher power to give them such a gift as Raven's voice.

"You have power in your own right. You have strength within your soul. Dreams are attainable, and made of solid gold." The women sang together. At its conclusion, Raven kissed the old woman's forehead and walked to the fridge for some orange juice.

"You're all so stinkin' cute, you make me sick," Que quipped. Dee looked over and grinned at Que before taking in Lilly.

"Well, that's what salt life and sunshine will do for you," she declared with a wink as she noticed the newcomer. "Well, now, come here child and let me get a good look at *you*."

"So you are the one and only Dee?" Lilly asked while walking over to her.

"Yep, that's me, and you're the Lilly-pad that saved that beautiful child," Dee responded, gesturing to Abby's mother.

Lilly smiled, taking her proffered hands, and leaned in for a quick hug. The woman's floral scent hypnotized her, and the doctor fell head over heels in love. Dee patted her cheek and turned back to the counter.

"Well now, let's sit and eat," Dee said, and turned holding a large stack of blueberry pancakes, and set them on the table. "And talk about the plan of attack for the next few days."

The surgeon sat and at her turn, forked two large pancakes onto her plate, before reaching for the pot of coffee, and smiled at Raven, to await the details.

"Well, at nine, there's a meet and greet with the photographer to go over the final list of events. I have to tell the cake decorator to change the frosted flowers to real ones. I got an email this morning talking about frosted flowers. I have no idea where that one came from, so somewhere there's been a miscommunication. But I can just call her for that. Then meet the wedding planner about twelve-thirty at the Hanalei Pier and get some lunch. Oh, then the last thing we need to do is meet with the reception manager." She sipped her juice. "Did I tell you already that the reception is within walking distance from the pier?"

"How does the day of the wedding go?" Que asked, nodding her head and forking a bite of blueberry pancake into her mouth.

"We'll go to the reception house to get ready. It's this big, beautiful place, and the yard is amazing. Not as spectacular as Dee's, but big and amazing enough for all the guests. That'll be around ten a.m. Finn, Nate, and Wyatt will get ready at Nate's house."

"Who's Nate?" Lilly asked.

"He's Finn's best friend. They started SeaHunt together."

"Technically, he thinks he's my boss," Finn supplied.

"I would love to see what you do, Finn," Lilly said. "Do you think the kids and I could swing by sometime before we go home?"

"Sure. I'll take you out to meet Kaimi," Finn said, indicating his favorite Hawai'ian Monk Seal.

"Is he the baby that survived?" Lilly asked.

"Yes, he's adorable," Raven supplied, and gave her fiancé a smile.

"So, what's after Nate's?" Wyatt asked.

"Um, we go over to the pier, get married, and…"

"Get lei'd," Finn offered, encouraging Dee to hit her grandson upside the head.

"The kahu"—Raven giggled—"will proclaim us husband and wife and then we'll go have an amazing party."

"What's a kahu? Is that like a minister?" Lilly asked, intrigued.

"Yeah, kind of. He's like a holy man," Finn said. "Rave and I decided not to tell anyone from the mainland too much about the service because we wanted it traditional and have that surprise factor."

"I was hoping you guys could come today too," Raven said to the room, as three sleepy children shuffled around the corner. Chelsea held her well-loved teddy bear by a foot, so it dragged close behind her.

"Oh," Lilly said, "well the kids. Maybe I should…"

"Who wants to go to the beach after breakfast?" Dee yelled to the trio of youngsters.

"Me!" The collective squeal rang across the kitchen, as three sets of hands rose high the air with desperation.

"What time were you going over to Hanalei?" Dee inquired. She looked at the bedraggled group of adults and smiled. "*All* of you should go. I can watch the children. You can go make a day of it." Both mothers started to protest when Dee flicked a hand upward, dispelling their concerns. "Nonsense," she replied. "You girls haven't seen that part of the island and there's lots to do over there. Besides"—she grinned at Raven and Finn—"I'm a phenomenal swimmer and it'll give me some practice for when I have some great-grandkids."

"Dee," Raven chided, "we aren't even married, yet."

"We'll get working on that immediately," Finn said in perfect synchronization, and winked at his fiancée, wrapping his arms around her.

Wyatt rolled his eyes, as Lilly tried to smile, the deep wriggling taunting her belly once more.

Chapter Five

The morning, already warm and humid, found Colt and Tua running along the Ke Ala Hale Makalae trail. Colt glanced down at his feet pounding on the red clay surface of the path from time to time, then returned his gaze to the waves breaking across the beach. The group had spent four days on the island already, and he enjoyed getting to know his new teammates. When training camp started the next week, he'd begin with a level of acceptance he'd yet to experience in his chosen career. Both Colt and Tua had taken to running each morning, and though the large man ran slower, he had endurance and agility for a man of his size. It's what made him excel as a Seattle Warrior Offensive Tackle.

"So, ya about ready to get started?" Tua asked, breathing heavy as their feet made a cadence.

"Yeah, I think so," Colt responded. "How does Mitchell run his practices?"

"All the days have a theme. Oh, sorry, sir," Tua said, sidestepping an elderly tourist in their path.

"Derek told me all that. I meant like how does he match everyone up?"

"You never know who he'll pair you up with at practice. He likes to change it up a lot. Something tells me he'll match you with Williams at first and often."

"Why's that?" Colt grunted.

"There's always tension when you and Eli meet up in games," Tua responded of the Warriors' free safety. "Mitchell knows it and by now he's already heard about the tension at Derek's for sure. That sonofabitch knows everything before it happens. So, he's gonna want to diffuse it early on."

"Fuckin' Eli."

"Yeah," Tua breathed. "Eli's young and full of shit. He thinks he's got to say something about everything."

"He always beefin' with someone?"

"Yeah. And then besides Derek, and myself...naturally...he's loved on the team. Now, you come along, and bring fan love with you across the whole league, he thinks you threaten his status, and he's gonna try you. We're in for a powder keg. Word of advice?"

Here it comes. Colt rolled his eyes, not answering.

"Try to make a new start, but just know some idiots are gonna try you. They're gonna stir the shit just to taunt you out and make it interesting. Create drama, ya know?"

"You going to have this little heart to heart with Williams too or am I special?" Colt rebuked.

"I already did"—Tua looked over at his new teammate—"before we left." He puffed out a deep breath, as they came to a stop back at the car, and both men raised their arms, locking hands behind their heads. "We have all the pieces this year, Colt, all the potential. How many more years you think you got in ya?" When Colt just shrugged, Tua said, "I know I'm on my way out in the next couple two or three, and I want those years culminating in rings and cha-ching. Ya feel me?"

57

The large man reached into the open car window and pulled out two cold waters from a cooler, throwing one to his new friend. Still breathing hard, Colt uncapped the bottle and drank deeply, draining the contents. When finished, he crumpled the plastic tight in his fist, and threw it into a nearby trash can before turning to face the ocean. Placing his hands on his hips, he closed his eyes and inhaled. The briny, fresh scent smelled like perfume to his nostrils.

"I can't make any promises. People like Williams chap my ass, and I don't take shit…not from anyone."

"Yeah, I get that," Tua said, turning to watch the water too. "All's I'm saying is don't start it. Keep your head down a little. There's plenty of guys on the team that have your back. Not to mention, Derek and I. Hell, we can't stand Eli either. There's not many on offense that can. He's a showboat and all-around arrogant asshole. But he is talented, and he's got loyalty from everyone on defense, and I do mean everyone, so don't go looking for too much love there. I meant what I said." The wind picked up and the man's voice rose in volume. "We've got everything we need to make a serious run here and I for one won't let anyone fuck that up. This isn't about you or any of the bullshit they've said about you. It's about winning."

When his audience didn't respond, the big man turned to him and lifted a hand.

"You hearin' me?"

Colt looked at the hand before clasping it. "Yeah, I hear ya, man."

"Well, all right." Tua slapped a large hand on Colt's shoulder and squeezed. "There's a game of touch back on the beach with our name on it."

****

Built in 1892, the Hanalei Pier stood as a testament to romance. The covered planks jutted out three-hundred and forty feet into the crystal aquamarine waters of Hanalei Bay. A light fog settled in the cove with the curious misty mountains peeking through at intervals.

Lilly sighed from the beach, and watched Raven and Finn walk hand in hand down the pier with Dianne, the wedding planner, and Wyatt, in tow. Que wrapped an arm around Lilly's tiny waist.

"They look so happy, don't they?"

"Yeah," Lilly agreed just as something hit Que in the temple with great force, causing her head to snap back and for her to cry out in pain. Lilly looked down at the football, lying prone and guilty in the sand, as realization hit her.

"Oh my God, Que! Are you okay?"

She examined Que's head and neck checking for injuries, with rapid authority. A small goose egg already formed just above her right temple. A tiny cut opened in her eyebrow, from her broken sunglasses now laying in the sand, causing a small bead of blood to well up.

Used to the recklessness of her son and his friends regarding the sport, Lilly turned, gearing up for an impressive tongue lashing to teenagers.

"What in the hell…" she bellowed, turning around and smacking her face into the sweaty muscular chest of a massive redhead. Refusing to let the fourteen-inch height difference and the hundred and sixty pounds of additional weight intimidate her, Lilly balled her small fists on her hips, shifted her gaze up, and narrowed her eyes.

"What in the hell is the matter with you? You're on a crowded beach with a bunch of young children and families. You're a grown-ass man. Can't you catch a football?" When he stared down at her in fascinated disbelief, she continued. "There is a wide-open park just over there," she said, stabbing her finger in the general vicinity. "Maybe you and your little friends"— she looked over at all the massive men in his group, but continued undaunted—"should go over there and pull your heads out of your asses."

Not saying another word, she turned to re-examine Que, but noticed the man didn't move or speak, just displayed a broad patronizing grin at her. Lilly recognized she must sound like a tiny teacup Chihuahua yipping at a Saint Bernard. The redhead glanced over to a large Samoan man trying his best to sprint over to Que. The man seemed to have thrown the off pass, if his flood of apologies were any sign. Another large man ran to join the fray calling out even more apologies, but Lilly tested her friend's vision before they arrived. By the time they did, Lilly satisfied herself that Que didn't seem to have a concussion or other injuries, barring slight embarrassment.

"Oh wow, Doc M.?"

Lilly, who turned to continue her diatribe, swallowed the words at the sound of her nickname. She shifted her gaze to the smaller of the giant men and tried to place him into context, when it rolled and clicked into her consciousness.

"Derek?" She hesitated, then looked over at the Samoan man and recognized him too. "Aulelei?"

"Yeah." Derek laughed. "What're you doing

here?"

Wyatt, Finn, and Raven ended their meeting when they saw Que get hit, and ran over to check on her. By the time they arrived, Tua had all but plucked her up off the sand, still murmuring profound apologies and asking for forgiveness.

"Ah," Lilly started, at a momentary loss. "My friends are getting married, so we came over for a few days."

"Oh wow, that's fantastic." he nodded at Finn and Raven, then looked at Que. "She gonna be okay?"

"Holy shit." Wyatt laughed and gaped at the three men. Finn noticed the celebrities too, and aped his brother-in-law's expression.

"Wow, Derek Watson, how you doing, man?" Finn raised a hand, and the player clasped it with warmth, before extending it to Wyatt.

During the entire exchange Lilly noticed Colt kept his eyes, and amused smile fixed on her. She narrowed her own eyes, which only looked to amuse him more.

"Colton Stone, I heard Seattle got lucky," Finn blurted, extending a hand.

At this proclamation, the giant ginger shifted his gaze and shook hands with the would-be groom. He looked back at Lilly with a smile, perhaps expecting an impressed gasp at his celebrity status. *He'll be waiting until somewhere beyond the twelfth of never.*

Aulelei looked like he died of embarrassment at the botched throw and horrified that it connected with the stunning African queen. He became clumsy and started to babble.

"That was all my fault, I-I'm so sorry, we were just fuck...er...screwing around and it got away from me."

Que laughed, looking embarrassed herself. "It's okay, baby, I'm fine. Really." She glanced around at everyone watching her, and waved them off. "Seriously, I'm good."

Tua gave her a skeptical look, then smiled sheepishly.

"Well, maybe I should make it up to you and buy you a drink?"

"Sure," Wyatt and Finn said in unison.

Lilly rolled her eyes and crossed her arms over her chest with frustration. She sucked in her cheeks while pursing her lips, and cocked her head to the side. Raven giggled at Que's blush and urged them all to get drinks.

"Why don't you all go over to the Tahiti Blue," the singer suggested. "And I'll meet up with you in about fifteen minutes."

Lilly could tell Raven didn't want to stand in the way of anyone's fun, but also needed to finish her tasks. Finn turned, as if remembering the reason for being there.

"Oh, babe. Sure, let's go get the rest of the…"

"No." She laughed, seeming to understand where her man wanted to be. "It won't take me long. We've already done your part, so go have fun. Really."

Colt turned to Lilly and raised his eyebrows in challenge.

"I'll go with you, Rave," she said with cool detachment. Something interesting passed over the large man's features, but she couldn't discern what.

"I'll come too." Que hesitated, then took a step closer to the girls.

"No!" both women responded in unison.

Lilly wanted her to take a moment to rest, and it

was clear Raven wanted her to continue her conversation with the large man looking at her like a lost, little puppy. Raven's eyes shifted from Que to Lilly and at last, to Colt's.

"Football player," Lilly heard her murmur. "That's a kind of modern-day gladiator." Her eyes widened. "A warrior."

Lilly drew her brows together, puzzled at the statement, then looked at Finn. The couple began an entire conversation without speaking. The whole thing looked bizarre. Lilly turned back to observe the men from the football team already walking down the beach a little. Derek called out to his wife, whom the doctor met many times during their work together, and the two women exchanged waves before Katie ran to join the small party.

"He's kinda hot," Raven observed as they watched the group walk away.

"Yes," Lilly teased. "You're a very lucky woman. Could you be any more in lust?"

"Not Finn." Raven laughed. "Although look at his ass."

"Oh my God," Lilly responded but let her gaze drop to take in the request, then raised her eyebrows in appreciation. "Who are you talking about then?"

"The giant redhead. I think he's into you."

"No, he's not." Just then Colt glanced back, and the corner of his mouth drew up.

"Oh...My...God, look at that!" Raven squeaked. "He is *so* into you."

"Stop it. They're a bunch of self-entitled jocks. Well, except for Aulelei and Derek. They're fantastic. *Children's* is both their charities. Aulelei works with

63

Oncology, and the neurology patients are Derek's primary cause."

"Oh that's right," Raven said. "He was in the hospital that day, when Abby had her operation? He came in with a really large group, didn't he?"

Lilly thought for a moment, trying to remember back to the day in the hospital when she first met the little girl and her family.

"Oh yeah. He and his wife, Katie." She gave a nod of her head to indicate the woman slipping her hand into the quarterback's. "They're a super sweet couple and they really care about the kids. It isn't just for show."

"Uh huh, and what about the other guy?"

"I have no clue who he is but the guys seem to."

"Would Aulelei be good for Que? Is he nice?"

"Oh yeah. He's got an absolute heart of gold," she divulged, then turned to look at her friend. "Are you one of those crazy ladies who aren't content unless everyone around you is married with a bunch of babies?"

"Maybe a little." Raven giggled.

"Come on," Lilly said, chuckling. "Let's go see your reception area."

"Yeah." Raven padded across the soft sand.

Lilly took one last look at the retreating tight end, and raised her eyebrows again, before following her friend.

****

"Your woman looks like Raven Hunter," Tua called back to Finn, looking impressed.

"His woman *is* Raven Hunter, sugar," Que responded, with a wink.

"No shit?" Tua started to laugh, then realized he cursed and said, "Oh, sorry."

Que just gave him a smile and told him how the couple met. Wyatt, Katie, and Finn walked behind them, with Colt and Derek close behind the trio.

Finn clasped hands with the owner of Tahiti Blue and asked to be seated outside. The hostess escorted them to a large table, and Finn allowed everyone to go ahead of him, following behind Colt and Derek.

"Who's the little spitfire with the black hair?" Colt asked his teammate, as they approached the table. "She a real doctor?"

"Yeah, she's a phenomenal doctor," Derek replied. "She's a pediatric cardiothoracic surgeon at the children's hospital in Seattle and highly respected." Finn smiled at the waitress who waited to hand out menus, as the group found their seats, and continued to listen. "Remember when we were talking about my charity?" Derek asked, pulling out a chair for his wife.

"Yeah."

"Well, like I said, a lot of the departments' events cross over, and neuro and cardio cross all the time. Everyone wants to help the kids." He smiled at his wife who returned it, before turning back to Colt.

"Do you have any?" Finn interjected, sitting on the other side of the quarterback's wife.

"What? Kids?" Colt responded.

"No." Finn laughed. "Charities?"

"Oh." The TE's pale skin flushed a little. "No. I've been thinking about it though." He opted for the seat across from Finn that sandwiched Que between himself and Tua.

"You should. You can make a real difference at the

hospital. For example"—Derek took a menu from the hostess with a smile—"I know Lilly's department doesn't have a Warrior on it now that Cooper left the team. He's transferring his support to a local hospital in LA, but it won't be long before someone else takes it."

"She's that good, huh?"

"Lilly saved my daughter's life about a year ago," Que breathed. "She had to perform surgery for HCM."

"What's that?" Tua asked. "HCM?"

"Obstructive Hypertrophic Cardiomyopathy," Que answered and told the group of listeners how Abby had collapsed on the basketball court. "They had to rush her to the hospital. Her heart stopped twice in the ambulance before we even got there. By the time I met Lilly, I was hysterical and ready to tear down the hospital for answers."

Que told Finn she never had an ounce of doubt the surgeon would do anything other than what she said she would.

"Is your daughter okay now?" Tua asked, eyes full of concern.

"Yes." She beamed at him, eyes glassy with tears. "She's one hundred percent perfect."

"Tough as nails," Wyatt confirmed, and looked around the table. He found Finn's eyes, and indicated Que needed a change of topic.

"So, are you guys just vacationing before the season starts?" Finn asked.

"These guys were coming already," Colt offered. "I just got into Seattle a couple of weeks ago."

"We needed a little time to get to know him," Tua confirmed, sliding his arm onto the back of Que's chair.

"Well, I can tell you we're pumped for the season,

man," Wyatt said in a rush.

"You guys all live in Seattle too?" Derek asked.

"I live here," Finn supplied. "Born and raised. Rave and I will live here after we get married, the day after tomorrow. But Wyatt, Que, and Lilly all live in Seattle."

As the table settled down to talk football, Finn cast surreptitious glances at Colt who seemed to listen but not contribute much to the conversation. *A football player*. He thought of the violent behavior this particular tight end displayed on the field. Finn ruminated he could more than fit the bill for a modern-day warrior, to use Raven's words. He turned to Derek's wife.

"So, how long are you guys here for?"

"Just a few more days," she offered.

"You should all come then."

"Come?"

"To our wedding. We're having it on the pier, the day after tomorrow. The reception's just down the street. We'd love to have you guys there. The wedding's going to be very casual, just us and a few hundred of Rave's fans, news trucks, and all." He laughed. "No, we've made it as private as we can for being on a public beach, but the party will be secluded and phenomenal."

Que's face lit up as she turned back to Tua and smiled in invitation. At the thought of a wedding, Katie's eyes also lit up. She looked at her husband, and Derek glanced over at Colt. The redhead seemed to ponder the idea for a moment then gave a shrug of approval.

"That would be great," Derek said. "We'd love to

come."

"Perfect," Finn said, eyeing Colt, then just under his breath confirmed. "That'll be just perfect."

Chapter Six

Lilly walked across a desolate landscape in a wedding dress. It wasn't her dress, the one she wore when she married David, but stark white, and made of several layers of a gauzy, sheer voile. Ruby red dirt, the consistency of talcum powder, clung to her hem as she padded across its surface. Parched but not from thirst, she tried to identify the source of the deficiency; the earth trembled. Lilly scanned the landscape, and in the distance, a man dressed in a gray flannel suit walked toward her. She moved closer, raising a hand to shield her eyes from the bright, almost white, sun. Her hand lowered to her mouth in shock, as she recognized her late husband. Overcome with disbelief and sheer relief, she ran to him, but as she took a few steps, his hand dissolved into the red dust.

"David?" She stopped, reaching out a hand, and he mirrored the image with his other hand.

She stepped forward and his arm dissolved too, blowing away from him in the warm wind. David looked from it, back to her, then past her, to something that stood behind his wife. When Lilly turned, the man from the beach stood before her at attention, like a man in the military, but not any force from the modern century, or even the one previous. Behind him stood a thousand warriors, hunched with spears and primed for battle. Lilly looked back to her husband, who smiled and once more reached out for her hand. Extending one of hers out to him, she took two more steps, but as she did, he turned diaphanous.

"No!" she pleaded. "David, wait! Wait a minute. Don't leave yet."

"He will not prevail."

She swung around to glare at Colt with loathsome anger, but upon seeing him, it turned to white fear. He looked ruthless, yet resplendent in battle armor. Trojan now, he wore a chest plate of pure gold and its reflection shone like glass. The helmet placed on his head had waves of flame cascading down, where otherwise there should have been horse hair.

"You are mine now," he stated with simplicity. "Come, mortal, for your life will be that of royalty."

"Lilly," David said, voice weak with fatigue.

She whipped back around and saw he now knelt, head bowed, turning into the red talcum powder of the dirt, settling lightly upon the earth. Hundreds of thousands of people laid to rest the same way revealed themselves to her beneath her feet. Dropping to her knees in her gown, she placed her face in her hands and sobbed. When the first tear hit the dirt, millions of lilies sprouted from the earth, their happy faces tilted in the direction of the sun.

"Come now. Weep no more, for I am here," the warrior said, holding a sword that dripped with blood, and the gray flannel suit laid at his feet.

"No!" she screamed.

Lilly woke bolt upright, trying with desperation to catch her breath. Slick with perspiration, she scanned the room for her husband. Realizing he wasn't there, she hiccupped with frustration and tried to slow her breathing and jack-rabbiting heart. Peeling the blanket off her body, she walked to the window and looked up into the sky. Cloudless, the night wasn't black but inky blue, and the stars shone like diamonds dripped onto its surface. Five stars glowed brighter than the others. She blinked and opened her eyes wider. The stars pulsated, as she stood transfixed. They seemed to deepen and grow, consuming her, until she blinked again, and they'd disappeared. Turning, Lilly looked back toward her bed and raised a hand to her temple. *What the hell's going on with me?*

****

The day before Raven's wedding, Lilly wanted to give her friend that perfect bubble, where happiness, excitement, and fairy tale glitter clung to everything and everyone. She took time to collect herself after the dream and dressed in running clothes. Pulling her hair into a short, stumpy ponytail, she walked into the kitchen, in search of coffee. She found the bride sitting alone on the veranda, reading a note.

"Wyatt and Finn took the kids to see some famous trees in some dinosaur movie," Raven said without looking up.

"What? They're gone?" Lilly asked, shocked she hadn't heard her children, as they had as much stealth as a political rally. She looked around. "Is Que up yet?"

"No," Raven almost sang, elongating the vowel, and lowered the note. "She stayed out *all* night."

"Out? Out where?"

"Out…with the big guy." She reached for her coffee mug.

"What? Oh, my God…Aulelei?" Raven closed her

eyes and nodded, a grin spreading across her face. "Oh my God," Lilly repeated, starting to laugh. "Well, I guess that answers our question. Does she really like him?"

"I guess so." Raven sipped, then smiled over her cup of coffee, beaming.

"So, what about this morning? Is she coming?"

"She texted me and said she'd meet us later. I told her to just have fun. All the stuff is just a lot of little details now. She already knows what she's supposed to do, and I'd much rather her hang out with him. It's been a while since there's been a nice guy in her life."

Raven loved her friends well. Lilly smiled. It had been so long since she'd had a friend like her. Though, on paper, the doctor had more in common with Que, being single mothers, she'd always felt a stronger, more intimate connection with Raven.

"Well," Lilly said. "Would it be okay if I still come? I want to run but it's been awhile since I've seen last-minute wedding preparations in action, and I'd love to help if I can."

"Oh, Lil, I'd love it too," Raven exclaimed. "I'll tell you what, I'll even run with you first. Just don't go too fast and kill me before I make it down the aisle."

Lilly grinned. "Deal."

****

"Did you have a big wedding?" Raven asked, an hour and a half later, as they drove through the rainforest to the Hanalei Pier.

"No, not by today's standards. There were about fifty guests, maybe."

"Where was it?"

"At my parents' church on Beacon Hill in Seattle.

It was a beautiful summer day, everything in bloom."

"What do your parents do?"

"My father's a neurosurgeon and mother's an ICU charge nurse."

Lilly glanced over at her friend and saw the wheels turning. "Yeah, I always got along better with David's parents. She used to be a photographer and his dad's an architect, like David was."

"Wow, that is a lot of following in parents' footsteps."

"Yeah. Except with David and his dad, Ryan, they never expected or planned for it. They both had this desire to create something that lasts. Ryan and Danielle, David's mom, are the most lovely, down-to-earth people you could ever meet."

"And your folks?"

"Successful, generous, and very hardworking. There are never any fights or disagreements, they are just very career-driven. I've never doubted their love for me or my sister, Rose. She's a psychiatrist and runs her practice over in the Wallingford district. They're just not demonstrative at all. It would never occur to my parents to do something frivolous, let's say, and their expectations are high. Father's very precise."

"Precise?"

"Well, I just mean he's an intelligent man. A genius really, with an IQ of like one-sixty-seven. So, he sees things through a scientific and analytical filter...very fact-driven. Which, in his line of work, is a good thing."

"And your mom?"

"So, Mother's also very clinical. As a woman, she wants to be top in her field, and can give any doctor a run for their money. She's just gone back to school to become a nurse practitioner and isn't super warm and fuzzy, and I'm okay with that."

"But?" Raven prompted.

"But I'm the oldest and I didn't even know what my period was when it happened."

"What?"

"Well, in all fairness, I was pretty young, but I didn't even know what it was, and I thought I was dying." Raven snorted and Lilly laughed at the absurdity of it too. "Stop it!" the doctor exclaimed. "It isn't funny. I hid in the bathroom for hours, holding my underwear, wondering how I was going to tell them I was dying." Raven snorted again as tears ran down her face, causing Lilly to do the same.

"So, what happened?" Raven asked, trying to collect herself. Lilly looked out at the canopies of the trees and saw a colorful rainbow.

"I called Danielle, who was appalled I wasn't told what to expect. She educated me very assiduously about the facts of life. They lived next door to us."

"Oh Lil." Raven sighed. "That's beautiful. Awful about the period, but I guess if I'm being honest, Wyatt's the one that had to explain things to me, then Que confirmed it."

"That's an incredible relationship you have with your brother."

"Yeah, I don't know if it's just a twin thing or if our circumstances made us close."

"Maybe both."

"Tell me about David. How did the two of you meet?"

"Well, like I said, we grew up together. His mom

was like a mother to me."

"Oh, that's so sweet. Childhood sweethearts?"

"No, we didn't like each other much, actually."

"Oh."

"He thought I was prissy, and I thought he was a jerk until sometime around eighth grade."

"Was it, we like each other, so we're going to act like we hate each other, things?"

"Maybe. David was beautiful and I mean beautiful. Super athletic. Every girl in our school absolutely *loved* him, and he ignored me there, but at home he treated me like a bratty little sister."

"So, how did it turn around?"

"I've always loved to run. It was like an escape for me. I started running cross-country in middle school, all the way through college. He showed up at one of my first races." She looked out the window again, remembering. "He'd come to watch his best friend, Anthony, run but his race was after mine. So, they were all standing around, when I walked by to get into position. I unzipped my warm-ups and I'm not gonna lie, running gave me a great tush. I caught him looking as I warmed up with this weird expression on his face."

"Like a lust-sick puppy?"

"I didn't know what it was. I was a young, naïve girl, with no roadmap to the opposite sex. He stood at the finish line waiting for me and never even watched Anthony's race. It had been a long while since we played companionably in a mud puddle together, so it felt weird at first. When I went to his house, I had always hung out with Olivia and Danielle, and now his mom was telling us to leave the door open."

"She just knew?"

"Yeah, even before we did. Anyway, we clicked, and before long we were kissing, then dating and learning about sex, graduating, and going to college."

"Did you go to the same college?"

"Yes. I was advanced two years in school. So, even though we were two years apart chronologically, we went to college at the same time. I got accepted to Ivy League West, and he was Ivy League East. But, after the first year he moved to California with me and we finished our college experience together."

"Wow, that's some serious brain power between the two of you."

"Oh I don't know. We were both overachievers, for sure. We did four years of college together, and he did two more for his Master's, before going to work at Ryan's firm. I had four years of med school after college, and we got married before I started my surgical residency."

"How long is a surgical residency?"

"Five years."

"Oh wow! So, when did the kiddos come?"

"After my residency, and smack in the middle of my cardiothoracic fellowship. We knew we didn't want to wait too long before having kids. I was thirty and knew it would be another five years before I was done with school."

"Five more?"

"Yeah, cardiothoracic fellowship for three years, then pediatric cardiothoracic fellowship for two. So, we planned for Trav, but nothing prepared us for Chelsea coming so soon after."

"How far apart are they?"

"Eleven months."

"Oh, shit." Raven laughed.

"Oh, shit, is right." Lilly giggled. "That was a rough time, I'm not gonna lie. But David being David said we weren't going to stop or put my education on hold. He told Ryan about the challenges we were facing, and they built a little add-on to the house and set up an at-home office."

"That's lovely."

"Ryan and Danielle wanted grandkids, so they were over-the-moon to do it." Lilly looked wistfully out the window. "In some ways it was such a blessing because David got to spend so much time with Travis and Chelsea. Everything was truly perfect." Lilly watched the road tunnel through the rainforest canopies. "And then he got sick, right after I finished my pediatric fellowship. In fact, I had just received my letter saying after twenty-eight years of attending one school or another, I was totally legit. We had a few months of everything settling down into a quasi-normal life, when he started showing symptoms."

Raven looked over at her and the quiet settled there too. "It was cancer, right?"

Lilly nodded her head and glanced over at Raven's serious face, deciding. "No, we aren't going to do this today." She took a deep breath. "I promise, sometime I'll tell you all about David, but not now. Not today."

"I want to see."

"See what?"

"A picture of him."

"Oh." Smiling, Lilly tapped her phone and the sleeping screen awakened. She held it up into Raven's field of vision. Thick golden hair waved around a magnificent face. His eyes, blue and clear as sapphires, looked just like both his children. A strong and masculine face claimed a square jaw, with a slight cleft denting his chin. In the photo, he held a football helmet and his body was muscular, yet lean, with youth.

"Captain of the football team?" Raven queried.

"Yep and quarterback."

"Wow," Raven said a little dreamily. "Well, you're right, he was beautiful."

"Yeah, he was perfect," Lilly commented looking at the picture with love.

****

Colt ran along the beach, breathing hard. The morning turned awkward when he started to rib Tua about his date with the beautiful woman from the beach, and at a noise, saw the woman dwarfed in one of Tua's T-shirts. At a total loss for words, he gave an embarrassed grunt good morning and walked straight back to his room, changed, and went for a run as the couple giggled.

His feet pounded out their cadence on the sand, and he looked out to the water before a movement caught the corner of his vision. An incredible looking blonde ran toward him. Her perfect breasts seemed to be trying to break free from the captivity of her jogging bra. A large burly man, whose head swiveled from side to side, like some sort of bodyguard, trailed her.

As she neared, he realized he'd had his hands on those perfect breasts, not to mention just about every other imaginable surface of the Hollywood starlet, and stopped. She glanced up, trying not to make eye contact, when recognition snapped into her eyes and she stopped too.

"Colt?" She grinned.

"What in the hell are you doing here, Cap?"

"Oh my God." She scanned his sweaty body from head to toe, laughing before looking back into his eyes. "A friend of mine's getting married here tomorrow."

"Let me guess, Raven Hunter?"

"Yeah," she exhaled a little breathless. "Do you know her?"

"Not really. I just met her and her boyfriend a couple of days ago."

"Fiancé, darling."

"Whatever."

His eyes traveled down her, causing her lids to lower and pupils to dilate, on cue. A relationship built on sex and convenience, they also enjoyed a friendship, along with the benefits. When each found others to spend time with, they parted ways, to stay loyal to their new lovers. In fact, it was the only romantic relationship he'd ever had that ended and began with friendship. The starlet's security guard turned his back with discretion.

"Lookin' good, Cap."

"Feelin' good, Colt," she all but purred.

He opened his arms, and she walked into them smiling, before tilting her head back for a quick kiss.

****

Lilly walked just in front of Raven on the Hanalei Pier. Her eye caught the flash of Colt's, bright copper hair blazing in the sun. He embraced a woman that looked like she'd stepped out of Eden itself. Halting, she caused Raven to run into her. Confused, Raven looked at Lilly, then followed her gaze to the couple still locked in a steamy embrace.

"Oh, well now."

Lilly looked up and down the beach. People with kids dotted the surface, and the two carried on with no sense of shame, creating a spectacle. Jealousy flamed into her face with such ferocity, she stepped back, and drew in a sharp intake of breath, before trying to release it slowly.

"Wow, is that..." Raven eyed the couple in a growing recognition. "Oh God, that's Caprice, and..." She looked harder. "Is that the guy from the beach?" She whipped her gaze back to Lilly's.

"The football player, yeah," retorted Lilly, full of judgement. "He's the one that..."

"Caprice! Is that you?" Raven called out to the couple.

"Shh, Raven!" hissed Lilly. "What're you doing? They're going to think we're watching them."

The couple parted and turned toward the women. Caprice held a hand up to shade her eyes, seeing Raven, but Colt's eyes seemed to fasten on Lilly. The surgeon looked away and became enthralled with the white, fluffy clouds circling above them, and brought her hand to her neck.

"Rave?" the starlet called. "Hey there!" She bounced her way over to them. "What're you doing over here? I thought you were on the south side?"

"I am." Raven laughed. "But it was early, and I had to get some last-minute things done. Lilly"—she gestured to her friend—"said she'd come too but only if I ran with her first."

Caprice turned her attention to Lilly, giggling. "I hear you. I have to go out early too or I wouldn't get any exercise in at all."

Lilly spared only a glance for Caprice before

turning to Colt with a denunciatory glare.

"Yes, the price of fame I suppose. I just have two kids and work schedule to work around, not an entourage." Shocked at her own snarkiness and implied put down, Lilly blushed and tried to backpedal. "I...sorry, I just meant I don't have to contend with fans."

"Yes," Caprice said with cool irritation, obviously accustomed to women behaving rude and hateful toward her. "This is my friend, Colton Stone."

"Yeah, we met a couple of days ago," he replied, holding Lilly's eyes in challenge. "What, no hug?"

Lilly felt her face flush again. Seemingly aware of the undercurrent, Raven tried to deflect the tension.

"Well, this is where we'll be in twenty-four hours."

"Oh, show me, show me, show me!" Caprice giggled again and took Raven's arm so fast, the man and woman found themselves alone in an instant.

"So, I guess we haven't been officially introduced yet. It's just been a lot of intense eye connecting," he said, baiting her. He stood close, forcing her to look up his imposing chest. "I'm Colton Stone." He held out a hand to shake.

"Lillian Morgan," she said quickly, and took a step back. She turned toward the direction the women had gone, showing him her back.

"Lilly, you need any help with that? It's gotta be a little painful."

"What?" She turned around again. He'd slipped his hands onto his hips, chest sparkling with perspiration.

"That stick up your ass."

"I'm sorry, what did you say?"

"Don't get me wrong, you're sexy as hell when

you're mad, but I don't know what I did to piss you off so much."

Regaining her sense of speech in warp speed, yet unable to retrieve which words to say first, she stuttered with fury.

"H-has… Do… Has anyone ever told you, you're an asshole?"

"Sure. All the ti…"

"Who in the hell talks like that to someone they've just met?"

"What are you most pissed about? The stick thing, or telling you you're sexy when you get mad? It was supposed to be a compliment."

"You're making lewd comments, when your girlfriend is right over there."

"Caprice?" he laughed. "She's not my girlfriend. Well, not anymore anyway. It's been a while. Now it's just…"

"Seriously, am I being punked right now?" Lilly spat with anger and moved to walk away and rejoin Raven.

"Okay, well, I'll see you tomorrow. We can pick this up again then."

Lilly whipped around. "What do you mean?"

"Didn't they tell you? They invited us to their wedding." He gave her possibly the sexiest grin she'd ever seen.

She opened her mouth to say something, but words failed her. She closed it again, leaving the giant redhead to watch her retreat in silence.

Chapter Seven

Raven stood in front of a full-length mirror, staring at her reflection. Thin straps held the form fitting bodice in place over her curves, while leaving her toned back exposed, and the full, soft, gossamer skirt, to gently float around her with each movement.

Que's reflection stepped behind her in the mirror and glowed, in her own strapless, rose-gold-colored gown. Puffy corkscrew curls sprung out in a riotous mop, except those contained behind the doughy petals of white, rose, and yellow Plumeria flowers. Raven looked harder and discovered a bloom in her best friend's cheeks that wasn't there before.

"You look happy, Que."

"I know." The mother gave a dreamy sigh. "He's a real gentleman, and I haven't had one of those in a long, long time. And my God what that man can do with his…"

"Eh hem." Wyatt cleared his throat, and both women jumped and turned. "The man could crush me like a bug, or at the very least make me piddle on the carpet. So, don't say it out loud or I'll have to go over there and fail miserably at defending your honor."

"Did you say piddle?" Que whooped and walked over to him. She kissed him on the cheek. "Don't worry about defending my honor. That's been tainted damn near fifteen years now. You know that." Que continued to chuckle and left the room.

"Well?" Raven asked, smoothing her hands down the bodice of her dress. "Is he going to turn around and run screaming?"

"No," Wyatt whispered. Walking over to her, he kissed her on the forehead. "I think his heart might explode in his chest though."

He opened his mouth again, but more words seemed to fail him. He just laid a hand on his heart, and Raven did the same. They remained quiet for a moment.

"Mom and Dad should be here doing this," he murmured, moving a stray lock of hair from her eye and tucking it behind her ear. "Because I know I'm gonna mess it up,"

"Wy…"

"Just wait a minute and let me get this out." He searched her face with his warm hazel eyes. "I honestly can't believe this day came. I always hoped it would, but at least with Fortner, I knew I still had you. Your heart, ya know?"

"You'll always have my heart."

"That's not what I mean." He closed his eyes a moment and gave a slight shake of his head. "I…it's just it's always felt like it was my job to protect you, us. You know? I mean we always had each other's back but I kinda feel like I'm out of a job now. Don't get me wrong, I know Taylor's the right guy, it's not that. You guys will be fantastic together. It's just…I don't know, it's not just the two of us anymore." Her eyes filled with tears. "No, Rave, that's a good thing. It's a great thing!" He smiled, while looking a little anxious. "I told you I'd screw this up."

"You aren't." She laughed. "I know you've always felt that burden, Wy. And you're right, you've always taken care of us. I'd like to think in the past few months I've learned to take care of myself but…"

"You have." He stooped to eye level and grasped her hands. "It's been so awesome to watch. Both Que and I think so."

"Well, I wasn't kidding. You're my brother, and you'll always have part of my heart. Like, literally, we share DNA." They laughed at each other and Wyatt cleared his throat.

"Okay, so I'm guessing this dress is new. What's blue?" he asked.

"Um, it's in my lingerie," she said, not quite meeting his eye.

"Fine," he said and moved on. "What's borrowed and old?"

Raven touched her hair where a golden woven haku encircled her up-do with fresh Plumeria.

"Dee wore this wreath in her hair for her wedding and she did the flowers, so that should cover old, I guess, and borrowed."

"Well, I have something you can borrow."

"Really?"

Raven watched as her twin pulled out a black velvet jewelry case and opened the lid, revealing his gold medallion, re-strung on a thin gold chain.

"I thought maybe since you didn't have yours anymore, you might want to borrow mine today."

A thousand words passed between the siblings, without speaking. She opened the box, and a gold medallion lay there, with a lyre embossed on one side and an arrow on the other. The last piece of their mother, Isabelle, who died in a car crash by a drunk driver when the twins only counted eight years. The devastation would alter the course of the children's existence forever. It altered again when they ran away from their abusive, adoptive family to Washington state and met fellow homeless runaway, Que Jackson, on the streets of downtown Seattle.

Raven closed her eyes, recalling her own medallion, and how through a twist of fate, she could no longer count it as her own. She never told her brother the magic that brought the gold to life on her neck. How it fell onto an old wooden box and melted into a groove on the top. She had a small scar, a distortion of the lyre's shape faintly burned into her flesh now, but the rest she didn't think he'd ever believe. Chatting with the apparition of her long-lost ancestor Apollo, who just floated out of the same box? No, she could never figure out the exact right way to phrase it.

Now she looked at her brother with radiant joy and happiness, at his gift. He clasped it around her neck and looked at her in the mirror, as it nestled into her pikake lei, as if made for that purpose.

"So, how about you? You sure about all of this? We could make a break for it?" he teased.

"No, I'm sure." She smiled back at him in contentment.

"Well then, let's do it." He raised her hand to his lips, then tucked it into the crook of his arm before escorting her to her new life.

****

Lilly smiled at Finn who looked at his grandmother

with anxious excitement, and Dee winked back at him. Looking magnificent in his soft white shirt, tan slacks, rose sash, and maile lei, Finn glanced over at his best man, Nate. His friend also smiled back which seemed to reassure the groom even more.

"Just keep breathing, man," Lilly heard Nate advise. "And for Christ's sake don't lock your knees or you could faint."

"I will not faint," Finn said with indignation.

Nate chuckled as the town car pulled up at the end of the pier. Wyatt stepped out in an outfit similar to the bridegroom and his best man. He reached out a hand and Abby jumped out first, looking confident in her appearance. Not noticing the crowd's attention, she spun in a circle making her dress twirl. Wyatt reached in again withdrawing Que. Lilly noticed Aulelei, sitting next to Derek and Katie. His eyes never left Que as she walked down the aisle with her daughter, who dribbled Plumeria blossoms onto the pier. At last, he offered a hand to Raven, who stepped out of the car, a vision of grace. The sun shone down on her, turning her hair into radiant spun gold.

They had hired security to keep the fans and media at bay, but it didn't stop the crowd from standing behind the barriers, two hundred yards away. An uproarious cheer from fans resounded, and numerous camera shutters clicked, as Raven gave a quick wave before turning and spotting her love. From that moment, neither Raven nor Finn seemed to care who watched or what they did. Lilly's heart tripped, as the familiar pang of longing and desire echoed inside her.

The kahu blew into a conch shell to announce the bride's arrival, then the music started and the bridal party processed. Lilly's eyes couldn't help but fall on Colt, sitting just a few rows behind her. Caprice whispered something in his ear, causing him to smile.

Lilly scanned the actress's outfit. The woman's body, all luscious curves, displayed Hawai'ian florals in her silk sarong. Strawberry-gold cascaded down her back with a small section of her hair secured loose behind her ear with a Plumeria bloom. Brilliant ocean-blue eyes disappeared behind large tortoise shell sunglasses as she slipped them on.

Colt watched Raven glide down the aisle, and as she passed, for a just a moment, he gave the bride a broad, genuine smile. Somehow that gesture of acknowledging something sweet and beautiful touched Lilly. When the bride neared her, his gaze snapped to hers and the air between them sizzled. He gave a nod of his head and smiled again. To her supreme bafflement, she smiled back, before she could stop herself. Unaware of the byplay, Caprice touched his bicep, and seeing the gesture caused Lilly to look away again.

****

Colt watched the bride as she reached her groom and the service began. He always felt overwhelmed and bewildered by people that made this kind of commitment to one another. From time to time, he couldn't help but let his eyes travel from the couple to the petite woman he'd met at the beach. Something about the little firecracker pulled at him.

Her dress, the color of soft amethyst, appeared to be silk or some other such sensual material. It showcased her toned shoulders without the sleeves or straps to mar them. Light freckles danced over her cheeks, shoulders, and crests of her small breasts, whose rise and fall quickened when she got irritated.

"Isn't she beautiful?" Caprice whispered into his ear.

"She's all right," he answered, trying to sound matter-of-fact, then realized the actress spoke about the bride, not the dark-haired woman.

Caprice hadn't heard him but when he looked to his other side, Tua gave him an ear-to-ear grin. Without a doubt, the tackle understood who he'd been talking about.

"What?" Colt charged.

"What?" the large man parroted under his breath. He nodded in Lilly's direction.

"Okay, she's hot," Colt admitted. "Not that you'd notice."

"Damn straight." Tua laughed and nodded his head toward Que. "At least they both live in Seattle."

"You know her too, right?"

"Doc M.? Yeah."

"Shh!" Caprice scolded.

The men turned with the small congregation and watched as the couple exchanged vows and rings. The kahu twined their hands with a maile vine, admonishing anyone that would try to separate the duo. As Raven and Finn exchanged rings and leis with each other, and their families, the kahu led a collective in a chant, honoring the union. They exchanged a smoldering kiss, and the ceremony ended.

Now newlyweds, the couple walked back down the aisle, followed by Wyatt, Dee, Abby, and Que, who gave Tua a playful wink. As Caprice moved past Colt, her large breasts brushed against him. She followed them with fingers trailing across his chest. Tua slapped

Colt on the shoulder, a little harder than necessary.

"Whew-e," Tua said watching. "It's going to be a great night."

Chapter Eight

Lilly traversed the crowd to the bar and asked for a glass of Malbec. When she received her request, she turned and watched the Hula dancers move with grace and elegance to the sound of steel guitars. The day had been perfect for her friends. She grinned at Abby and Chelsea, who burst into uncontrollable giggles as they tried to make their bodies move like the dancers. She sipped her wine and notes of pepper, plum, and black currant glided over her tongue and down her throat. Scanning the crowd, Lilly tried to locate her son and caught him sitting at a table alone, with a strange expression on his face. Frowning, she focused on him. He appeared to be almost having a daydream, without outright stars in his eyes. She followed his eye line expecting to see a cute little girl capturing his attention. Instead she discovered Colt.

He wore his tan chinos well, and a chambray shirt with the top two buttons unbuttoned. The sleeves rolled up with defiance, revealed strong forearms with rope-like veins that moved as he raised his drink to his lips. The conversation he exchanged with Finn seemed captivating. *Why did he have to irritate her and turn her on at the same time?* Lilly reached her son just as Abby and Chelsea ran up with three huge slices of cake.

"Wait a minute. Weren't you two just dancing?"

"They cut up the cake, Mama!" Chelsea said with her mouth full of dessert.

"Right. Okay, well what are you three up to after cake?"

Travis looked at her with pure hero worship on his face. In fact, she couldn't remember the last time he looked so happy.

"Mom?" he gushed in excitement.

"What?" she said mimicking his excitement back.

"Guess who's here, and he's really, super famous?"

"We already know. Raven," Abby said, rolling her eyes. "And, in case you hadn't noticed"—she gestured over at her godmother—"she's a girl."

"Duh, I know she's a girl. I wasn't talking about her."

"Who is it you think is famous, son?" Lilly asked, stroking his soft honey-colored hair.

"I don't think he's famous, I *know* he's famous. Look." Travis pointed over to Colt, now relaxing in a chair and responding to something Derek had asked him. "That's Colton Stone. We just got him and he's worth a lot of money."

"Oh yeah?"

"Yeah, and…"

"Mama, did you know a real live princess is here?"

"A princess?" Lilly looked around trying to understand, as both her children chattered away. She looked in the direction her daughter's eyes had gone. Caprice, in her high wedge heels, perfect mani-pedi and flawless tan.

A princess? A cow more-like. Lilly blanched at the direction her thoughts had just taken. It was not like her at all to think such a thing toward another woman, and the emotions bewildered her. She bounced her eyes over to the newlyweds, who danced, only having eyes for each other. *They don't seem to be bothered by anything.* An arm slid around her waist, causing her to jump, as Que stood next to her and sighed.

"I'm ecstatic for them."

"Yeah, it's fantastic," Lilly said, still distracted by trying to analyze her thoughts. She drew her brows together and felt some shame.

"Mmm, Mmm, Mmm, Mmm, Mmm," Que sang.

The surgeon's mind re-engaged and noticed Tua step over to talk with Colt, as Caprice shimmied down to sit next to him. The large man checked on Que every couple of seconds, so Lilly turned to conspire with her.

"You've got a boyfriend," Lilly sang, nudging her. "You like him?"

"Yeah." Que grinned at the man. "He's sweet to me. When we get back to Seattle, he's gonna take me and Ab out so he can get to know her a little, too."

"Wow," Lilly exclaimed, shocked. "That's just... wow... I don't know...fast."

"Eh, maybe?"

"Don't you wanna get to know him a little bit before introducing him into your life with Ab?"

"Why?"

"Why?" she repeated, a little bewildered. "Well...I guess I haven't dated all that much since David died." She tried to phrase it so as not to offend her friend. "With the kids being so young and...I don't know. I guess I'd worry they'd think I'm trying to replace him or that they'd get attached and it could turn out bad."

"Oh." Que gave an airy wave of dismissal. "Well, Abby never had a dad to start with. I hooked up with her father for only a little while." Que eyed Lilly, perhaps to see if judgement did in fact, come. When it didn't seem to, she continued, "I was always getting tangled up with losers, but then I met Eric. He had a steady job, and was really nice. After six months, I found out the shithead was married, so, I dumped his ass, then found out I was pregnant and nothing else mattered. Abby knows all about it, and she's always had Wyatt to fill the void."

"Why didn't you and Wyatt ever…"

Que laughed so hard, her eyes teared. "Girl, please. He's my brother, and I've never looked at him any other way. He's the best man I know though, and that's why *you* should be looking at him. For me, that's too bizarre to even think about."

"So, why this guy, and why so quick?"

"No, I hear you, I do but…I don't know, I just have a great feeling about him. I think he's awesome." She looked back at her friend's worried face. "It's not like I'm marrying the guy, Lil. But I'm also not living my life on the sidelines either. I could never do that. He's interesting, sweet, and terrific in bed, if you know what I mean."

"Oh God, Que Jackson!" Lilly hissed and looked around, laughing.

"Yeah buddy." Que guffawed, slapping her leg. "He's good." She raised her eyebrows at her friend, then still chuckling, lowered her voice. "Come on now. I'm putting my heart out there, Lilly, because I think he's a great guy. If things don't work out, they don't work out and I just found one more guy that's not *the one*. But you can tell just by looking at him, he wouldn't hurt a fly."

Lilly looked over at the man in question. He was positively enormous and looked like he could wrestle a lion, let alone swat a few thousand flies.

"I think he's the type that would want to stay cool, you know?" Que continued. When her friend remained silent, Que ventured, "And what about you?"

"What about me?" Lilly said and scanned Que's laughing eyes.

"Girl, you know Red hasn't taken his eyes off you since he got here."

"Funny," Lilly retorted, "I haven't seen him take his eyes off Venus yet, let alone notice anyone around him." Lilly paused. "He's so…"

"Sexy? Hot? Mysterious…"

"Irritating," Lilly decided.

"Oh, well now, don't hold back, honey, tell me how you feel." Lilly laughed and Que just rolled her eyes at her. "Christ, you need to live a little, Doc." That hurt. Lilly felt like she'd been elbowed in the stomach. "I'm sorry," Que countered, seeing she stepped off the mark. "But it doesn't have to be all serious. In fact, it's supposed to be fun."

"I'm not sure I'm ready for a long-term relationship."

"Honey, I just said it doesn't have be hard and forever. It's just gotta be hard for one night." Que guffawed again, as Lilly turned crimson.

The dance floor opened and Tua walked over to ask the maid of honor for a dance. Lilly watched her slide into his arms, and the couple swayed across the dance floor, leaving loneliness to consume her. Deciding to refresh her drink, the doctor made her way back to the bar and accidentally bumped into Caprice, spilling some of her wine on the actress.

"Oh, excuse me."

"No harm done," Caprice stated, making a show of wiping at her sarong. "After all it's just a dress."

"Yes." Lilly couldn't help but look at the woman's incredible chest, then down at what looked like mere speed bumps below her own décolletage in comparison.

Four teenage girls approached and asked the starlet for her autograph. Caprice obliged, then smiled at Colt as he walked over holding three glasses of champagne.

"Ugh. It's so frustrating when you're just trying to blend in," the actress complained, taking a glass.

Lilly spared only another glance at Caprice before turning an irritated look at Colt. He eyed her back in challenge and handed her a glass of champagne. Playing with ideas on how to remove herself from the situation, Lilly looked up as Raven appeared, breathless and glowing.

"Everyone having fun?"

"Darling, you look gorgeous," Caprice chirped. "I can't believe you're a married woman now."

"I know." Raven laughed. "It feels like yesterday I was slapping Donovan with you cheering me on." The women seemed to share the private joke before Raven asked, "So, *is* everyone having a good time? Can I get anybody anything?"

"Ugh," Caprice said. "Don't be so boring. It's your wedding day, for crying out loud, go be spoiled."

"What? I just wanted to know if I could get you something."

"Yes. You can get me the hell out of this judgey, tension-filled conversation"—she raised a hand at her two companions—"and introduce me to your hot, new hubby."

"You've met Finn before."

"Yes, but I was naked, remember?"

"How could anyone forget," Raven volleyed. "Come on, let's go."

"Thank God," Caprice bubbled, and turned a gimlet eye on Lilly, who had the decency to look abashed.

Colt grabbed the champagne from Lilly's hand and set both flutes down on a table before wrapping an arm around her waist and drawing her in for a dance. "Are we having our first fight?" Colt asked.

"We have nothing," she hissed, and decided to play the dance out rather than make a scene. The fact that her body wanted to vibrate pressed against him was irrelevant.

"Are you still mad because I said you're sexy?"

"I don't *need* you to tell me I'm sexy."

"Fantastic, a woman with no self-esteem issues." He looked down at her and smiled. "Maybe…"

"Mom?" Travis stood next to her looking shy but hopeful.

Knowing a disaster in the making, she stopped dancing and turned back to Colt, with a look of sheer desperation. *Please, God, don't let this man be an asshole to my baby.*

"Oh honey, um" She bit her bottom lip and looked at her son, then back at Colt's shocked face, before she bent down to the boy's level. "Okay, so, Colt." She looked up, her voice holding a note of warning. "Ah, this is my son, Travis Morgan… *He's eight.*"

She widened her eyes, just in case the football player didn't grasp the magnitude of the feelings involved. Before he could retort, she turned back to her son.

"Travis, this is Mr. Stone." The boy looked up at him with wide eyes and a dreamy smile.

"Ah, hey Travis." He extended a hand and seemed surprised to find the boy had a firm handshake. "Nice to meet you, pal."

"Hello, Mr. Stone," Travis all but whispered.

"Ah, naw, we're…friends now. Just call me Colt."

"Ah, no, it's Mr. Stone," Lilly corrected.

Colt smirked at her, as her son tried to find words but failed. Seeming to be used to the reaction, Colt helped him out.

"So, ya like football?"

"Yes, sir," Travis exclaimed. "It's my whole life. I want to be a quar-, ah, I'm gonna try out to be a tight end, in like a month." He looked at Lilly to make sure he had his dates straight and she nodded in agreement.

"Really?" He grinned. "Ya sure you don't want to be a quarterback?"

"Naw." Travis tried for nonchalance. "Quarterbacks are really olderrated, I wanna do what you do." Lilly felt a sharp pang to her heart, hearing her son dismiss his father's football position without a flicker of remorse.

"Olderrated. Right," Colt said, as if considering the merits of the statement.

Relieved to see Stone could understand and act with sensitivity to a young fan, Lilly gave Colt her first real smile, and filled it with gratitude. An awkward look passed over his features before giving her a genuine smile back.

"Well, I could give you a few pointers sometime, if

you want them. Have you met Derek Watson or Aulelei Tua yet?"

"N-No sir."

"Well, before the night's over I'll introduce you."

Tears filled the boy's eyes and Colt's eyes widened, horror stricken. Lilly supposed, that to a man, the only thing worse than a woman crying helpless tears was a little boy full of uncontrolled emotion. However, before she could do anything, Chelsea approached. Colt's expression changed again, yet this time, to wonder. He looked as if the most beautiful creature on Earth had just entered his life, which to Lilly's biased opinion, had. Chelsea grabbed the large man's hand and pulled on it.

"Hello. My name is Chelsea Victoria Morgan and I'm seven and a half." She held up the correct fingers in illustration, trying to bend one middle finger. "And Travis is my brother and he turned eight and a half. And this is my mama." Her soft golden curls swung around her angelic face as she grabbed Lilly's hand and balanced on one foot, while swinging her other leg back and forth. Her large, round, crystal blue eyes sparkled at him. "Are you a giant? Do you want to pick me up and dance with me?" She let go of her mother's hand and raised both arms up to him.

"Ah…"

Colt blushed and blinked at the little vision. Lilly chuckled at her youngest and felt sheer relief at her timing, so her boy could pull himself together. She placed an arm around her son's shoulders, then cocked her head at Colt with interest and challenge. She tried to deduce what he would make of all this new information, and her little spark plug. Believing he would become overwhelmed with the lot of them, she smirked with superiority and waited for him to flee to the nearest drink and the busty blonde bombshell. However, when his eyes flicked back down to hers and saw what they contained, he just raised his eyebrows.

"I'd be a fool to blow off such a beautiful woman," he responded, gazing down at her little angel, then leaned down to secure her in his arms.

"I'm not a women." Chelsea giggled and ran her soft hand over Colt's stubble. "I'm a little girl."

"Little girl?" Colt laughed despite himself. "Well, okay, blondie, let's go tear up the dance floor." He glanced back at Travis who looked devastated at being replaced by his little sister. "Then we'll talk some football, and I'll make those introductions, okay, Bud?"

The boy beamed back, and Colt looked at Lilly with smug satisfaction, before he disappeared with Chelsea on the dance floor. Lilly tilted her head to the side and furrowed her brow but couldn't help a little smile.

Chapter Nine

Colt ran along on the beach for what seemed like a long time. He could taste the salty tang of the ocean, as each new wave crashed against the rocks, spraying into the air. In time, the sand turned into a very fine red powder and he stopped. Looking out, the landscape had become arid, and in the distance, a mirage shimmered. In it, he could make out three people. To the left, Chelsea danced and twirled in various stages of life—as a young girl, as a teenager, as an adult woman, and as an elderly woman. On the right, Travis played football, also in different stages of life. Lilly stood in the middle. He knew it to be the woman, Lilly, even though she looked like a flower, roots digging deep into the soil. Her scent seemed to drug him, and he craved her with an almost feral desire. He moved toward her and the children, but his father stepped into his path. Andrew turned dark and manifested into thousands of black smoky serpent-like bindings.

"You cannot have them," his father's voice whispered, dark and taunting.

"Naw, man, they don't want him," argued another collection of dark bands, assembled behind him. Turning, he recognized Elijah Williams.

Colt shifted toward the trio who all smiled and beckoned to him.

"Fuck that," Colt retorted, looking back at each mass, "and fuck you." He sprinted toward the family, but the black serpents followed him, whispering.

As he neared them, the blackness tried to hold him back. Determined and covered in red powder, he pushed harder and soon reached the family. Their pristine appearance looked so pure to him that he didn't want to touch them.

"Will you dance with me?" Chelsea asked, as she approached.

"Will you teach me?" Travis asked, eyes large and hopeful.

"Will you love me?" asked the lily, bending with gentle fragility in the breeze.

Their voices and requests melted over him like music and he reached out to touch them. Chelsea, the closest, reached her small hand out first and when he touched the delicate fingertips made of light, they blackened. She screamed, as black seeped into her perfect skin and darkened her veins, sending the color up under her skin. Travis reached out to help his sister but when his hand brushed Colt's, the darkness seeped into him too. Both children screamed in agonizing pain.

Andrew Stone and Eli kept whispering ugliness and despair into Colt's ear and laying blackened hands upon each of his shoulders. The veins under the children's perfect skin started bursting, and the darkness devoured their bodies.

Lilly crystallized, her feet rooted deep underground. She couldn't move to help her children or stop Colt from ruining them. He tried to take a step back, but an imaginary force propelled him a step closer.

"No!" he yelled at the powers that claimed him, "Stop!"

He continued moving toward Lilly. However, before he reached her, the black bindings seeped into the soil and he could only watch in helplessness as they slithered into her roots. As they entered her, she screamed and reached out for him, but eluded his grasp by inches. The base of her perfect white petals...saturated deeper. Cobalt blues and deep purples seeped into the petals like ink swimming through water. Lilly's freckles dotted along the colors until the bud bloomed, and Lilly appeared naked and vulnerable. She arched her back out, as if stabbed in the back from behind. Landing on her hands and knees on sharp jagged rocks, her skin punctured and bled, turning blue, then purple, then black iridescence, until she vanished. Colt struggled in vain to move but couldn't. His father and Eli held him so secure. He could only watch with impotence, as both children turned to ash.

Colt came awake with pain exploding in his head. He winced and tried to hold what could only be two pieces together.

"Jesus," he groaned, and swung his legs to the side, planting his feet on the floor and elbows on his knees. He cradled his aching head and shifted his eyes to the clock, a quarter past two in the morning.

After the worst subsided, he stood naked and walked to the sliding door in his room that exited onto the beach. He blinked at the clear blackness, bright with stars, and slid opened the barrier. A warm breeze seduced and floated around his body, as energy seemed to spark in the air. The crashing of waves on the beach comforted Colt as he looked up and swore five stars illuminated brighter than the others. He blinked, and they disappeared.

Early the next morning, his team packed up and left for Seattle. Colt decided to stay on an extra day to see Finn's work and go out on the water. He relished the quiet, a run, and a cup of coffee on the back deck. At nine, he drove the hour and a half south to Hanapepe Bay, and the SeaHunt Research facility.

"Morning?" he called out to the newlyweds, stowing gear. "You sure you guys want to do this today? It feels like you should be going somewhere glamourous."

"Hey." Finn looked up from setting down a large cooler. "No way, we're excited to take you guys out. With our schedules Raven and I decided to wait on the honeymoon for a little while."

Mrs. Taylor looked over too and smiled, replying, "We stayed on the boat last night and brought it down this morning. It'll be a lot more comfortable than that." She pointed to a smaller, metal, utilitarian vessel that looked more set up for Finn's work but less for comfort. "Besides," she went on, "I hope you don't mind but we have three more joining us. Lilly and the kids wanted to come out today too."

"That's great," Colt replied, happy he'd see her again before he left. "I don't suppose you've got coffee around here, do ya?"

"Sure," Finn replied, hopping off the boat. "I was just going there myself. I'll take ya." He leaned over the rail and kissed Raven, brushing back her hair. "You want anything, babe?"

"Um, how about a triple grande, nonfat caram…"

"Caramel macchiato, with extra caramel drizzle," he finished. "You got it."

"Wow, this married thing is awesome," she replied and grabbed his shirt, bunching it in her fists and pulling him back for another kiss.

Colt turned his back and wondered if he made a mistake coming today. A car pulled into the parking lot, and Lilly and her kids bounced out. She turned toward the boat and even though she wore dark sunglasses, he knew the minute her eyes landed on him. They hadn't told her he would be joining them, either. The thought made him smile. As the kids ran over and began to talk and jump all at once, Lilly approached, laden with towels and a heavy beach bag, which Colt took off her shoulder.

"Ah, thanks," she said. "I didn't know you were coming today."

"Right back at ya. Hope you aren't too disappointed," he replied and watched her face blush. *Anger or embarrassment?* He didn't have a clue.

"Hey," Finn said and grabbed the stuff from football player. "Colt and I wanted coffee, but maybe you two could go get it and I'll help Rave get the kids outfitted in the right life jackets and stuff."

"Oh, I can do that," Lilly blurted out.

"You could, but you don't know where everything is," he responded. "If you help Colt, we should be ready by the time you get down there."

"Oh, sure," she said. "Just tell me what kind you want."

He relayed the orders and directions about where to go, then ran down to the boat with the kids to join his wife. Lilly turned to Colt, his red hair sparking in the sun.

"Hey, Doc."

"Hello." She turned and started to briskly walk to the coffee shack.

"Great day," Colt said, looking up at the sky, his long legs keeping up with her effortlessly. "The kids look excited."

"They are," Lilly answered, intent on her mission.

"Hey." He reached out a restraining hand to her elbow and stopped her. "So, are we good? I think we got off to a bad start, but it felt better last night. I was hoping we can move on."

"Sure." She turned to continue walking but hesitated and looked back at him. "Just so you know, a lot of men think speaking to women that way is flattering, but it really isn't."

"Oh, God, you're one of those."

"What?" When he said nothing, and just began to walk again, she ran to catch up, and stopped him by raising a hand to his chest. "If you mean I have self-respect, a level of intelligence, and two children to raise, then you'd be right. I wouldn't want someone speaking to my daughter that way, any more than I'd want my son thinking it was okay to do so." She stood her ground and placed her hands on her hips. "I set the standard for those two little people, Mr. Stone, and I don't necessarily want it set at the lowest common denominator."

"Fair enough."

"Okay." She gave a nod of her head and resumed her trek to the coffee shack. He walked the rest of the way with her in silence. As he ordered the drinks, he felt her eyes on him, but when he'd look at her, she'd glance away quickly. He paid for the beverages and they waited for their order, sitting at a picnic table.

"So, what *is* your story?" he asked. When she merely eyed him, he said, "What?"

"Why do you want to know my story?"

"I think you're interesting...intimidating as hell, but interesting."

"I'm not intimidating."

"Lady, you're terrifying." She gave a genuine laugh, and he smiled at the sound. *Progress.* "Maybe when we get back I can take you to dinner."

"After today, I'm sure we won't be spending too much time together."

They called the order, and the couple both stood at the same time, inches apart. The desire to kiss her suffused through him. Resisting his natural urge, he took her hand instead and brought it to his lips. Lilly's eyes widened at the romantic gesture.

"I think you're wrong," he said, holding their hands up and threading their fingers together. His thumb dipped in and stroked lightly up her palm, and she shivered. He whispered, "I think we'll be spending a lot more time together."

He studied her clouded green eyes, and for just a moment saw desire in them. Grinning, he took the drinks and whistled as he walked back down to the pier.

Chapter Ten

Dee, Finn, and Raven sat on the quiet beach, drinking wine and watching the sunset.

"So, does anyone have any doubts it's Lilly and Colt?" Raven asked.

"No," Finn replied. "But I don't think it will be easy getting those two together either. They seem like opposites, don't they? Did Lilly even like the guy? Yesterday was a little awkward after they got back from getting coffee."

"Yeah, but you said it didn't feel anger, right?" Dee asked her new granddaughter. "More like bafflement."

"Yeah," Raven said. "Sometimes, I'd look over at Lilly and have no idea what she was thinking. Also, she and Caprice had some interesting moments at the wedding. I don't think they liked each other much."

"What happened?" Finn asked

"Nothing really happened, but Lilly was definitely not acting like herself. Que thought she might like Colt but was trying hard not to."

"Sometimes opposites attract," Dee added with a wink. "With what we know about Ares and Hera, it would be appropriate for their personalities to cause a little bru-ha-ha."

"I'm not sure that's even the real problem though,"

Raven interjected.

"What do you think the problem is?" Finn asked.

"I'm not sure if Lilly's truly let go of David, or maybe she just feels guilt or something and it prevents her from getting back out there. We talked about him in the car before the wedding, and he's pretty flawless in her mind."

"That's hard for a guy to compete with," Finn suggested, sipping his wine. "And Colt's already a little rough around the edges."

"That boy's so rough, he could give my leg hair a run for its money," Dee quipped.

"Ew," Finn said with horror, as Raven guffawed.

"Well," Raven said, still chuckling, "he may be rough, but I think he's very sharp. You two seemed to be getting along."

"Yeah, he's a lot cooler and down to earth than I thought he'd be. It surprised me when he said he wanted to see SeaHunt and what we do there."

"Oh, and you should have seen it, Dee," Raven cried out enthusiastically. "Everyone went absolutely nuts when we found Kaimi!"

"Yeah," Finn laughed, warming to the mention his favorite Hawai'ian Monk Seal. "Kaimi was eating it up too." He sipped his wine. "Colt also said if we're ever in Seattle and want to go to a game, to give him a call and he'd arrange tickets."

"He gave you his phone number?"

"Yeah, he was interested in our benefit and if it doesn't conflict with their season schedule he'd come back for it."

"Oh, honey, that's really cool," Raven said. "I'll invite Lilly too maybe. Maybe they'll be into each other by then."

"I watched him at the reception." Dee sipped her wine. "I think he's smitten with the good doctor and her little peanuts."

"Right?" Raven agreed, then frowned a little. "We can't forget Travis and Chelsea in all this. It has to be right for them too or I don't see how we can push it."

"Those kids had no problem with Colt that I could see," Dee said. "In fact, just the opposite."

"No, but did Colt have a problem with the kids?" Finn queried. "He's a single guy, who has a little history with women and creating drama wherever he goes. It's one of the reasons they traded him."

"Wait." Raven looked at him, worried. "What happened?"

"Texas traded Colt to the Warriors."

"Right? He's a…what is he again?"

"He's a tight end."

"And what does a tight end do?"

Dee bit down hard on her lower lip with her teeth. No doubt a myriad of playful retorts danced in her mind. Finn saw it and gave the barest hint of a smile at the cluelessness of his adorable new wife when it came to sports. A tragedy he'd have to remedy.

"He's part of the offense and a pretty amazing player." Finn drew patterns in the sand with a stick. "Colt can catch anything, but he can also block. He's super fast, super tall, and you might have noticed super strong."

"Yes, I did notice that," Raven said, giving her husband a wink. "But they traded him?"

"Well, to be clear he's probably the best that's ever played his position. He's broken all but one record.

He's got..."

"Finn, stay on track," Dee coaxed, before her grandson worked himself up to a fever pitch. "Right. So, yeah, he's amazing. He plays with a single-minded determination and is downright brutal on offense. Ruthless even."

"So, if he's so good, why did the other team agree to let him go?"

"Well, there's several reasons. Some say he's at the end of his career or on the downhill slide of it."

"So, he doesn't do that well anymore?"

"No, that's the weird thing, he's as consistent as he's always been." Finn thought about that for a moment.

"So, why would they let him go then?"

"Well, owners and coaches have to think about the future. Not only how long a guy has left to play, but will he play well. The players are all trying to get the best deal they can before they're out, to tide them over for the rest of their lives. They've got young guys coming in every year and only have so much money."

"So much money?"

"Yeah, so the other thing about football is each team only gets so much money. It isn't like one team can have billions and another team, ten bucks. It's got to be fair," Finn explained.

"How much money does each team get?"

"I think this next season is somewhere around a hundred and ninety-one million."

Raven spewed out her wine, choking. Finn leaned back and patted her back, as Dee laughed and reached out for her own wine glass before it spilled. When she collected herself, Raven wiped her face with a towel.

"So," she said clearing her throat, "you're saying each team gets a hundred and ninety-one million dollars?" When they both nodded, she asked, "How many teams are there?"

"Thirty-two," they both said in unison.

"So that's..." Raven tried to do the sum in her head. Rattled, she took out her cell phone and asked it to calculate the total.

"Thirty-two times one hundred and ninety-one million dollars equals six billion, one-hundred and twelve million dollars," reported a computerized female voice.

"She said that like it was no big deal!" Raven said appalled. "Every year that's what they pay?" Raven stood up and paced. "A trillion dollars in debt, six hundred thousand people homeless, and we pay a bunch of guys six billion dollars to beat the crap out of each other?" When the couple nodded again, Raven asked again, "Six billion?"

"One could say you make a lot of money just for singing." Finn laughed and handed her a fresh glass of wine.

"Yeah but I, I..."

Chuckling, he pulled her down, so she sat between his legs and leaned back onto his chest.

"There's a lot of reasons those guys get paid that kind of money. Talent is only one of them." He kissed the top of her head, then rested his chin on it and looked out at the sun melting into the earth. "Those guys play hard, and a lot of times they play injured. They break bones, dislocate joints, get concussions, the effects of which go far beyond the years they play. I think you'd be hard-pressed to find a career football athlete who doesn't have something wrong with him for the rest of his life."

"So they make extra money to cover it all."

"Something like that. Don't get me wrong, it's an exorbitant amount of money, and sometimes it's blown on cars, women, sometimes drugs. Anything they want, but the smart ones invest it for what they'll need later."

"So he's older and more expensive to keep on the roster?" she asked.

"Exactly, but even that isn't insurmountable. The thing is, Colt's got a reputation for creating drama in the locker room. He doesn't get along with people very well. He's hard-headed, has a hair trigger temper, and is known for his high standards."

"What's wrong with having high standards?"

"Nothing if you're doing it supportively, but when you belittle someone at practice for not doing things the way you think they should...Well, they're grown ass men with a lot of pride and don't like to be disrespected. Teams need to be a cohesive unit, almost like the military. A lot of the game's mental, just like any team sport, and they've got to have each other's backs and depend on each other. You got a guy who isn't a team player and can be divisive, then that can affect morale and create all kinds of shit for a team.

"Not to mention Colt's good and knows it, so people get jealous of that," Dee added.

Silence fell on the trio, alone with their thoughts.

"You don't think he'd hurt them, do you?" Raven asked.

"The kids and Lilly?" Finn asked. "No, I don't he'd hurt them intentionally. And certainly, not physically, if that's what you mean. He's known for bravado with women, not meanness. Women love him. And I think if the kids turned him off, he wouldn't have hung around, he'd have just moved on."

"Well, I think he was interested," Dee chortled.

Finn stood up and lit a fire in the small pit they'd created earlier for the purpose. The warm blaze flickered into life.

"So," Raven said, watching him work. "I guess if we haven't heard about him killing anyone in the next couple of weeks, we'll know just how easy or hard this will be. How're you coming along with the historian search, Dee?"

"Well, it's been hard. There's a lot to understand and I don't even know if I'm pointed in the right direction. Then I try to call people and they either give me these long dramatic stories or think I'm some dingbat ole lady trying to…God only knows what."

"Weren't the gods dramatic people, or apparitions or entities, or whatever the hell they were?" Finn asked.

"Oh, they were nuttier than fruitcakes, but through my research there're stories from good sources, like the Iliad or Homer, and then there're all kinds of myths and legends that don't have a lot support. I mean it's not like you can go on Greekgodgenealogy.com, like the normal people one," Dee quipped. "I try to find a story and then see if it's supported at least four or five times before I take it too seriously. There's just so much made up stuff."

"Hey, a few months ago we thought it was *all* made up, so we've made progress," Finn retorted. Raven grinned at him as he regained his seat behind her.

"Maybe we should look at this from a different

angle," Raven offered, leaning back against his chest. "Maybe we should look at the conjunction thing first."

"Well, as to that I found a pretty well renowned astrophysicist," Dee said.

"That's fantastic," Raven encouraged. "Who is it?"

"Well, there's a tiny wrinkle."

"What?"

"The information I got was from a few years back and he doesn't seem to do it anymore."

"Doesn't do what anymore?" Finn asked. "How do you just stop being an astrophysicist?"

"He's a pilot now."

"What kind of pilot, like for NASA or something?" Raven asked.

"Nope, he gave it all up to fly Nathanael Aetos around."

"The mogul guy in New York?" Finn clarified, and Dee nodded.

"Why would he give up being a rocket scientist to be a pilot for Nathanael Aetos?" Raven wondered.

"I can give you about fifty billion reasons why," Finn retorted.

"Yes, but how much does an astrophysicist make and how much does a pilot make?" Raven asked. "It can't be all about money."

"Astrophysicists' median wage is about a hundred and twenty thousand a year, according to Occupational Codex."

In the time they had been talking, Dee pulled up two screens on her cell phone. Finn blinked at the old woman with incredulity. When they started this whole odyssey a year ago, his grandmother could barely turn on a computer.

"And," the older woman continued with pride, "pilots' range, depending on what they do, from seventy k to a hundred and forty k."

"A hundred and forty thousand dollars to be a pilot?" Finn wiggled his chin on top of his wife's head. "Honey, I'm in the wrong business."

"Well, if anyone can get someone to listen, it's you, Dee." The singer giggled.

"I'm not sure if that's true, but all he can say is no, right? And even then, I won't let him get away with it. We might want to wait until things die down a little before concentrating on him though," she said, and thought for a moment before continuing. "Have you given any thought about how you intend to confront Lilly and Colt?"

The couple looked at each other with consternation.

"Well," Raven began, "Caprice might be a way in for Colt. She told me they date off and on, but have always remained good friends. Maybe we can, I don't know, all get together and start building on this quasi-friendship." Raven looked back at Finn, "I'm sure that'll be hard for you to endure, won't it, Finn?"

"If I must make friends with a famous football hero, I'll just have to make time and suffer through it."

****

Later that night Raven lay on Finn's chest, fresh from making love, his fingers playing in her long silky hair fanned out over their intertwined bodies.

"Do you feel like we're doing things the right way?"

"Did you have an orgasm?"

"Shut up." She smiled and breathed in his cologne.

116

"I mean, is it wrong to become friends with everyone and try to make choices for them regarding the rest of their lives?"

"You mean for the greater good?"

"Yeah." She sat up on an elbow, leaving her other hand on his chest. "I mean what if we're wrong? What if this isn't the right person for Lilly and her kids?"

"You think something should happen to let us know we're on the right track?"

"I don't know. You'd think the gods would have something in place, with so much at stake." Her fingers curled his chest hair. "I mean what made you think to look at this whole thing more seriously?"

"Besides Vapor Chick and the huge dude that came outta the box?"

"Yes." She laughed. "Besides that."

"Well"—he sat up a little, and adjusted his pillow to a more comfortable position before replying—"I guess it was a dream I had."

Raven sat up quickly and crisscrossed her legs. "I had dreams too, all the time, weird ones."

"What were yours about?"

"No, you first."

"Well." Finn took a deep breath and let it out slowly. "I don't know, in one I was just walking and Poseidon was there and he said a bunch of stuff I didn't understand at the time and can't remember it all now but at the end, I remember a raven flying away."

"One of mine was about a waterfall and a cliff and there was a dolphin and a swan in it."

"So, what does all that mean?"

"I have no idea," she admitted. After a moment, she asked, "You know for sure it was Poseidon talking to you?"

"Not at the time, but after everything shook out, I know *now* it was the same guy."

"And I know I was talking to Apollo too. Again, I didn't get it at the time either, until later. We really do need to write this stuff down. What doesn't make sense at the time might mean something big later."

He nodded as his mind started to work faster, and he felt like they were on to something that just eluded their grasp. Raven looked up at him like things just clicked into place and bloomed on her face.

"The raven," she said. "Was it just a raven or was it me?"

"I mean, I thought of you because it *was* a raven, but no, I think it was just an ordinary black raven."

"Okay, wait a minute."

She jumped off the bed naked and ran for the kitchen table. Grabbing her laptop, she sat down at the kitchen table and started to type. Finn moved behind her to look over her shoulder, and saw Apollo printed in the search engine of their favorite website about the gods. His wife clicked the sun god's name again and read, placing a finger under one word. Raven. She opened another window and typed in Poseidon, before telling him her thoughts.

"Okay, some of Apollo's sacred objects were a lyre, a laurel wreath, swans, and ravens." She clicked to the next tab. "Poseidon's were tridents, dolphins, and horses. All of those were in the various dreams I had, the second I stepped on this island."

"Yeah? Mine too." They looked at each other for a long moment.

"Do you think we're right?" she asked.

"Only one way to find out." He reached arms around her and typed in Hera's name, then Raven read out loud.

"Okay, so Hera's sacred objects are pomegranates, peacocks or peacock feathers, a diadem, cows, lotus, and...oh my God."

"What?" he asked, trying to catch up.

"A lily."

"Lilies?" Finn reiterated. A chill ran up his spine and zinged out to his extremities.

"Yeah," she confirmed, visibly shaken too. He reached around her again and typed, Ares.

"Ares...Ares..." he read. "Okay, his sacred objects are a sword shield, spear and..." She watched her husband read in expectation. "A helmet."

"A helmet," she blurted, and looked at the screen. "A helmet. Like a football helmet?"

"Well, not exactly. It's more like a Trojan helmet, but for these times, yeah. I mean I guess it could be a military helmet with the weapons and stuff."

"Except, now he's a Warrior, right? A Seattle Warrior."

"Okay," Finn said, straightening up, as she turned to look at him. "I'm officially freaked out."

"Freaked out but convinced," she said. "They're talking to us through our dreams."

Chapter Eleven

"So *Chéri*, I heard you received another one."

Lilly looked up from scrubbing her fingernails. Dr. Moussa Koffi, one of her favorite colleagues, strode into the scrub room and picked up a cellophane-wrapped kit. He and his family had immigrated from the Ivory Coast, just five years earlier, and he'd worked hard to become a respected pediatric pulmonary-thoracic surgeon. He threw his mask into a bin.

"Sorry?" Lilly countered, confused, and scrubbed underneath her thumbnail with laser-point precision.

"I heard the cardiac unit received a new benefactor but that he would only work with you." The doctor opened the cellophane and withdrew the items.

"What're you talking about, Moussa?"

Now, Koffi looked confused and paused in his ministrations.

"Colton Stone," he said in his heavy French accent. "He is making your department his charity, no? But will only work with you. Did you not know this?"

Lilly frowned, returned to her scrubbing, and shook her head. Colt called her at the office twice since they'd been back. He asked her to dinner the first time, which she refused. The second time, he left a message asking the same thing, and she didn't call him back. Deciding she knew what he wanted, and being an intelligent

120

woman, with two children, wouldn't indulge him. The fact he made her nervous and turned her on at the same time, didn't matter or not much anyway. "I heard it was one point five million dollars."

Lilly dropped her soap and couldn't catch it before her fingers touched the bottom of the sink. *Damn it.* She released a deep sigh before grabbing another soap pack and beginning the scrubbing process all over again.

"Where did you hear that?"

"Dickerson," he returned, speaking of their Chief of Surgery.

"Dickerson knows?"

"Yes. He was just now at the table with several of us and mentioned it."

"Why does the guy only want to work with me?"

"I do not know, *ami.* It was our hope you could answer that question for us." He raised his eyebrows expecting an answer, but she wouldn't meet his eye.

"I have no idea. I only met him a couple times."

"You must have made an impression, no?"

"I guess," she retorted. "What did you have today?"

"Congenital Lobular Emphysema."

"How did it present?"

"Two-week-old female, two-point-one kilo, obvious respiratory distress. Her O-two sat was eighty percent on room air. Decreased air entry and crepitations on the right."

"Chest x-ray?"

"Yes, overdistention of the right lung. A prominent mediastinal shift with compression and atelectasis. At first we thought RTI, complicated with a pneumothorax but after everything, we realized it was more consistent with CLE." He continued to watch his hands as he scrubbed. "So, we did a right posterolateral thoracotomy and upper lobectomy, then ligated her patent ductus arteriosus."

"Aww, poor baby."

"Yes, well I am positive missing a lobe of her lung and removing the threat of the extra blood flow is a small price to pay for the alternative."

"It is," she agreed. "And how's Mom?"

"Young. Very young and alone, but also handling everything with grace and asks relevant questions. Not hysterical at all, just wants what is best for her little girl."

"That helps." She smiled.

"Yes, it certainly does." As he scrubbed, Koffi looked over at his friend. "And what do you have today, *Chéri*?"

"Primary repair of the tetralogy of Fallot."

"Fairly simple, how old?"

"Fourteen months." She looked at her colleague with trepidation. "So, what did Dickerson say?"

"That Mr. Stone was taking you to dinner."

Lilly guffawed before she could help herself at the prospect of trying to entertain Colt for an evening.

"Well, *Chéri*, you did not hear it from me, but I think some serious ass-kissing is in your near future."

Like hell. Lilly grimaced, drawing her brows together and clenching her jaw. However, the thought of him, like so many times before, caused her to flush. She raised her hands and backed through the doors into OR three.

****

"Yes, come in Doctor Morgan," Chief of Surgery

122

Alan Dickerson said three hours later. "Please, have a seat." He gestured to a high wing-back chair.

"Thank you. I think I know what this is in regard to, sir, and I don't think Colton Stone is a good fit for me or the department."

"What do you mean, good fit? He's giving this hospital and your program one and a half million dollars. How on earth does that not fit for you, Dr. Morgan?"

"No, I just meant I met him in Hawai'i at a friend's wedding and we didn't get on very well."

"Well, you're not dating the man for Christ's sake, Dr. Morgan. You're accepting his contributions to save children's lives. He must have viewed the encounter differently." The man peered over his black-rimmed spectacles at her. "I'm trying to ascertain how that doesn't fit in with your goals or the goals of this hospital?"

"No, I just mean...I think he wants to, um..."

"Listen, this is a huge donation. He's a high-profile celebrity that's new to this city and highly coveted. Furthermore, he's willing to participate in benefits and raise money for your cardiothoracic unit. So, we *will* accommodate him in any way that we can." Dickerson looked at her steely eyed. "His only request was he wants to work with you. If there's a problem with him pursuing you outside the professional realm, then we can tackle that if and when it happens." He removed his glasses and rubbed his reddened eyelids. "Look, Lillian, I understand what you're saying. Believe me, if there's a problem, the hospital and myself will support you. However, if he's looking to boost his public profile and make a fresh start here in Seattle, which is what he indicated to me, then we need to support that as well, don't we? And I need not tell you how this will benefit the children and by extension your program, now do I?"

"No, sir," Lilly responded on a vanquished sigh. "All right, when's this happening?"

****

Two days later, she sat across from Colt at an elegant table in the Grand Seattle Bistro. Dressed in an immaculate navy-blue suit, he grinned at her sour look.

"What, no 'thank you, Mr. Stone, for your most kind and generous donation?' "

"Thank you, Mr. Stone, for your very kind and generous donation," Lilly parroted, voice dripping with sarcasm. "Did you think you could buy a date with me and I'd swoon, somehow overwhelmed by your sex appeal, celebrity, and money."

"You think I'm sexy?" Colt gave her a wolfish grin.

"What. No. I…"

"Then appealing?" Colt sipped his Scotch and looked over its rim at her. "Just for the record, anytime you want to take this to the bedroom, because of my celebrity, Doc, all ya gotta do is ask." His eyes glittered under the lights.

Trying to think of something witty to say but failing, Lilly gulped more wine, playing for time. His eyes traveled to the lariat necklace trailing down between her small breasts. For reasons that only irritated her further, she blushed. He chuckled, as if knowing her thoughts.

"Why do you do that?" she asked, a miserable edge to her voice.

"What?"

"Try to unsettle me by speaking in lewd innuendos?"

"Like a Neanderthal?"

She leaned forward laying clenched fists upon the table. "I'm not one of your bimbos, Colt, or even someone that thinks *you're* something because you can catch a football."

"That would be a groupie," he quipped.

"Look, shall we end this right now?" Lilly stood, and a waiter rushed over to help her with her chair. "As much as my department and the children need your support, it's clear you have no real interest in their cause."

"Wait." Colt stood too, looking chastened. "I'm sorry. It's a defense mechanism." When she only continued to stare, he said, "Look, I told you before, you intimidate the hell out of me, and that doesn't happen very often." He held her eyes and the simple statement eased her. When the waiter asked if he should retrieve her coat, she declined and sat back down to wait him out. He sat too and after a moment, said, "You are right about one thing. I have no fuc- ah, no clue how to talk to you." He looked away and let his eyes roam the elegant room. "Most women I've dealt with are more into me and what I do than I'm into them."

"Is that supposed to make me feel pity or charmed?"

"What? No," he said quickly. "Look, it's obvious you're used to a certain type of guy, right? Does that make you a conceited snob? I mean shit, Lilly"—he leaned back in his chair—"aren't you making a bunch of judgements about me, too?"

Admonished, Lilly lowered her eyes. "Yes," she

admitted after some thought, and sipped her water. "Yes. I guess I am. For that, I'm very sorry, Mr. Stone."

"Okay, well, whatever. Why don't we just start over? I'll be more respectful and maybe you can cut me some slack for trying." When she said nothing, he ventured, "Despite what you think, I am interested in this. I've been thinking about it since I moved here and started talking about it with Watson and Tua. Before I even met you, by the way." Surprised, she smiled at him, which he returned. "I've never really thought of myself as some kind of philanthropist but when I got here, I made up my mind it would be different."

"Different?"

"Just…Why don't you tell me a little more about what the money goes for?"

"Well." She sipped her wine, took a deep breath and let it out slow. "Some of it will go toward people who can't afford the surgeries. Many times, families come from all over the state, the country, or even other countries, and surgeries and recuperations can take a very long time. We're dealing with children, and some families give up their jobs, especially single parents, to be here with their little ones."

Colt sat up and leaned his forearms on the table. "And this Pearson House helps with that?"

"The Pearson House takes on a lot of these kinds of situations. Whole families can stay there, and they provide food and accommodations for them all, but that's only part of the problem." She sipped her wine again, and set it down before ticking things off on her fingers. "The medications, tests, surgeries, and hospital stays are expensive. One or both parents are no longer working and away from home and their support systems. So, you've got food, lodging, transportation, and no one at home paying the bills. You've got healthy siblings needing to uproot their lives too. There's that emotional and psychological component, which can be overlooked but just as incapacitating." Lilly sat forward now too. "Your money would go to that, for a start. We allocate a specific yearly endowment to them. However, a chunk will also go toward new equipment, research, and technology. We've been looking into a surgical robot, made special for pediatric patients, but their price tag is astronomical."

"I always thought the money went into some giant pool and paid salaries and drugs ya can't pronounce."

"I think many people wonder about that, but no most of it will go to the families and research. I think the pharmaceuticals take more than their share but they aren't part of this. My department is ranked fourth in the nation. We've worked extraordinarily hard for that accomplishment and strive every day for higher." She considered him. "Not unlike you, I guess. Just a different type of game."

"Wait. Did you just say that we might have something in common?" Colt asked, grinning.

"Maybe," Lilly conceded and smiled. "But the work is very challenging, Mr. Stone."

"Would you stop it with the Mr. Stone."

"I like to keep my professional and personal lives separate."

"So, when we go out on our second date, you'll call me Colt?"

"This isn't a date, Colt."

"See there." He slapped the table, making an elderly couple next to them jump. "I guess we're making progress already."

"We aren't at the Steak Pit," Lilly hissed at him. "Can you please try to act with some decorum?"

"Only if you call me Colt."

"Fine," she said through gritted teeth and looked around. "Colt."

Colt watched her with a huge grin and soft eyes. "Damn, I think I might be crazy about you," he confessed.

"Is that right?"

"Yeah, I think so."

"Well, what about you?"

"You're crazy about me too?"

"No." She laughed despite herself. "Why do you play football?"

"It's all I've ever known." When she only observed him, he said, "My old man started me out in it from the time I could walk. He played in high school and wanted to go pro but got hurt."

"So, he put everything into his son, to get *his* dream?" She watched his eyes darken, and he shifted in his chair.

"Something like that."

"Is he proud of you now?"

"Sometimes."

"Sometimes? What does that mean?"

"If I do well, he's happy for a time. I could probably do better, but he won't give me too much crap about it." He sipped his whiskey.

"And if you do bad?"

"I never do bad," he said, a little too quickly, then grinned at her. She smiled but waited him out. "If I didn't perform the way he thought I should, he wouldn't talk to me until the next game. He hadn't spoken to me in weeks since I got traded. Called me up right before I left for Hawai'i."

"So, he withdraws his love because of a game and how you play?"

"A little messed up, but it did make me a better player." He reached for his Scotch again and sipped it.

"And what about your mom?"

"Ah." Colt looked away from her and at the other elegant tables. "She died when I was, what... eighteen...breast cancer."

"Oh, Colt, I'm so sorry," she replied. Quiet prevailed for several moments before she asked, "Do you enjoy playing football?"

"Wow." He thought for a moment. "No one's ever asked me that before. I guess, football's always made sense to me. Like I said, he'd get mad when I didn't do well, and that was his standard. To everyone else I was great and got a lot of recognition for the way I played." He smoothed a large broad hand over his tie. "There aren't too many jobs in the world where you get to take out your aggression physically and get paid a lot of money to do it."

"Did you go to college?"

"Yep."

"Break all the records?"

"First-round draft pick." He shifted gears. "This is going to be my fourteenth season, which is rare for a tight end."

"Because it's physical?"

"Yeah, QB's, kickers, punters, they all have longer careers because they aren't beat up as much."

"Do you ever think about giving it up?"

"Sometimes. I'm not sure what I'd do," he added. "But yeah, sometimes. If I have it my way, this'll be the last team I play for. So, I bought the big house, working on setting up some charities." He gestured to her. "Trying for a fresh start, so we'll see."

The waiter placed their meals in front of them. After he left, the couple remained quiet, sipping their refreshments. Lilly realized she'd relaxed, and watched Colt over the rim of her wine glass. He cut into his steak, then lifted his eyes to hers.

"Okay, so besides the money, tell me what else I can do to help."

Chapter Twelve

Colt caught the game-winning touchdown and stood in the end zone, arms raised to receive his due praise. Thousands of fans poured out onto the field and encircled him, chanting his name but not touching him. The Warrior cheerleaders approached in their skimpy teal and bright blue uniforms.

One by one, the girls stroked his chest, ran their hands over his body, and undressed before him. When they got to bare skin, they stepped just out of his reach and opened their circle to reveal Lilly standing before him, also clad in a cheerleaders' uniform. His eyes traveled up her body. In that moment, he wanted to take her and tried shedding his gear, singular in his desire. However, Lilly held up a hand to stop him and an invisible force prohibited his progress. He could smell her scent and feel desire radiate from her. The cheerleaders writhed and moaned all around them, almost orgasmic from unseen lovers, as fans continued to cheer.

Colt's body temperature heated until his helmet, now that of a Trojan, melted and became part of his skull. Painful, thick, fire plumes ignited from the sides of his head and curved toward the sky, until they solidified in a solid line down the middle of the helmet. Black snake-like smoke wafted up from the earth and encircled his ankles and wrists, locking him into place. The smoke turned into bindings and massaged tentacles over his chest and phallus.

He looked over at Lilly, who now knelt helpless as her skin became dusky, then turned a brilliant shade of blue. However, the color became an iridescent hue that reminded him of something just outside the confines of his mind. Her skin bubbled, separated, and formed into thousands of compact hairs. Small points protruded from her shoulders and down her arms until they freed themselves from the surface of her skin, as she screamed. Several long, hollow shoots grew, lengthening into the elegant, arching rods, as more buds sprouted from them and turned into thready feathers. As the feathers lengthened, green and blue eyes opened in intervals. At a screech of transformation, Lilly turned into a peacock, whose tail plumed out in a perfect fan. A feathered diadem lifted from her skull and the beautiful eyes all blinked at him. He wanted to mate with her, devour her, possess her, and bellowed out an unearthly warrior battle cry. Breaking his bonds, he charged at her.

Colt jerked awake, in a cold sweat, confused, agitated, and hard with desire. Glancing around his bedroom, he reoriented himself and tried to correlate anything he dreamed with his present reality and came up with nothing. Well not quite nothing, he grunted— he wanted to have sex with her, and a bunch of naked cheerleaders watching wouldn't be the worst thing, maybe even taking part. Frustrated, he realized it wasn't true. He wanted her, and only her. Breathing in deeply, he let his hand fall on his erection, knowing somehow, he would make it happen.

****

"Hut! Hut!" Derek shouted, as his offense fanned out into their positions during Friday's practice.

Colt sprinted and saw the linebacker, Dominic Brown, coming at him hard, then dip low. At the last second, Colt leapt, hurdling over his body, and continued to run into the end zone. He gave a wolfish grin at the man he'd beaten, and high-fived several players all laughing and congratulating him on his athleticism. Indignant on his friend's behalf, Eli Williams charged. The free safety ran in Colt's periphery, blind-siding his nemesis by hitting his helmet to Colt's with full force. Taken unaware, the tight end landed hard on the turf, causing a significant impact to his cranium and causing stars to blink into existence behind his eyes.

Colt shook his head to clear it, then surged to his feet. Snapping off his helmet, he threw it to the ground and attacked, thrusting his shoulder into Eli's mid-section. Raising up, Colt pummeled the man's face again and again. Eli's nose gave a satisfying crack, causing it to bleed in a crimson gush, as Colt's knuckles abraded. Tua, who had been blocking, ran over and used his massive frame to pull the TE off his attacker and hold his arms back.

Other players ran over to join the melee, dividing their allegiance. Those that had seen what happened joined Colt. Those loyal to Eli vented their anger. However, seeing blind rage in Colt's whiskey-colored eyes, some backed away appreciating they might actually burst into flame.

"Chill, man," Tua grunted and pushed Colt into some of his allies for restraint, before turning to the safety. "What the fuck're you doing man!" he screamed. "This is just a practice, Williams. What the fuck're you doing, hitting him like that?"

Williams, who had fallen, got to his feet and pushed back on Tua.

Bill Mitchell, the Warriors' head coach, bellowed into the mouthpiece of his headset, broadcasting his displeasure over the speakers.

"Enough!" the coach yelled, as some players continued to fight. "I said enough, God damn it! One more punch and you'll find your asses benched, I don't give a shit who you are!"

Murderous, Colt tried to breathe through the red haze clouding his mind. Dizzy and nauseous, his head felt like it would explode. Shaking it one more time, he tried to behave as if his teammate hadn't just rung his bell. Concussion protocol wasn't what he wanted to experience before the opening game. When Colt glanced over, the head coach stared back at him.

"Shit," Colt muttered. He spit out a glob of blood and saliva pooled in his mouth and tried a reassuring smile at the coaching staff, even giving Mitchell a thumbs up.

****

Bill clenched his jaw before he turned to his players. Some lay on the ground, others restrained, and still others holding various body parts, yet all in various stages of outrage.

"Get up...Now!" Bill ordered through gritted teeth, and slowly the men stood. "What in the hell's the matter with you? You're on the same damn team for chrissake! Opening night is the day after tomorrow, gentlemen. Start acting like it. Williams, Stone, in my office, now! Jason," he handed the headset to his offensive coach, "run suicides until they puke."

Without another word, he stalked off to his office, with the requested players trailing behind him. He clenched his jaw as the first whistle blew and heard the team grunt out their displeasure as they ran. By the time the duo arrived at his office, the coach, already seated and hunched over, steepled his fingers in front of him, lay his elbows on the chair rests. Bill gazed down at the myriad of papers, plays and schedules scattered across his desk. They were nothing compared to the tension that plagued his entire pre-season.

Mitchell was ecstatic when he realized they'd acquired the final piece to his offensive puzzle. Aware of the baggage that followed Colt, over the past couple of months the head coach also saw a man trying to change. It was his celebrity and past that caused problems.

Eli, the up and comer of his rookie season two years prior, stood out among his peers. The accolades were well deserved but rather than handling them with grace, Williams let them go to his head. In fact, his behavior was very similar to a young Colton Stone, and in the prior season the safety cemented his popularity and place on the team and among the Seattle fans. Although Eli claimed outrage and vengeance at Stone for having an extramarital affair with a friend's wife, Bill suspected it was more about Colt sharing his limelight. Hoping it would settle itself out, Mitchell realized it wasn't going to happen, and had enough of indulging it.

"I'm not having this bullshit on my team anymore!" He looked at both his players. "You boys have problems; you figure a way to work them out. But I will not have this cancer proliferating my team anymore."

"You better cut the cancer out then," Eli said, smirking over at Colt, confident the coach sided with him.

"That mean you, Eli?" Colt sneered back. "Cause as far as I can tell, you're the one that keeps running your mouth."

"Enough!" Mitchell bellowed. "Williams, Brown was beat. It was a solid play, and he was beat. Don't ever fucking target another member of my team again. The season starts in two days; everyone needs to be a single unit. Do you understand me?"

Eli clenched his jaw and started a clever retort, but Mitchell had already moved on, pointing at Colt.

"You've created animosity and discord on this team since you got here, Stone. Running your mouth every bit as much as he has. Arrogant and angry. I'm done with it. Show-boating to show-boat isn't what we do here. Everything is a team. There are no individuals, and everyone is replaceable."

"We've got young impressionable guys coming up," Mitchell continued. "Your example can guide those rookies. They look at the two of you for clues on how to behave. And what they see is how to be uptight assholes! You don't like each other. I don't give a shit. You got feelings, go see a shrink. But I'm telling you right now, the acting out will cease and desist. Do you both understand me?" He pointed at each man, and when he received reluctant nods from each, he jerked his chin toward the door. "Now, get out of my office."

****

Darkness fell two hours later, as Colt stopped at a deserted gas station for fuel on his way home. He replaced the pump on the lever when a deep rumble and glossy SUV emerged from the Seattle fog. It pulled up alongside him and Eli and Dominic stepped out. *Damn, that little shit is determined.* Colt rolled his eyes and replaced the cap on his gas tank. Brown moved around behind him and waited.

"Ya guys bring me flowers?" Colt asked.

"Oh flowers'll be blooming soon enough," Eli growled menacingly. "You can count on it."

"What's your problem, Williams? Why are you such a prick?"

"Darren's a friend of mine, and I don't want you here."

"Well, tough shit, the contract's signed, with a great bonus I might add." He closed the fuel tank door. "Nothing happened between me and Lisa. She said all that shit because she wanted two guys fighting over her. She's a bitch, and whatever happened between the two of them had nothing to do with me."

"That's not what Darren said," Eli said, and both men moved in closer.

"Well, Darren's a fucking idiot."

Without warning, Colt turned and cold-cocked Brown, sending him sprawling on the ground. Eli didn't hesitate and punched Colt three times hard in the kidney. Howling in anger, Colt turned and punched Eli in the face, splitting his eyebrow. The safety stumbled back before rushing forward again, and landed another punch to Colt's mid-section. The redhead grabbed Eli's shirt and pushed him up against the gas pump, fire igniting in his eyes, as they reflected off Eli's. Colt pummeled the lanky man's solar plexus, until he heard wheezing cut through the red haze of his mind and knew he could kill these men if he wanted to. It scared him enough to back off a few steps, but not lower his guard. Eli stood holding his ribs, one eye already swelling shut.

Energy sizzled around Colt, whispering and encouraging his violence. He glared at each man steely eyed, before collecting himself.

"That's it, we're done here," he growled. "Stay the fuck away from me, Williams, and I'll stay away from you?"

Eli hissed out a breath and spat out blood and what looked like a capped tooth. When he looked at his teammate again, Colt saw unbridled fear. Apparently, Eli witnessed the frenzy in his eyes too.

Colt discovered his fists clenched and opened them to let the blood seep back in. Looking around the dimly lit station and then past the circle of light, he saw what looked like black ribbons of energy or smoke moving in the darkness. Shaking his head to clear his vision, he looked again, and it was gone. He wondered if he had received a concussion after all. Eyeing the men, he walked back to his car.

"Don't forget to ice tonight fellas. You'll want to be in tip top shape for Sunday's game."

He folded his long frame into the driver's seat before shifting it into gear and balding the tires as he left the station. On the way home, his cell phone rang and the car display illuminated his father's number, so he hit decline. After dancing with one devil, he wasn't willing to step into the fire again so quickly.

Still riding on the red wave of anger, he tried to

think about other things. Lilly filled his mind and to his surprise, became the cooling salve that slowed his breathing.

Chapter Thirteen

"Travis, stop spinning right now and come pick up your ninja attack people," Lilly ordered.

"Yeah, and the binoculars," Chelsea demanded.

"Shut up," Travis barked back at his sister.

"Travis David, we do not say shut up." Lilly then turned to her daughter. "Chelsea, I think I'll be Mommy today, okay? Thank you *very* much."

"Fine," both children intoned in unison.

Travis continued to spin as Chelsea secured her mother's stethoscope and tried to listen to the desk's heartbeat.

"I can't hear anything, Mama." Exasperated, Lilly went over to the little girl and placed the disc square on her own chest. "Wow," Chelsea yelled over the plugs in her ears. "It's going really fast."

"Yes," Lilly said in frustration, "it is, sweetheart."

The mother gave another silent curse to her children's babysitter for canceling on her yet again. Finding a new one moved to the top of her priority list. She tried to focus on her patient's chart and finish her notes.

"Wow, it looks like powerful minds are at work in here," Colt said, leaning against the door frame.

Three heads popped up with different levels of enthusiasm. Chelsea jumped up and ran over to the giant man, lifting her arms for a hug. Smitten, Colt obliged, and the little girl surprised him by kissing him on the mouth. Excited, yet unsure about what to do or say, Travis moved closer with trepidation, until Colt ruffled his hair and the boy gave him a hug too.

"H-hello Mr. Stone."

"Remember, I told ya to call me Colt?"

"Yes sir, Colt." Travis looked like he'd float away on the request.

"Ah," Lilly said standing up. "No, it's Mr. Stone."

Colt smiled at him, then darted an exasperated look at Lilly. She gazed back at him with a confident expression. Over the past two weeks, the player had created a habit of showing up unannounced at the hospital. He'd seen patients, signed autographs, and twice cajoled Lilly into going to lunch with him. However, this was the first time he'd seen the kids since Hawai'i.

A quick scan of her office revealed the uncommon clutter of open charts, her white lab coat falling off a chair, and toys strewn all over the floor. When she looked back at Colt, he appeared satisfied with the mess, as if happy to see her capable of it. He looked at her children, who now each hung off a bicep, before he glanced up at her again.

"Hey, I wanted to talk to you about a notice I got."

"The benefit?"

"Yeah, but first, I'm super hungry. I worked hard today and was wondering if anyone could show me where the cafeteria is?" The boy and girl let go of his arm and raised their hands.

"I can show you," Travis replied. "I know exactly where it is."

"I know too," Chelsea said.

"Okay, well do they have donuts or ice cream there?"

"Yeah," Travis replied. "They have a whole bunch of flavors too."

"And I can take you," Chelsea decided.

He looked at Lilly, but asked the kids, "Well, you might need to have some with me, 'cause I *hate* eating alone. Do you think your mom can do without you for an hour?"

"Yeah!" they both exclaimed in unison, then looked at their mother with large, pleading eyes.

"Oh, I don't think…"

"Please, Mommy," Chelsea sang.

"Please," Travis intoned at the same time as his sister.

She had no real reason to refuse. She hadn't shared her kids with Colt, and now they looked at her with exuberant hope in their eyes. Staying cooped up in her office for two hours watching her do paperwork on a coveted day off from school left both children bored to the point of distraction. She eyed Colt with dubiousness, searching her mom radar for any warning bells regarding Colt and her children. The radar remained silent, and the benefits of peace and quiet beckoned, so she relented.

"Okay, but if you misbehave, even a little bit, Mr. Stone…"

"It's Colt," he reminded her.

"*Mr. Stone* will bring you back immediately. Deal?"

She rose and walked around her desk as the kids agreed and disappeared down the hall. Colt turned and

142

left the office too. However, when she got to the door, prepared to call out her thanks, he re-appeared above her. A large hand came around the back of her neck and pulled her in for a kiss. His lips, soft and sensual, opened hers, and drew in her bottom lip, before she allowed his tongue to mingle with hers. He broke the kiss as quickly as it began and smiled at her.

"You're welcome."

He turned and whistled as she stood for a moment dumbfounded. The trio walked down the hall as Colt secured both of her children's hands in his own. Deciding it wouldn't hurt, her eyes dropped and ran over the denim covering his ass. She gripped her bottom lip with her teeth, to savor the kiss. Drawing in a lung full of air, she released it in a puff and returned to her work. This time the barest hint of a smile tugged at the corners of her mouth.

****

Colt watched as Travis attacked his ice cream sundae with a single-minded determination only a young, growing boy could possess.

"And I told Emily that she couldn't choose blueberry frosting for her birthday cupcakes because I already chosed it for mine and it's not polite to be a copycat. Then, Ashley said if I'm going to play with her quick baking oven then Jasmine couldn't play with her doll and…"

Colt's eyes widened like a statue in perpetual surprise. The little girl hadn't stopped talking since they'd arrived in the cafeteria. How such a small being could go on so long without drawing breath, he didn't have a clue.

"So," Colt interrupted, taking a spoonful of soft-serve before he did harm to himself, "you guys always live in Seattle?"

"Yeah," Travis replied around a mouthful of ice cream. "We always lived in our same house."

"We probably won't ever move 'cause Daddy died there," Chelsea contributed.

"Died?" Colt asked startled, assuming the children's mother and father had gotten divorced. "When did he die?"

"Almost four years, plus some ago," Travis said with a touch of quiet sadness. "I was four."

"I was three, but Mama says we both have his hair and his eyes, so he isn't gone for real." She seemed to ponder her own words for a moment. "I'm not sure when he gave them to us though."

"He got the cancer," Travis supplied.

"Yeah, in his panties. Panties number four."

"It was his pancreas, dummy."

"I'm not a dummy." She tried to hit her brother, with a hand still holding a spoon containing ice cream. It flew off the spoon and plopped onto the floor. Travis attempted to hit his sister back.

"Hey, cool it," Colt refereed, raising a suppressing hand. "Dude, you never hit girls, never, no matter what, you feel me?" Travis lowered his eyes in shame. Colt assumed he'd been warned against this before. "Chelsea, it's not cool to hit boys either," he warned, then as an afterthought said, "unless they try to hurt you, then kick the shit out of 'em."

"You said a cursed word," the little girl scolded, scandalized.

"Sorry." Wanting to lighten the mood, Colt searched for inspiration. He looked around the cream-colored walls. Three blue and yellow stripes swirled on them and the whole place smelled like hospital antiseptic.

"Hey, you guys want to come to opening night Sunday?"

"Really? You'd let *us* come?" Travis asked, staring at him in open mouthed wonder.

"Sure. I just moved here, and I don't have any fans yet. I need a cheering section."

"Oh, that's not true. Almost all my friends like you best."

"Can I wear my cheerleader costume?" Chelsea's freckles seem to sparkle on her nose and cheeks, just like Lilly's.

Christ, I'm a goner. "Sure. We'll have to figure something out with your mom though."

"I don't think my mom likes football anymore."

"Why not?"

"Cause my dad was a quarterback in high school and college and he was really good."

"What was his name?"

"David Allen Morgan," he recited. "He played in California."

"Really?" Colt thought Travis exaggerated his father's ability but made a mental note to look him up later. For a fleeting second, Colt felt guilty for learning about Lilly through her kids, but he just couldn't help himself. "Your mom didn't want to get married again?"

"No," Chelsea said, climbing into the large man's lap and running her hand up and down the stubble of his rusty beard. "'Cause she said Daddy was perfect. She might still be sad but I'm not sad anymore and told her we need a new daddy."

"Ah…S-so, the game. Do you guys have jerseys?" Colt asked, changing the topic before those beautiful blue eyes inquired if he wanted the job.

"I have number twenty-seven, that's Elijah Williams. He's the best safety in the *whole* league."

"That so?" retorted Colt.

"Yeah, do you know him too?"

"Yep," Colt confirmed. He would remedy the jersey situation as soon as possible. Chelsea began playing with his face and making different expressions with his mouth, then giggling.

"I don't have one of those, but I can still come, right?"

"One what?"

"A jersey."

"Sure." As the little girl contorted his face again, he pretended to take a bite out of her and she giggled. "Okay, so we'll just have to find a way to tell your mom now."

"Tell Mom what?" Lilly asked, standing in the doorway.

The trio looked as guilty as gluttons over a cookie jar when they all turned and grinned at her with innocent expressions.

"Mommy!" Chelsea exclaimed and hopped off Colt's lap, running to her mother. "Colt says we can go to our first real ever football game!"

"Oh, really." Lilly blinked up at Colt with stunned irritation spreading across her face.

"Please, Mom, can we go?" Travis asked.

"Please, Mommy," Chelsea joined in.

She continued to stare at the man who looked back at her with innocence and challenge at the same time.

She'd be cursing him for sure but couldn't refuse him either.

"When is it?"

"Sunday."

"In two days, Sunday? But I'm on call."

"Really?" Colt's face fell. He hadn't thought about that.

"No, but I could've been," she muttered.

"So," he said, lips twitching into a cocky smile, "I guess I'll see you Sunday?"

She looked at her kids, grinning at her with large pleading eyes.

"What time should we be there?"

"I'll send a car."

"No," she said. "I'm capable of driving us."

"Lilly, it will be a zoo. You'll pay fifty or sixty bucks for parking or have to park a mile away and walk with these two."

The look that crossed her face told him he'd won.

Chapter Fourteen

"Mom, look at that!" Travis pointed as they passed yet another life-sized depiction of a Warrior's player.

"That is so incredibly cool!" Lilly responded, with patience only a devoted mother could have, hearing the same thing repeated several times in a row in rapid succession.

She smiled at her two precocious children and Abby. They pressed their bellies against the back of the limo seat, fogging up the window glass with each excited breath. The Morgans all wore new jerseys with 'Stone' emblazoned on the back above the number eighty-seven.

"Can you believe this?" Que asked. "It's crazy. What in the hell are we doing here, Lil?"

"Absolutely no clue."

Relieved to find out that Tua had invited Que and Abby, Lilly relaxed a little when the stretch limo arrived that morning. The Jacksons each wore the tackle's jersey with the number 'seventy-seven' affixed to it.

"Mommy, we are really rich," Chelsea stated as she turned to sit back down. "Aren't we?"

"No," her mother informed her, drawing her brows together.

"But Colt is, right?" Travis asked, turning around

too.

"I have no idea," Lilly responded. "But I *do* know it's very rude to ask. I also told you, his name is Mr. Stone, not Colt."

"He told me to call him that because we're friends now."

"You're not…" she paused. *Damn. Damn him for knowing I can't contradict that.* "Yes, honey, but little kids shouldn't call…" The car door opened, causing her to jump. She hadn't realized they stopped.

"Ms. Morgan, Ms. Jackson." The chauffeur extended a hand to help each mother out of the car. He gestured to a young woman in her thirties carrying a clipboard and wearing a headset. Her high ponytail swung as she looked up and smiled at them. "This is Brittany McDonald. She'll be explaining where to go and what to do next."

Lilly tried to extend a hand containing a tip, but the driver denied it, and said he'd been more than compensated. She pressed her lips together hard and returned the bills to her wallet. Since they awoke that morning, they received a box full of Colt's jerseys, sweatshirts, scarves, headbands, beads, and every other piece of merchandise a fan would need to attend a game. Inside the box, a note explained a car would come to pick them up and to just follow the hostess's directions once they arrived.

Now the hostess escorted them into a players' suite at the north end-zone of the field. The atmosphere was charged with opulence and electricity. Creamy walls containing signed glossy photos of the players making incredible plays adorned the entry way. As the two families walked farther in, large screen televisions decorated each wall. A full bar and wait-staff waited to do the occupants' bidding. Katie, Derek's wife, walked over and embraced the doctor, then Que. She turned to the kids and told them to go out to the seats where her twins, Dillon and Daniel, waited for them. The mothers all smiled as the boys, two years older than Travis and Abby, welcomed the newcomers, giving them benefit of their wisdom, about the suite and stadium. The children came back into the suite and congregated around the large island full of snacks, plates, and noise makers.

"May I offer you ladies something to drink?" the concierge asked. "We have water, wine, beer, cocktails, soda, tea."

"I'll take an IPA, if you have one," Que said, raising a hand, then grinned as a waiter handed her one from his nearby cooler. "Wow! Thanks."

She wiggled her eyebrows at Lilly. When the man inclined his head for her order, Lilly asked for a glass of red wine, and he produced it in record time.

"Oh, Lord," Lilly noted, as she watched the kids walk by, talking in vivid animation, plates loaded with hotdogs, cotton candy, and large sodas.

"Yeah, they'll be sick in no time," Que quipped.

The three mothers walked to the outdoor seating with their drinks and looked around at all the people in the stands. Lilly couldn't help but feel a little excited as the enthusiasm became palpable. An individual screamed out a barbaric battle cry, provoking the remaining collective to answer with their own call to arms, three times in a row.

"You do this every week?" the surgeon yelled over to Katie. "It's so high energy. Aren't you exhausted by the time you get home with the kids?"

"Yeah, is it hard being married to a football hero?" Que followed.

"You get used to it," she called back. "Once we get in here, we're protected from the fans, but they love Derek and want to talk about him. You have to put blinders on or you'll be talking to everyone all game. Most of the time they take the hint and you can watch in peace. Now going to and from the grocery store is a whole other story, especially when Derek's with me." She laughed. "Most of the time it's positive though. The negative side is, thank God, minor."

"There will always be haters, hating just because they can," Que supplied.

"Exactly," Katie responded. "Don't worry," she told Lilly, placing a supportive hand on her arm. "You guys will get used to it."

Before Lilly could respond, the music rose in pitch, and they all stood. The cheerleaders lined up to form two rows at the entrance to a large tunnel, across the length of the field. Teal and bright blue smoke billowed out of cylinders, and the crowd roared as the announcer's voice blared over the speakers.

"Ladies and gentlemen, boys and girls, welcome to the season opening game night between the Arizona Hawkeyes and your very own Seattle Warriors!"

The overhead jumbo-tron illuminated and showed a vignette of amazing plays by the team from the previous year. A live archer shot a flaming arrow into a display that caught on fire, creating a ball of destruction that billowed up into the night. The music swelled, and eight flag bearers ran with enormous team banners trailing behind them. A loud, guttural scream sounded like a battle cry, and the Warriors football team ran out to take the field. The fans, already in a frenzy, worked themselves up to a fever pitch, watching their champions burst forth.

"And now your starters…"

"It's so loud," Lilly yelled.

"Oh honey, you ain't heard nothing yet," Que shouted back.

The speaker called out the starters, and one by one the players advanced.

"Number eighty-seven, the legendary Colton Stone," the announcer drawled out the vowels of Colt's name.

He entered the arena with his hands splayed out, palms up, looking massive in his gear, and the crowd chanted his name. She looked down at Travis whose enthusiasm radiated, causing Lilly's eyes to sting. She had to admit he looked impressive. Colt pointed at their suite, and brought his arms down and in, causing his muscles to bulge, as he screamed out a Warrior cry, and she couldn't help but grin. The announcer ran through the starters.

"Number seventy-seven, Aulelei Tua."

"Tua…Tua, Twoo-Ahh!" the crowd shouted, extending the last two syllables.

"And number four, your quarterback, Derek Watson," the announcer proclaimed. "Here's your Seattle Warriors!"

Lilly sat down, took a gulp of wine, and decided what the hell, she might as well enjoy herself. It promised to be a great night.

****

Colt stood in the tunnel in constant movement,

shifting his weight from side to side, kicking out his feet and trying to center himself the way he did before every game. His thoughts kept drifting to Lilly and the kids in the audience. Feeling nervous in a way he hadn't since his first pro game, Colt wanted to make an impression. No, he wanted his talent to impress her, and for her to acknowledge his place as top in his field, just as she achieved in hers.

When his number exploded over the speakers, he ran out onto the field. Waving his arms up and down, he roiled the crowd into a frenzy, and the overwhelming sound reverberated off the stands. He'd played in this stadium many times on the opposing side. No team enjoyed playing there because the overwhelming fan noise drowned out play calls and momentum. However, now these fans churned a contagious and consuming excitement for him, and he couldn't wait to play for them.

As the crowd continued to cheer, he raised his arms wide, turning in a slow circle and looked down field to the suites. He found the tiny shape of Lilly, clapping and raising hands to her mouth, to cheer for him. Feeling energized and invincible, he brought his arms down and screamed out a battle cry. The starters encircled Tua and wrapped their arms around each other's shoulders, pumping as a unit from side to side aggressively. Tua began to chant, and the team responded to his questions.

"Whose house?"

"Our house!"

"That's right. Nobody fucks with us in our house!" The team screeched a battle cry.

"Where we goin'?"

"55!" They yelled the seasons' championship game number.

"Where we goin'?"

"55!"

"That's right, we goin' all the way baby!" Tua yelled and again, the team screamed out their battle cry. "Now, what's our name?"

"Warriors!"

"What's our name?"

"Warriors!"

"What is our name?" he screamed as loud as he could.

"Warriors!"

"Let's kick some ass!"

Screaming out their battle cry for the third time, the team left the huddle and stood on the line for the National Anthem. At its conclusion, military fighter jets flew low and in formation, as fireworks sprayed atop the jumbo-tron. Colt took the field for the first time as a Seattle Warrior.

The home team won the coin toss and opted for the other team to receive first. In the opposing teams opening drive, Eli intercepted the ball and ran it down to their own thirty-yard line, before being caught and tackled. Despite his injuries from two nights before, the safety, high on adrenaline, mocked the opposing team for what he determined ineptitude and lack of talent.

As Colt ran out to his place, he thought he heard Eli say, "Don't choke out there, King Player."

Stone secured his helmet and at the snap, watched Derek run back looking for an open man, but the opponent kept a tight cover. He struggled to get out of the pocket and throw the football. Colt sprinted and created an opening. Almost taken down, the QB eluded his enemy and darted right, looking downfield. He saw Colt nearing the end zone, and the opponent gaining ground on him. Colt pointed a little left, and the ball sailed through the air in a perfect spiral. By the time it got to Colt, two sets of arms jumped up for the retrieval. They came down as a unit, but Colt raised the ball in a victorious touchdown and the stadium erupted into applause. Derek sprinted to the end zone and hit his helmet to his new tight end's.

"Not bad, rookie," he laughed. "Nice job, man."

Tua clanked his helmet against Colt's and smacked his butt.

"Legendary Stone."

The stadium speakers came to life asking the audience to light its fire. Colt looked at the largest screen and saw a new motto following his replay, reading, 'You Got Stoned,' and a horse's whinny, cementing the tight end's celebrity status in Seattle.

He ran toward the suite and threw the ball to Travis, something they would give him a fine for later, but he didn't care. Giving Lilly a wink, he returned to the game he loved.

****

About an hour after the winning conclusion, Derek, Tua, and Colt entered the players' suite. Both Katie and Que ran to their men and kissed them with varying degrees of heat. Travis and Chelsea ran to Colt, and he picked them up in his arms at the same time. Remaining where she stood, Lilly eyed the trio as Colt accepted their hugs and Chelsea's kiss. A queer feeling ran through her. A dichotomy of happiness at the undiluted joy and love her children displayed for this man they barely knew and guilt over something she couldn't identify. Colt beamed at her, and she smiled back, trying to decide if she should give him a hug. David crept into her mind and an instant pang of betrayal wafted over her, almost in accusation for her joy.

Colt seemed to consider her conflicting emotions, and she wondered if he realized he competed with a ghost at the height of perfection that no man could ever measure up to. Carrying his load, Colt walked over to her and touched a cheek to hers.

"Thanks for coming," he said in her ear, then set the kids down.

"Oh no, it was so amazing." She reached out a hand and stroked Chelsea's silky hair before allowing her gaze to connect with his.

"You were so awesome!" Travis cried. "You had two touchdowns and two hundred and thirty-six receiving yards."

"Two hundred thirty-six?" Colt asked. "Is that right?"

"Yeah, you didn't know? You had two hundred and thirty-six and everyone was so excited 'cause you're the new favorite now! Maybe even more than Derek Watson." He lowered his voice and looked over at the quarterback, talking to his family. "You're the best, Mr. Stone."

"My name is Colt." Exasperated, he glared at Lilly before looking back at her son. "You can call me Colt, and I will be angry from now on if you *don't* call me Colt."

Looking anxious, Travis eyed his mother, who laughed.

"Yes, okay, fine, Colt it is," she acquiesced.

Victorious, Colt swung Travis onto his shoulders and Lilly picked up Chelsea, before they said goodbye to the other couples, and walked to the garage. Lilly assumed they'd take the limo back home and was surprised when Colt led them to the players' level. He gestured to his SUV, and they climbed in to meet the Watsons, Tua, and the Jacksons, for pizza and ice cream, before the group separated and Colt drove them back to their house.

****

"Okay kids, run in and wash your face and brush your teeth," Lilly said, unhooking her seatbelt as they pulled into the driveway. Silence emanated from the back seat.

"Trav? Chels?"

Both Colt and Lilly looked in the back seat to see the boy and girl fast asleep, exhausted from the day's events.

"Well, I guess we wore them out," Lilly said, resigned.

Colt chuckled and glanced over at her looking at her children. He didn't think he'd seen anything more beautiful. She looked back at him too, their faces only inches apart. Without thinking, he reached up a hand to brush the hair back from her face, then leaned in and kissed her. When he pulled back, it surprised him to see the slightest smile tugging at her lips.

"Come on," he said, unhooking his seatbelt. "I'll help you get them inside?"

"Thanks. I'll get Chels, if you can handle Travis. I'm not sure I can lift him anymore."

"Sure. Here, give me the keys."

He felt the boy's heavy weight as he transported

her son to his bed. After he pulled up the covers and walked to the door, Colt looked back and caught the moon highlighting the boy's unwashed face. A boy with no worries. Entering the hallway, he narrowly avoided running into Lilly. Pillowed between her mother's breasts, Chelsea's small mouth lay open and emitted the softest hint of a snore.

"It was a great day," Colt said, stroking a hand in the little girl's soft springy curls.

"It was a great day," Lilly agreed. "Thanks again." She smiled and moved past him to lay her daughter down.

Colt brought in the rest of their things from the car. Feeling out of place and awkward in the toy dream house, he didn't know where to stand or how to act. Lilly came around the corner, taking a breath and running hands through her hair.

"Whew, out like a light," she reported, then noticed his domestic chore. "Oh, thanks for bringing all this in."

"Welcome."

"You were very generous in your gifts, Colt. You'd think Santa came early."

"No problem."

They stood just looking at each other for a moment. Wondering if she'd kick him out or let him stay for a drink, he waited, trying to anticipate her choice.

"So, um, I think I have some wine or water or something if you…"

"Sure."

"Great." Lilly walked to the kitchen where a small wine cabinet lay and selected a bottle of Merlot. "Do you like red?"

"Sure," he responded, looking at the wall of photos in her living room and coming upon one of a fair-haired man with eyes the color of sapphires. Travis and Chelsea's eyes.

So, this is the famous David. The man looked like a model, lean and athletic, handsome and all-American. The perfect family. His eyes examined Lilly, whose black hair fell in long layers to her waist. She looked young, happy, and in love. Travis, a toddler, sat atop his father's shoulders and Chelsea, just a baby, radiated in her mother's arms. They all laughed as if the viewer caught them in mid-joke, walking in an autumn forest.

"That was the last good day," Lilly said quietly, watching him. He turned and looked at her in question. She extended a glass of wine to him and he took it. "About a week after that picture we found out David had stage four pancreatic cancer."

"That's rough." He blew out a breath, then looked back at the picture. "How old are Travis and Chelsea here?"

"Four and three." Four and three, just like the kids said.

"I didn't know he died," Colt admitted. "The kids told me a couple of days ago in the cafeteria. I just thought you were divorced."

"Yeah."

"What...How long? Was it a..." he stopped and started, trying not to sound tactless.

"It was ten months."

"Ten months?" he parroted, surprised. "That's it?"

"That was it. We thought it was a gallbladder disease—many of the symptoms are the same or similar, but we missed it." She sighed. "I missed it."

He looked back at her and realized she blamed herself for what happened to her husband.

"You couldn't have known."

"I'm a doctor," she retorted. "I'm trained to know."

"Oh, bullshit." She drew her brows together and looked at him with irritation. Undaunted, he continued. "You were his wife, not his doctor." Glancing back at the picture, he drank from his glass. "He was a young guy...looked fit...father of two." Colt turned to look at her again. "Young, fit, fathers of two don't get stage four pancreatic cancer and die in ten months. He wasn't your patient, Lillian, and you weren't looking at him like a patient. He was your husband, and he died." Walking over to her, he caught a tear that escaped down her cheek with his finger. "See, I can be perceptive and caring when I want to be."

"How often is that exactly?" she asked, looking down with a small smile.

He set his glass on a table, then took hers and did the same. He cupped her face with both hands and forced her to look at him.

"Believe it or not, I'm wanting to more and more. That's a new thing for me."

"Colt." She took a breath, placed a hand on his, and backed up a little. "Look, I know you want something, but we're broken here, and I can't give you what you..."

"Bullshit."

"It's not bullshit. It's how I feel. I've got kids to think about and responsibilities. You want easy and I'm not that."

"You don't even know me, Lilly."

"I know. That's what I've been trying to say."

"No, that's what you're trying to use as an excuse. Those kids aren't damaged because of their dad, you are." When she only gaped at him, he threw caution to the wind. "Those kids have a mom who loves them and makes damn sure they aren't damaged. You're afraid to try, so you hide behind your dead husband."

"How dare you be so callous?"

"How dare you use your husband to get out of trying again?" He took a step toward her and she took a step back, knocking her head against the wall. She placed her hand on the spot of the pain as he approached. Removing her hand, he kissed the top of her head. "You're a beautiful, intelligent woman. Your life isn't over." She looked so small next to him, powerless. She lifted her head, as if to say something, and he saw tears shining in her eyes. Bending his head, he captured her mouth with his. Lilly made the most sensual sounds in her throat, making his blood heat and his body harden.

She placed her hands on the tensing pectorals of his chest, and bunched his shirt in her fists. He released her head and let his hands roam down and over her bottom, causing her to hum. Encouraged, he reached a hand up and found her small breast, squeezing an erect nipple through the jersey that bore his name. Long liquid pulls in his stomach intoxicated him as Lilly reached a hesitant hand around to cup his ass. She opened her eyes, and Colt knew the exact moment they found the photo of David behind him, and he cursed himself for not turning their bodies. She jerked back as if slapped, and stared into his eyes, like she'd never seen him before. Trying not to grimace as his penis strained in discomfort against the denim of his jeans, Colt clenched his jaw.

"Christ, Lilly," he said, trying to draw breath and stepped back.

"I'm so sorry. Colt...I can't do this. The kids are in the next room." She looked up at him with large, pleading, mossy-green eyes. "They could walk out here. How would I explain it? I-I can't even explain it." He moved back from her only a little to give her some room, then dipped his forehead to hers. He inhaled her scent, as she just closed her eyes. "I'm sorry. I'm not trying to play games with you, I promise. I just...I..."

"Be honest with me," he said, searching her eyes. "Do you like it when I touch you?"

"It scares me."

"But do you like it?" He ran his thumbs down the sides of her throat.

"I," she whispered and looked down. "I don't know."

"I'll take that as a yes." He kissed her forehead, then her eyelids, before poising a hair's breadth from her mouth. "Do you like it when I kiss you?"

"Colt." She cast her gaze down again, and he raised her chin, so their eyes would once more find each other. She nodded. Elation seared through him, yet he restrained himself.

"I want you. Lilly." He kissed her neck. "I want my hands on you." He kissed the tip of her nose. "I wanna watch you lose control." Feeling her body quiver, Colt stepped back, deciding to let her think, rather than frighten her. "You know how I feel. I'll try and back off a little but..." He walked to the front door, and when he opened it, the cool, clean crispness of the night floated in. Turning back to her, he said, "Just...Lil? Don't make either of us wait too long, okay?"

Without waiting for a response, he turned and walked out under the illumination of the moonlight.

Chapter Fifteen

The day had been a grind. Lilly's sitter had cancelled on her thirty minutes before the children's school day began, causing her to be late for morning rounds. Relief flooded over her when Que agreed to pick them up after school. Since she went to the game Sunday, the doctor didn't complete all the paperwork and chart notes from the week before, and the result lay strewn across her desk. More accumulated throughout the day, but she couldn't focus on it. One of her small patients experienced a complication with surgery, coded, and lost her life on the table in the early afternoon, an aspect of her career Lilly never learned how to accept.

She stared at a chart she should have completed two hours earlier, when Colt and his mind numbing kiss permeated her mental membrane. More than anything, the experience of the night before left her twitchy and confused about how to proceed. A headache of massive proportions swirled in her temples, leaving her close to tears, when a newspaper landed on her desk with an accusatory slap.

In the photo, Colt leaned into her in the players' suite, Travis and Chelsea in his arms. The angle of the photo implied a smoldering kiss to come. Lilly frowned at it, then looked up into the stormy steel-gray eyes of her sister-in-law, Olivia.

"What the hell is this?" she demanded. "Are you seeing him?"

The noise stabbed into Lilly's head like a needle spike, causing her to wince. She glanced back down at the paper, which appeared to be an expose on the town's new player. The caption under the picture read, *Colt and his new filly, Dr. Lillian Morgan.* She snapped her head back up, mind racing. *How in the hell did they have her name?* She considered it a small miracle they hadn't printed her children's names. When she looked up again, Olivia's angry face loomed in her entire field of vision.

"It's nothing, Liv. I met him at Raven Hunter's wedding a few months ago. Travis noticed him and began talking with him," she evaded. "He considered giving some time to a charity and became my department's benefactor."

"That's a fairly big leap to go from supporting your work, to you and the kids going to one of his games and kissing him for the newspapers."

"Olivia, I wasn't kissing him for the newspapers. He's a nice guy, who gave us tickets to the opening game. I told him how much Travis loves football. That's it. And I wasn't kissing him, I gave the guy a hug. That's just an unfortunate angle."

"That's it?" Olivia asked, throwing her coat and purse onto a chair. Her eyes studied the picture. "It sure doesn't look like it. You know what kind of guy he is, right? His reputation? Because I do. Joe said he's dangerous and has an anger problem. He's slept with like a million women."

"Olivia, it isn't like that."

"What in the hell would David think of you? Dating this guy makes a fool out of my brother, Lillian." Her sister-in-law's voice bordered on a screech, causing tiny explosions of pain to go off in Lilly's brain.

"Now, look," Lilly responded with heat. She rose from her seat to circle around the desk. "First off, I would do nothing to disrespect David's memory. I loved him more than anything else in this world, Olivia, and I miss him every single day of my life. I thank God I have two living reminders of him. So, do not ever suggest I didn't. Second, I'm not dating Colton Stone. He was extremely considerate to me and the kids and generous enough to create a very memorable day at the stadium for all of us. So, please stop creating drama where there is no stage."

"Then why is he carrying the kids and kissing you?"

"God damn it, I just told you he wasn't kissing me! It's the angle of the photographer, in this picture," she said, side-stepping the fact he kissed her later that night and she'd kissed him back. "He kissed my cheek. You know, like you say hello to a friend? The game just finished, they won, and he played well. Everyone was happy and excited."

"So...he's a friend?"

"Yes," Lilly hissed. "He is, and will remain one. Please don't ever come barging into my office again telling me who I can be friends with or how to live my life."

"And he's never kissed you?"

Lilly just stared at her. Rage bubbled inside her. "I'm done. Go home, Olivia."

"Well, okay. I'm sorry then." Olivia brightened. "You want to go get some lunch? How are the kids?"

Lilly clenched her jaw but wasn't up to the fight that would inevitably occur, so decided to let it go…yet again.

"I can't. I'm back-logged with charts. I had a terrible outcome today in surgery, and two more back-to-back surgeries tomorrow that I need to prepare for." *And there's not a snowball's chance in hell I could spend another minute, let alone an hour, in the same room with you right now.*

"Fine, and the kids?"

"The kids are great. Travis is playing football and Chelsea has a recital coming up."

"Great! Give me the details and I'll tell the folks. We'll all come."

"They'd love that. And how are Joe and the kids?"

"Oh, they're fantastic," Olivia replied. "They chose Helena for the homecoming court. I just know she'll win queen. I mean you should see the other girls. One has half her head shaved, and the other one is a total bitch, everyone knows that. Helena is the most talented by far. And Henry is taking the SATs next week. I'm sure he'll only need to take them once, he's so prepared. If that kid isn't the valedictorian, there *will* be hell to pay."

"Hmm," Lilly said, as she moved back behind her desk, without listening. With Olivia she never had to. The same words came out of her mouth every time they spoke anymore, and it made her sad they'd grown apart.

"Dad tell you he just got that new project downtown?"

Lilly heard the pause in the conversation, not the

actual question. "I'm sorry…what?"

"I said, did Dad tell you he got that new project downtown?"

"Ah…no. That's fantastic. He worked hard for that."

"And Mom's been going around room by room organizing, cleaning, and fixing everything up."

"What for?"

"She said she's been wanting to do it for a long time." Her voice quieted. "I think it keeps her busy and not thinking about…things."

"Yeah," Lilly whispered. Olivia had a way of sucking all the energy out of a room.

"Well," her sister-in-law said, now that she had the proper reverent feeling she intended. "I'm off. I'll let you get back to your chart…things. I just wanted to know what was going on." She shrugged on her coat and picked up her purse, as the doctor rose to say goodbye. "Just remember what I said, Lil. That guy is a complete player."

"Okay, Liv. Thank you for your concern."

The woman moved to leave, and Lilly reached to close the door, when Olivia turned around.

"David's watching over you and the kids. He might not be here in the flesh to see it, but he's watching all the same. Make sure what he sees makes him proud."

Lilly closed her eyes as anger raged inside her. Taking a deep breath, she tamped it down so she wouldn't start a fight, when peace was just inches away.

"That's all I've done since he died, Olivia. I'd like to think I've done him great honor and he's happy with how I've handled things."

"Sure, just…keep it in mind."

Her sister-in-law turned with a flourish and whipped out her cell phone as she walked down the hall, heels clicking on the light blue tile. The altercation left Lilly feeling as if she been dealt a physical blow to her gut. Circling back to her desk, she leaned back in her chair and closed her eyes again.

When Lilly arrived home that night, the kids all sat around the kitchen table doing homework as Que read to Chelsea.

"Hi," Lilly said on a sigh.

"Hey. There's chicken, angel hair pasta, and salad in the fridge."

"You're a life saver, Que. Thank you so much for this."

"It's all good. These guys were just getting ready to watch a show."

"I'm done," Travis said, closing his math book.

"I've got two more words," Abby said, her pink tongue sliding back between her teeth.

"Here, Trav," Que said, helping Chelsea down off her lap. "Why don't you guys go pick out a short one."

As the kids ran into the living room, Que walked to Lilly's cupboard and pulled out a bottle of wine.

"You look like you could use this."

Lilly placed her plate in the microwave and turned it on. She glanced at the bottle of wine and nodded, worried she'd make her headache worse, but decided not to care.

"Just a half glass."

"Done," Abby announced and raced into the living room to see what the Morgan kids selected.

"Bad day?" Que asked as she twisted the

corkscrew into the bottle's neck and pulled. It popped, and she relieved the bottle of two glasses of wine, as Lilly also grabbed a bottled water from the refrigerator.

"The worst, but it's over now. How was your day?"

"Great."

"Oh yeah?"

"Al sent me two dozen roses."

"Wow." The microwave pinged, and Lilly retrieved her food as both women settled down at the table.

"We're going away for a couple of nights."

"What about practice?"

"We'll work around it. We're going to this place in Bellingham and going to learn how to line dance."

"Line dance?" Lilly tried to picture the massive football player in boots and a flannel, and noticed Que's flushed face. "You really like him, huh?"

"I love him," she corrected. "I told him last night."

Lilly set her fork down and stared at her friend. "You told Aulelei you loved him last night?"

"Yep. It was our also our anniversary."

"Anniversary?" Lilly felt doubt bubble to the surface. Que had a daughter, responsibilities, and never once seemed to question the timing of any of her choices. "Isn't all this moving a little fast?"

"Oh, Christ, Lil! You sound like a broken record. Look, I don't need to approach dating like you do."

"How's that?"

"At a glacial pace."

"I just want to make sure…"

"Lilly, sloths move faster than you."

Angry, the doctor started to retort, then realized she'd just had this same conversation with Olivia.

However, in this scenario, Lilly was behaving exactly like her sister-in-law. She stopped talking and forked a mouthful of food into her mouth, reminding herself that she and Que had two very different approaches to life.

Chapter Sixteen

Sam Iverson and Colt settled into a booth at a sports pub, waiting for Colt's father. The elder called Colt and demanded a meeting. With understanding that Colt and his father didn't do well on their own, Sam made the meeting a priority and public, opting to stay with his star client and friend for moral support.

"You seem like you were born to play here," Sam said and gave a jovial smile to the waitress as she set down his drink. "Things workin' out well in the locker room?"

"Well enough," Colt hedged, and sipped his beer.

"Hmm, 'cause I heard a rumor."

"Oh yeah? What's that?"

"You pounded on Williams a little hard."

"Fucker jumped me at a gas station."

"This about Darren?"

"Man, I don't know what's going on. I've told him, there was nothing there. I tried ignoring him. He just will not let the shit go."

"You got friends here?"

"Yeah, they know the score."

"Good," Iverson said and sipped his Scotch. "You want me to talk to Mitchell?"

"God, no. At some point the shit's got to blow over."

"Glad to see you've got your priorities straight." A newspaper flopped down in front of him. "Who's the skirt?"

Colt glanced up to see his father looming over him. Disappointment shone through the player at his early arrival.

"Dad."

"Hello, Andrew." Sam raised a hand, which the elder Stone ignored. Sam turned it into a gun and pulled the trigger, but Andrew didn't seem to notice.

"Dropped the ball in the third," his father accused.

"Watson under-threw it," Colt returned.

"Always an excuse."

"Always a criticism."

"Aw, didn't know you're so sensitive, Mary."

"You flew three hours to be here, you gonna sit down or are you just gonna stand there disgusted and without purpose?"

Andrew drew in a breath and let it out, with force. The waitress started in his direction as he barked, "Get me a double jack straight up." He grabbed a chair from a nearby table and sat down. "So, who's the girl in the picture, Colt?"

Colt glanced down at the paper, not wanting to think about what Lilly would say. He gave a non-committal shrug.

"So, not only are you not taking my advice and focusing on football but now you're into it with some doctor and her brats?"

"Watch it, Andrew," Colt warned.

"Oh, did I overstep the mark? What the hell is some doctor doing takin' up with you?" The waitress placed his drink in front of the old man, but he didn't even look up. Colt gave her an appreciative smile.

"She's beautiful," Sam noted. "What kind of doctor?"

"Kids heart."

"Wow, good for you," his agent commented, and Colt smiled at him.

"Yeah, except she's gonna take your edge, your money, and then your career. Mark my words."

"Look," Colt growled, irritation erupting in him like a grease fire. "You invited yourself here tonight, but you don't have to be here. Why don't you just try to relax and enjoy your drink?"

"Truth hurt, Colt?"

"Whose truth?" Colt retorted, a red flush scurrying up his neck. "Damn, why can't you ever, just once be satisfied?"

"Jesus, but you're soft headed. Your mother…"

"Yeah, she'd be disappointed, she'd cry, she'd disown me, probably a good thing she's dead."

Andrew's hand shot out of nowhere and slapped his son, hard across the face, then stood face filled with fury. "Do not ever disrespect my wife again. Own the fact you're a piece of shit, and you'll always be a piece of shit."

He stood, drained his drink, and walked out of the bar, leaving his son molten with embarrassment and fury. Sam raised a restraining hand without touching him before Colt could stand and retaliate.

"Let him go, Colt," he advised.

"The asshole comes all this way, for five fucking minutes."

"Yeah, but he has to live in that world. Be thankful you only have to see him for five fucking minutes."

****

Andrew left the restaurant in a black rage. He'd never understand his son. All that God given talent, and he kept pissing it away. Andrew's dream since childhood included him in a pro uniform and living Colton's life. He too had been a modern-day gladiator, and by the time he'd come of age, his future appeared set and golden.

His senior, and second, year set to become an all-American, lay on the horizon. The most beautiful girl in town, and most prized achievement, stood by his side. And the letters of intent to play for colleges flooded his mailbox, until the game and tackle that changed his life.

As a wide receiver, Andrew took hits, but as he caught the ball and ran that fateful night under the lights, two opposing players ran into him. One broke his kneecap, and the other caused a fracture to his femur and pelvis. He lay there on his back, body broken, with the second player still lying on top of him. The boy looked down at him with ugly inhuman eyes, causing Andrew to draw in a deep breath and pain to sear through him. He cried out, and when he blinked again the boy vanished and his future now looked dark and bleak.

Everyone told him only one player hit him, but he didn't believe them. From that day, the only thing he kept was the love of a devoted woman, who remained the best part of him until her death. She bore him a son, and Andrew decided that son would carry the torch that elusive player snuffed out. As Colton talents grew, Andrew's heart blackened to charcoal. The boy became a natural, his gift pure. Where his father had to work hard, then lose his talent, Colt's ability came easily, and he seemed to take all of it for granted.

As the elder Stone took a taxi back to his hotel at the airport, he muttered curses at his son. By the time he opened the door to his room, changed, and poured himself another whiskey from the bottle he bought next door, his mood leveled out some. Lying down on his bed, he switched on late-night television and immediately fell asleep, snoring loudly.

The television flickered off, and his body twitched. Deep in his throat the secretions thickened, and his snores turned into wet, choking gasps. A small, black substance began to pool in his mouth, filling it. He convulsed, and the substance trickled out and down the sides of his neck, creating a web that wove up onto his face. The Okapnose threaded and wove down his body, cocooning him, and Andrew no longer breathed. When the last visage of it spewed from his mouth and tried to detach from its anchor, it could not do it. It pulled hard and writhed, like a snake being held by its tail, but the Dark Abyss held on. As an understanding of the limitation crystallized, a defiant scream bellowed from the depths below.

The black threads turned to smoke and vanished, causing the old man to gasp in a lung full of air and wake. He blinked around the room, trying to understand his whereabouts. Since that fateful night and his terrible accident, the same thing occurred too many times to count. Andrew looked at the television and viewed his son, in a recap of the game, catching a pass for a touchdown, as thousands cheered him on.

****

Colt returned home that night and flicked on the light in his office. Peeling off his jacket, he laid it on a chair. Instead of sitting behind the desk and checking emails, he sat in the small couch in front of it, thinking. His eyes fell on a picture, of his mom, dad, and him.

Eighteen years old, Colt sat at a desk holding a pen poised over a letter of intent to play D1 collegiate football. His beautiful mother looked at him with a smile, and though already sick, she radiated with pride. Her arm lay across his shoulders. His eyes flickered over to his father, who stood back and slightly away from the duo, arms folded across his chest, and a scowl plastered on his face. Colt relaxed his own face when he realized he wore the matching expression.

"Should've dumped your ass and never looked back," Colt said, then looked back at his mom.

Every day from the moment the diagnosis came to seconds before she passed, she made her son promise to watch over his father and take care of him. Even then, she must have known what their relationship would be. Yet she'd asked him not to give up on her husband. For the sake of her and that promise alone, he hadn't walked away. The thought of disappointing her, too painful to accept and his father knew it. Colt looked back at his dad. Plus, God help him, he wanted the old bastard's approval, and always had.

Chapter Seventeen

—Dinner?— Colt texted.
—Can't, long shift.— Lilly texted back.
—When then?—
—I'll let you know.—

Colt threw his cell on the shelf of his locker after practice with frustration. Lilly moved from hot to cold, then cold to hot. Just when he thought things progressed into more, she'd slam on the brakes for no apparent reason. He whipped the towel from his waist and dried off his chest. He spent time with her and the kids, but she never asked anything from him. Tua came around the corner naked, with his towel slung over his shoulder.

"Good practice," he said to Colt and reached to the top shelf of his locker, retrieving his deodorant.

"You too. What are you doing tonight?"

"Well, I *was* going out with Q and A, but your girl messed me up." Tua recapped his deodorant after using it and toweled off his body.

"Lilly? How?" Colt slid on his underwear and adjusted himself before grabbing his jeans.

"She's on call or something and having problems with her sitter. So, Que's getting all of them and hanging at Doc M's house 'til she gets home."

"She there now?"

"Yeah, I think so." Tua grabbed his cell phone and checked the time. "Should be."

"What were you guys going to do?"

"Gonna see a show at six." He threw an arm into his shirt, and then the other.

Colt thought for a moment and realized this might be a chance to prove to her he could help, while also helping out a friend at the same time. "Would it be cool if I went over there and took over?"

"Really? You'd do me that solid?"

"Sure." Colt laughed, throwing a hoody over his head. "You'll owe me one."

"You got it! Okay, I'll call her, or just come with me and we'll surprise her."

"Even better."

****

Lilly stopped by the grocery store to buy a bottle of wine and a pizza for her, Que, and the kids to share. She juggled the bottle, the pizza box, her purse, and her briefcase to the front door, but to her supreme frustration, discovered it locked. Blowing the hair out of her face, she moved to set some things down and retrieve her keys, when the door opened. Colt stood in the threshold in worn jeans and a soft blue hoodie looking down at her.

"Ah..." Lilly gaped, feeling an instant of sheer pleasure at seeing him, then disbelief and confusion. "What are you doing here?"

"Tua came over to get Que and Abby." He grabbed the things out of her hands, then stood back so she could enter her home.

Lilly looked around for Que to give her a glare of disapproval. When she only discovered her kids sitting at the table doing homework, her frown deepened.

"Where's Que?"

"Oh, I told them to go. They wanted to see a movie, and I said I'd wait."

"Mama!" Chelsea called and ran over to her, reaching up for a hug.

Lilly stooped to pick her up, as Travis spoke animatedly about the football instruction he'd received from his new hero.

"And *finally*, I threw a perfect spiral," he babbled.

"A perfect spiral, wow, that's awesome, baby." She bent and kissed the top of her son's head as she looked at Colt with resentment. He cocked his head to the side as if confused by her reaction. "Okay, well why don't both of you go wash your hands. I brought home pizza for dinner."

"Pizza!" They both squealed and stumbled over each other as they raced to clean up.

Colt leaned back against the counter, crossed his arms and ankles, and waited for her to say something.

"What are you doing here, Colt?"

"I told you."

"So, you, Tua, and Que decided all of this and didn't even ask my opinion?"

"Why? What's the problem?"

"Why? Because they're *my* kids, Colt," Lilly whispered, eyes firing. "I decide who takes care of them and what goes on in their lives."

"And I'm not okay to take care of them or be in their lives?" he whispered back.

"No…Yes…Look, I don't know…Come here." She grabbed his arm and pulled him into the living room, calling out for the kids to get started on their dinner. "I don't know what I feel about any of this, but I can tell you I *am* feeling a lot of pressure from you. The kids like you, and sometimes it feels like you're using them to get to me, and that I can't have."

Colt's neck flamed and he seemed to clench down on a strong emotion. He took a deep breath and spoke in a measured tone.

"You sure think a lot of yourself, don't ya Doc? Can't I just want to hang out with them? They're cool kids."

"Right. So, you haven't been trying to screw me since we met, at all."

"I don't need your kids to like me to fuck you, Lilly." His voice raised a little. "What the hell's going on?"

"Keep your voice down," she hissed.

"I like your kids, and they like me. We have a lot of fun together. So, what's your problem with that?"

She grabbed his hand and dragged him outside, under a burnt-out light by the garage. "You're making it impossible for me to say no to you because of them and it's pissing me off."

"Huh. So, you've been trying to say *no* to me this whole time, is that it?"

"We just met."

"We met almost four months ago."

"Well, I realize for you that might be an entire relationship, but I'm not like Que. I won't invite someone so completely into my life in two seconds."

"Four months," he retorted. "And I'm pretty sure I haven't asked you to bed yet."

"Oh, right."

"And the kids are, what? My evil plan to…what?"

"You being friends with them and encouraging them makes it harder on me, because…because…"

"Because, what?" he demanded. He used his body to invade her space a little.

She looked at his mouth, to his massive chest, then up to his eyes. "You are such a jerk sometimes."

Colt laughed derisively. "Yeah, well, you're a huge pain in my ass too." He looked down at her mouth. "Do you want me to leave Lil? Stay away from you and Travis and Chelsea?" He hovered inches from her. "Because I won't. You want me as much as I want you, and what's worse is you know it. It pisses me off to hear you say you think I'm using them to get to you. I was just trying to help, and I don't screw with kids' heads that way."

She said nothing, and he bent down to eye level. Considering his eyes, she only wanted to get lost there for a moment, and leaned over to kiss him. At first, he held back, but all the frustration inside her poured out and into the kiss, causing him to respond. She realized she'd missed him, but didn't want to.

"This you saying no, Lilly?" he asked, hands moving up her waist and onto her breast. "You want this to stop?"

"You're such an asshole," she gasped.

He laughed, and his tongue violated her mouth, dancing over it and seducing hers. Knowing she should push him away, she found she couldn't. His hands moved down to the hem of her pencil skirt and started to pull it up. She slammed her hands down to stop him, breathless, and looked around the darkened street for neighbors.

"We can't."

She swore his eyes ignited in front of her. Reaching up between her legs, he cupped her, and with helpless betrayal her body went damp. Decency battled against yearning, and still he studied her as he slipped a large middle finger into her panties, then inside her. She panted out a gasp at the violation, and need bubbled within her. It had been so long since she'd last felt that deep, primal ache of wanting. Her orgasm peaked, and she cried out, causing him to cover her mouth and swallow her plea. He removed his fingers, and for a moment she kept her eyes closed. Feeling like a coward, she opened them to face the intimacy, and still he watched her, with an expression she couldn't discern.

"Colt," she whispered, as realization about what they'd just done rushed in.

"Mom?" The couple gave a violent start to the simple question and searched each other's eyes before breaking apart. "Mom? Colt? Are you out here?" Travis called out.

Still breathless, Lilly shoved Colt back, and in a frenzy tried to straighten her skirt. Colt realized he'd be no help in her struggle for composure, so ran a hand through his hair, and took a deep breath. He left her and walked between the two cars.

"Oh, hey, man. I was helping your mom out, with some…s-stuff." He glanced back at her, and she darted a nervous plea back at him, running a hand down to smooth her hair. "But we're almost done talking. Did you get your homework done?"

"Yeah, I figured out that one hard one."

"Oh yeah," Colt said, feeling like someone had doused him and his member in cold water. "What did it wind up being?"

"Two hundred and twenty-four."

"Fantastic, bud!" He looked at Lilly. "Twenty-eight times eight," he informed her of the tricky equation. "Okay, well, I'm going to finish talking with your mom, then take off, okay."

Colt looked back at Lilly, now much more composed, albeit still a little breathless. She rounded the corner with a smile. "Hey, honey, let's go back inside. It's cold out here."

"You were gonna leave without saying goodbye?" Travis asked, and walked over toward Colt.

"Oh, just for today. Remember, we still have some other stuff to work on before your practice. Ah," he said, remembering Lilly's admonishment, and added, "if it works out. Okay?"

"Okay." Travis neared, and Colt realized his own body no longer betrayed him, so allowed the boy to advance and returned the boy's hug. "Thank you for today and everything, Colt."

Lilly's eyes stung with tears, mortified at what she had just done in her driveway, for God's sake. Just feet from her children. Angry at her desire and need for Colt, the release, and now scared at the vulnerability her little boy just exposed to him. She'd never in her life done anything as reckless as she just had, and it terrified and exhilarated her at the same time.

"You're welcome, pal. Come here, blondie," he called out to Chelsea, who had just come around the corner in her pink, paisley nightgown. "Come give me a hug then get back inside, where it's warm."

He met her halfway, when she launched herself at him, wrapping thin fragile arms around his neck and kissing his cheek and forehead. He set her down, and both kids scampered back into the house. Colt looked at Lilly, still smiling at their exuberance.

"I-I better go in," she stated and moved toward the house.

"I won't hurt them, Lilly...or you."

She stopped and looked at him. "I know you won't mean to, but..."

"We both know this has potential."

"I'm not sure that I know that."

"Yes, you do. You're just scared." He walked to his car and opened the door. "Your move, Doc." He slid into the driver's seat, started the engine, and drove away, his taillights disappearing in the darkness.

****

Lilly read stories and tucked her children into bed, as they babbled about the wonderful, Colton Stone. Pouring herself a cup of tea, she then sat in the dim light of her living room. She reviewed the fatal surgery again several times, trying to determine if she'd made an error somewhere. She hadn't, but only after exhausting all possibilities did she accept with sadness, that sometimes little ones died on the table. Her thoughts turned to Colt, and the fact she just had her first orgasm in four years by another's hand...literally. She laughed out loud then stifled it just as abrupt. Along with reckless, it had been fun, exciting, and daring.

Her blood hummed, rising in heat once more. She flushed and took a sip of tea to douse the rising inferno, when her cell phone rang. As a physician, Lilly always carried her phone nearby in case of an emergency with one of her patients. She looked at the display and a broad smile spread across her face because right then she needed a friend.

"Raven? How are you? Officially four months in, how's married life?"

"Fantastic!" Raven gushed. "I hadn't talked to you in a couple weeks and wanted to see how you guys were doing."

"We're great!" Lilly said, with a little too much enthusiasm, then realized how she sounded and tried to tone it down. "Busy as ever."

"Lil?" Raven said concerned. "You sound...I don't know...what's going on?"

"Nothing I," she started, then changed her mind and went with honesty. "I lost a patient a little while ago and we're closing the case. A little girl."

"Oh, Lil." Raven sighed. "Oh, honey. I can't imagine what that does to a surgeon. I'm so sorry, does..."

"And Olivia..."

"Olivia?" Raven asked. "Was that her mother?"

"David's sister."

"Oh," her friend said, as if surprised at the quick change of topic. "O-kay."

"She said if I go out with Colt, it's disrespecting David. But he showed us such a good time. And then there was a photographer, and it was such a bad angle. But then later, he kissed me, and okay, yeah, I didn't think I liked him before, or maybe it's just that I shouldn't. And my babysitter keeps flaking, and tonight...tonight..."

"I...ah..."

"No, I'm good. Seriously, I just, I..." Lilly stopped talking. Her words sounded frenetic and worrisome to her own ears. Suddenly, she wanted Raven's advice, but didn't know how to frame the question. Having an epiphany, she started with a slow, direct question. "When you met Finn, you said you weren't super responsive, right?"

"Well, if I'm being honest, I didn't want to be responsive, but I was. I was just scared."

"You didn't want to be though, right?"

"No, I guess I didn't want to be, but it was more the timing of the thing."

"What changed?"

"Okay. Lil, what's going on?" Raven asked, concern once more etched in her voice. "Wait, before you answer that, let me see if I got this all straight." She took a deep breath. "Colt asked you and the kids to go to a game. I already knew that because Que told me. And you must have had fun because you kissed, and a photographer took a picture of it? Is that right?"

"No, he didn't kiss me at the game, but he did later that night. At my house…in the living room."

"Okay, so how does…Olivia, was it? How does she know about it then?"

"The photographer put it on the front page of the sports section."

"Oh, shit."

"Yeah, oh, shit. But he didn't kiss me then, it was just the angle. He kissed me later that night, after he brought us home. But the picture looks like he's about to kiss me. But he wasn't. He was just going to kiss my cheek. And he was holding both the kids. And they said in the caption I was his new filly."

"Well, that's insulting," Raven said with disgust. "Not the almost kissing, but I don't like the whole 'filly' thing. I must admit the rest sounds kind of wonderful. So, what's the problem?"

"Olivia saw the paper and got pissed off and offended. She thinks I'm disrespecting David's memory by going out with a man like Colt."

"And…I'm sorry, what kind of man is that?"

"A womanizer who's known for his temper. She thinks I'm a horrible mother."

"That cannot be true."

"No, she didn't say that," Lilly admitted. "But she sure implied it."

"Okay, well first off, you aren't disrespecting David's memory at all. He loved you and would want you to be happy, wouldn't he?"

"Yes, but Colt is so different…In fact, he couldn't be further away from David if he tried."

"You told me he became the new benefactor to your department three months ago, right? How's all that going?"

"It's good, but I can't tell if it's just to have sex with me or if he really wants to do it."

"That's not very fair or nice to either of you."

"He's strong-willed, angry and…wild."

"Okay, well, that kinda sounds fun."

"Right, because you would've gone for someone like that?"

"Well, I didn't get that exactly, but Finn *is* a lot different from Donovan. In fact, they couldn't be further apart. I know what you're saying, Lilly, but sometimes different is exciting, and that's okay too."

"I have kids to worry about."

"Has he given you any sign he doesn't like your kids, or that you have something to worry about where they're concerned?"

"No."

"Well?" Raven paused. "You can tell me to mind my own business, but have you been intimate yet?"

"No, absolutely not. I told you he just kissed me."

"And you said you kissed him back? And you said something about tonight. What happened tonight?" When she received a long pause in response, she asked, "Lil?"

"Yes."

"Well?"

"He, ah…" She paused, then said in quiet horror at her behavior, "He sort of got me off—" She paused again. "—in the driveway."

"What?" Raven expelled a breathy laugh.

"It just happened."

"It just happened?"

"Yeah."

"But you liked it?"

"Yes," she admitted. "But it wasn't sex."

"Well, whatever it is, it's fantastic, and your sister-in-law should just butt out if she can't be supportive. Seriously, it isn't cool to dump on you like that. You deserve all the fun you can have. Go enjoy him. And if he's wild, that's got to bubble over into good sex, don't ya think?"

"Maybe. I'll probably get an STD. He's got to have something, right?"

"Lilly, come on, that's not okay," Raven admonished but giggled. "I, of all people, know how the media can distort a personality. They have a special knack for dramatizing small things to make them look very different from what they really are. Most of what they print is total bullshit."

"His reputation seems…"

"The only way you'll know anything real about him is to talk to him directly about it. Trust me on that. It's what's fair. And if he has a past…Well, who doesn't? No one's perfect. It's just…"

"David was perfect," Lilly murmured.

"David was perfect," Raven parroted. "Really, Lil? Was he perfect or has he just passed on?"

"What's that supposed to mean?"

"You know both of my parents died in a car wreck when I was eight, right?" When her friend affirmed it, Raven went on. "They became the ideal. They became almost God like to me. When I married Donovan, I thought I'd found that security again. Almost like a father figure. I'm not proud of it, but there it is." She sighed, then continued. "When Wyatt and I were in foster care, they matched us with an awful man. But frankly, even if they'd placed us with a good and nurturing family, I'm not sure I would have accepted that either."

"Because they weren't your parents, who represented your entire world. Then they were taken from you tragically, which immortalized them as saints forever," Lilly said, as if quoting from a textbook.

"Well, I couldn't have said that better myself." She paused, letting the silence grow. "And don't you think you've done the same thing with David? Not that he wasn't a good man, I'm sure he was, but he *was just* a man. He wasn't a saint." Raven rushed on. "He's the father of your children, and you guys were married for fifteen years. You grew up together, spent all those formative years with each other, had all your firsts together. And then he died from a horrible, despicable disease that you couldn't fix."

"Couldn't fix? Raven, I couldn't even diagnose it."

"Well, hell, Lilly, you really are a horrible person," she said with a venom that surprised Lilly. "How dare you look at a strong healthy man and see cancer rather the flu or an injury?"

"I'm paid to see that, Raven." Lilly's eyes filled with tears and flooded over.

"You're a cardiologist."

"I'm a doctor." She sniffed and reached for some tissues.

"You are a pediatric cardiothoracic surgeon," she stated, then seemed to search for inspiration. Her voice turned a little icy. "You must hate your family, not to mention David's. How have you overcome that?"

Lilly blew her nose in a tissue, then paused, confused, and spoke in a croaky voice.

"What?"

"How did you overcome the hate you have for them or have you?"

"Raven, what in the hell are you talking about? I don't hate my family."

"What about David's?"

"Why would I hate them?"

"Well, your dad's a neurosurgeon, right?"

"So?"

"So, that's a fancy doctor. How come he didn't pick up on David's condition? Or what about your mom? She's an ICU nurse for chrissake. She must have seen hundreds of cases of pancreatic cancer."

Lilly shook her head, getting angry. "I know what you're trying to do, and it's not going to…"

"Sure you do because your sister's a psychiatrist. She's probably told you all about it. Then there's David's family."

"D-don't start with Ryan and Danielle."

"They were so close, their little nuclear family. You even said those two did everything for their kids. Shouldn't they also share some of this burden, because they sure as hell didn't see any changes in him either? Or maybe they did and hid it from you for some unfathomable reason."

"Raven, know you're pissing me off."

"Really, why? Why, Lilly? Have I injected a dose of reality you can't fight?" Raven yelled. She took a very deep breath and let it out slowly. When she spoke again, she seemed back in control. "Or maybe it was rotten luck. Horrible rotten luck, and it was part of a circle of life that you couldn't prevent. A woman dedicated to saving lives. You couldn't protect him, Travis, or Chelsea. You couldn't even protect yourself from the pain of that loss."

"I know. I hear you," she relented. "It's been almost four and a half years. I guess I should be over him…"

"What? Over him?" Raven said, confused. "Of course, you shouldn't be over him, Lilly. There's a reason there's a hole. He was a special unique person, who had a very special and unique spirit and energy. That energy isn't physically there anymore, and you miss that. Of course, you miss that. I'm sure you ache for it. I know that pain, Lilly. You can't fill the hole because you're not supposed to. Stop putting everything into tidy boxes."

"The kids are moving on. I'm not sure if they even

remember him anymore."

"Kids are such amazing, resilient survivors, aren't they? Wyatt and I survived. Finn and Que survived. You could never replace David, not in your eyes or in the eyes of your children. Maybe there's room to let a different spirit in though. A different kind of energy."

"Colt couldn't be more different." Lilly chuckled. "He's huge and loud. David was lithe and soft spoken. Colt's demanding and I don't know, manly. David was patient, kind, and we were a unit. Colt's a gladiator, David was an architect. They kiss different, they look different, and they act different."

"Well, maybe you should stop comparing them. That's not very fair either," Raven responded. "You said the kids like him?"

"They love him, and they're getting attached, which scares the hell out of me, given the type of man he is."

"And what type is that?"

"He could tire of us and leave, just like that." She snapped her fingers. "He's lived his whole life with no strings attached."

"And you know that for a fact?"

"He has his playboy mansion, toys, groupies."

"I don't know, but *if* that's true, and that's a big if, it sounds incredibly lonely to me." Raven paused. "Do you think he likes the kids?"

"Yes, I know he does. He wants to help Travis with football, and I think Chels wants to marry him."

"Well, that's good, and anyone would be hard pressed to find a man that little girl couldn't wrap around her finger."

"You aren't kidding." Lilly laughed again. She

paused for a moment before asking, "So, you're saying I should go for it?"

"I'm saying you should be over-the-moon happy. If for no other reason than you deserve it, and your kids deserve to see you happy. If Colt does that for you, then hell yes you should go for it. Besides, I'm coming to see you in a week."

"What? You are?"

"Yep, it's a bye week, and Que and Aulelei wanted to get away, so we're watching Ab."

A stab of guilt, hurt, and anger vibrated through Lilly at the women's friendship. After Colt left, she called and voiced her displeasure to Que for leaving him with her kids and not telling her. Que responded by giving a benign apology for not telling her the new plan, then adding insult to injury didn't ask for help in return. No, she called Raven. Lilly couldn't blame her, she guessed, but why did she feel like the heel rather than Que? The other mother just went on living her exciting, blessed life, feeling no uncertainty with her new relationship or to Lilly's way of thinking, a real remorse for her faux pas. She paused, confounded by her vitriolic emotion. *What in God's name is happening to me?*

"So, we're coming over, except first we're going to California," Raven was saying.

Lilly sipped her wine and gave a slight shake of her head. The negative emotion had, again, only lasted a bleak second before slithering away into the ether again.

"Oh," she asked, re-engaging. "Why California?"

"Caprice is having her big thirtieth birthday bash and asked us to come. She asked if I'd sing a little too, and then Dee needs to meet with someone. Anyway, we're coming. And then we'll babysit, so you can get laid."

"Raven…"

"Just do some thinking on it, Lil."

They disconnected and Lilly closed her eyes and could think of nothing else but Colt's fingers inside her, and sighed despite herself.

Chapter Eighteen

"Hello, this is Kyle Evans," came the modulated voice down Dee's receiver. "I understand you have a question on the Great Conjunction of Saturn and Jupiter, miss, ah…"

"Taylor, but please, call me Dee."

"Well, Dee, just to let you know, I don't do this anymore. I stopped working for the institute a few years ago."

"Yes, sir, I do know that but I'm doing this project and I need an expert on it."

"Well, I'm sorry but…"

"It's just…well…I've only got a little time left and I need to see this completed before I die," Dee crossed her fingers behind her back during the long pause her statement created. "Please, Mr. Evans, hear me out. It would mean such a great deal to me if you could just spare the smallest amount of time."

"Okay," Evans said. "Well, in that case, you better call me Kyle. How can I help you, Dee?"

"Well, Kyle, first, I guess I just want to understand what it is."

"What?"

"The Great Conjunction," Dee said. "I understand you are the absolute master of all this."

She hit the speaker feature on her phone and

engaged a small recorder as Kyle gave a genuine laugh.

"Oh come on now, Dee. Ya already hooked me, you don't have to kiss my ass too."

Relieved he could see through her facade, she smiled into the phone. "You gotta deal."

"Okay, so let's see if I can give you the less technical answer."

"Yes, please. The easier the better."

"So, the most simplistic way to explain it is a Great Conjunction occurs every eighteen to twenty years. And what happens is it takes Jupiter about twelve years to fully orbit the sun and it takes Saturn about thirty. So, when they both align with the sun, it's known as a Great Conjunction."

"So one happens every eighteen to twenty years?" Dee asked, a little confused which conjunction did Themis mean? "Are there ever more?" she queried.

"More what?"

"More planets that can align.

"Oh, well there are, but the occurrences become more and more rare."

"How many are there?"

"How many what? Planets, you mean?"

"Yes."

"Well, you've got the terrestrial planets, Mercury, Venus, Earth and Mars Then the giant planets, Jupiter, Saturn, Uranus and Neptune. Then countless dwarf planets, the most famous being Pluto, Ceres, and Eris. From there, more sub categories and so on."

"The Sun isn't?"

"The Sun's a star."

"Oh, right. Okay, and what's the Immaculate Conjunction?"

"I'm sorry, the what?"

"The Immaculate Conjunction?"

"Immaculate Conjunction?" Kyle queried, sounding confused. "Ah, I'm sorry I don't think I know that one." She tried to collect her thoughts. "Dee, are you still there?" he asked. "Did you have any more questions?"

"Yeah, but I think I'm gonna need to talk with someone about which ones are the right ones to ask and get back to you if that's all right?" She paused. "Actually, I have one slightly unrelated question. Do you have just a minute more?"

"Sure. Shoot." He chuckled.

"I wonder if you know anyone that's an expert on Greek mythology?"

"When you say Greek mythology, are you asking about the stars and mythology, like the zodiac signs?"

Dee's rolled her eyes. What must he think of her?

"Well, no, it's more about the Greek gods themselves. The stories, you know, the mythology. But I need someone that really knows what they're talking about."

"Oh, okay, well I can tell you the absolute expert on that is Dr. Raymond Butler, at the California Public Library," Kyle said. "He used to teach Greek mythology in the Midwest, and he's the best there is."

"Really? You aren't trying to get me off the phone now?"

"No ma'am." Kyle laughed again, and recited Ray's work number, divulging, "I took all of his history classes, but Greek mythology was everyone's favorite because he had such a passion for it. Believe me, he's your man."

"Oh that would be fantastic. You don't know what it means to me."

"No problem at all, Dee. It's been a pleasure." He paused, before saying, "You know, if you're interested in Greek mythology and the planets. Many of the gods had their own."

"Their own what? Planet?"

"Yep. Planet, stars, asteroids."

"Can you tell me which ones?" Dee asked, excited.

"Well I can tell you some of the planets, and some asteroids. I'd have to look up others. Why don't you give me your email and I'll send it to you?"

"Would you?" Dee asked, voice full of gratitude. "You've been so much help, and I'm sorry to have taken up so much of your time."

"Not at all. What did you say that last thing was? Conjunction? What did you call it?"

"The Immaculate Conjunction."

"Okay, I'll see if I can't find something on that too."

She rattled off her email, and the moment she disconnected the phone with the scientist dialed the number Kyle gave her. She knew this connection would lead somewhere important. She could just feel it.

****

The doors to the prestigious library had yet to open, and Pachelbel's Canon in D had nothing on the pleasure the silence brought to Dr. Raymond Butler. As he returned volumes of books to their resting places, the smell of dust and old parchment filled the air.

The older man could hear his own footsteps shuffle on the ecru marble floor, along with the book trolley and its one painfully squeaky wheel. He made a note to oil it as he slipped a copy of H. G. Wells' *Time Machine*, into the final channel. Turning, he began the laborious process of making his way back to the main information desk, aware of the pain of his left leg behind him.

When he woke that morning, he understood today would be a bad day on the famous scale of one to ten. Most days he hovered at a six or seven, spending an hour each morning to manipulate and stretch out the painful limb full of contracture and old grafted skin. However, on days like today, the pain deepened in severity, straight into the marrow of his bone.

Ray glanced up at the clock, then at the sunlight streaming in through the stained-glass windows, displacing dust motes. He nodded at the desk clerk to unlock the front doors and allow the patrons access to his sanctuary.

As the first students, locals, tourists, and educators made their way in, Ray hobbled to his office. He pulled down his favorite coffee cup, like he did every morning, and filled it with the pre-brewed coffee, his first of many throughout the day. Unwrapping a customary scone, he ate with a single-mindedness at his desk. When finished, he brushed any remaining crumbs onto the paper napkin, balled it up, and threw it into the trash before washing his hands in a tiny sink. As he dried them, he glanced up into the mirror affixed above the sink and caught himself unaware.

He stared back in horror with his only redeeming feature, fired-whiskey eyes. His coarse hair, streaked with generous silver and tied back in a thong, hung between his shoulder blades, and bushy side burns connected to a patchy, grizzled beard. Deep, corrugated grooves furrowed across his face and eyes. In fact, he looked as ancient as time itself.

Ray made a game of watching people's faces as they scanned a room, passed over him, then snapped back in recognition of something disrupting the normal order of life. Immediately they averted their eyes again, in hopes of avoiding any contact with the strange mutilated man before them. Soon, they'd speak in whispers, point and stare at his face, his leg, his burns. The dichotomy of thick and thin skin crisscrossing each other almost in animation. Other areas looked like the skin melted and swirled together, deviating in color. The burns covered the complete left side of his face, courteous enough to spare his eye and forehead. He wore his hair long to camouflage the bald spot where the fire had done its worst, forever kissing away the ability to grow new life. All these characteristics inspired him to spend as little time as possible on the library floor during hours of operation.

Grunting, he turned back toward his desk and logged onto his computer. Thus began his day, every day, six days a week. They closed on Sunday, much to his chagrin. However, many times he still found himself there in its embrace. Ray had no family, few friends, and a standoff, surly disposition.

However, what he lacked in appearance he more than made up for in intelligence, and yearned to live most of his life in the past. Before the accident that forever change his life, he'd been a professor in the heart of the Midwest. His specialty, European history, paid the bills, but didn't feed his obsession—Greek Mythology. Since the accident, he no longer indulged that joy. He signed onto the search engine as his phone extension rang.

"Dr. Raymond Butler."

"Ray Butler?"

"Ah," he answered as he pulled up an email requesting a copy of a rare volume from another library. "This is Dr. Raymond Butler," he repeated.

"Hello there, my name is Dee Taylor, and I live out here on the island of Kaua'i."

She paused as if expecting an exclamation or proclamation about how wonderful it must be to live in a tropical environment.

"Yes," he asked in a rush.

"Well, I wanted to ask for your help on a project I'm working on involving Greek mythology. Do you have a second?'

"No. Not really." The last thing he'd indulge in was chit chat with another human being.

"Ah, well, I'm an old woman that's dying, and it's my final wish to get this information." Unmoved, he said nothing, and she tried a different tack. "Your friend Kyle told me to call you."

"I'm sorry, who?" Ray evaded. *I will absolutely kill that boy.*

"Kyle Evans, the scientist."

"I don't know any Kyle Evans, the scientist, and am afraid I don't have time to help you right now, Ms. Taylor."

"It's Dee, and I don't think you understand. This won't take long." She paused. "And if now isn't a good time I can call back later."

"I don't believe that will be necessary, Ms. Taylor. I think we've resolved the phone call, don't you?"

"Well, no, not to my way of thinking, I don't," she

retorted. "You haven't said yes yet. When that happens, well then by God we'll have it all resolved. Now, stop being an asshole." He blinked. *What an exasperating woman.* Visions of an old rotund person sitting in a house that smelled of deep fried canned meat and old cats filled his mind. "Now look," she said. "This here is important."

"Is it life threatening? Because if the answer is no then…"

"Yes, damn it!" she snapped with anger. "As a matter of fact it is."

He held the receiver away from his ear, then rubbed it on his forehead. He could feel the beginnings of a headache coming on.

"Okay. Well, to put a fine point on it, right now there are numerous projects and tasks that I am responsible for and committed to. I do not have the adequate time to take on another task. I feel as if I am making myself perfectly clear when I say that I am not interested in participating in your…project. Now, I trust this will put an end to this inquiry. Goodbye, Ms. Taylor," he stated with emphasis and replaced the receiver, then muttered, "Christ."

****

"Well, of all the nerve…" Dee spat and tossed her cell phone onto the kitchen counter with a clatter. "That rude, condescending…asshole."

The man didn't even listen to me! After all the research, time, and effort, and he won't even listen. To understand the nuances of the prophecy, and the Greek world of the gods, they needed someone knowledgeable. This man had been the first real lead, and he didn't care, nor would he do anything out of his way to help. She would need to know all the questions she'd want answered and be ready, when the time came again.

"Oh, and that time's coming, because when the going gets tough, the tough take out their biggest shit-kickers," Dee spat out to the room. She picked up her cell phone again and stabbed in the digits. "Little prick," she muttered and waited for someone to pick up. "Yes, hello there. I need a ticket from Kaua'i, Hawai'i to Los Angeles, California please."

Chapter Nineteen

Caprice Starr glided to a small landing at the top of a short, marble staircase. Her blood-red sequined dress hugged every generous curve. Thick, bouncy, strawberry-blonde hair waved glorious around her pale, toned shoulders.

"Thank you, everyone, so much for coming!" she shouted to the crowd of seventy people. "I can't tell you what an incredible honor it is to have all of you here celebrating yet another year of this crazy experience with me." A cheer rumbled over the guests, and she winked. "I have prepared an exclusive surprise for you and an incredible birthday treat for myself." She gave a dramatic pause as the crowd speculated on what entertainment their extravagant hostess had provided. "Teeny hint. I can tell you it wasn't easy because all she wanted to do was stay on her little island, with her hot, sexy new husband, but..." Understanding weaved through the collective now, as excitement started to bubble. "Ladies and gentlemen, I give you the one and only, Raven!"

The lights dimmed, and a spotlight showcased the singer sitting at Caprice's white grand piano, in a strapless, periwinkle gown of silk. Thunderous applause welcomed her, as Raven smiled and bowed her head with grace.

"Hello," she spoke into the mic, her voice deep and sultry. "It's my honor to play for you all tonight, and I'd like to wish my beautiful friend a very happy birthday and an incredible year to come."

She performed as photographers and guests turned the living room into a world of strobe lights. Caprice blew a kiss to her, smiling, then walked down the stairs and passed through the living room, when she seemed to spot Colt watching her and the proceedings from the doorway. He wore sunglasses, a dark leather jacket. and worn faded jeans, looking every bit the sports hero. A grin exploded across her face as she ambled over to him and held out her arms for an embrace. He moved into it and she kissed him on the mouth. In the same moment, a photographer covering the event snapped their picture.

"I didn't think you'd actually come."

"I wasn't sure either but decided what the hell, I'll take a charter in the morning."

Colt wanted to go home. In fact, he yearned for it, as he hadn't spoken with or seen Lilly since that night by the garage. He'd driven home angry at her remarks, and sexually frustrated, trying to decide what a guy had to do to warrant a fresh start without judgements and opinions? Last night, they played a game and had a bye the next week, so he stayed in L.A. for Caprice's party.

"I watched," she purred. "Congratulations."

"Thanks."

"What happened in the fourth?"

A fight occurred between Colt and the L.A. cornerback. The man had done some trash talking after interfering in Derek's pass to Colt. The TE retaliated by making comments about the man's mother. Furious, the corner ripped off Colt's helmet and threw him to the ground, as another teammate clipped him in the head with his cleat. A fight ensued, and all involved fined, with one ejection for the man with the cleat.

"He's always been a punk." Colt shrugged off the two steri-strips holding the skin at his eyebrow together.

"And you've always had a temper, my love." When he only looked around the room, she ran a hand through his hair, making him look at her. "Colt, we've known and cared about each other a long time now and in a bunch of delicious ways, right?"

"I guess." He met her eye. "Yeah."

"You're playing hurt, aren't you?" He started to look away again, but she took his chin in her hand. "Something's going on, I can see it. Have they checked you out?"

"I'm fine."

"In the past few games…"

"Cap, I'm fine," he snapped. "What d'ya got to drink around here?" He spotted the bar. "I'm gettin' one. You want something?"

She shook her head, and he made his way to the counter.

"What can I get you, Mr. Stone?" A lanky bartender with a handlebar moustache grinned at the Warrior, a little awestruck.

"Ya got a beer?"

"Yes, sir."

"Make it two." Colt turned to see Finn approach and shook his hand.

"Hey, man, I didn't know you'd be here tonight," Colt said, then gestured toward Raven at the piano.

"Yeah, Caprice asked Raven to sing," Finn replied. "Great game today. It must suck when you have them back-to-back like that."

"Yeah, ya feel it a little more on Friday for sure."

"Michaels ring your bell?"

"He's a knob. It was a cheap shot kicking me in the head." Colt tipped back his beer again. "Fun staring him down when he got ejected though."

"What happens when something like that goes down? Do you have to go through protocol?" Finn asked, regarding the tests a player must go through when a suspected concussion has occurred.

"Naw, it was the last play," Colt said before changing topics. "Your wife's crazy talented."

"She is." Finn turned to look at her too.

"How'd the two of you meet?" Colt looked at him. "Seems like an odd combo."

"It's a long story." Finn laughed. "The highlighted version is she came to the island to take a break from it all and I can be irresistible when I want to be. We're heading your way next."

Colt raised his beer and sipped. Finn aped the motion and then just waited.

"To see Doc?"

"Yeah," Finn confirmed. "Que and Aulelei are going away tomorrow for a few days and we're taking care of Abby too." He sipped his beer and considered. "So, the cardiothoracic unit. That about the donation or the doctor?"

Colt wanted to reply with a dismissive retort but looked over at the marine biologist and knew he had his number.

"I guess both," he said, trying to play it cool.

"What do you know about her?"

"Lilly?" Finn eyed him with a smile. "Not much. What do you want to know?"

"What's the deal with the dead husband?"

"I honestly don't know very much about him. He died before we met her. I *do* know she hasn't dated in a very long time. So, you must be doing something right."

"I don't know about that. She's an enigma wrapped up in a conundrum, man."

"Aren't they all? What about the kids?"

"They're cool." Colt's face lit up.

"So, you like her?"

"Honestly, I don't know what to think."

"I'm listening," Finn said, before taking another swig of his beer.

"We were…we just." Colt paused, feeling like a first-class idiot. He stood in the middle of a party talking to a guy he didn't know; about things he didn't speak of. He eyed Finn, who looked back. His startling eyes seemed to spark, and Colt felt a connection. Not male bonding bullshit, but something deeper, an authenticity or confirmation that they knew each other. Maybe because Colt met him the same time he met Lilly. "Sometimes, we seem like we're all good."

"And other times?"

"I don't know, it feels like I'm competing with a dead guy all the time. And…I don't know, this isn't my usual scene."

"God, I know how you feel." Finn laughed. "Just over a year ago I was a very content bachelor, or at least I thought I was. Women, job I loved, and a life that made perfect sense to me. Then this shy, little introvert came into my life and everything changed." He paused and looked at Raven before turning to Colt. "And I mean *everything* upended."

"And you're good with that?"

"Well." Finn chuckled again. "Having any girl you want is awesome until it isn't anymore. Having one that gets you and makes you want to be a better person, it's…I don't know…amazing. She, like, filled something up I didn't know was missing. Now that I see it though, it was this insane, huge thing. I know that's lame, but it's the best I can come up with."

Colt nodded and drank from his beer, looking over at Raven too. She closed her eyes, feeling the music, and when she opened them again, she sought her husband. Colt looked back at Finn, who now stared at his wife, and the football player couldn't have broken the connection if he tried. After a moment, she finished the song, and the crowd erupted into applause.

Finn looked back at Colt and grinned. "Nope, not one thing about it I regret."

"The two best looking guys in the room are looking at each other," Caprice admonished. She took Colt's beer, sipped from it, then returned it to him.

Feeling uncomfortable with her observation, the men turned toward the room and away from each other, causing Caprice to laugh at their testosterone.

A man in a dark suit approached the starlet and whispered in her ear. The color seemed to drain from her face as she listened and both Colt and Finn looked at each other, concerned. When the suit took her arm, and started to lead her away, Colt took her other arm.

"Hold up," he snarled, and turned to his hostess. "What's going on here?"

Caprice glanced around at the surrounding people who laughed, clinked glasses, and carried on their conversations without hearing the drama.

"It's fine, honey. Nothing I can talk about right now, but I'll tell you later."

"No, tell me now."

"No, I said I'll tell you later." She jerked her arm from his grasp and preceded the man out.

Colt followed her with his eyes until she left the room, then scanned the crowd. He turned to see Raven approach Finn, her set over, and smile up at him. He leaned in to kiss her, both lost in each other. A group of women stood close by gathering their courage to approach him, and Colt realized that soon, they'd corner him for the rest of the evening. He set his glass down on a waiter's tray and sought a clear path to the front door.

****

After the party, Caprice, Raven, and Finn sat on the couches drinking cognacs by the fire. The newlyweds stayed in one of the star's many guest rooms. Raven asked her friend if she could borrow a sweater. As the singer walked into the starlet's closet, she searched for the garment. Upon finding one she straightened, then saw a strange doll sitting on Caprice's jewelry cabinet. Underneath it, was a small pile of papers with scrawled writing, warning, *your day is coming*. The doll looked like Caprice. A decapitated Caprice. Shocked, Raven ran back to the living room and thrust the doll and papers at her friend.

"What's all this?"

"Oh that." Caprice looked at the lot and paled. She recovered herself quickly, and took a deep breath, before laughing it off. "It seems I have a stalker with an overzealous imagination."

"Overzealous imagination? That's a death threat. When did this start?"

"Oh, honey, you've had crazy fans too."

"I've never had a death threat."

"That you know of. Believe me, Donovan's a shit, but he would never have let something like that get back to you." She tucked her legs under her, sipped her drink, and looked at their worried faces. "Listen to me, Raven. I'm not an idiot, and I have this in hand. Seriously, I've got the authorities involved and hired a personal detail. They've got some leads and seem very confident they'll catch him. I won't make anything easy for him, I promise."

"When did it start?" Finn asked.

"About six months ago," she told him, then added, "It's only been letters."

"And a decapitated doll," Raven exclaimed, handing the object to Finn.

"If it involves the police, why don't they have all this in evidence?" Finn asked.

"They do. Those are copies."

"And the doll?"

"It came to the gate during the party." Caprice looked uncomfortable. "My lead security came and told me. I'll call the authorities in the morning."

"Caprice, this is serious," Raven warned.

"It starts off like regular fan mail and just get nastier," Finn observed, as he scanned the notes. "How'd they get your address? Isn't it unlisted?"

"Yes, darling, but the die-hards always find a way. The media don't help either. Sometimes, I think they find out where we live and hand it out like candy in hopes something nasty happens just so they can get a story."

"Wait, this came here to your personal address." Raven asked, eyes darting around the room, as if the perpetrator would jump out from behind a curtain.

"It's not a huge secret where I live, Rave. It was outside the gate." Caprice looked at their dubious faces. "So," she said, taking a deep breath, "did Colt leave pissy?"

"I don't know," Raven said. "I never even got to say hello."

"He's just mad at me."

"Why?" the couple asked in unison.

"I called him out because I think he's playing concussed. Then, I didn't tell him what this was all about"—she gestured to the papers—"the second he asked about it."

"But I thought they didn't let them do that anymore. Wasn't there a movie or research or something done about that?" Raven asked.

"There was, but it wouldn't be the first-time Colt played hurt. He, like everyone else, knows how to play the system," Caprice reported.

"I know there's been fights and that last game…" Finn began.

"I think it was harder than it looked," Caprice noted. "It looked like another time he got hit hard when we were dating. And it's happening when he's overlooked or can fade into the background. He told me once how he or a teammate will create a thing somewhere else, so they forget about the protocol." She drank again. "It's just what he does. What he's always done. But I'd be willing to bet if you were to watch a video of just Colt during each game, he's had a lot of head and neck injuries over the years. So, I just called him out, and he must've gotten mad and left. Which now pisses me off because I didn't get a birthday-beni."

"A what?" Raven laughed.

"A birthday beni. If we aren't with anyone, we give each other a birth…Oh never mind," Caprice said, with a wave of her hand. The couple looked at each other with worried expressions and the actress saw it.

"Okay, what was that?"

"What?" Raven asked.

"You gave each other meaningful looks, like you were being all judgey."

"We aren't judging, Caprice, I promise. It's just…"

"Oh," Caprice said understanding. "Is he seeing someone? He hasn't mention it to me."

"He is, and she's a friend of ours," Finn revealed.

"Oh! Well, seriously guys, there's nothing going on. Colt and I had a wild, hot ride and then flashed out almost as quick. We understand each other very well though, and he's one of my best friends. I want him to be happy and healthy, if he can be, especially with someone that loves him." She gave a feline grin. "Now, who is she?"

"You don't know her." Raven laughed.

"Hmm, does she live in Washington?"

"Yeah."

"Could she be a heart surgeon?"

"How d'you know that?"

"There was a thing about it in the paper. Wait!" Caprice exclaimed. "Is it that teeny-tiny thing that shot blow-dart-death stares at me at your wedding? The one he donated all that money to?" When the couple just looked at each other, she giggled in awe. "I'm right, aren't I? Well, I'll be damned. She's got kids too. Colt a daddy? Ho-ly shit."

"It's still new so…" Raven studied her friend. "Caprice, you've got to stay out of it."

"You think I'd ruin something that would make him happy?"

"No, but I see meddling all over your face."

"No you don't," She smiled then sobered and paused. "It's just…what do they have in common? He's a football player, she's a heart surgeon. He's a very eligible bachelor, she's a mother of two. I'll give you, they both have tempers, and I think she gets jealous as a green pea, but they don't exactly scream longevity, do they?"

"Maybe stability and family is something Colt wants," Raven suggested.

"Oh, for sure it is, but whether he can acquire and hang onto it is something else. And his way of life…on the road, groupies outside every hotel room door. Fame, celebrity…come on, Rave, you must admit, it's a heady cocktail."

"I've never been in it for the fame and celebrity."

"No? So, you'd be content sitting in your living room, singing your songs to the walls." Caprice gestured at her with her drink. "It's in your blood, honey, and just because you don't crave the attention like some of us do, your music needs to be heard. Could the lovely doctor ever be okay with that, the attention? I mean, tonight alone there were hundreds of photographs taken. When Colt came in, I kissed him. It was nothing, just how we say hello, but if someone sells that and she sees it, would she understand or accept it?"

"Well, could you blame her? You give each other birthday benis."

Caprice snorted. "Not for years now, and if you notice darling...he's not here. That should speak volumes."

Chapter Twenty

"Yes, Sheila?" Ray asked with frustration into the intercom.

"Hi, Dr. Butler. There's a Ms. Dee Taylor here, wishing to speak with you. She doesn't have an appointment, though."

"Who?" he asked, knowing he should know the name. His secretary's mouth muffled, before coming back on the line.

"Ms. Dee Taylor, from Hawai'i? She said you should know her from her phone calls and sparkling personality." Sheila giggled. When her boss said nothing, the secretary sobered. "I'm sorry, sir, should I send her back?"

Ray sat in his chair dumfounded, then closed his eyes for patience. "You have got to be kidding me," he announced to the empty room.

The thought of refusing the blasted woman teased his mind, but he reconsidered. A woman that traveled twenty-seven hundred miles to meet with him wasn't an ordinary woman. He didn't think he'd be able to reject her with such severity, no matter how much he wanted to. At least now he could listen to what she had to say to pacify her, then politely say no. Hell, no.

"Fine," he snapped. "Send her in."

Ray stood, put on his jacket, then smoothed down

217

his hair. He always liked to be standing when someone new entered his office. First, because it wasn't always easy maneuvering up out of the chair when he'd been sitting awhile, like he had today. Second, when people saw him for the first time, they tended to be shocked by his appearance. So, taking the time to sit back down, his eyes could shift from the horror reflected on their faces, and give the person time to recover. He'd only just smoothed a hand down his coat, when a knock rapped on his door.

"Yes, come."

The door opened and the most eccentric woman he'd ever seen materialized in the doorway. Eccentric and very petite. The woman appeared to be in her mid-seventies and deeply tan. Understandable, given the climate in which she lived. However, her skin appeared soft, crepey and creamy all at the same time. Radiant eyes sparkled back at him, and two long silver French braids framed her face. A rather ridiculous hat adorned her head, with exotic flowers encircling its brim and—real cumquats woven through the petals? She looked fit, but he couldn't be sure for the hot pink muumuu she wore, with large teal and orange flowers splashed across it.

Dee extended a hand and shook Ray's with enthusiasm, her soft pink lips turning into the happiest smile he'd ever seen. If his deformity horrified her or made her uncomfortable, she didn't disclose it in her actions, demeanor, or speech. In fact, he wasn't sure if she noticed it at all.

"Ah…Ms. Taylor?" he offered.

"Yes, yes, I'm Dee, and you're Ray. Now let's move on, because you're *such* a busy man."

"Ah, no," the gentleman said with a frown. "I prefer Dr. Butler, if you don't mind. It keeps things professional."

"No."

He furrowed his brow and shook his head in disbelief at her total takeover of his office. He opened his mouth to object to the intimate personal use of his name again, but Dee just rolled her eyes.

"No, I'm not gonna call you Dr. Butler. It's just too much of a mouthful, and Raymond's just too stuffy. So, to me you'll just be Ray. Now listen," she said. "I've been trying for two weeks to talk to you. I've been nice, I've been charming, and I've been patient. You, in return, have been pompous, arrogant, and just plain rude."

"Is that a fact?" he asked and sat down, leaning back in his chair to study her.

"Yes, sir, it sure is." She nodded her head as if to emphasize the point. "Now, I respect the fact you're a real busy man, I do. In fact, I wouldn't even bother you if I didn't have a real emergency that needed your professional help."

"An emergency?" he queried. "Forgive me, Ms. Taylor…"

"God damn it, I said to call me Dee."

"Dee," he confirmed, looking at her like a bomb that could explode at any moment. "Well, Dee, in history there aren't many emergencies, thus being so long in the past. Now, if you have some deadline"—he looked at her with skepticism—"perhaps, taking some class?"

"No," she retorted. "Now, please, just be quiet for a second and let me tell you what's what without your judging commentary for a few minutes."

He tensed and pressed his lips together in a hard line. His wife used to say the same thing to him, and he didn't want to smile at this woman. Despite the dismay at being entertained, Ray's curiosity about what she had to say seeped through. He took in a deep breath and let it out on a sigh, before giving a nod of his head to relinquish the floor.

"I'd like to know some information about Greek mythology, and I understand you're the best."

"Best? Well, I don't know about…sorry," he said when she glared at him.

"Specifically, I need a lot of information and advice on the Greek gods. Individual Greek gods."

"And you are coming to me?" He paused, taking her in. "And from whom did you get my name?"

"Well, I already told you if you'd attempted to listen to me before, but it was Kyle Evans," she snapped, as if not amused at the pompousness returning to his voice. "Now, *there's* a nice and helpful young man."

"Kyle?" Ray thought of his young friend. "Kyle told you to contact me?"

"Yes, he said you used to teach Greek mythology and there was nobody more qualified than you."

"Why were you looking for Greek mythology information through Kyle?"

"Well, I went to him for the stars. Mainly about the Immaculate Conjunction. He's a big deal in astrology. First rate."

Ray burst out laughing before he could stop himself. "Kyle is an astronomer, not an astrologer."

"Well, what's the damn difference?"

"Well, astronomers deal with the study outside the scope of earth's atmosphere, and astrologers like to believe they can tell people their future."

He took off his wire-rimmed spectacles and polished the glass with a microfiber cloth just for that purpose.

"All right, Dee." He sighed, in exasperation. "Why don't you tell me exactly what you're looking for."

"Okay. So, I'm writing a book on Greek mythology and I need to know some insider information on some—er—characters," she said in a quick cadence.

"What's the premise?" he asked, pushing his spectacles back up the bridge of his nose.

"The what?"

"Premise. What's the premise of your book? Is it a story of fiction or non-fiction?"

"Oh, I see. Well, I haven't decided yet. It could be probably either or both." She cleared her throat, and he knew the story he'd hear would be complete bullshit but let it play out. "So, it's a story about Cronus making an evil spell or prophecy on Zeus and all the others. He's super pissed because Zeus locked him up and all. So, he puts a curse on him that if all the generations can't get their shit together and complete some tasks, then he'll kick the crap out of them."

"Dee?" Ray's eyes narrowed at her vulgarity.

"Yes?"

"Why don't you cut the garbage and stop wasting my time?"

"What d'ya mean?" she retorted, removing her hat and flinging it onto his desk.

A large lump gathered in his throat as the light

danced off her silver hair. He tried to swallow it down, but it remained in stubborn defiance.

"I mean, why don't you just tell me what's going on here?"

"Oh…" she started. "Well, I want to understand about the Titan, Cronus. How his children took over everything and threw him down into Tartarus." She looked up as if confirming she had the story correct. He gave her a nod, although surprised she knew even that much. "Well, I imagine that pissed him off, right? I mean he worked so hard to steal the kingdom from his daddy. Then, here comes his own kid, just out of nowhere, and takes it from him a little while later. Pouf'—She snapped her fingers.—"just like that."

Amused by her description of the events, he chanced speaking.

"Well, it wasn't just—" He hesitated "—pouf." He drew his eyebrows together at the term. "Titanomachy lasted ten years." Ray's lips formed into a genuine smile at the priceless look of incredulity on her face.

"Titan what?"

"Titanomachy. It was several battles that occurred in Thessaly, over the course of a ten-year period, between the Titans and the Olympians." She looked completely thrown off her game and when she didn't respond, he continued. "The Titans, and some older Primordials, based on Mount Othrys, fought the younger generation and their allies."

"Okay, so there! What is that? A Primordial, what are they? I thought Zeus slipped his daddy some stuff to make him throw up all his kids? I don't know this other stuff?" Dee looked at him expectantly as he reached for his coffee. "And my grandson said something about

Cronus cutting off his daddy's pecker and throwing it away before *he* took everything over."

Ray choked on his coffee, not prepared for the crude observation. He gagged and hacked until Dee came over and thumped him hard on the back. Blood filled his face as he tried to free the liquid from his lungs and trachea. Recovered, yet scandalized, he looked at her with irritation as she blinked back at him innocently.

"Is that not what happened then?" She waited, but when no response came, she reclaimed her seat. "Look, Ray, I know I came barging in here and disrupted your whole peaceful, quiet day. It's just this is super important," Dee continued. "And I can't tell you why yet. I need to understand all of this first."

Ray gazed back at her for a long while, then took in a deep breath and provided the narrative on his most beloved topic.

"All right. I will try to give you the briefest rundown on Greek mythology. You have the Primordials, and there are several of them. The two most important to our story are Gaia, or Mother Earth, and Uranus, also known as Sky and Cosmos."

"Okay, so just wait there. This is what I don't get. They ruled these things and said what's what with them?"

"No, they *are* these things. Gaia is Mother Earth, and Mother Earth is Gaia. Almost like the spirit or personification of what you know it to be. It's an abstract idea to be sure." When she nodded, he continued, "Gaia bore Uranus, via immaculate conception, then took him for her husband. They mated and had children, and call the collective group the

Titans, among others.

"Uranus threw some of their children, more creature-like, into Tartarus, which infuriated Gaia, and she demanded their release. When her husband, Uranus, refused, she went to her remaining children and held out a cutting tool, called a scythe. She asked them to castrate the mighty god and dethrone him. Only one of her children, Cronus, took up the challenge. He promised his mother he would release her imprisoned children and create a new realm."

Ray stood up, forgetting about his appearance, and shuffled as he spoke.

"Gaia lay in wait, calling to Uranus. When he appeared, Cronus severed off his father's...ah... genitalia and cast them out into the sea, thus becoming the new ruler and a Titan king. However, the betrayal enraged Uranus, so he created a prophecy."

Dee sat up so quick, it caused him to jump. She nodded at him to continue and he eyed her with wary concern.

"Th-The prophecy said that Cronus's children would also take over the throne from their father. Well"—he readjusted his small, square spectacles on his long straight nose—"Cronus became paranoid. He re-imprisoned some of Gaia's children and took one of his six sisters, Rhea, for his wife."

"Okay," Dee said, irritated, and held up a hand. "So, Gaia started everything. She has a kid and then takes him for her husband. She and the husband, slash son, have a bunch of kids and he sends some of them to prison. Mama bear gets pissed and tells her kids to dismember dad. And one does, but all the kids are siblings and they all marry each other too? So, what is it with all the rape and incest? Why not find a little variety for the bloodline?"

Ray blinked at her for a few seconds. "There was no one else," he stated. "There were Primordials, who had children, who became gods, deities, person-ifications, and so on. It isn't unlike the theory of Adam and Eve. The early days, and all the theories of how the world began, and who created it, using what method." When she only stared back at him, he went for a different approach. "You can't think of the Greek gods as human. Think of them as concepts, essences, or personifications."

"Oh, okay, I guess I see. They are people-spirits? But everything seems so brutal and impersonal."

"Well, there you may be right. The Greek gods are selfish beings. They are arrogant and entitled. The only beings to match their power are other gods." He resumed his pacing. "They mate with humans or mortals sometimes, but those are only pawns in a very strategic game. Mortal lovers, husbands, wives, children…it doesn't matter, mortals are all expendable and easily killed on a whim, whenever a particular god is feeling…ah…"

"Pre-menstrual?" Dee suggested.

He turned again to look at her and she smiled back at his prudishness. Clearing his throat, he continued as if an unruly student had interrupted a class.

"Cronus decided the best way to stop his children would be to eat them immediately after their birth, much to the chagrin of Rhea. Tired of having all her children taken from her, she developed a plan to hide the youngest away. Once she delivered, she presented it to Cronus. However, instead of the babe, she gave him several large rocks in a blanket. Cronus, not interested in the children, only what they represented, gobbled the bundle down without even looking. That last child was Zeus."

Dee, who had been leaning forward, hanging on each word, now sat up and leaned back in her chair.

"Zeus," she confirmed, and he nodded his head. "Who were the other children? Zeus's brothers and sisters?"

"Well, first is Hestia and…"

"Hestia, what's he god of?"

"*She* is goddess Hearth Fire, Home, and Domesticity."

"Okay, so she's the oldest."

"In a way."

"In a way? What does that mean?"

"Here, let me finish and then I'll see if I can explain it." She nodded, and he began again. "Next comes Demeter."

"Yes," Dee said with a smile. "I know about her. Goddess of agriculture and the harvest."

"That's correct. Then there's Hera, goddess Marriage, Women, and Childbirth. Next in line is Hades, god Underworld, among many other things. Hades, Poseidon, who is next in line, and god Sea, and then Zeus, all split the areas into three sub realms. Heaven and earth, the sea and oceans, and the underground. They drew lots in the beginning, to see who would rule which realm."

"Okay, so Hades drew the underworld, Poseidon drew the sea, and then Zeus drew earth and heaven."

"He rules over earth, but is also the supreme ruler over everything, which includes the heavens. The three brothers hold a sacred bond together and are incredibly powerful as a unit. But even they have their brotherly battles." Ray stopped pacing and leaned on his desk.

"Okay, one thing I noticed when you were talking was you said Hera, goddess Marriage and Children. Not Hera, she's the goddess of marriage and children. Do you mean to say it like that?"

"Yes. Like I said before, she *is* those things not *of* those things. It's her name, her whole name. Now, remember I told you their birth order? Well, once Zeus came of age, he came under his father's use. Cronus, not understanding who he was, made him his cupbearer. Within the ruler's wine, Zeus mixed mustard seeds, and other things, causing the ruler to vomit copious amounts, thereby regurgitating his offspring one by one in reverse order. First, was Poseidon, then Hades, Hera, Demeter, and at last, Hestia. So, Hestia was the first, and last born."

Ray turned and walked behind the desk before sitting down again, with a painful grimace. Dee appeared to assimilate what he'd said. Standing, she walked over to his full coffee pot and took down another mug. Pouring herself a cup and then one for Ray, she replaced the carafe, handed him a mug, and resettled herself onto the plush chair.

"Dee, I think we've covered just about…"

"So where does Themis fit in?"

"Themis?"

"Yeah, I've read she was a sister, or an aunt, or even Zeus's wife. Are you going to tell me she's all three now?"

"Themis is a child of Gaia."

"So, Cronus's sister and Zeus's aunt?" When he

nodded his head in affirmation, she stated, "And she was a prophet?"

"She is Divine Law, Order, Fairness, and Customs."

"So, a judge?"

"If you like. In truth, she's high counsel to Zeus, and has no discord with anyone. She decides what is right and wrong. Moreover, she *is* right and wrong, if we continue to think in the abstract. There is a special sword Themis covets, that cuts fact from fiction."

"What if there was a spat between parties, like a gray area?"

"There's never a gray area. She wears a blind across her eyes to be fair, so she can't make a personal judgement, even if she wants to."

"Okay, but was she was a prophet?"

"She has the uncanny ability to tell the future. So, her mother made her the Oracle of Delphi, enabling her the ability to create oracles and prophecies."

Silence saturated the room and Ray jolted when he looked at the clock and discovered they'd been talking for over an hour.

"If I may, what's the nature of your project? I mean you say this is a matter of life and death, yet you're speaking of people in the Golden and Silver Ages. What could be so urgent about that? Please, don't insult my intelligence by saying you're writing a book again."

"Well, you speak like they're here now so…"

"For me, and for many others, they are. Greek mythology, in essence, is my religion."

When she didn't respond, he raised his eyebrows. *Well, Chuckie, the ball is in your court.* Dee looked stymied and searched the ceiling for inspiration.

"But," she began. "Okay, maybe it isn't...What if...How about you answer a hypothetical for me?"

"If I can," he returned, then added with a little snark, "it's your proverbial dime."

"Let's just say, because of being overthrown, Cronus got so pissed he made his own prophecy, to get revenge?"

"Well, let's see, there are a lot of theories regarding the afterlife of Cronus." Ray leaned back in his chair and held his cup of coffee. "Some think he's imprisoned for eternity deep in the cave of Nyx, within Tartarus. Some believe Zeus, feeling magnanimous, allowed Cronus to enter and rule over the Elysium, which is also in the Underworld. Still others believe he escaped to Latium, the birthplace of Rome, where he ascended to king and created the law of that land."

"How is it open for interpretation?" Dee asked in frustration. "I mean, it either happened, or it didn't."

"Dee, Greek mythology isn't an exact study. I mean, all the stories criss-cross, depending on who tells the story. Is it the Greeks or the Romans? Was it Homer or Hesiod? These stories overlap and run parallel with one another. Those of us that made it our life's work have our own interpretations about the correct path, but I will again refer you to modern day religion. How many religions are there in the world? Who is right and who is wrong? Or is everyone right?"

"What do you mean?"

"Most religions feel there is a higher being and a set of rules that their higher being wants you to walk in. All the rules have similarities and truths. Many are the same."

"Wait, wait, wait...What the hell are you talking

about now?"

"Buddhism has the five precepts. Islam has the five pillars. Christianity, Mormonism—Latter-Day Saints—believe in the ten commandments. And what are these things? Don't harm others, trust in God alone, don't steal, don't commit adultery, don't lie, but pray, fast, love. The rules differ with how creation began and what God looks like, but I think you'll agree, religion should be a good thing, correct?"

"It is a good thing."

"Yes, I agree. It can keep people civilized and in their humanity. However, what about when it's taken out of context?"

"What do you mean?"

"I mean, what happens when evil occurs in the name of God and the perpetrators say that it is their religious purpose?"

"That would be bad."

"Yes, terrible," Ray confirmed. "We've seen that, haven't we? The Greek gods are powerful, but they are also fallible. That's what makes them endearing to humans. Like us, they are selfish, spiteful, and can make mistakes."

"Can the gods be taught?" Dee asked.

"By what measure?"

"Can us mere mortals teach them?"

"Teach them what?" Ray wanted to know.

"I don't know, teach them to stay in the light, don't commit adultery, be nice people." Dee jolted in her seat as if struck by one of Zeus's thunderbolts. "Yes, teach them," she murmured.

"All I'm saying," Ray said, getting frustrated, "is there are different versions, and different storytellers.

The Greeks have their take on mythology, but so do the Romans. Were they different or were they all one being?"

"Okay, fine. So, Cronus, he could have made a prophecy."

"No, Uranus made the prophecy."

"That's not what I'm asking, Doc," Dee snapped. "I'm asking, was it *possible* for Cronus to make a prophecy?"

"There's no record of him ever having the ability to speak or write to the oracle."

"Could he have help? Maybe something to do with time and place?"

"Cronus was Harvest."

"Wait, I thought he was god of time?"

"Cronus, of Greek mythology, is god Harvest. However, Chronos, also of Greek mythology, was the personification of time, and Cronus's predecessor. They are often substituted for one another in error, and some even believe they, themselves, changed positions frequently to create confusion and subterfuges."

Dee gave a quick rattle of her head, as if the information was too overwhelming. "They could do that?"

"Some believe so. They were both incredibly powerful gods."

"Okay, okay, so let's just say this is one of those times and Cronus was Time. Now if he wanted to make a prophecy and couldn't do it himself, how would he go about it?"

"I'm sorry Ms. Ta...um, Dee. He didn't do that, and I'm not sure that he ever could."

"So he couldn't, but Themis could?"

"Possibly."

"Who else could? Anyone?"

"Themis had the ability. Her sister, Phoebe, also did and then, I guess Apollo would have been next in terms of gifts." Ray looked at her puzzled. "I still don't see what…"

"Okay, so Cronus couldn't. Themis and Apollo wouldn't because they don't want to help him out," Dee muttered again.

"Excuse me?"

"What? Oh, nothing." Dee glanced over at him. "What about Phoebe? Who's that chick?"

"Dee," he said, sounding exasperated to his own ears. "We have been discussing this for a very long time now. I have pressing work that needs completion, and must insist…"

"I know, Doc, I know. Okay, just a few more questions please, then I'll get out of your hair."

He rolled his eyes in frustration and sighed in heavy resignation. "Phoebe is goddess Bright Intellect and Prophecy. So, imagine oracular intellect. She is gifted at reading or understanding prophecies," he said.

Ray watched her in fascination, as the wheels in her mind turned. Life or death, that's what she first said, and the woman definitely acted as if her life depended on these answers.

"Okay, now, I really do need to get on. I trust I was of some help to you?"

"No wait," Dee pleaded. To Ray's horror, tears glistened in her eyes. "I need you to help me but I can't tell you why. At least…I can't tell you yet."

"I'm very sorry," he said, as if de-fusing a bomb. "But no. My plate is very full at the moment."

"Are you married?"

"Am I what?"

"Married, are you married? Gotta big family?"

"No," he said, his voice raw with pain.

"Well, I don't have a big family either, but we've been through a lot and have more to go through yet." She looked at him, eyes pleading. "Something's happened. Something I can't tell you and something you'd never believe, even if I did."

She took a deep breath and pressed on. "Is it possible…I know I've taken up more of your time, than I've had a right to, but would you be willing to meet me for a drink later, and I'll see if I can explain it?"

"No."

"No?" She looked at him in disbelief. "Whatcha mean no?" Ray smiled despite himself, wondering how many people ever dared to say that word to this woman. "Now look," Dee said in obvious frustration. "I have something that'll knock your socks off, Doc. Seriously, I will blow away your big brain with all its fancy education. If it doesn't, I'll eat my hat."

He eyed the item in question, still laying on his desk like a dead animal. It looked bigger than she did. She snatched it off the desk and replaced it on her head.

"I don't drink," he informed her.

"Ever or just tonight?"

"Ever, and I'm busy tonight."

"Oh, okay, so we won't drink. I can pick up some Chinese or something and bring it to your pad a different night."

"My…my house?"

"Yes, it has to be some place private. I'll pay for dinner and everything. You give me one more hour and a meal and if you want me to leave after that, I will, no questions asked. And you won't ever see me again."

Sure, I'll believe that when I see it. He almost refused her but somehow, he couldn't form the words. No one spoke to him like the gods were real. The curiosity to hear the punchline to this joke overwhelmed him, but he needed to think.

"Call me tomorrow and I will have an answer for you." The gods help him if he didn't.

Chapter Twenty-One

Lilly stood in an open field. She turned and could see nothing but green rolling hills in every direction and smelled fresh-cut grass. Boulders dotted along the landscape and behind one she heard garbled sounds. As she neared, pain and anger rose within her, though she didn't know why.

A large boulder loomed in front of her, a helmet with a large fire plume lay on its side in the grass at the base. Next to it, a shield and armor glistened in the sun. The noises grew louder, and as she walked farther around the rock, a large, lean, muscular man covered a woman, engaging in mind-blowing sex.

Mortified, Lilly turned to leave, and the man jerked into an awareness of her, and turned his head to reveal Colt's face. Under him a woman sprawled naked, voluptuous, and perfect...Caprice. She didn't know what to say, but felt a flaming anger ignite within her. Sharp pain emanated from her back and she turned to see a fan of feathers extending out from her. Shocked, she traced them to the center of her back. Looking down, bright blue, iridescent feathers covered a bird's chest. She wasn't human.

"You must win him, if we are to survive."

Lilly looked up, and standing on a rock, in front of the most amazing throne she'd ever seen, stood a woman. Regal, statuesque, and beautiful. When she turned back to Colt, he'd turned back to his lovemaking.

"Who are you?" Lilly asked.

"I am the way."

"The way to what?" She looked back at Colt and screamed, "Stop it!"

Colt withdrew from Caprice and stood, glorious and sated. He collected several pebbles and flung them at Lilly one by one.

"Go!" he shouted, as Caprice giggled.

Enraged, Lilly screamed and charged them both.

She woke up with a gasp and stared at the ceiling. Raising her arms, she tried to study them in the darkened room. Feeling that they weren't feathers anymore, she exhaled a sigh and sat up. Reaching for her glass of water, she took greedy gulps and tried to regain her senses. Never in her life had she had a dream like that. So bizarre, yet so vivid and real, and the dark air seemed to swirl around her.

****

"Grandma!" The Morgan children burst from the car and ran toward their grandmother's outstretched arms.

"Hello! Hello!" Danielle Morgan exclaimed. "Come here, my sweet angels."

As she hugged and kissed them, Lilly's father-in-law, Ryan, leaned in with a smile and kissed her cheek.

"Hello, love."

"Hi, Dad. Wow, you've got a great tan. The time down under certainly did you some good."

"It was fantastic. I almost didn't want to come back, but then I started itching for my board." Ryan winked and Lilly grinned knowing the old architect's deep passion for his craft.

"Hello, darling." Danielle reached a hand out and squeezed Lilly's. "How are you? It feels like it's been weeks and weeks."

"It has." Lilly chuckled, and called out, "Here, Trav, Chelsea, help me…"

The kids, already running toward the couple's Red Heeler, Lefty, and Golden Retriever, Chance, never looked back, and the trio watched them with affection.

"Ah, here now, let them go. What do you got in here?" Ryan asked.

"Oh, just the lemon meringue pie and a green bean casserole."

"My favorites."

Once settled inside their modest, cozy kitchen, Danielle asked Lilly if she wanted a glass of wine while she finished preparing the evening meal.

"I'd love it." Lilly walked to the cupboard and retrieved a glass for her and her mother-in-law. She opened a bottle of pinot noir and poured out. Setting a glass beside Danielle, she gazed through the window and watched her children play in the backyard with their grandfather and the dogs. "So, the cruise was fun, huh?"

"Yes, it was fantastic to get away for a while. Ryan's been working much too hard lately, and it was good for us to get away for a bit."

"Liv told me he got that downtown project. It's off Seneca, right?" Danielle nodded. "And she said you've been working on the house."

"Yes. I decided to go room by room and get rid of some stuff. It's been a long time since I've done that."

She paused and sipped her beverage. "Before we left, I also made the decision to start tackling some of David's things."

"You did?" Lilly stopped herself from taking another sip and looked at her. "How did it go?"

"It was hard, but also cathartic, which is more than I'd ever thought I'd have. Then, we went on our great trip and Ryan and I had some wonderful conversations about him and Liv, all of you really, that didn't end in tears. Novel, I know," she sighed, with a smile. "It was nice to just remember him and think about things like we would've had he still been here with you and the kids. Does that make sense?"

"Absolutely."

"It was nice." Danielle paused again and looked at her daughter-in-law. "How are you and the kids doing?"

"We're good. The kids are growing like weeds. I'm busier than ever. My sitter quit on me after being a flake for months, and I'm trying to find a suitable replacement. It's hard with my schedule and being on call, both to look for someone and then that someone being cool with same schedule."

"Can I help?"

"Oh no. Don't get me wrong, we'd love it, but it's way too far to come. I'll figure it all out. Que's been fantastic, helping me out. When she can stop making googley eyes at her boyfriend long enough."

"Who's she seeing?"

"Aulelei Tua—he plays football."

"Like a coach or something?"

"No." Lilly chuckled. "He *plays* football for the Seattle Warriors."

"Oh, you're kidding?"

"Nope. I think she's over-the-moon, and Abby looks like she's on cloud nine, too. The two of them are leaving on a romantic getaway and Raven and Finn are coming in tonight to take care of Abby."

"Wow, well good for her." Danielle sipped her glass of wine. "How long are the Taylors in town for?"

"Two weeks. Through Halloween."

"And what about you?" Mrs. Morgan eyed her daughter-in-law. "Are you seeing anyone?"

"What?" Lilly's head jerked up. "No, well, I…"

"Honey." Danielle set her glass down, looking concerned. "It's okay if you are, you know. We saw the paper, and I hope you know it's fine with us."

"I…Nothing happened…I mean…"

"Lillian, look at me." Danielle grabbed her daughter-in-law's hands. "Ryan and I want that for you, and so did David. Please tell me you understand that?"

"Olivia said that…"

"Oh, I can just guess what Olivia said," Danielle interrupted her, then stood and began to assemble the salad for dinner. "Honey, Olivia would be just fine with everyone standing still for David. It makes her feel less guilty for her own life marching on. None of us wanted David to go but I can tell you, now, I'm thankful he did. I, for one, couldn't stand to see him suffer anymore."

Lilly looked at her with a little skepticism.

"All right, if I'm being one hundred percent honest and you had dated right after he'd died, it might have been hard for me. But I can also tell you he and I talked about it a lot when he was sick. He pleaded with me to make sure you found love again." She smiled as the fresh ingredients blended together, creating a colorful masterpiece.

"He said that?"

"He did. It was very important to him, for you and the kids to be happy." Danielle set the bowl aside and leaned on the counter. "So, if you're dragging your heels because you think we won't approve or that somehow you're betraying David, you couldn't be more wrong. Please, don't put that burden on us."

She walked to the open window to call the playful trio to dinner. Lilly sipped her wine, eyes falling on a picture of their wedding day. Their eyes beaming out at the viewer, without any comprehension of things to come. Her vision tunneled.

David stood in the kitchen before her, dressed in his wedding clothes.

Lilly gasped as her eyes came back into focus. She blinked and scanned the room, but he wasn't there. The kids, dogs, and her in-laws all spoke and barked at once and didn't seem to notice the small drama unfold in the kitchen. Her heartbeat drummed in her chest, as she looked back at the photo and swore she smelled his aftershave.

****

Later that night Lilly opened the door to the Taylors'. Que had dropped Abby off earlier, and the kids now played a board game and giggled over their ice cream sundaes.

"Come in," the mother exclaimed, giving a hug to each of them. "I'm so glad you guys are here."

"Here you go," Finn said, handing her the newspaper she'd missed on the front porch.

"Oh thanks. The kids are in the rec room. You guys want something to drink?" she asked throwing the paper on the dining room table.

"I'd kill for a giant glass of water," Raven admitted.

"You got it. Finn?"

Finn brought a finger to his lips as a sign he wanted to surprise her offspring. He raced in like a banshee, eliciting yelps of fear, then pleasure, causing a melee to break out. Chuckling, Lilly gestured Raven to the table and returned with two glasses of water.

"So, how was the party? Was it all glamorous and fun?"

"Yeah, it was." Raven hesitated. "About that, Lil, I just wanted to tell you who we ran into…"

"That sonofabitch!" Lilly stared down at a thumbnail photo of Colt and Caprice in a deep embrace and what appeared to be a smoldering kiss. Noting the page number, she flipped to the page where the larger picture loomed, and noted the caption.

On again, off again lovers, Caprice Starr and Colton Stone, are back on at her birthday extravaganza. Sources close to the power couple say they've been serious for some time and are already hinting at wedding bells.

"Lil."

Fire consumed her. *Did he think he could make a fool of her?* Lilly's stomach tightened and her heart felt like it darkened.

"Colt was at Caprice's birthday party?" Lilly accused.

"Yeah, he was, but Lilly, they're just friends, really, there's nothing more."

"He's kissing her," Lilly spat. "He's kissing her, Raven…In the God damn paper!"

"No," Raven implored. "They were just saying hello. It's just what they all do in L.A."

"Oh, that's bullshit and you know it. Did he stay the night with her?"

"What? No. In fact, he left before I could even say hello to him. He just stopped by to wish Caprice a happy birthday."

"And?"

"And nothing. I think he was mad and left."

"Mad because she didn't have sex with him?"

Raven stared at her in disbelief. Lilly's anger seemed extreme to her own ears, and she felt helpless to control it.

"No, Lil," she said, trying to diffuse the tension. "Caprice thinks he's playing hurt and he didn't like her calling him out on it."

That brought the doctor up short. *Playing hurt?* She had noticed nothing. However, she didn't enjoy watching the violent game either.

"They go way back. I promise you they're only friends."

"I thought you didn't know Colt?"

"Well, I don't...not really, but I do know Caprice...very well. And she told me they were an item in the past, but would be ecstatic for each other if they found happiness with other people."

"Then why are they kissing?"

"Lilly," Raven changed tactics, "are you jealous?"

"What? No."

"Then why are you so furious? I've never heard you talk like this before. You're angry, upset and...jealous."

"I-I can't help it. I guess it's in my nature."

"Since when?"

"Since…" Lilly thought for a moment.

Jealousy and anger. Jealous over Que's relationship. Angry over Colt's budding relationship with her children. Jealousy about Caprice. Furious with David. That brought her up short. Furious with David? She never had been before.

"Lil?"

"I don't know what's going on with me. I just…"

Raven went out on a limb and took her hand.

"Have you been having dreams, Lilly?"

"What? Where'd that come from?" The surgeon's head spun. "Why would you ask me something like that?"

"I'm just curious. Not feeling like yourself? Maybe having weird dreams? Feeling like things are out of control?"

"Are you telling me you somehow know what that's about?" Lilly laughed with unease. "Who's the doctor here?"

"Maybe you should ask yourself why," Raven suggested.

"Why what?"

"Why you're so jealous and angry?" When her friend didn't respond, Raven continued, "Do you love him?"

Lilly looked down at the photo in the newspaper and her eyes stung. She rested her forehead in her hand and tried to massage the question away.

"Lil?"

"Of course not."

"Shouldn't you find out?" Raven asked, ignoring her answer.

"I can't get into a relationship with him. I've got my practice and the kids they…"

"Love him?" Raven supplied.

"I don't want them to love him," Lilly spat.

"Why?"

"David wouldn't have…" Lilly began, then started to cry.

"Oh, honey." Raven, full of sympathy, leaned forward more. "Do you honestly believe David would want you to be alone for the rest of your life? For the kids to not have a father figure?"

"No," Lilly admitted, Danielle's words ringing in her head. "I don't know. I can't…this is all happening way too fast."

"Maybe," Raven supplied, "you should go talk to him."

"What do you mean?"

"Maybe have, I don't know, a conversation about your feelings and all your concerns. The little I know about the man is that he's complicated, but then again, so are you, aren't you? Maybe he needs something and doesn't know what it is any more than you do. Maybe the universe is saying something to both of you."

"So, now we're delving into karma and fate?" Lilly asked with sarcasm.

"Well, why not? Finn and I had no business being together, yet here we are. I just think maybe the two of you need to have a frank conversation. Not knowing where each other stands has got to be as confusing as hell. Besides that, when do you two ever get a second to just spend time together alone?"

"Mama!" Chelsea called. "I want more ice cream!"

"No Chels, you've had enough," Lilly called out.

"Come on, go. Finn and I got the kids."

"I…"

"Lilly, go!"

"What do I say about where I'm going? They'll want to come."

"Just go. I'll tell them you got called into work. Don't worry about them. We'll play some games and have fun. They won't even know you're gone."

"Yeah, great, now I'm lying to my kids."

"No you're not. I am."

"I *am* glad you guys came," Lilly said. "It's been really weird around here lately."

"Me too, and Lil…" Raven grabbed her hand as the woman stood. "I want you to know something else."

"What?"

"I'm always here for you, I promise. You can talk to me about anything, no matter how crazy or weird it sounds. I promise, I'll believe you."

As Lilly drove to Colt's house, her friend's words sank in. *I'll believe you.* What an odd thing to say, as if she had insight into her dreams and secret thoughts. Thinking about the other things Raven said and the reason for it, anger bloomed in her all over again. Damn it, she'd understand this and get things settled tonight.

Chapter Twenty-Two

When Dee arrived, the professor looked shocked to see she'd brought a roll-away suitcase. Speechless, he opened the door a little wider, and she wheeled it in. She knew the case looked like its owner. Bizarre. It had a tie-dyed lacquered surface and one wheel that jumped around, as if possessing a separate mind. Once over the threshold, she held up a large bag, emblazoned with *The Golden Peacock Fusion Restaurant,* on its filmy surface.

"Told ya I'd bring dinner. I'm a phenomenal cook though, so next time I'll make ya my specialty," she said, rolling the suitcase into the pristine and tidy living room.

Still in disbelief he'd agreed to this encounter, Dee turned and grinned at the man.

"I'm guessing, in one hour's time we will part ways and I won't see you again, Dee. That was our arrangement, correct?"

"Yes, sir. Well, let's eat and then we'll get started on that hour."

He quirked an eyebrow, and she gave him her best innocent expression, at extending one hour into two. At the very least, she didn't imagine she'd bore him.

"Fine," he snapped with rigid acceptance. "May I offer you something to drink?"

"Hmm, well what do you have?"

"Tea, coffee, water, or milk."

"What kind of tea?"

"I have English breakfast or Chamomile."

"All right, lets both go for the Chamomile. It'll be more soothing."

"I'm having coffee."

"No, have the tea, Doc. Trust me."

A quarter of an hour later and tea in hand, Dee laid out plates and utensils. She opened containers and began preparing her chopsticks. He looked at her perplexed, as she rubbed the edges of the wooden sticks together.

"When you take them apart and rub them together like this," she said, "it takes away the sharp, raw edges, so you don't get slivers."

"Ah, I see," he said and ran his eyes down the length of her body.

She'd changed. The dress, though still a muumuu, looked more subdued in various shades of blue. When she sat down to eat, she removed her hat and her long silver hair slid down onto her shoulders.

"You haven't always lived in California, right?" she began.

"Correct."

"Oh, where are you from originally?"

"Back East mostly, a little in the midwest."

"Ah." When he didn't elaborate, she said, "I live on Kaua'i, and have since just after I was born. My grandson, Finn, lives there with me. He's a newlywed. Married only a few months now. Raven, his wife, she's a famous musician."

"Raven?" he asked, fork raised halfway to his

mouth. "Are you speaking of the singer, Raven Hunter?"

"Yes, that's right." She looked down to scoop up some pork fried rice. "Do you like her music?" He didn't respond, just used a fork to cut a bite off an egg roll, so she continued. "Well, they married on the island but Raven and her twin brother, Wyatt, are from here in Seattle."

Ray stopped eating again and looked over at her, with irritation, and Dee tried to backtrack. The man said he didn't have a family and his life hadn't looked easy. Not wanting to make him angry before she even got started, she wiped her hands and mouth on a napkin and began.

"Okay, well first off, I have to tell you, what I'm going to say will sound absolutely unbelievable. In fact, you won't believe me at all, not a word of it. You're going to think I'm certifiably insane. The only thing I can tell you…Well, promise you, is that it's true, as true as I am sitting here talking to you now. I've had nothing to drink. I've never done drugs and I'm not a mental case, even though I know you think I am." she acknowledged as he had the decency to blush. He lowered his eyes as if chastened, then gave a slight nod of his head and sipped his tea.

"Okay. So, last year…"

Dee explained how she'd been in her garden and the very air swirled, creating a large water spout in the ocean, complete with a beam of bright sunshine illuminating the inside of the tube. She had moments in life when impressions would flow in and out of her mind. She knew some people would call it psychic, but Dee never thought of it that way. This particular event involved her grandson, and though she didn't know her at the time, Raven.

Dee described how a force pulled her to her bedroom and a box, handed down from generation to generation. It had resided in her closet untouched, for years. Yet now, it called to her with conviction and desperation.

She looked at Ray, who in turn looked back at her with skepticism and irritation at the direction the evening had turned. She wondered how long she had before he threw her out.

Standing up, she walked to the suitcase and unzipped it, revealing the old box.

"My mother gave me this a long time ago. She said it never opened for anyone, ever. The instructions handed down were if it was intended to open for you it would." She looked at him. "It did."

Now looking intrigued, Ray took it from her outstretched hands, upside down. As he tried to turn it over, she shook her head and gestured for him to read aloud.

"Those that now rule will rue a day, when those they command refuse to pray. An old, most powerful foe will find a way, to escape the bonds of yesterday. And with him will turn one once trusted; that gods persecuted, belittled and neglected. Mighty gods shackled and toil never to be heard." Ray paused and searched her eyes. When she didn't break the connection, but just nodded, he looked down again. "Mighty gods shackled and toil never to be heard; from Tartarus's grip, deep in the abyss of the Underworld. There they will remain for as long as time rules, until the last bead of their blood is collected and cooled. The outcome they fear, fate could yet reject; if the children of tomorrow's lives intersect. And in their quest, three discoveries must be found, or the deities will face the Moirai and be cut to the underground."

"The Moirai?" Ray queried and stared at the old script confused. If nothing else, she could tell he understood the box contained historical significance on its own. Coming from the era it did, seemed to intrigue him. Turning it over, he examined it, then looked back up at Dee.

"Just keep reading," she pleaded.

He took a deep breath and read. "First, god and mortal alike, a weakness to conquer; and only from there the key may the children conjure. Second, something gods have naught to know; selflessness, devotion, and love-eternal the hardest to sow. The final discovery for this quest to take place, is when all children are in the same time and same space. Five arrows to join around heart's blood of great hope, it will lay; Perhaps even more, only I, Themis, can command, at the end of the last day. Many eras have tried to face success and prevail, only to miss the connections and fail. Brothers may harness drops of their power to advise in this cause, because it is written in Themis' divine law. For only then will the threat be defeated, and to the Isle of Blest, the remaining gods be seated. And though their time of rule may end; full assimilation of immortal blood, this Oracle will send. For even if one pure drop remains, ascending the steps, Olympians may again reign."

He finished and shook his head a little, as if the spell broke and reality flooded back in. "What is this…a joke?"

"No." Dee released a disappointed breath. Somehow she hoped a miracle would occur and he would see it and be willing to help. "Believe me, I know how it sounds."

"How what sounds?" he demanded. "What exactly are you trying to have me believe, Dee?"

She took a large breath and jumped in with both feet. "Someone gave me this box, or gave someone in my family this box, a very long time ago…I think it was Themis."

"Themis?" he queried, voice dripping with sarcasm. "What? Did she knock on the door and say she was selling little wooden prophecies?"

"No, she came out of my closet."

"Your closet." He laughed now. "Right. A Greek personification, a deity, rose out of your shoes and said, 'Dee Taylor I need you to go on a quest.' " Another laugh burbled from his register and bellowed out.

"Look!" Dee snapped. "You don't believe me, that's fine. I certainly know how it all sounds. Finn and Raven didn't believe me either, not for a very long time. Most people don't take me too seriously, and I can accept that. I have my faults, but lying ain't one of them. Things happened, and if you'd been standing in my home a little over a year ago, you sure as hell wouldn't be laughing now either. You'd be shitting your God damn pants, Doc. So, don't treat me like some kind of freak." She gave him a gimlet stare. "This happened. You can choose not to believe it, but just because you don't believe it, does not mean it didn't happen. Laughing at me is cruel. It's hurtful, and no matter what you think you know about me, I don't deserve your cruelty."

****

Ray stopped laughing. Experiencing his share of names, including freak, he knew what it felt like to be laughed at, poked, and even to make kids cry just at the sight of him. He'd built up barriers just to protect himself from the pain of it. Now, this beautiful woman sounded resigned that she didn't measure up, and he'd confirmed it with his laughter, but Christ, Jesus...The Greek gods? What in the hell could he say to that? *But you believe in them too,* a small voice said and he flinched.

"My apologies, Dee. I didn't mean to imply..."

"Forget it," she said, took a drink, and continued. "When I got to my room and pulled out the box, the pain in my body evaporated." She looked at him with emphasis. "You're my age, Ray. I'm sure you know what it's like to wake up with aches and pain in your joints."

He gave a nod.

"Well, that pain left my body...just leaked right out. I took hold of the box and noticed my arm." She held it out, to display large, fat freckles, from sun damage, and raised blue veins snaking across her hands. "All of this went away. My skin was clear...young. And my vision, I don't know, just focused somehow. I didn't need my glasses at all. I sat on the floor cross-legged, for chrissake.

"I've never been able to open this box before, but it just opened. A weird lady...floated...out of it. She was the most beautiful thing I'd ever seen. And had this thing around her eyes...and a sword. Her voice was beautiful too, like a song. I'd never heard anything so damned beautiful in my life, Ray. Then, she started talking about prophecies and whatnot. Do I look like someone that would know anything about Greek gods? I run a floral and garden market and wear muumuus. She told me Cronus was plotting to overthrow everything. How he would unleash the last evils on the world. She said all the gods...everyone...would go to Tartarus if he got out. The real bad part of Tartarus. Zeus, Hades, Poseidon, all of them, will all go in there and have eternal damnation. She said, we have until the Immaculate Conjunction. Sh-she..." Her voice wobbled, and she took a deep breath to settle it. "Themis said the brothers are the only ones that can come back a little longer and give some extra guidance, but we don't know what questions to ask." Dee searched the room for inspiration. "Apollo and Poseidon are now in the Elysium. They have to wait there until everyone else gets there or until one of the gods is captured, and down they all go."

"Apollo and Poseidon?"

"Poseidon, his descendent is my grandson, Finn. Raven is from Apollo, and I," she said, placing a hand close to her heart with pride, "I'm from Demeter."

"Demeter?"

"Themis said she sent Demeter because she...Themis, and Demeter share an affinity for life and death. Children of life and children of death." She lowered her voice and hung her head. "It's a long story but I have a child in death, my son, Matthew. And I have a child in life, Finn." She lifted her head and scanned his face. "I raised him. Believe me, Ray, I know how this sounds. It's crazy and insane and not possible. I was hallucinating or drunk. I had a stroke, or I'm just old and senile. Finn and Raven's favorite at the time was I had a very elaborate dream. But deep down in there"—she laid a hand on his chest—"I know you believe in them too and made it your life's work. You talk about them in the present tense. You know their stories, their history."

She looked down, as if only now registering she'd bridged the distance between them, and removed her hand, sliding back into her chair. Taking a deep breath, she let it out and settled the box on her lap once more.

"It wasn't until after a lot of hardship, and them finding each other, that Finn and Raven believed it too. And when they did, and we got back to the house, they each grabbed a handle of the chest This medallion that always hung around Raven's neck heated up. It made a small burn on her neck." She pointed to her own neck. "And there's a little scar there even now. Her mother, who died, gave her the necklace, and it just melted into the box, here." She pointed to the metal.

A cold shiver zinged up Ray's spine. Ray looked down at the box again, eyeing the gold metal settled into a groove on top of the box, creating a small arrowhead. An enormous sense of foreboding overtook him, unsettling him even more. He shook his head, as if to ward off the feeling. Some of the incredulous things she said made sense.

The Moirai and the significance that time would assign to them. The brothers and Themis having extra abilities, weren't mainstream ideas. Most novices had no notion of Themis or what she could do, knowing only the commercial symbol, Lady Justice. They didn't understand the significance of that or her or the brothers.

The box itself intrigued him. It looked the part.

Ancient as time, with the metal straps worn into a fine patina. On the top, several symbols lay engraved upon the surface. Who and what they represented he understood with immediate understanding. Dee seemed to notice where his gaze fell, and she moved it closer for him to see.

"I've got some of them figured out already," she said with only a slight hesitation. "I know this trident; Finn has the exact same thing on his back. A tattoo he got when he was twenty. And this"—she pointed to the lyre—"this was on the medallion that Raven's mother gave to her. The exact same thing, Ray. And her brother, her twin brother, Wyatt, has an identical one. Raven and Wyatt. Apollo and Artemis. Although, we aren't sure Wyatt's the other half. It could be someone different. It's just a pretty big coincidence. It burned her as it melted and moved along the chest to settle here." She pointed to the arrowhead.

Ray looked up in sharp anger and sat back in his chair.

"Wait! A-And these wings have to be Hermes. I'm sure of it. The cornucopia has to be from my line." She knelt before him, looking up into his disbelieving eyes. "I told you, I know how this sounds. It's impossible, and it's not logical at all, but I swear to you on the most important thing in my life, my grandson, that this is real. What I'm saying to you is true." She glanced down at the chest. "I'm not sure what a lot of the other ones are, but…"

Dee looked back at his face with tears in her eyes, and she must have seen the refusal in his eyes because she hung her head and gave a quick nod.

"Okay," she whispered and stood up. "Okay, I

understand. I do. Thank you for all of your time, Dr. Butler. I know I'm a pain in the ass."

The sound of the formal title on Dee's lips brought him up short. She started collecting her things, and he didn't know what to say. She drew down the flap, and darkness closed in on the box, forever removing it from his presence. Maybe he could help her with the symbols.

"The owl is a sacred symbol for Athena," he whispered, so quiet she almost missed it. Glancing up, she stared at him in disbelief.

"I'm sorry?"

"The owl on that etching." He gestured, and she withdrew the box again. "The owl is a sacred symbol for Athena, goddess Strategic War." He looked at the other symbols. "This here is a shield." He traced the outline of the coat of arms. "A sacred object for Ares, Violent War." He pointed to the dove about to perch on the top of the cornucopia. "That symbol is Aphrodite's dove. And this"—he pointed to a small bow and arrow—"is a bow and arrow for the hunter, Artemis." He looked up at Dee. "Her symbol would not be a lyre. You're right, the lyre is Apollo's."

"The rings represent Hera, Marriage. This"—he peered at the carving, enthralled at the game—"this anvil represents Hephaestus."

"Wait. Who? Hefus?

"No, Hay-fey-stoo-s." He smiled. "Hephaestus, Fire and Metallurgy. He's a blacksmith that creates all the magical things for the other gods, like the winged shoes for Hermes." He pointed to the wings. "He also helped forge the thunderbolts with the Cyclopes for Zeus himself." Ray's brows furrowed as he rubbed a finger over the thunderbolt in the center. He discovered a goblet. "This here"—he pointed to it—"would be Dionysus's goblet, god Wine. This fire here"—he ran a finger along the groove—"Hestia...Hearth-Fire."

He looked over at Dee and clarified, "Hestia is the sister of Zeus. Only twelve gods sat on Mount Olympus. Zeus, Hera, Poseidon, Aphrodite, Ares, Hermes, Athena, Artemis, Apollo, Hestia, Demeter, and Hephaestus."

"What about Hades?"

"Hades is a god and a powerful one, but he lives and spends his time in the Underworld, not on Olympus. It's a common misunderstanding." Ray pointed to the other pronged staff on the carving that represented the dark god, then went back to the blacksmith. "Hephaestus was, at one time, cast off Olympus but allowed to return at a later date. However, Hestia is the only goddess who gave up her spot on Olympus to Dionysus."

"Why would she do that?"

"Some say she despised her family and wanted a more simple life among the mortals. They all revered her...the mortals, I mean. She brings forth the hearth fire and gives them the ability to heat their homes and cook their meat. She provides the ability to see in the dark and didn't subject the mortals to her whims. They absolutely revered her."

"And what about this?" Dee gestured to a large orb surrounding the thunderbolt.

"My guess would be it's an oracle."

Dee nodded, as if that made perfect sense. *She truly believes what she's saying.*

"And this?" She pointed to the star.

"That…" Ray studied it. "I'm not sure. It could represent many things. You said something about a conjunction, but I didn't recognize the name."

"Yes, the Immaculate Conjunction, and no, Kyle didn't know it either."

"Kyle didn't know it?" Ray asked, lifting his head.

"No, but he said he'd look into it for me."

"It could be something about hunting or direction."

"Direction? Like to a specific place?"

"Maybe."

"Like same time and space? Like what the prophecy said?"

"Maybe," he said again.

Dee looked over at him, as if trying to gauge his feelings. She remained silent, but clearly desperate for his help.

"Ray, when this happened, it threw all of us in a tailspin. When Finn and Raven committed to each other, they each touched the chest at the same time and Themis returned…" Ray's gaze popped back up to Dee. "She wasn't the only one," the older woman blurted. "Poseidon and Apollo came through, too. Apollo said nothing and exploded into these little tiny beads of light. Poseidon, well, he was one intimidating son of a bitch who only talked to Finn. We could only ask him a few questions, but we didn't know what to ask. He said only he, Hades, and Zeus could talk to us in the end like that."

"Zeus? As in…Zeus?"

"Yeah. The thing is, this is hard enough on its own. It's impossible, but we have to get ten more people to understand how important this is. Not only that, but believe in it and take on their role. It was hard enough with someone I've known, taken care of, and loved his whole life. Finn gave me the benefit of the doubt, but now we're talking strangers." She stopped and looked down. "People that have no reason to trust us and every reason to call the cops or looney bin."

When he only nodded, she continued.

"We don't know the right questions to ask or even where to begin. Poseidon said Raven had already met the next person. Themis said, Ares and Hera would be next. Raven thinks Hera's is a pediatric heart surgeon in Seattle. She's a widow with two children. The Ares's guy, well, we *think* it's Colton Stone." Ray didn't react, and she continued, "The tight end for the Seattle Warriors?"

Ray had to admit the soundness of her interpretation, yet it was a little too much upheaval in his tidy little life. He understood on a gut level, utter discord lay at the odd woman's proclamations.

"And again, we think Wyatt, Raven's brother, could be another one, we just don't know yet and haven't brought it up to him. Apollo and Artemis, twins. Raven and Wyatt, twins."

"You said their mother gave them these medallions. Has anyone asked her where she got them?"

"No." Dee lowered her eyes in regret. "No, their mama and daddy were killed at a very young age. They had no family or kin, so went into the foster system."

"But the new family, the one that took them in, do they know their history?" Ray's eyes searched hers, but saw the reality.

"No, the new dad beat them within an inch of their lives, and they ran away when they were teenagers,"

Dee spat out in anger, then seemed to realize what she said. "Oh God, Ray. Please...I shouldn't have told you that. No one, and I mean no one, knows that part of their life. Please, don't ever tell anyone I said that, please."

"Who would I tell?" Ray's eyes burned with anger.

"Oh, I'm sorry, I'm not making a judgement," Dee countered. "It's just Raven is a celebrity and something like this...Well, Johnny Q. Public and those horrible tabloids would love to get their hands on something like that." Dee looked worried. "Not to mention, I just betrayed a trust and I don't do that." She raised a hand to her forehead. "I just don't understand what's gotten into me lately. This has been a complete nightmare, from start to finish. The one saving grace is that Raven and Finn found each other. A yin to the other's yang, and that's been a beautiful thing to watch."

She looked over at him.

"If you believe even the smallest measure of this and agree to work with us, know we're already deep into the second pair. It's happening right now. Work with us, and I promise you'll be a believer. If we can just get back to the box opening, you will be a believer. I promise. I'm begging you, Ray, please help us."

He looked deep into Dee's expressive blueberry eyes, searching for hints of mockery or ridicule. She only revealed a woman in dire straits, who seemed to believe everything she said. He took in her appearance and the lengths she'd undergone to impress him, and the chest she clung to on her lap. He couldn't deny it had properties he couldn't identify. If nothing else, a rare piece of history that suggested the Silver or Bronze Age. He stood before chuckling and coming to a decision.

"I can't believe I'm doing this." He looked into her hopeful eyes. "All right, Dee, you win. If you get to whatever stage this box opens at, I'll show up and observe. You have my word."

Chapter Twenty-Three

Colt looked at himself in the mirror one last time. Khaki slacks, white-collared shirt with a green sweater vest. His close-cropped copper hair lit in the sun, and the gentle wind blew across his clean-shaven face. Pulling out a watch on a chain, he checked the time, and replaced it in his vest pocket. He poured scented after-shave into the palm of his hand and slapped it on his cheeks, neck and clothes.

"Are you coming?" he heard her call to him and smiled.

As Colt walked around the corner, Travis, dressed like him, gazed at him with hero worship in his eyes. Lilly, in a bright yellow sundress, hair long and pulled back, knelt fluffing out Chelsea's curls in the sunlight. The little girl noticed Colt and ran to him, arms wide. As she approached, he crouched down and opened his arms. She giggled and ran faster.

"Daddy!"

His heart exploded with joy as he waited to receive her, but she ran past him. Confused, he spun around. Just behind and to his left stood David, dressed in perfect imitation of Colt. Lilly and Travis ran past the redhead, and he reached out to take her hand. She shook him off with irritation and kept running for her husband. A football appeared in Colt's hands and he called to Travis saying he could work some drills with him, but the boy never even turned around. They encircled David, smiling. The family man wrapped diaphanous arms around his children, laughing, but they didn't seem to notice. He reached over and placed a hand around Lilly's neck, drawing her in for a gentle kiss. They lingered and when he pulled away, Lilly looked up at him with utter devotion. She tried to hug his transparent frame, and as she did, David looked over to Colt grinning with victory.

"You have no business here."

He turned back to his family as the football player's vision darkened and tunneled. Liquid mercury poured from Colt's ears and moved up the sides of his head. It separated and fingered out into bars that covered his eyes. When he turned his head, a long plume of fire trailed over his shoulder, and he felt the fire arch in a high mohawk on his helmet. His clothes burned away, and he stood naked before the family, body consumed in flames. Mercury seeped from his pores and created armor, encasing the fire. David pushed his family away and screamed something ancient, and primordial. Thousands of men, who looked like his father, sprang from the earth and stood in a protective arch around David, who turned into a warrior woman.

Colt screamed and began cutting down the army. When he cut down one man, three more would rise. Colt knew he needed to cut down David...the woman. He slashed and brawled until the man and woman separated into two people. She sidestepped Colt, smiled, then disappeared. David fell to his knees, cowering and begging for his life.

"Please," he sobbed, "they're my family. They're mine."

Colt loomed above him, heavy sword raised.

"No, they belong to me now," he stated with simple appraisal and brought the weapon down, severing the man's head from his body.

As the man fell, black serpent-like ribbons streamed out from the opening in his neck and slithered their way across the floor. Colt turned to watch and screamed out his victorious war cry, when Lilly sprawled out on the ground, with millions of pomegranate seeds pouring from a gaping wound across her own heart. He cried out and saw Travis lying across his father's body, as if he'd tried to protect him. And Chelsea. The little girl had angel wings outlined in blood, her crystal blue eyes staring unseeing up at the sky. When he approached, and looked close, fire flamed in her pupils. His fire. His form reflected in the darkening pools. He raised his head, and all the slain men, his father, morphed into the trio. Hundreds of Lilly, Travis, and Chelsea clones cut down. He ran to the most prominent Lilly, and large barbs poked under the surface of the skin until they pierced the surface and exposed themselves to the light. The barbs sprouted fine feathers, as bird-like feet grew from her own. A hooked beak elongated, and black ribbons formed into eyes until soon a vulture screeched out its anger. He ran to the next body and just before he could reach it, another vulture appeared. Soon each body transformed into a vulture, like a tsunami wave and when only acres of the birds remained, the collective flapped their wings and took flight. As they did, their talons clung to the earth, ripping away its surface. A starry landscape remained with faraway planets aligning and a large super nova exploded. Colt felt innate fear as a darkness, and a dank, sticky plague, seeped its way across Earth.

Colt convulsed awake. *Real or not real?* No…people didn't sprout wings or morph into other people. He'd fallen asleep in his soft leather chair. Scanning the darkened room, he scrubbed a hand over his face, stood and walked out onto the deck and the cold night air. A light snow had fallen, and his bare feet sizzled against it, as though fire still burned in his blood. He'd murdered that man. Murdered them all because they didn't want him. Wouldn't have him. He didn't remember ever having a dream so vivid and saturated in colors. His icy breath unfurled in a thin stream in front of his face. Somewhere in the depths of his makeshift bed his cell phone rang. Running inside, Colt hit mute on the television, before looking at the phone and seeing his agent's name on the display.

"Sam," he said, taking a deep breath and releasing it with a quick verocity. "What's up, man?"

"Just checking in. How're things going?"

"Good…good," Colt said, still shaking himself awake.

"Okay, well how's your head?"

"What about it?"

"Colt, come on. You said you'd check it out."

"Jesus, you too? Everyone just needs to lay off. I'm fine."

"If you have multiple people saying it, maybe *you* should be the one listening."

"Yes, Mother. Anything else?"

"Sports Beat is asking about that broadcaster position again."

"I'm a player, Sam. I want to play, not talk about playing."

A buzz rang down his intercom, indicating someone at his gate. He looked into the security screen and saw Lilly.

"I gotta go. Someone a lot better looking and a whole lot more interesting just arrived," he stated, buzzing her in.

"Fine," his agent laughed. "Have fun but we aren't finished with this yet."

"I am," Colt said and hung up.

He'd never seen Lilly in ratty jeans, an old T-shirt, or even tennis shoes before, but to his eyes, she'd never looked more beautiful.

"I'd swear, you'd make a potato sack look good, Lil."

She narrowed her eyes at him and walked into the room, looking awestruck at the expanse. As she walked by, he raised his eyebrows and genuflected at her ass clad in worn denim.

"This place is huge," she stated, scanning the area. He remained silent and just watched her walk amongst his things. When she paused at the helmet and crossed swords, she asked, "Why do you have such a big house?"

"I don't know. I guess because I can." He stepped down into the living room. "Wanna drink?"

"Sure. Whiskey if you have it."

"Whiskey?" he asked, just to make sure. He'd never seen her drink whiskey either.

As he left to bar tend, she opened the slider door to the patio, and after preparing their drinks, he joined her. The pool light floated up to glow against her face, causing his heart to tighten a little inside his chest.

"It's really beautiful here."

"It is," he agreed, and handed her the drink before looking out onto Lake Washington. "So, you came. Does that mean…"

He ran a gentle hand down her arm, but she moved away. Dropping his head, Colt filled his cheeks with air, then let it out slowly. Somehow, he should've known it wouldn't be that simple.

"I want to talk to you about the other day," she said.

"Okay, so about the garage?" he said, as she paced along the patio, and he followed her movement.

"Why were you kissing Caprice?"

"What?" Genuine bafflement blossomed on his face, thinking about their last evening together. "When did I…Oh, the party? That was nothing." He waved a hand in dismissal.

"Nothing? It sure as hell looked like something."

"It wasn't, just sayin' hello."

"Really," she laughed. "That's your excuse?"

"Excuse? Why would I…" Understanding flooded his face, and he grinned. "Are you jealous, Lillian?"

"Don't be absurd."

"Absurd?"

"I just don't appreciate you doing what you did to me one night, then moving on to her because I said no. It's rude."

"Rude?" Colt smiled at her. "As far as I can remember you never used the word, no."

"I won't stand for this, Colt."

"Stand for what?"

"I'm not one of your groupies. I won't let you

exploit me or my kids."

"Okay, now you're pissing me off, Doc," Colt barked, his face flushing crimson.

"Well, I don't give a shit, Colt. You don't get to have your cake and eat it too."

"What the hell does that mean?"

"You can't have your whore one night and me the next."

Colt slammed down his drink and covered the distance to Lilly in two strides.

"Do not call Caprice a whore. You can be mad because of how a photo appears. You can bitch at me about my motives. Hell, you can even vomit your jealous rants if it makes you feel better. But Caprice is a phenomenal person to an insane number of people and as much as I like you, Lilly, I won't let you go all evil bitch hate on her."

"Evil bitch hate?"

"Yeah. I wouldn't allow anyone to talk about you that way, and I won't let anyone say it about her either. Do you understand me?"

"Oh, I understand."

"You understand dick, Lilly," he spat, anger and emotion now flaring inside him. "I want you, not Caprice. I should think that's very clear by now."

"Do you?" She set her glass down on the table and walked back indoors.

"Where are you going?" Colt followed.

"Home. This was a huge mistake."

"Stop!" he barked, catching her around the waist. "Why are you here?"

"I've been trying to answer that since I left my house."

"And?"

"And, if that had been me in the paper, out of context, how would it have made you feel?" He peered into her eyes, now seeing the hurt, and realized his mistake.

"You're right," he breathed and looked away for a moment before returning his gaze to her. "If I saw that, I'd kill the guy." He scanned her face. "Is that what you want to hear?"

When she didn't respond, he placed his hands on the sides of her face, tilting her head up to his and asked again, "Why are you here, Lilly?"

"I…" She looked at him with desperation.

"You have to say it." When she continued to look conflicted, he shouted, "Say it, damn it!"

"I want you to make love to me."

Relief spread through his entire body and he leaned in to kiss her. She only hesitated a moment before kissing him back. Reaching down, he stripped off her T-shirt to reveal a delicate undershirt that barely covered her. When he stooped to take one erect nipple into his mouth through the silk and lace, Lilly threaded fingers through his hair and tilted her head back with a cry of delicious pleasure. Colt's large fingers encircled her waist, and he stood, lifting her into the air, while she wrapped her legs around his torso and drew his bottom lip into her mouth. Groaning, he turned with Lilly in his arms, and made his way to the bedroom. The moment his bare feet hit the plush carpet, he set her down, and she lifted his shirt to lay kisses on his chest and abdomen, while unzipping his jeans.

Her warm breath swirled over his broad, massive chest, and in sudden torment, he couldn't wait to be inside her, and laid her on the bed. With heroic effort, he paused, kneeling between her thighs and rubbing his thumb over her clit. She moaned and writhed, and he waited and watched. When he knew she'd soon explode, he sheathed himself inside her, feeling her body absorb him in a hard grip.

Lilly screamed, eyes and mouth wide with pleasure, as the orgasm ignited within her. She arched her back, and he captured first one nipple and then the other. Lilly moved her hands across his back and down to cup his bottom, trying to bring him even closer. In a fever, Colt pumped inside her, feeling her body pulsate around him, her whimpers and pants seductive in his ear. His own orgasm built, moving and beating to the surface, until it crested and broke, filling her.

"Jesus...Christ!" he groaned and buried himself deeper inside, as they locked in frozen unison.

They stared at each other, chests heaving, as the rest of his orgasm rippled between them, then he rested his forehead on hers and closed his eyes. With reluctance, he disengaged himself after a moment, and rolled over onto his back, pulling her with him. Lilly laid her cheek against his chest, and the room felt heavy. Colt looked down at his new lover as she stared out into space.

"You okay?"

"Yeah." She smiled.

"Regret it?"

"No." She looked up at him. "You?"

"Hell, no."

She chuckled, then sobered. "I'm sorry. I just didn't know what to think."

"Lilly, I get it." He tilted her chin up. "There's

been no one since I met you. That's the God's honest truth. Okay?"

Consternation spread across her face. "I...honestly I'm not..." She sighed. "Despite recent events to the contrary, I'm not a jealous person..."

"Listen, I get it," he said again. "I don't want you putting anyone else in our bed either."

"Do I look like a person who juggles multiple lovers?"

"No, but it's easy to find fault with people that are living. I've got enough of my own without shoving a saint at me for comparison." Colt brought a gentle hand down on her head and stroked her glossy hair.

"David wasn't a saint," she replied, looking up at him.

"At this point he's damn close." He laughed and ran a hand through his own hair, then onto his chest. His gaze shifted to the ceiling. "Do we have a deal?"

"Yes," she responded and smiled up at him, causing him to grin back while biting his bottom lip. "But the last time I made love to anyone *was* over four years ago."

"That's a long time," he said with incredulity.

"Yeah."

"No wonder you're so uptight." At his statement, she looked up at him, irritated.

"What?" Lilly retorted. "I'm not uptight."

"You've been bitchy."

"I don't know too many women that would be okay with their boyfriends kissing their old girlfriends on the mouth every time they see them."

"They would if they trusted them. Wait, did you just call me your boyfriend?" Colt rolled over, pinning her hands above her head. "Is that what I am?"

"I don't know," she said, with a girlish giggle.

"No, I like it. It's like we're going steady." He kissed the sides of her neck and collarbone, then nipped her bottom lip. "Are we going steady, Lil?"

"Yeah, I guess we are." Lilly giggled again. "The kids'll love it."

"Where are they now?"

Colt looked down at her breasts, distracted. He dipped his head low and took a nipple in his mouth. Lilly closed her eyes and seemed to like the sensations.

"Raven and Finn came into town for a couple of weeks and they're with them. Maybe..." She gasped. "Maybe we can all get together and have dinner," she panted. "You want to?"

"Sure," he said, taking the other nipple in his mouth. "When?"

"Mmm, next Sunday?"

He stopped and looked at her. "Tua and I play on Sunday."

"Oh, course you do. Sorry. When do you get finished?"

"It's in Texas."

"Oh. I'm sorry, I should know these things."

"Actually..." He laughed and got within eye level. He brushed the hair from her face before kissing her again. "I love that you *don't* know about these things. It's nice." He considered her face. "How about Monday night? It's a quieter day."

"Okay, that's Halloween, but I'll set it up at my house for after trick or treating."

"Oh, I forgot about Halloween. What are they going as?"

"Travis is going as a football player, surprise, surprise. And Chels is going as a butterfly."

"Cute."

"Yeah. Thanks to you, Trav already has his costume. He's going as you."

"He is?" An enormous rush of pleasure flooded into Colt.

"Okay, well don't let it go to your head," she warned.

"How long do I get you for?"

"I need to be home before the kids wake up."

"That's a long time." He grinned.

"Yes, it is," she laughed.

Colt pulled the blankets away and took in the length of his new lover. He rolled onto his side, propping his head up with one hand while running the other across the thin silver stretch marks on her otherwise taut belly.

"Do they bother you?" she asked.

"Do they bother me?" he asked, perplexed. "You don't strike me as someone insecure about their body, Lil."

"It's not that, it's just, I don't know." She tried to collect her thoughts. "When you're married, and have kids together, you accept stretch marks and body changes because the result is your children, but..."

"But, if they aren't your kids you couldn't possibly understand what a woman has to go through to get them?" he asked, irritated. "It's your body, Lil. If you hadn't noticed, I've got plenty of my own scars. Do they offend you?"

"No." She looked at the abrasions and scars of a man in a punishing line of work.

"Then stop before you piss me off."

"Okay." She laughed and scanned the hard muscles of his body much in the same way he'd scanned hers.

She let her fingers trace patterns over his erect nipples and abdomen, then trailed down his chest and lower, watching their progress. When they reached their mark, she flicked her eyes back up to his with increasing desire. Her fingers played over him, causing a muscle spasm under his skin. She grinned and took him in her hand, stroking with a soft rhythm.

"I'm more worried about you being so tiny," he admitted, closing his eyes on a groan. "I'm afraid I'll hurt you."

Realizing he once more strained with need, Lilly rolled him over and straddled his hips, impaling her body on his.

"Why don't we risk it," she murmured back.

"The benefits of going steady?"

"Absolutely."

Chapter Twenty-Four

Pain exploded from Colt's scrotum, causing him to first cry out, then peer through a blinding white-hot rage. Playing Colt's old team, he reached for Derek's overthrown pass but it tipped off his fingers, causing players from both teams to converge and try to retrieve it. As Colt's arms wrapped around the ball, he drew it close to his body. One by one, two and three-hundred-pound men fell on top of him. Common tactics of retrieval tried to rip the ball from his hands, or encourage him to drop it. As most men had two chinks in their armor, Colt felt a hand grab one of those chinks and apply pressure. He grunted and kicked out, hearing a muffle moan from the culprit, as the referees peeled off the players to see who had won the ball. The reduced weight only allowed the increased desire to throttle whoever had grabbed his man bits.

As the last man rolled off, Colt noticed the Texas team's safety, Darren Carlson take off his helmet and rub an abraded cheekbone. Darren and Colt had been adversaries from the start. When the former's wife suggested the latter had seduced her into sex, Darren spread venom about Colt's character throughout the team. It led to more tension, fights, discord, and division on the team. Colt, though innocent of the charges, yet guilty of creating the consistent animosity and negative press for the team, did not receive the benefit of the doubt. The coach, who also disliked Colt, gave an ultimatum to the owner, resulting in the TE's trade to Seattle. Now, as the two men's gazes connected, Darren smirked at Colt. He grinned because he thought Colt would only do so much about the dirty tactic in front of the refs, the teams, and the seventy-five thousand Texas fans, and soon discovered the wrongness of that thought.

Colt threw his helmet to the side and charged his onetime teammate, knocking his thick body to the ground. Darren's helmet popped off and rolled away looking guilty. Tua, watching Colt's mannerisms consistent with an attack every man fears, tried to diffuse the situation before it escalated. Darren popped up first almost dancing and gesticulating with his hands in a wild frenzy, much like the crowd who all seemed to be on their feet.

"Yeah man, come on. That's all you know, ain't it?" Darren taunted, knowing what the outcome would be. "Hey, Stone, who's the tasty bitch in the paper?" Darren bumped Colt's chest with his own, his stale breath pungent as spit flew. "Rollin' another man's wife again?"

"Fuck you, Carlson," Colt said through gritted teeth, as shocks of pain still zinged through his gut.

"What's that?" the safety grinned. "You want me to fuck her? That's some kinky shit there, bro, but I'd be happy to make your bitch moan. Better yet why don't you...ack!"

Colt had leaned back and punched the man in the throat, then grabbed his jersey with both hands as the man wheezed.

"Say another word and I will fucking end you, cocksucker," he growled with a low menace in his nemesis's ear.

Before anything else could be spoken, both teams joined the melee, with Tua and Derek pulling Colt off the man, who still gasped for breath.

"How we doin' fellas? Great play, great effort." Tua placed restraining hands on Colt's arms and pulled him back. "So great to see y'all getting along." He flinched as he considered Colt's eyes. "Shit man, chill. Ref's coming, rein it in. You hear me?"

Colt slapped his hand away and pushed off his friend. He circled around, trying to look for another opportunity to attack.

The referees ejected both men from the game, and as both coaches sprang to life arguing their player's case, the replay showed the entire play revisited in slow motion. Viewers could see Darren reach up between Colt's legs, and though unclear what he did, the result looked clear enough. They showed Darren speaking with what looked like anger and taunting, then Colt's violent reaction. The crowd rained debris down on the tight end, as he walked back to the visitor's locker room.

Colt punched through the double doors enraged, as pain still pulsed in his groin. He couldn't seem to win and didn't understand how to prevent these scenarios from happening. His reputation for a quick temper and easy fight just continued to work against him. Even now, as he tried to turn it around with the Seattle team, things never seemed to go his way. It didn't help that the episodes of anger felt like a borderline possession.

When the Warriors re-entered the locker room,

they found Colt showered and dressed. Eli pushed his way toward Colt, but the offense blocked his path, so he screamed out obscenities and threats on behalf of his friend. When the team's coach walked in, his face the color of a dusky eggplant, he headed straight back to an abandoned room. An assistant coach informed Colt that Mitchell requested his immediate presence. Resigned, Colt sauntered into the room and slammed the door as he squared off to his coach.

"What?" Colt demanded of Mitchell. "What can I do for you? What bullshit hoops do I have to jump through now?"

Mitchell watched the man rant, seeing rage and vengeance seep up his pale skin. The coach said nothing, just observed. After a short time, he spoke with a deadly quiet voice.

"You think I don't get you?" Mitchell queried, bringing Colt up short. "That I don't know what happens at the bottom of that pile. You forget who I am, Colt. Once upon a time I *was* you. I had a shitty father, too. They misread me, took me out of context. I was young and dumb, and fought against those early choices my whole career." Mitchell took off his hat and walked a few steps away, scratching his head. He put the ball cap back on and turned to his player. "I gotta punish you for fighting because we have zero tolerance. If I let you get away with it, then it sets a bad precedent. But here's the thing…You aren't that young and dumb anymore. At some point, you have to compartmentalize this shit."

"He grabbed my fucking…"

"I know what he did! Hell, everyone knows what he did. Do you think Bob Franklin's gonna let him get away with that shit?"

"That coach fuckin' hated me from the second…"

"Yeah, I'm aware. Shocker 'cause you're such an easy person to like."

"How long?"

"I'm not kidding, Stone. Contain yourself on this team. I'm not sure what penalties the league will hand down."

"How…long?"

"One game. It's against the Greywolves. You'll be fine, you won't even miss it."

"Fine." Colt started to leave the room, when his coach spoke again.

"It's not the only reason." Colt turned and looked at Mitchell, with the question on his face. "Don't think I haven't noticed the hits you've been taking. The aggravation, the increased anger. This break will also allow your body to heal. It'll do you some good."

"Whatever." He turned to the door again.

"Colt"—Bill turned and set his clipboard down—"I will not kiss your ass and beg you to be here. I see the progress you've made. You're on time, you don't hold back in practice. You've tried to use some restraint from acting out on the Williams drama. Yes, I noticed," he confirmed when Colt's gaze snapped up to his coach. "You're one of the all-time greats, and you aren't even finished yet. I hope you'll ride out your career with us. I can see getting angry and pushing back when you've been sack-tapped, but Jesus, you punched the man in the fucking throat. That's not football, and it sure as hell isn't this team. I don't know how many more years you want to go, but you don't want to end it doing that kind of shit."

When Colt said nothing, just crossed his arms on his chest, Mitchell walked up to him and clamped a hand on his shoulder.

"Go out with some class and on your own terms, son, not anyone else's."

The coach left him in the quiet room and Colt paced like a jungle cat. After a time, he stopped and leaned his forehead on the cold brick wall, tired. Since the age of ten, he played football. All the frustrations of his childhood, losing his mother, the impossible standards of his father. Football had been his escape. Lilly filled his mind. Watching her with her children, looking over at him, catching him looking at her and smiling. In that moment, he just wanted to talk this through with her and ask her opinion. They had offered him coaching positions and sports commentary whenever he retired, but could he do it? Could he walk away from it all and be content with the decision? Taking a deep breath, he listened to the organized media chaos in the other room, knowing full well they waited for his sound bite. Straightening, he walked to the door and punched his way through it. Immediately, cameras and reporters deluged him, asking all their questions at once.

"Colt…Colt?" one eager sportscaster shouted above the others. "Did this fight have anything to do with allegations of an affair with Lisa Carlson?"

At first Colt just smiled, getting ready to deflect, but thought better of it. It was time to change the perception.

"Okay, look," he began in a measured voice, "I've said this to Darren, and I've said it to the team. I don't know why Lisa singled me out. There's nothing between Darren's wife and myself, and there never has been. She had her own reasons for making up the lie, and that's it. The fact is, only Lisa and Darren know the reason they split up and it's between the two of them and it has nothing to do with me."

"So, the fight *was* about Mrs. Carlson?"

"No, man, I was at the bottom of the pile and Darren couldn't keep his fucking hands off my balls. He's a piece of shit and will always be a piece of shit."

Colt turned his back and as he walked out of the locker room toward the bus, he smiled at the fans once his, that now booed him. Tomorrow he would see Lilly and the kids, they'd have a barbeque, and he would leave this encounter at the field house.

****

The next evening, Colt arrived and a beautiful butterfly, a ferocious football player, and a quirky cowgirl greeted him at the door.

"Colt!" all three squealed.

"You got here just in time to go trick or treating," Travis informed him.

"Mommy was just getting our flashlights," Chelsea continued.

He walked in and shook hands with the guys before giving the women a hug and Lilly a smoldering kiss, causing cat-calls.

"Sorry I'm late," he said, rubbing her arms.

"You're not. They just ate, and it takes a while to get things moving." Lilly turned to hand out the flashlights, then asked, "Does everyone have their pillowcases for candy?" She received an enthusiastic confirmation.

"Does everyone have their flasks to endure this

evening's festivities?" Que murmured to the adults, and she received an equally enthusiastic confirmation.

Bundled and ready, the children took turns asking for treats at each house, while the adults waited on the sidewalk. The mothers checked in intervals to make sure their children thanked the goody contributors. After two hours, the excitement waned, and the kids grew tired. Colt picked up Chelsea, who instantly fell asleep on his shoulder, arms wrapped around his neck, as they made the walk back to the Morgan house. Colt placed Chelsea in her bed, while Travis and Abby started to count their candy. The adults moved into the kitchen and their own dinner. About halfway to its conclusion, Tua gave a dramatic clearing of his throat.

"Ladies and gentlemen, I've got an announcement to make."

"Ya got traded," Colt quipped.

"Now why in the hell would they ever get rid of me? I'm not some short-tempered ginger."

"That's right, baby, you're a glorious teddy bear," Que confirmed.

"That's right. So a few days ago, I took my queen up north, and we had so much fun I asked her if she wanted to make it permanent."

"You're moving to Bellingham?" Raven looked between them confused.

"No, not the place." Tua gave a deep melodic laugh.

"Nope," Que said beaming and extending a hand, now containing a large two-carat yellow diamond engagement ring. "I'm getting married, girl!"

"What?" Raven asked, incredulously taking Que's hand in her own. "Oh God, Que. Oh my God!" The two women hugged.

Stunned, Lilly, stood up and hugged Que too. Wyatt extended a hand to Tua, who shook it, grinning.

"Welcome to the family, man," Wyatt said, looking happy for the couple.

"Thanks, Wy, excited to be here, bro."

He turned to Colt, who stood by quietly and in obvious surprise. Giving a slight incredulous shake of his head, he reached up a hand, and the large tackle gripped it, bumping shoulders with his friend and teammate.

"Congratulations," Colt said, almost as a question, then added, "that's fast, man."

"Yeah, but when you know, you know."

"When are you doing it?" Raven asked.

"After the championship," Tua responded.

"Where at?" Raven asked, threading arms with her friend.

"We don't know yet," Que said, laughing. "I'm gonna start planning though."

"What about Kaua'i?"

"Oh Rave, I didn't want to like put you guys out or anything."

"Are you kidding!" Raven exclaimed. "We would love it. I still have all my contacts. I mean if you want them. You certainly don't have to use any of them, but say the word and they are yours."

"Oh God, I'd love it," Que exclaimed. "I just didn't know if you'd think that was weird."

"No, not at all. Do you want the pier because if so that'll take a little time but…"

Lilly listened to the women make plans and tried to be excited, yet felt unsuccessful. The irritation came from Que's complete certainty of her situation. The fact their relationship evolved so quickly and seemed so careless intensified the emotion. She looked over at Colt, who looked just as perplexed as she did. She re-engaged her mind when she heard Que's next requests.

"I was hoping Wyatt would walk me down the aisle and that you and Lil would be my bridesmaids. The girls could be flower girls and I'd love it if Travis would be the ring bearer."

"And I'm going to ask my brother to be best man, but I was hoping you'd stand up with me too, Colt."

All eyes turned to the tight end who looked shell-shocked at the request.

"Ah, sure man, whatever you want."

"Well then," Wyatt said, raising a glass, "to my sister and Aulelei, I'm so happy you found each other." They all raised their glasses to the couple.

The evening progressed around how Tua proposed to both Que and Abby. When the kids came in after separating all the candy, the little girl showed everyone the beautiful gold necklace Aulelei had presented her with, and the request that she allow him to adopt her.

Eventually, the men moved on, debating different flavors of candy with the kids, as Raven, Que, and Lilly topped off their wine and sat at the table.

"I can't believe this, Que. I'm so happy for you. He's going to be such a great guy for you."

"He is and an incredible dad for Ab." Que's eyes teared up. "I couldn't believe it when he gave her the necklace and paperwork. He didn't even tell me what he was planning."

"He didn't ask you first about adopting Abby?" Lilly asked, a little stunned. "Are you okay with that?"

"Absolutely," Que confirmed a little stiffly. "It has nothing to do with me. He knew the score with her dad. I never even saw the dude the week after we conceived Ab and I found out about his wife. I didn't even know I was pregnant yet. Anyway, it's her choice if she wants him to be her daddy, but of course, I'm thrilled she does."

Lilly couldn't believe the mother could be so cavalier about such an important decision. She studied Que, beaming across the room at her affianced. Her friend embodied a free spirit. It was what she loved about Que. However, Lilly judged her ability to make monumental life decisions with the flip of a hand. Could it work between them with such little information? Tua leaned over to kiss her and she beamed back at him. Apparently so.

Colt looked as dumbfounded as Lilly felt about the abruptness of the couple's announcement. After all, they all met the same day, and now Tua would get an instant family. As everyone left to go home and their hotel, Abby ran to her big man and received an instant boost in the air. She squealed with joy and locked her arms around his large neck, kissing his cheek.

"Wow," was all Lilly could say as he approached and waved goodbye.

"Yeah," Colt laughed. "Wow." He turned to stand behind her and rubbed her arms with his hands. "I should get going too, unless you need help cleaning up?" When she shook her head, he kissed her and slid a gentle thumb down her jawline. "Talk to you tomorrow?"

"Yeah."

She stood in the open door, as he climbed in his car

and drove away, then caught herself smiling and realized she was happy…content…and that terrified her.

****

As Colt walked inside his home, his cell phone rang and without thinking, answered it without looking at the caller display.

"Hello?" He heard what sounded like a wounded animal down the line. He withdrew the phone from his ear and noticed the caller id. *Andrew Stone*. "Dad?" He heard heavy panting. "Dad?"

"What?" his father demanded. "What do you want from me?"

"You called me," Colt said, throwing his bag on the kitchen island. "You all right, man?"

"I'm fine," he snapped. "It's that fucking kid from Friday. He broke my fucking leg and ended everything, now he won't leave me alone."

"What?" Colt was baffled. Friday? Was the old man talking about high school? "Dad, I'm gonna call you an ambulance. Hold on."

"You'll do no such fucking thing!" Andrew spat, snapping out of whatever happened to him, and sounding like himself again. "What's the matter with you, boy?"

"Okay, what the fuck just happened? You were just talking some crazy shit."

"I said I'm fine, damn it." The line disconnected and Colt stared about it in disbelief. "What the hell?" Blinking he looked back at the phone and entered his manager's digits.

"Hey, Colt, what's up, man?"

Colt relayed what happened with his father and

asked Sam to schedule some appointments to figure out what was going on. His friend agreed and said he'd get back to him, and as he disconnected, Colt felt an unease descend.

****

The Taylors drove to their hotel, and Raven couldn't stop telling Finn stories about Que and all the dramas and adventures they'd all had to endure together. She was over the moon for her best friend and her goddaughter's happiness.

"Did you see Colt's face?" Finn asked, as he slid the hotel room key card into the slot and opened the door.

"Did you see Lilly's?" Raven countered, walking in and throwing her purse onto the bed. "I thought she was going to be apoplectic. I can't read either of them very well."

"Me either. They both keep it pretty tight to the chest, don't they?" Finn walked over to the mini bar. "You want anything?"

"I'd love a water."

"I have a better feeling about the whole thing, though." He retrieved two waters from the fridge and opened one before handing it to her. "More than I did before."

"Why's that?" She sipped from the bottle, recapped it, and set it down on the night stand before sitting on the bed to remove her shoes.

"He's intense, but not near as much as he first was." He opened a dresser drawer and withdrew a Dobb kit before moving toward the bathroom.

"I don't know. He still seems intense to me." Raven looked in the other dresser drawer and withdrew

287

an aquamarine slip. She stripped off her clothes and slid into the teddy before taking out her own cosmetic bag and retrieving her toothbrush.

"But a little less, right," Finn said around brushing his teeth. He spat into the sink and smiled at her appearance in the bathroom. "He's not that arrogant guy that he was when we first met him. I think he likes her, a lot. So, that leaves Lilly."

He rinsed his toothbrush and replaced it before stripping off his T-shirt and jeans, then stood behind her. He wrapped his arms around her waist while she brushed, spit, and rinsed out her mouth.

"I think David stands in her way still, but even that's changing. They slept together, you know."

"Ya think?" He laughed, causing her to quirk an eyebrow at him in the mirror's reflection. She set her things down and turned to him, wrapping her arms around his neck.

"So, what do you think I should say to her?" she asked.

"About what?"

"About the whole prophecy thing? If they love each other, or even have strong feelings for each other, shouldn't we say something?"

"Hell no, baby," Finn blurted. He began to laugh but stepped back to look at her when he realized she was serious. "You tell her something like that now, she'll drop not only him, but us too, in a nanosecond."

"Okay, but we need to do this right."

"Well, I think it's optimistic that sex turns into love in the span of a few days?"

"Why couldn't it? It happened to us, didn't it?"

"Yeah, but Dee was using her voodoo charm to

push us together. Not to mention Vapor Chick and all those weird dreams."

"I think she's been having dreams too. I wonder if he has."

"We talked about meeting for a beer before we go tomorrow night. I could try to work it in."

"You think she and Que are getting along?"

"Why?"

"I don't know. I couldn't tell if she was happy for her or not. You know there're things about Lilly that are a complete one eighty from the woman I first met a year ago. I don't know if I just didn't know her or..." She paused.

"Or what?"

She pulled away and walked out of the bathroom, to the bed. Tucking one leg under her she sat, and Finn mimicked the posture.

"When I first met her, she was this super strong, confident, funny woman and I guess professionally that hasn't changed, but...I don't know. The jealous thing, and insecurity, I just wonder. I just..." She stopped. "God, I don't know how to say it because it sounds crazy."

"Just say it. Believe me, I'm not judging."

"Okay, well, if she's Hera, and Hera had all kinds of issues with jealousy and her marriage. Zeus was almost like an absent spouse, and so is David."

"I'm following."

"Okay, so, the first adjective anyone ever assigns to Hera when asked is jealousy, and Ares was all about the violent anger."

"Yeah, but Colt's a football player. He has to be a hard-core individual."

"Okay, well, you told me he punched a man in the throat, Finn. Is that normal? Does he do that all the time?"

"No."

"Okay, well, what if the other world is reaching into this one, physically, somehow?"

"Rave, come on. How would that be possible? It's a different time and place."

"How do we know that?"

"Um, because it's documented as being in the past."

"But what if this prophecy thing runs in some kind of parallel universe, not in the usual way?"

"Come on."

"Come on, what? We think of things like *we* think they should be, but none of this is normal, Finn. None of it. And Themis said we'd be having repercussions or it would affect our world, or something like that."

"All right," he agreed. "Let's just say that's true. What can we do about it?"

"I have no idea."

"Exactly."

Chapter Twenty-Five

A sizeable commotion came from the center of the cardiothoracic wing. The large, colorful rec center heralded a sanctuary for young patients to play with other kids outside their hospital rooms, while still receiving medical support. Though meant to be fun, it still contained a large measure of quiet reserve.

Lilly peeked in during her lunch break and hoped she wouldn't see a patient in distress. What she saw caused her to yelp. The more mobile kids appeared to be wrestling in a large pile. Considering the IV's, stitches, not to mention most underwent procedures and surgeries, with blood pressure indications, Lilly reacted without the slightest hesitation.

"E-nough!" Lilly commanded like a drill sergeant.

In an instant that voice compelled the pile to collapse, and a behemoth to erupt from its center. Lilly's mouth dropped open when a massive redhead she recognized stood up grinning at her.

"Hey, Doc." He turned and looked around at his frightened minions. "Everyone say hi to Doc M."

A chorus of hellos washed over Lilly, but her laser beam death stare just narrowed even further on Colt.

"What in the hell are you doing? This is a hospital for God's sake!" She turned to some nurses and barked out orders. "Get these children to their rooms…Now!"

Other aides joined, and soon they separated the breathless bodies, exuding over-bright expressions of joy. Lilly had to admit as she identified them that she'd cleared this group for more activity, and even if it looked aggressive, it wasn't. Eyes glistening with excitement and joy, each youngster fist-bumped Colt while the chastened personnel escorted the children back to their rooms with haste. When no one remained, Lilly turned to glare at Colt. Furious, she jerked her head in a silent, yet emphatic command to follow. She slammed the door to her office, and leaving a mere three inches of space between them, stared him down, stabbing a finger onto his chest.

"Have you lost your mind?" she yelled. "Those kids are sick. Either coming out of or going into surgery! Elevating some of their BP's could actually kill them!"

The nurses observed for this very thing, but it still irritated her that no one bothered to inform her of the proceedings, and it wasn't under her control. There would be hell to pay for everyone involved.

"They were having fun," he retorted. "It looked worse than it was. We were all having a great time until…"

"Until what?" she spat. "Until I swooped in and injected a wet blanket of reality?"

"I just wanted to make them feel normal for a second."

"At blatant disregard for their health and safety."

"That's ridiculous, Doc," he retorted, bringing her up short. "You honestly think I didn't make sure it was as safe as possible before I went in there and made those kids feel their age again?"

"Tell me something, Colt. Where exactly did you fit in your medical training? While you were beating the hell out of the other boys in your stupid little games?"

He clenched his jaw and inflated his chest. "I just meant that I asked the nurses..." He sneered through gritted teeth.

"The nurses?"

"Yes...the nurses. They looked on all the computers or chart things or whatever..."

"Chart things?"

"Yes, damn it, you know what the hell I mean. And they said they could handle it. I didn't start a fucking scrimmage, we just wrestled a little. They were having fun. None of their machines even beeped."

For some reason, that last statement made Lilly want to laugh. Playing for time, she turned back toward her desk and took in a deep breath, trying to relax. She had reacted out of fear, only seeing the uncharacteristic activity rather than level of exertion. She blushed with mild embarrassment. Of course, the kids had fun—a huge, red giant came to play with them.

Colt leaned with his back against the door, legs crossed at the ankles and arms folded across his chest. The look of smug self-importance, combined with the restless, sexy swagger, caused desire, anger, and confusion to burst inside her. Deciding on anger, she moved until again she stood a hair's breadth away from his chest. Tilting her chin up to look at him with all the authority her small stature could muster, she placed her ineffectual fists on her hips.

"Look, if you cannot act with the proper decorum in *my* department, then I will have no choice but to drop your service here and now. That would be a huge shame for these kids, but I will do it. For their safety, I will do it."

His eyes scanned her face, taking in her freckles, eyes, hair, and at last her mouth.

"Christ, you're beautiful Lilly," he murmured, bringing her up short in her rage. "All I want to do right now is fuck you on your desk."

Dumbfounded, she stared at him until her gaze turned from shock to disbelief. "Are you kidding me with this?" He looked at her mouth again, and she shook her head. "You are…This isn't some daytime soap, Colt. We don't fling each other down on desks, while yelling stat, as we have sex. And…and…"

His eyes sparked, she noted. *He was enjoying this*. She could no more stop her eyes from flicking toward her desk, any more than he seemed capable of stopping his reaction because of it. Colt uncrossed his ankles and arms so quickly that when she glanced back at him, his large hands framed her face. Too stunned to protest, Lilly only had time to register his wide mouth before it claimed hers.

She told herself to pull away and she would…in a moment…she would. His massive arms wrapped around her tiny waist, the kiss full of hunger. Without a moment to ponder its consequences, Colt freed a hand and without ceremony or grace swiped the contents of her desk onto the floor and set her on its surface.

Lilly tried to speak but couldn't find words. She wanted to laugh at the total cliché he made of her office. Instead, a traitorous moan escaped from her throat as he slid a hand down from it and cupped her breast. His tongue danced with hers as his other hand trailed down her neck, over her clavicle. Lilly looked down as his aggression pulled apart her blouse, popping off a button. It rolled onto the floor and spun in a spastic circle before stopping. A heartbeat later, he hiked up her skirt.

"Wait!" she panted, breaking away from him. A black ribbon of haze seemed to ooze over the recesses of her mind, when a noise went off like cannon fire. "Colt...stop."

Her beeper went off again in urgent demand, ending their kiss. She pushed him away and reached for the device. Yanking open the door, and disregarding her state of undress, she called out over her shoulder.

"I have to go," she called and sprinted down the hall, as a team of four sprinted into her wake.

****

Colt stood there for a handful of seconds collecting himself. He could hear the flurry of activity, just a short distance away. Straightening his clothes, he glanced around Lilly's office and the upheaval he'd brought to it. Looking back down the hall in the direction she'd run, he followed without thinking, leaving the ruined office behind him.

A crowd of nine or ten people surrounded the tiny doctor and followed every one of her commands without hesitation. She had only done up enough buttons for decency sake. On the table, a little girl not much older than Chelsea, and bearing a striking resemblance to her, lay prone on the examining table. Lilly raised heart paddles, affixed them to the top and side of the girl's chest, and screamed, "Clear."

The little one convulsed with the shock, and for the first time since meeting her, Colt understood what the woman did for a living. Not something on television or a movie where the dying patient might show up on an awards show thanking his mother, but real. Important. Her job, in fact, personified life or death and it not only humbled but awed him. He realized how small his life was compared to hers.

The patient's heartbeat returned, and Lilly handed the paddles back to one of her nurses. She called out more acronyms and orders before noticing Colt and approaching him.

"I'm sorry, Colt, but I have to go," she said, all business, as she raced once more back down the hall. "I have to call to see if the sitter can come. This one needs surgery. Shit."

She opened her office door with a bang. At first, she just turned and looked at the mess, as if trying to determine what happened in there.

He followed and watched her wade over to her desk, pick up her cell phone, and punch in digits. Stepping over more charts, she opened a cupboard and removed a scrub top before hitting the speaker option and placing the phone on her desk.

"Oh hi, this is Dr. Morgan." Lilly stripped off her ruined blouse and drew the scrub top down over her bra. "Is there a way you can pick up the kids today and run them where they need to go, I…" She listened and her face fell. "Okay. No, don't worry. It's last minute, I get it." She listened again as she retrieved some scrub bottoms from the same cupboard. "Okay, see you tomorrow then. Bye."

A nurse ran in as Lilly stripped off her skirt and relayed a bunch of acronyms and numbers, to which Lilly responded in some code. She turned to the phone on her desk, depressed a button, and one-handed slipped on the hospital scrubs.

"Tracy?" she said, breathless.

"Yes, doctor?"

"Hey, can you get Mrs. Morgan on the phone? I need her to pick up the kids."

"Where do they need to go?" Colt asked, bringing Lilly up short.

"What?"

"The kids. Just tell me when and where and I'll take them."

"Oh no, Colt, I couldn't ask you to do that."

"Lilly, I'm here, and done for the day. I can take them wherever they need to go."

The mother looked at Colt, finger still depressing the intercom button. She bit the inside of her bottom lip.

"Okay. Never mind, Tracy. I've got it covered. Thanks." She looked at Colt and tied the strings of her scrub pants. "It's a lot," she warned.

"I offered."

"Okay, ask Tracy, my assistant out there to text you their schedules and we'll meet up at the house when I'm done. It could be late."

"All right. I was going to meet Finn for a beer before they leave but I'll call and blow it off."

"No, you should still be able to, depending on the time. You don't have to stay while they're at practice."

"Practice?"

"Yeah, ah." She looked around distracted, then grabbed her stethoscope. "Travis has football and Chelsea has dance for an hour and a half."

"Okay."

"Okay." She looked around her office and its

dishevelment, breathless. "I'm sorry, but I have to go. I'll see you later." She hurried to the door and started to disappear around it when she stopped and smiled at him. "Colt?"

"Yeah?"

"Just remember one thing."

"What?"

"You asked for it."

****

Colt watched from his car as Travis and Chelsea walked out of their elementary school hand in hand. Chelsea spoke with her usual animation, as her older brother listened with indulgence. For a moment, he just watched them and felt...fulfilled. He frowned at the unaccustomed feeling. Travis lifted his head on a swivel to look for his mother. After scanning and failing to see her, the boy said something to his sister, who also looked around. What did that feel like to have someone they could depend on so completely? Colt thought of his father and frowned. He heard nothing since his last bizarre phone call, but knew Sam had spoken with him several times. Clenching his jaw, he stepped out of the car, and when Travis's gaze swept past him, then snapped back to him in a double take, Colt lifted his hand in a wave.

Sister forgotten, Travis flung her hand aside and ran for Colt. Perplexed, Chelsea's eyes followed her brother until she discovered who he ran for. She started yelling his name and dashed for him too. Travis appeared as if he'd leap into Colt's arms, but got shy at the last moment and hung back. Chelsea, having no such compunction, launched herself at him and kissed his cheeks.

"Hey, blondie," Colt laughed.

"Hi, Colt!" she exclaimed, then planted a loud smacking kiss on his mouth, causing a blush to creep up his neck.

Unsure of how to proceed, Colt patted her back, then opened the door and swung her into her seat, hooking the seatbelt himself. He backed out and turned to Travis who kept staring at him.

"Ya getting in?"

"Where's Mom?"

"She had to go into surgery with an emergency and sh...stuff." Wariness flooded the boy's face, compelling Colt to say, "honest."

"Where's Hen?"

"Where's a hen?" Colt asked, baffled.

"No, where's Henny, our sitter?"

"Oh. You're kidding, that's her name?"

"Yeah."

"Well, that's unfortunate."

"Where is she?"

"I guess she had something going on."

"What about Raven and Finn?"

"They're busy."

"What about Que?"

"Working, I guess," Colt said, getting rather amused. "Anyway, I talked to your mom, and I asked if I could come get you instead." When Travis said nothing, Colt continued, "So, ya getting in or what?"

"What's the secret password?"

"The what?"

"The secret password. Mom told us a password, so we'd know if she wanted us to leave with someone."

"Of course she did," Colt retorted, exasperated.

"Well, she must have forgotten to give me the secret password. So, we're at an impasse." He looked at Chelsea, bobbing up and down with excitement from her seat, then back at the boys' cynical face. "So, what? You think I'm out to kidnap you or something? Don't we know each other by now?"

"It's not easy being green," Chelsea said in a loud whisper. "Tell him, it's not easy being green, Colt."

"Chelsea!" Travis yelled. "Ya aren't 'sposed to tell."

Fascinated that his little idol worshipper had fizzled out on him, but proud of the boy's dedication, Colt tried to put the boy at ease. He pulled out his cell phone, dialed Lilly's cell, then hit speaker. She picked up immediately.

"Colt, I'm just going in, is everything okay? Did you find the school? Oh, God I knew…"

"Relax, I'm here. Blondie's in the backseat but Travis said I don't know the secret password and won't get in the car."

"Oh no," she chuckled. "I'm so sorry. Everything so chaotic, I forgot to tell the school. I didn't think the kids would question it but it's…"

"Mom, Chelsea told him it already."

"Oh, honey. I'm really sorry. I'm so proud of you for standing up and not bending. That's so good of you. Chelsea and I will talk later."

"But Mama, it's Colt."

"You're so right, honey. Actually, you're both right and we never talked about this scenario. I'm so sorry. Colt said he wanted to take you to all your stuff today. So, can you guys help him out? I hope to be home by eight o'clock to tuck you in, okay?"

"Okay, Mommy," Chelsea sang. "Can you bring us a cookie with the pink icing?

"Yes, I'll get you one for your lunches tomorrow, okay?"

"Okay."

"Trav?"

"Okay."

"'Kay, well, I have to take care of a little girl that's super sick, so call and leave me a message if you need anything and remember your manners. I love you."

"Love you," the kids sang back, and a tight constriction flooded into Colt's chest.

"All right," Colt said, sliding his phone into his back pocket. "So, we all good?"

"Yeah, I'm sorry."

"No, it's fine, pal. It's smart to be careful, you did great." The boy beamed with the praise. "So, where to first?" he asked, sliding into the driver's seat and starting the car.

"Well, we go home and get our bags and do our homework," Travis replied.

"Your homework? Don't you do that at night?"

"No, we have to do it first thing," Chelsea said with authority.

"We get to also have our snack and then we gotta do our chores."

"Chores!" Colt exclaimed, indignant on their behalf. "You don't get to chill at all? How long does it take you to do all that?"

"About an hour."

"An hour?"

"Yeah," Travis giggled.

"Okay, well, how much homework ya got

301

tonight?"

"Mostly it's spelling words and math problems."

"Mine is coloring butterflies, and then I need to think of things that start with the letter B. I want them to be sparkly blue," Chelsea informed him. "Cause buh, buh, buh-loo."

"Nice!" Colt said, grinning at her. "So, are your bags already packed for practice or do we need to do that?" Colt asked Travis.

"Yeah, they're already packed."

"Well, we're going to do a slight change of plan."

"What kind of change?"

"We'll go get your bags, then we're going to the park, but first we need ice cream."

"Ice cream!" the kids both squealed in unison and began vibrating in their seats. "Really?"

"Absolutely."

"But what about our homework?" Travis asked, sounding like his mother.

"We'll do it at the park. Besides, I thought we could work on some football."

Colt looked in the rearview mirror at Travis, whose eyes shone radiant, and he knew he'd said the right thing.

"You remembered."

"Sure, kid. How could I forget?"

When they arrived at the park, Chelsea found some friends and ran to give them hugs.

"Chelsea," Colt called. "Don't go far, okay?"

"I won't." The girls giggled and whispered behind their hands at Colt before running for the swings.

"All right, Trav," Colt said as he caught the boy's wobbling pass. "You gotta relax your right arm and keep your left arm close to your body. Throw the ball up over the top like this, then follow through, snapping your thumb down, for the spiral." They passed it back and forth until Travis had it down.

A while later, Colt took out his phone to check the time and realized they'd been there an hour and fifteen minutes. Looking over to the swings, he realized he hadn't heard Chelsea's giggle in a while, and he turned rigid with fear. She wasn't there. He looked around in a panic before seeing her run behind a tree playing hide and seek with her friends. Sucking in a relieved breath, he gestured for Travis to come, as he ran to scoop her up.

Colt helped Chelsea into the back seat and discovered she hadn't finished her ice cream in her excitement and had left it on his leather seats.

"Chels, what's this?"

"I got full."

"So, why didn't you tell me? I would have thrown it away.

"'Cause I wanted it later."

He clenched his jaw and snapped the buckle into place before grabbing the sweet mess with his bare hands and dumping it into a nearby trash can. He reached for the bottled water in his cup holder and rinsed off his hands as well as he could.

By the time they got to Travis's football practice, Colt's hands kept sticking to the steering wheel. He rinsed off his hands again, and then the steering wheel, before walking Travis to the field. Parents and kids alike spotted the football player and began to run for him. Not wanting to disrupt practice, Colt promised to stay and meet the boys and their coach when he returned for pick up. The player hurried back to the car and slid into the seat when he glanced into the rearview mirror, then averted his eyes in horror.

"Chels! What in the hell're you doing?"

The tiny dancer stood in the back seat naked.

"I gotta wear my tights and stuff."

"Well." He looked up, helpless, as fans began running toward his sports car, their cell phones held aloft to record the celebrity. In a knee jerk reaction, he locked the doors. Noticing the screen he used to block out the sun on hot days, Colt unfolded it and stuck it in the front window. He thanked the heavens for tinted windows. He glanced back at Chelsea who now had her leotard on backwards and was glaring at her mistake. She started to remove them again.

"Wait," Colt said and looked around. "Here." He threw her his coat. "Get in your seat and put on your seatbelt, then put that over you, okay."

"But I'm not ready yet."

"I know but we got people outside that wanna take my picture and you can't be sitting there like that. It's just for a second then we'll get it all sorted out, okay?"

"Okay," she said a little dubious and climbed into her seat, clicking the belt closed.

"Now put the coat on, up over your head." He removed the screen and peeled out of the parking lot before the throng could surround them any further. "Holy shit," he muttered under his breath. "Why did you do that in the car?"

"I always do it in the car."

Colt searched for a more appropriate place and feeling uncomfortable helped Chelsea get dressed. They continued on their way to her ballet class, when the little girl started belting out the latest animated cartoon song, but after a short time, went quiet.

"Do you think I'm pretty, Colt?"

"Gorgeous," Colt responded without hesitation.

"Same as Mommy?"

"Absolutely. You might even leave her in the dust," he replied, and she giggled.

"Do you like Travis?"

"Sure," Colt replied, a little hesitant now, unsure of where this conversation headed. "He's cool, isn't he?"

"Yes. Do you ever want to be a daddy?"

"Ah," he halted. "Sure...I guess...someday."

Chelsea was quiet for a long time as Colt held his breath.

"Do you think you want to be *my* new daddy?"

And there it was...out there. It shocked him that no didn't instantly roll off his tongue. This little girl, as close to perfection as he'd ever seen, asked to be his. The thought of calling her his left a lump in his throat. Feeling undeserving of such a precious gift, his thoughts also drifted to Travis. A boy to teach football and life to. Small boys idolizing him happened every day with thousands of fans doing just that. However, not one that could be his...*But he isn't yours,* his father's frosty voice beckoned in his head, *none of them are.*

"Colt?"

"Um." Colt snapped back into the moment and searched for inspiration. "Well, I..." His cell phone rang, and he grabbed for it like a dehydrated man on the Sahara Desert grasping at a glass of ice water.

"Hello."

"Hey Colt, it's Finn. We still on for a beer before I

go back?"

"Yeah, you there already?"

"Yeah."

"Okay, I'm dropping Chelsea off at ballet. I'll be there in ten."

"You got it."

They disconnected and Colt checked the rearview mirror, noting that the girl had gone back to singing. He took a deep breath and rolled his eyes to heaven, crisis averted for now.

****

Andrew Stone walked out of yet another doctor's office snarling. At first furious with his son for scheduling these visits, Andrew eventually embraced them. Something was happening to him and he wanted to know what, but the so-called professionals had nothing.

"The tests were inconclusive, Mr. Stone, as to what is causing these episodes you describe."

"Well, what good does that do? I can't account for the time, I'm blacking out."

"Yes," the doctor responded. "And I'll circle back to what I told you before, Mr. Stone, and suggest treatment for your alcohol use."

"You said my liver stuff was fine."

"No. I said it's crossed over into concerning. The numbers are…"

"You said it was barely in the red."

"It is but it won't stay that way forever. You have to stop drinking."

"It's not my damn drinking," Andrew snapped. "Yes, I drink but that's not what this is. I pass out and feel weird. It's not right."

The doctor turned to his medical chart and withdrew a pamphlet. "You wanted an answer, it's my professional opinion…"

"Damn it, and damn you. You're no fucking use to anyone at all."

Andrew left the building cursing. As he walked out the automatic sliding door, he turned his collar up to the biting wind, walked to his car, and started the motor. His front windshield fogged, and he switched on the defrost before reaching into his side pocket and dialing Colt's number.

"This is Stone, leave a message," drawled out Colt's voice, then a beep sounded.

"Answer your fucking phone," his father commanded. It remained quiet, and Andrew growled. "Tell that stupid coach of yours to run you on more routes. Then I want you to command that ball…Command it, son." When no reply came, the old man switched off the phone and turned on his windshield wipers.

As the condensation swiped away, a face loomed two inches off the glass. Andrew started violently as he recognized the football player that hit him his senior year of football. His eyes, dead and his face dusky, exactly the way he'd been. The old man closed his eyes and when he opened them again, the boy grinned, then opened his mouth and black snake-like objects came out of his mouth, covering the windshield, and blanketing Andrew in darkness.

Chapter Twenty-Six

Finn debated the merits of solar energy with a local, as he waited for Colt to arrive. Colt called out for a beer, which the bartender brought him and left with an autograph. Having the exact scenario happen innumerable times with his wife, Finn took it in stride.

"Are you domesticated then?" Finn asked, when they were alone again.

"Shit," Colt said on a laugh. "I think I might be. Those little shits are exhausting."

"How long you got?" Finn laughed and sipped his beer.

"About an hour."

"Need something to eat?"

"Naw," Colt responded, grabbing a bowl of pretzels and stuffing one in his mouth. "This'll do."

"No practice?"

"We watched film and lifted today. So, it's an early day."

"And now you're babysitting? That's awesome. You're right about one thing. The smaller they are, the more they can take out of you. Where did you go?"

Colt ticked off on his fingers. "School, house, ice cream, park, football practice, and ballet practice. Oh, and I might be in the paper tomorrow, with a headline saying I'm some kind of pedophile or something."

"What?" Finn started laughing. "Why's that?"

Colt leaned back in his seat, resting his hands on his thighs.

"I'm dropping off Travis at his practice and blondie decides that's the time to strip down naked and change into her dance stuff in the backseat of my car."

"Oh, God."

"Right?"

Finn chuckled and took another pull off his beer. He reached over and scooped out several pretzels himself and crunched on one. "How do all the single moms do it?" he wondered.

"Special place in Heaven for sure."

Colt sipped his beer, and Finn looked around the pub, trying to think of an opening, now that they had a time crunch. He just needed some way to get a foot in the door, however slight.

"Well, at least you'll sleep good tonight," he suggested.

"Yeah, for sure."

"It's been hard to sleep here. I'm used to the island."

"Yeah, I bet. This babysitting gig might be a blessing in disguise, 'cause I've been sleeping like shit lately."

Boom! Finn smiled and gave the football player his full attention. "Why's that?"

"Oh man, every time you get to this place in the season you can't help but think of getting to playoffs."

Shit, not the prophecy at all, just football. Natural, under the circumstances.

"Not to mention all the crazy-ass weird dreams I've been having since I got here."

Yes! One down, one to go. Finn decided on a course of action.

"What sort of dreams?"

"Just…stupid, nonsense ones."

"And what about Lilly?"

"What about Lilly?"

"Well, I mean you just said you've been taking the kids to stuff. Has to be new for ya too."

"Yeah, but weirdly enough, I'm getting used to it." Colt grabbed more pretzels and grinned. "You guys gonna have kids?"

"Yeah, but there's just too much going on right now so we want to wait a little."

"Makes sense. It's crazy about Que and Tua, huh?" Colt said, sounding conversational. "Seems fast to me."

"Raven and I moved fast, too."

"Oh, yeah?"

"Yeah. Luckily, we realized early we didn't want to be apart, you know?"

"Huh. Actually, I have no idea. The only woman I ever lived with was my mom, when I was in high school."

Frustrated, and knowing he could only push so far, Finn decided not to speak and see what would happen. He didn't have to wait long.

"Is Raven one of those girls that's crazy or is she down to earth?"

"Well, she's a celebrity, so I'm sure you know what that's like. We have more cars driving by the house now, but most of the time people keep a respectful distance. It helps that we're on one of the more remote islands. All that being said, she *is* down to earth, she's amazing." He sipped his beer. "What about

Lilly?"

"She's complicated." Colt replied, considering his beer.

"Complicated how?"

"I can't tell which way's up half the time, or what she wants. You know what I mean?" He looked at Finn. "It's like she just can't let herself be cool, with the dead husband and all."

"You want to be with her?"

"Yeah."

"And the kids?"

"Yeah." Colt laughed.

"Maybe she's worth the effort then." Colt said nothing, and Finn tried to observe him through his lashes. "I haven't known Lilly all that much longer than you, but I have seen what she's made of, and to go through everything she has, it's incredible. She's incredible. Maybe it's complicated, because you're just a little confused by it. Hell, I know I was."

"No, she's just complicated," Colt laughed, as did Finn.

"She lives in a tidy world, man," Finn said. "I know she was upset after that fight on the field. She isn't used to that kind of thing. I mean, from what I know, David was a low-key guy. Celebrity and its craziness are hard things to assimilate to when you aren't used to it, believe me. When that has never been your world, it's intrusive and awkward. I almost split when I saw what happened behind the scenes and what it did to Rave."

"So, you telling me to walk away?"

"Oh, hell no. Just recognize that she hasn't lived in your world for decades, like you have. She doesn't understand it, and she has kids to think about. And you haven't lived her life, which has its own drama because of what she's been through, and what she does for a living. But her life with her kids is simple, right? When's the last time you had simple?"

"What's simple?" Colt drained his glass.

"Uh-huh, exactly. You want another one?"

"Naw, I'm picking up the kids."

Finn just smiled and tilted his head to another swallow.

****

Colt picked up Chelsea and then Travis, taking the time to sign shirts, shoes, and even a mom's chest. Lilly's boy beamed with pride as Colt helped the coach carry gear to his truck.

"Thanks again for giving the team tickets," the coach said. "The boys will have a great time."

"No worries." They said goodbye and Colt folded his body into the car. "All right, so we done with everything now?"

"Yep, now we just go home and take our bath," Travis informed him, as Chelsea started belting out the same songs she'd sung all afternoon.

"Well, you can do all that with your mom. I'm good for a video game. What games ya got at home?"

"We only have baby games."

Colt looked over at Travis, who peered out the window, looking mournful. He grinned at the boy, then noticed a store that would carry what he wanted.

Chapter Twenty-Seven

When Lilly got home that evening, she found the trio in the living room. With one hand, Colt played a video game with Travis, but in the other hand he held a small plastic tea cup, with Chelsea chatting away beside him.

She leaned against the doorjamb and tried not to laugh. Her heart skipped a beat and she felt herself fall over the ledge. Sensing someone, Colt turned his head and noticed her. His first instinct looked like tension, as if he needed to protect her babies from an unwanted intruder. However, he settled into recognition and smiled, albeit a little wild from so much domesticity.

Chelsea looked up to see why her large playmate hadn't drunk from his tea cup yet, then followed his line of sight.

"Mama!" She jumped up and ran into her mother's waiting arms.

Travis looked up from his game and smiled. He laid down his controller and rushed to his mom, where an outstretched arm reached out for him, too. Lilly stroked her fingers through Chelsea's soft downy curls and wiped a small smudge of chocolate ice cream from Travis's lip.

"Mom. Colt, bought me Madigan 54, and we've been playing it for over a whole hour now."

"And he bought me a tea set, Mommy. I have it right here. Do you want some tea, Mommy?"

"And we just ordered a pizza," Travis continued. "And he said we get to watch a movie and eat in the living room even." The boy encapsulated the whole room with his gestures.

"Oh he did?" Lilly looked over at Colt's sheepish smile.

"And we're going to have tea."

"No we aren't, we're gonna have root beer, right Colt?"

She continued to smile at Colt and raised her eyebrows at his plan.

"Oh, come on," he implored. "Live a little. Eat off china or eat dessert first or whatever the saying is."

"All right, you win," she laughed, relenting, and sat next to Colt on the floor, as the kids jumped up and down, screaming their excitement. "So, what are we going to watch?"

"Revenge of the Zombies," Travis didn't hesitate.

"No, we are not."

"I want to watch Princess Desiree."

"No, that's a girl one."

"How about Revenge of the Titans?" Colt suggested.

"What's that about?" Travis asked.

"Football, of course."

"Yeah!"

"And," Colt said, looking at Chelsea disappointed face, "there's a girl football player too."

"Girls can't play football," Chelsea retorted.

"Says who?" Lilly demanded. "Of course they can."

Colt and Travis looked at each other with dubiousness. Lilly bumped Colt with her elbow.

"Absolutely," Colt reassured her. "Actually, I can't tell you the ending, but the girl in this movie has a really important role."

"Really?"

"Yep and"—he looked at Lilly, raising his eyebrows—"there's even kissing."

"Ew," Travis said, repulsed.

When the pizza came, Lilly spread out a tablecloth on the floor. Colt sat with his back leaned against the big couch and his legs outstretched before him crossed at the ankles. One of his arms stretched protectively over Chelsea as she snuggled up to his side. Lilly sat on the floor on the other side. At one point, desperate to ask questions, Travis stretched out on Colt's lap, and mimicked his idol's posture. A sharp pang seared through Lilly as she took in the scene and glanced up. David smiled down on them from his picture, and she closed her eyes, exhausted from the day.

David lay in the hospital bed in the center of the living room. His body, shrunken to half its normal size, his skin waxy and jaundiced, his breaths shallow and slow. Travis and Chelsea cried, appearing to know their champion would soon leave their lives forever. Tears slid down David's cheeks as he said goodnight to his children, and watched them leave, as if trying to commit every detail to memory.

Lilly spent time tucking them in that night, so once they fell asleep, they wouldn't wake until morning. She and David would have the time remaining together. She returned to her husband. First, sitting on the small bed next to him, then crawling in beside him. The aroma of the lavender lotion she'd rubbed into his skin permeated her nostrils. It forever stayed with her as a permanent reminder of the night. However, under that she smelled death coming and silent tears rolled down her cheeks and onto his chest.

"They down?" *David panted in wispy gasps.*

"They are now, but they weren't happy about it."

"It's weird...being here..." *he wheezed.*

"Weird? Weird how?"

"Knowing tomorrow...all this will be gone."

"David..."

"I want you...to be happy, Lil." *David panted and winced a little in pain.*

Lilly laughed with derision.

"Happy? Oh, honey." *She looked up at him.* "I'm not going to be happy for a long time. But I will take care of us, I promise you that." *He grimaced in pain again.* "Do you need more?" *she asked and gestured toward his pain meds.*

"No."

"David, please..."

"No...if I'm...down to hours...I...want them... clear."

She didn't want the burden of causing him to linger in pain, for fear of leaving her and the kids in anguish. She collected herself and looked up at him smiling.

"I'll make sure we're okay, honey, I promise you that."

"Be...happy...Lil. Be...happy again...okay?"

"David...I don't think..."

"Someone...good to you...and...the kids. Okay?"

She nodded and lay in bed with him intending to witness his passing. However, he waited until she slept, waking two hours later to find David Allen Morgan had taken his last breath. She woke to his body cooling and sobbed as her heart broke.

When Lilly opened her eyes again, she swore shadows scurried away into the walls as she looked around the room. Colt carried her little girl's limp body down the hall toward her bedroom. Looking around, she noticed he'd already brought Travis to his bed as well. Rousing herself enough to walk over and select a bottle of wine from the rack, Lilly searched for the corkscrew. Moving the utensils around, she found it, just as Colt walked back into the room.

"Wow, did we all conk out on you? What a great date."

Colt came up behind her and grabbed her hips, moving them back into his pelvis. She breathed out and leaned back into his chest. One of his hands snaked around her rib cage and moved to her breast squeezing, the other moved between her legs. Lilly's breath came up fast, but she stepped out of his hold and turned to face him.

"What's wrong?" he asked.

A red blush suffused up his neck, his whiskey-colored eyes dilated, and a large erection strained against his jeans. She knew she could let it happen like this. She could let him take her. It would be hot, exciting, and sexy as hell, but she decided the waters needed testing. Not to mention she had kids now sleeping in the next room.

"Do you trust me, Colt?"

"What?"

"Do you trust me?"

"What the hell kind of question is that?"

"A simple one."

"Yeah, I trust you. What's wrong?"

"Nothing's wrong." Leaving the wine, she took his hand and led him to her room. Once inside he pressed her against the closed door and hastened to kiss her, but again, she gave him a gentle push away. "No," she said, with a feline smile.

"No what!" he said irritated. "The kids are out, I promise."

She took his hand and led him to the bed, pushing him to sit. He looked unsure about what to do, almost embarrassed and out of his element. Lilly knelt and took off his socks, then stood and removed her blouse and slacks. Colt stood too, and splayed his hands over her bottom, drawing her near. She placed her hands on his and moved his arms to his sides before unzipping and removing his pants.

"Okay, what the hell is this?" he asked, exasperated. "I can't touch you?"

"I don't want this to be fast."

"It doesn't have to be fast."

"I know. Because tonight *I'm* setting the pace."

****

Colt panicked a little. He understood easy sex. Down and dirty sex. However, Lilly made him sit again, then slowly straddled his lap. The heat from her center seduced his member. She kissed him with soft tenderness, as her hands moved to his face, and she kissed his forehead. Nobody but his mother had ever kissed his forehead. Colt just stared at her, closing his lids only when she kissed them. Walking her hands forward, she caused him to lie down on the bed and kissed along his jawline. The jasmine scent of her perfume, mixed with her need, wafted over him, and he tried to touch her. However, each time he did, she stretched his hands above his head. Kissing his neck, she moved lower and used her tongue to circle both of his nipples, and each turned into a stiff nub. Lilly ran a gentle hand down the strong muscles of his abdomen and lower, before clasping it around him, and causing him to jerk.

"Jesus."

She moved down him until her mouth found the tip of his shaft and closed her mouth over him. He groaned, unable to leave his hands on the bed, and fisted them into her hair. Colt watched her drift up and down, applying rhythmic pressure as she went. Her gaze moved to his. Terrified he'd lose it, he pulled her face away and moved her up his body. She guided his fullness into her and clamped down hard around him. Colt took in a deep breath, feeling her body stroke him. She leaned down so the tips of her small breasts played across his chest in a gentle caress, then seduced him with a passionate kiss. He realized, no one had ever made love to him before, no one, except her. He opened his eyes and felt her almost bewitching him, daring him to not look back. They laced their fingers together as her small body made slow circles and danced on top of him.

"Do you do things fast because you're afraid, Colt?"

Surprised, he didn't know what to say to the odd question. Talking about anything other than the parts involved during sex wasn't something he did.

"Ah…what do you mean?"

Her eyes closed, and she gasped a little before

opening them again and continued to grind against him.

"You move fast. Almost shocking. Aggressive, like you're in a battle," she panted. "Is that so you can push 'em out of bed and don't have to feel anything?"

His temper spiked a little and with intention thrust deeper inside her. She gasped and made the most incredible noise, as she arched her back, causing him to groan and gentle once more.

"I don't want you out of my bed, Lilly. I want you in it. Under me."

"But over you, and slow, isn't…"

"Maybe going fast keeps me from having to have a conversation, when we should just be fuckin'."

"Maybe." She stopped, causing him to have a pang of panic. He sat up, placing his hands on her hips and looked into her eyes, breathing hard. "I'm not interested in just fucking, Colton," she informed him.

"Yeah, I'm getting that."

"I'm also not a twenty-year-old groupie." She placed her small hands on his shoulders.

"Is that what you're worried about? That I think you're a groupie?"

When she said nothing, Colt wrapped an arm around her hips, keeping them engaged, and laid her back down on the bed with gentle ease. Supporting himself on his elbows he brushed the hair back from her face. A tidal wave of emotion flooded over him.

"I'm in love with you, Lilly," he stated, surprising even himself. Her eyes widened, as they stayed poised for a moment. He splayed his hand out on her cheek, breathing out a laugh. "I never thought I'd ever say that to another person in my life, but I do. I love you and it scares the hell out of me."

"Makes you feel vulnerable."

"An understatement, but yeah." He moved inside her again, to the rhythm she set.

"I know how you feel."

"Because?" he asked with hesitation.

"I love you too."

"Yeah?" He grinned.

"Yeah." She breathed out a laugh.

"Say it again."

"What? No," she giggled, as he quickly thrust inside her twice.

"Come on, tell me again."

She stopped laughing and smiled.

"I love you, Colton." He closed his eyes and fell over the edge.

Chapter Twenty-Eight

Colt woke early the next morning. He wanted to shower and leave before the kids woke up and started asking questions that he didn't know if either of them wanted to answer yet. However, upon exiting Lilly's bathroom, a towel slung low on his hips, he almost bumped into them running into her room. Lilly sat up in a panic, tucking the surrounding blankets around her naked body, and looked up at him terrified.

"Colt!" Chelsea squealed and launched herself at him.

Towel secure, Colt flung his arms out just in time to catch the little girl and lift her into his arms. She kissed his face and wrapped her arms around his neck.

"Did you sleep over?"

"Ah."

Colt made the mistake of looking at Travis, who eyed his naked chest with something akin to awe. Collecting himself, the boy glared at Colt with outright anger before looking at his mother and deducing the evening's activities.

"Oh God," Lilly said with such quiet fear he almost didn't hear her.

"What're you doing here?" Travis commanded of Colt.

Unaccustomed to hearing the boy speak to him

with anything other than hero worship, Colt stood baffled.

"I…"

"Leave!" He emphasized the command with a finger pointed at the door.

"Travis David!" Lilly scolded. "Do not speak to…"

"Why not? He's not my dad!" Travis yelled, then screamed at Colt. "You aren't my dad!"

The boy turned and fled. Lilly grabbed her robe and threw it on before running after him. Chelsea turned Colt's face to hers.

"You can be my daddy, if you want to be." She kissed him all over his face, then wiggled her nose against his.

What the hell, Colt thought, cold fear moving through his gut.

****

Lilly snatched Travis by the arm when they got to his room, and spun him around. "Travis David Morgan, what was that about?" It wasn't the exact scenario she foresaw when introducing another man into her children's lives. The shame that thunder-clapped within her gave way to worry now, more than anything else.

"You had sex with him. I know it!" Travis accused, and pointed a finger at the door she'd just come through.

"I…where did you hear that word?" When he didn't answer, she reached a hand out to his shoulder. "How do you know about…"

"I'm nine, Mom. I know what sex is, and you had it with him, and he isn't Dad. You aren't even married."

Oh, great, what had she done? How would she ever be able to look her son in the eye and tell him no sex before marriage now? She took in a deep breath and decided for honesty.

"Okay. Travis. I really care about Colt. Things um, things are...well, things are complicated."

"He doesn't like us at all. He just wants to have sex with you."

"Travis, that is enough," she said, giving him a small shake. "I will not have you speaking to me that way. Collect yourself and then we can talk." His eyes glistened with defiance, and she softened. "I thought you liked Colt?"

"I did, but he was just lying and now he's gonna go too."

"What? Of course, he won't..."

"He was helping me, and we were having fun. But now he'll like you more than me and then if you get married, he's gonna go away, too," the boy sobbed.

"Travis, sweetheart." She held her son close to her and rocked him, stroking his hair. "Shh. Shh."

When the worst of it subsided, she pulled him away and pushed his sweaty hair off his forehead. She sat down on the bed with him and turned to face him.

"Okay. So, help me understand this. You think if Colt and I are together that he won't want to do things with you anymore?" Travis burrowed his face in her arms, nodding his head. "Honey, Colt loves hanging out with you. He has fun showing you football and everything. His friendship with you is separate from me. He would never just leave you." She closed her eyes and prayed for the truth of it.

"But what if he died?" he asked, and a new ache crushed her heart.

"Sweetheart, what happened to Daddy was awful,

rotten luck." She turned his face to look at her. "Sometimes people's bodies just betray them. It's like I told you, a bunch of cells in Daddy's pancreas turned against him. He couldn't control it. He didn't want it. All he wanted was to be here with us, but they wouldn't let him do that. Just because Daddy got sick, doesn't mean Colt will get sick or anyone else we know for that matter. It was a random thing. I know that's incredibly unfair, but it's part of who we are as human beings."

"But maybe he just wants to be with you and doesn't really like us, 'cause we aren't his kids. Tyler Markie said his stepdad doesn't like them at all."

"Okay, well first off, that's sad if it's true, but we don't know if it *is* true. Second, Colt and I are not getting married, and even if we did, that's a long way away. And third, I would never be with anyone that didn't love you as much as I do. Do you understand me? You, me, and Chelsea all come together, like one big packaged deal, yeah?"

"Yeah." Travis sniffed and wiped his watery nose on the back of his pajamas.

"Right?" she asked and tickled him. He went into fits of giggling. "Right?"

"Right." He started to belly laugh, the music of the angels to Lilly.

"Now maybe we should go see what Colt and Chels are up to, then make some pancakes."

"Chocolate chip?"

"Absolutely."

****

After a tense breakfast, where everyone but Chelsea felt a little uncomfortable, Colt asked Travis if he wanted to work on some football. When the boy gave a sedate nod, they went into the backyard and tossed the ball back and forth. After several moments, Colt decided he should start.

"Hey man, I'm sorry you're upset." When Travis said nothing, Colt clenched his jaw, clueless about what to say next.

"I'm sorry that I yelled too," Travis murmured.

Colt stopped for only a moment before resuming their play. "Sometimes it's good to yell."

"I'm not supposed to."

"Yeah, well I deserved it." Travis's eyes grew wide, not expecting the surrender. "I should have talked about things with you, man to man, so you knew what was going on. I'm sure it surprised you. But"—Colt held the ball and looked at Travis—"I love your mom, Travis. Do you understand me?"

"But you probably sometimes wish me and Chelsea weren't here."

"What? Why would you say that?"

"'Cause then it would be just you and Mom."

"Naw, you guys are fun and your Mom doesn't know how to throw a football." When the boy tried to hide a grin, Colt gave a relieved sigh. "Right?"

"Right." They threw the ball back and forth again, in silence.

"So, we cool?"

"Yeah."

"Don't you guys have school?"

"It's late start but I have to get ready."

"Okay, well we'll practice more later then."

Travis grinned at him, then ran over and gave him a hug. Colt gave his back a pat, then watched him run inside as Lilly came out. She walked to him and drew him in for a gentle kiss.

"Thank you," she said. "So, want control of your life again yet?"

He just smiled, not knowing if he'd had it since the day he met her.

As Colt drove to practice, contentment plastered on his face. His cell phone rang, and he answered it without looking.

"It's Stone."

"Colton."

"Hey, Sam."

"Where are you at right now?"

"Parking at the ATC." Colt shifted gears and looked out at the water as he pulled into the training facility's parking lot. "You aren't here in Seattle, are you?"

"Ah, no I'm home."

"Okay, well, I'm about to go in. Ya have something fast for me?" Colt stepped out of his car and walked to the trunk. He popped it open and grabbed his gear bag.

"Colt, I ah...I got a call from a Dr. Harold Parkinson in Oregon."

"Oregon?"

"Yeah, he's the primary guy working with your dad."

Colt slung the bag over his shoulder, then stopped his forward progression. Something about his agent's voice clicked in.

"What's he got? Cancer? Stroke?"

"He, ah...he passed out in his car after his appointment, and I guess someone saw him after hours and tapped on his window." Colt looked out at the water again, waiting. "He died, Colt. The doctor didn't know how to get ahold of you before now. I guess he's been passing out and stuff." Sam stopped talking and just waited. Colt swallowed hard and looked down at the pavement.

"Yeah...okay. Thanks, Sam." He disconnected the call and shoved the phone into his back pocket. Looking back toward the water, Colt now stared without seeing it. "Sonofabitch...You always get the last fuckin' word, don't you?"

****

By the time Raven and Finn returned home exhaustion had set in. Dee, already home on an earlier flight, pulled up in her older model sedan to pick them up at the airport. After they transferred the luggage and closed the doors, Finn lay back in his seat groaning.

"I'd kill for a coffee, Dee," Raven said as she hooked her seatbelt.

"Keanu's Coffee coming up," Dee sang and pulled into their favorite coffee shack.

"Well?" Finn asked after they'd ordered their drinks. He reached out and snatched three green grapes off the bunch his grandmother had bundled on her floppy hat.

"Hey," she scolded, with a grin. "He said he'd help."

"He did?" Raven asked with incredulity, then whooped. "Did you...what did you say? Did you tell him everything?"

"Yep. He thinks I'm madder than a serial killer with a turkey baster. I think he took a little pity on the old, crazy lady."

"Okay, so, now what?" her grandson asked, as they

paid for their drinks and got back on the highway.

"Well, he said he'd come observe when the time came. If we can get that far."

"You mean if they can open the chest?" Raven asked.

"Yes," Dee confirmed. "I think I baffled him, but I also think curiosity got the better of him. The chest too, just because it's an old relic."

"Did he show any signs of believing *anything?*" Finn asked.

"Well, he's a hoity-toity type. All Mr. Snooty Boots, so it was hard to tell, but I think he's had some real bad stuff happen to him too."

"What do you mean?" Raven leaned forward in her seat.

"He's had some kind of accident. He's burned on one side and has a hard time walking around."

"Burned?" Raven sat up, upset. "That sounds bad."

"To look at him, I'd guess it was life threatening at the time. He didn't talk about it, and I didn't ask."

"Did you look him up?" Finn asked.

"No, not yet."

"Ray Butler, right?" Raven tapped buttons on her cell phone.

"Dr. Raymond Butler," Dee corrected.

"So, why do you think he'll help us? If he's like you say, it doesn't seem like he'd even entertain the idea," Finn asked.

"I think he just wanted me out of his hair, so agreed to get rid of me. I don't know, maybe we made a small connection. Like, when I told him it wasn't just me and that the two of you are onboard now." Dee signaled and turned into their driveway. "Your medallion melting and the fact he could see it on the top of the chest helped too. I think letting him know I wasn't just an old dingbat but others believed in it too helped a lot. I mean, who knows, he may completely flake out on me."

"Okay, so he doesn't have any social media," Raven informed them, reading. "In fact, aside from the library's website, I can't find him at all."

"Maybe type in his name and the word accident, or, God, maybe he got attacked by someone?" Finn said.

"No, I think it was an accident. He doesn't drink a drop, so maybe that has something to do with it." Dee opened her car door and got out then gave a few excited hops. "Oh. Oh. And he said he's from back East, originally."

"Did he say where?" Raven asked, pecking away at her phone.

"No." Dee's face fell. "He's private. Very cynical and prickly. Though he *did* tell me about the markings on the top, and who everyone was."

Finn grabbed their luggage, and the trio walked inside. He set them down and stood in front of the chest now sitting on the dining room table, where Dee unpacked it the night before. His grandmother walked over too, with Raven in tow. The older woman explained the different symbols as the doctor saw them. At the conclusion, Dee looked back at Raven, still reading something on her phone.

"Anything?"

"Nothing. No accidents, not even a mention of his name which is weird."

"No," Finn said. "It just means he's a super private guy. What about the astrophysicist? Did he get back to you on the Immaculate Conjunction thing?"

"Yes, he said he never heard of it. But like I said before, maybe it's a god thing, and it will only happen one time or something. Ray never heard of it either."

"Wait!" Raven exclaimed. "How old is he?"

"My age." Dee moved toward her but Raven's shoulders fell.

"Oops, no, this guy's last name is Ray and he's like sixty-five or something. What is this?" Raven looked through the document, confused. "Um, well, anyway, it's not him." Deciding she could discover no more, she put the phone down.

"And how are things going with Lilly and Colt?" Dee asked.

"Good, I think anyway," Raven said.

"Yeah, they like each other, but they're trying to figure things out." Finn hefted the chest and turned for Dee's room to store it once more on her closet shelf.

"But they seem to be moving forward and the kids like him?" Dee asked, turning to Raven.

"Yes," Raven giggled. "I'm not sure who's more love struck, the kids or Colt."

Dee breathed in a sigh of relief.

Chapter Twenty-Nine

Chelsea, Colt, and Lilly sat in the top row of the crowded bleachers, watching Travis play in his flag football game. Even though Colt wore dark glasses and a baseball hat, fans still approached him to sign autographs and take selfies.

News of his father broke days after the discovery of his body. Surprised she read about it in the paper and not from Colt, Lilly tried to talk to him about it, but he shrugged it off, saying he and his father never saw eye to eye.

Lilly knew Colt suffered, but also knew he wouldn't appreciate her pushing, so bided her time. Another group of teenagers approached, asking for Colt's autograph, and again he refused them, saying he wanted to watch Travis play. They left, disappointed.

"Don't you ever get tired of all that?" Lilly asked.

"I don't know. I guess I'm just used to it now. You kind of plug extra time in your day knowing it's just going to happen whether or not you like it." He watched Travis rather than look at her. "It can get annoying and inconvenient sometimes, but it's part of the deal."

Travis whipped his hand out and retrieved the opponent's flag, causing his family to reward him with whistles and cheers.

"Hello, mind if we sit up here?"

A man with two boys, one also dressed as a player, and a few years older than Travis, gestured to the few empty spots in front of the trio.

"Go for it," Colt said, removing his feet from the seat.

"Timothy?" Lilly asked, surprised.

The thirteen-year-old turned around, and recognizing his doctor blessed her with a huge grin.

"Hey Doc M."

"Well, hey! Come here and give me a hug. How are you guys doing?" The boy ran over and embraced her hard as his father looked on, smiling.

"Well, Dr. Morgan. I'm so sorry I didn't recognize you there. You're out of your white coat."

"Yeah, they let me out of it every once in a while. Hello, Peter, is your son playing today?" she asked, gesturing toward the other boy sitting with his father.

"Yes, James here is right after this one. Do you have a kid out there?" The man turned to peer out onto the field.

"Yes, number twelve, my son, Travis." She pointed at him. "This is my daughter, Chelsea, and my, um…this is Colt," she said gesturing, to the redhead. "Colt. Peter."

"Christ, you look just like…" The man stopped and peered more closely. He looked back at his two sons who recognized the famous football player before their dad did. "Sorry, right, ah, Mr. Stone, we're huge fans."

"It's Colt."

"Can we get your autograph?" asked Timothy.

"I'm sorry, bud. After the game I'll sign some. I want to be here for Travis right now."

"Oh, of course," the father responded. "Sorry."

"Dad, can we get some popcorn?" James asked, hopping from one foot to the other, with his hand extended.

"Sure." The man dug into his jeans pocket and withdrew a twenty-dollar bill, handing it to his son.

The boys scrambled back down the steps, glancing back at Colt. Lilly wondered how long it would be before the entire park knew he sat in the bleachers.

"So, how's he doing?" Lilly asked after the boys had gone.

"Tim? He's good. A lot of adjustments, primarily with activity." Peter addressed Colt. "He was born with Marfan Syndrome."

The tight end looked to Lilly, confused.

"It's a connective tissue disorder. Children are born with it, but some don't show clear signs or have many problems until they're older. The aorta enlarges and pumps the blood out to the rest of the body a little too quickly."

"He's not able to play sports anymore, which devastated him. But we discovered he likes art, and he's exceptional at it."

"That's wonderful," the doctor gushed. "I'm so glad to hear that. And how's the team doing?" She turned to Colt again. "Peter also coaches the high school football team."

"That's great!" Colt exclaimed. "How're they doing?"

"Right now, we're six and three. If we win our game next week, we move on to state."

"Nice."

"You guys have two more in regular season?

Feeling good about it?"

"Yep." Colt shifted his body and watched Travis, leaning his body forward as if it could give the boy more speed.

"Playoffs?"

"We should. We've got all the right moving parts."

"Well, I hope you do. Before I go, I'd love to go to state and watch you guys go to the championship in the same season."

"Go?" Lilly asked. "Where're you going?"

"Denver. We're moving to the big leagues."

"College?"

"Yep, my final season here and then we leave after the school year. Mike Henderson's taking over."

"Oh, he's great," Lilly said.

"He is." Peter looked out onto the field where a member of Travis's team had the flag removed from his belt. A groan emanated from the crowd, and Peter frowned in sympathy. He turned back to Colt. "I don't suppose you'd come to the gym and speak to the boys before next game, would ya?"

"Sure." Colt shrugged without hesitation. "When?"

Surprised by the answer, Peter said, "Absolutely anytime you can fit it in after three p.m., or I guess, early in the morning works too."

They planned it out and continued to watch Travis's game until the final whistle blew. Saying their goodbyes, Lilly, Colt, and Chelsea made their way to the field where fans bombarded him. Instead of paying them any mind, he extended a fist out to Lilly's son and gave him a fist bump before throwing a hand on his shoulder and giving it a loving squeeze.

****

After dinner that night, Lilly gave the kids their bath, read them a story, and put them to bed before she walked back toward the rec room.

"Sam, just take care of it okay. It doesn't matter what it costs, if that's what he wanted," he said, then listened.

Lilly stopped just before rounding the corner. She could see Colt's reflection in the room's window. He paced like a huge cat.

"Okay, when do they want it by?" He listened. "Fine, just make it happen so we can be done with it." He turned and looked out the window, then must have seen her reflection, for he walked over to where she stood and swung an arm out to draw her close. Lilly leaned into him, smelling his cologne. "Sam, I gotta go. Okay, thanks man. Bye."

"Sorry, I kind of walked in on you," she said.

"It's fine." He smiled and kissed her. "Kids down?"

"Down for the count. Was that Sam, your agent?"

"Yeah, he's taking care of my dad's stuff."

"You don't want to?" she asked. "It might give you some closure to do some of it."

"You analyzing me, Doc?" He walked over to the couch and sat.

"Only a little." She sat next to him, then thinking better of it turned to face him. "I know there's stuff between you and your dad, but can you talk about any of it?"

"Lil, I told you it's done, it's over. I don't need to talk about it or anything." She sat quietly and he seemed to realize she wouldn't let it go. "Okay, the long and short of it is, he was a bastard. He was a football hero in his small town and he got hurt. It happens all the time. Guys couldn't cut it in college or the big leagues for whatever reason, and they spend their life drunk, talking about the good ol' days." He tucked her hair behind her ear. "*I* was lucky enough to get him for a dad," he said with a note of sarcasm. "All he wanted me to do was what he couldn't, then got pissed off when I did. I know it sounds super harsh, but it's a good thing he's dead. He's happier, trust me."

"That can't be any good for you though," she prompted. "You don't get closure."

"Not everyone needs closure, Lil."

"More often than not, they do."

"Uh huh, and how well is that working for you?"

"Great, now we're deflecting," she retorted.

"I didn't want to talk about this in the first place," he countered, then softened. "Look, I'm gonna head out." He stood and walked to the kitchen to put his glass in the sink.

"You're leaving? Just like that?" she asked, following him.

"I can't stay tonight anyway, babe. We have a game tomorrow." He grabbed her hands and wrapped them around his waist. "Or did you forget you were coming?" He framed her face with his hands and drew her in for a kiss.

"You don't want to…" she started, then let the suggestion hang in the air.

"I *do* want to," he said running his hands over her ass. "But I need an edge tomorrow and having sex with you tonight would not make that edge a very sharp one."

"Guys really do that?"

"Of course."

She laughed, and he kissed her again, then wrapped his arms around her waist and lifted her from the floor, walking with her through the kitchen and to the front door. He kissed her deeply a final time, then set her on her feet.

"I'll tell you what," she said, with a mischievous smile. "You lose tomorrow, and you don't get it for a week."

"That's more like it. Make me angry at 'em, baby." He chuckled and disappeared into the night.

Chapter Thirty

The air chilled overnight, and the landscape turned into a snow-dusted wonderland. Rather than a limo, the Taylors, the Jacksons, and Wyatt all drove to the game together and watched from the player's suite with Derek's family.

The Warriors played the Cyclones, and the defense just allowed another touchdown, causing momentum to shift from the home to the visiting team.

Derek, Tua, and Colt snapped on their helmets, as the offense went out to receive the return kick. Looking downfield, Colt could just make out the jubilant forms of the kids jumping up and down. He smiled and turned to Derek, ready to hear the play call. Derek raised his voice above the throng, called the play, and everyone took their positions. The Cyclones converged at the signal and forced Derek out of the pocket. He scanned the field looking for an opportunity. Fake pumping toward Colt, the quarterback hung onto the ball and ran hard. He slid into safety as the Cyclones' cornerback leapt over his defenseless form.

After two more plays, the offense made it down to the forty-two-yard line and snapped the ball. Derek ran backwards but slipped. Colt, watched the two men covering him step forward to attack, thinking a turnover or sack would occur, so he ran hard for the end zone.

As the enemy converged, Derek stepped back, saw Colt, and threw the ball toward him with everything he had. Colt watched the ball and ran hard, arms pumping. As his foot crossed the end zone, he leapt up to retrieve it. Securing his arms around the leather in mid-air, he just needed to land and remain its keeper. On his way down, a rookie from the Cyclones, seeing a chance for glory, dipped his head. However, the player didn't see his own teammate on the other side do the same thing. Colt tried to brace himself for what happened next. The two opponents' heads still lowered, hit their helmets to Colt's defenseless form. The clack of all three helmets hitting together gave a loud reverberation across the stadium. Colt's head snapped back, his body flipped, and he landed hard on his head in the turf. An intense pain shot through his system, like his head shattered through a windshield, and his world went dark.

****

A collective gasp waved over the crowd, and Lilly brought a hand to her mouth. One of the two reckless men stood and shook his head not twenty feet from the player's suite. The other sat on the ground but remained conscious. Only Colt's body didn't move. Que placed a hand on Lilly's shoulder as she moved by her toward the children.

"Oh my God," Katie said under her breath.

The team, coaches, and trainers ran over to Colt's lifeless form while Lilly watched in helpless horror. Both Travis and Chelsea broke away from Que and ran to their mother crying, and crawled onto her lap for reassurance. Her eyes filled with tears as she prayed and wrapped her arms around her babies.

"Is Colt hurt, Mama?" Chelsea asked, tears

swimming in her big blue eyes.

"Yes, baby."

"Why doesn't he get up, Mom?" Travis cried out. "Did he die? Mom, did he die?" He cried harder now, and Lilly pulled him to her chest, stroking his damp hair.

"Shh, no baby, he didn't die," she whispered, then cleared her throat, and said with more assurance, "We just have to wait and see what they say."

Her gaze darted to Derek, but he still looked down at Colt. She kept searching until they snapped to Tua, looking for some kind, any kind, of an update or reassurance. He just looked back, helpless, before he knelt by Colt's left side and placed a hand on his foot. Trainers and doctors knelt over the player, shielding him from the crowd.

****

Mystical bonds clasped around Colt's hands, feet, and torso. He opened his eyes but only saw darkness. He heard whispers scurrying all around him and felt cold, and blind? *Why couldn't he see?* He tried to think but his thoughts muddied. Blinking, Colt saw his father before him covered in some kind of thin sticky webbing. The old man stared at his son with dead, black eyes. Panicked, he closed his eyes hard, then opened them again, and the man vanished. He saw blurry movements through a haze, and then the crowd started to infiltrate his consciousness. *Football. A game. They played a game. Did it end?* He couldn't remember. Pain leeched in, permeating each cell of his brain, and he could feel bile building in the back of his throat. At last, he remembered Lilly and the kids in the suite, watching this…watching him. He jerked as if to sit up.

"Colt, this is Dr. Lewis. Lay still a minute, bud," the team physician instructed. "Can you hear me?"

"Colt? We're right here with ya, brother," Tua called.

"We're getting the cart for you, Colt," Lewis said. "Can you hear me? Can you see me?"

"No cart," Colt croaked, and tried to sit up again.

"Sorry, bud, but you don't get a say in this one."

"Fuck you," Colt said and pushed against the restraining hands. "Get your fucking hands off me. I'm not leaving this field on a God damn cart."

"Stone, stay put," Derek commanded.

"No. I got people here and they're worried. Either help me sit up or move, so I can do it myself."

"You might have a neck injury, Colt," Bill Mitchell growled. "Now stay down. We're doing this the right way."

Colt sat up and twisted his neck to look at Lilly, causing the surrounding men to suck in air with dramatic concern. The crowd roared their approval and the TE gave them a weary thumbs up. His gaze connected with Lilly and the kids wrapped tight in their mother's arms. He waved at them hoping to convey his soundness. He moved to stand up and several pairs of restraining hands tried to push him down.

"Get your fucking hands off me!" he yelled, loud enough for the suites to hear.

Kneeling, he looked at Tua, who immediately moved to his side, resigned. Derek moved to the other side, and Colt stood on shaking legs. He snarled at the cart driver and walked unsteadily off the field. As they walked, he murmured his thanks to the men for their solidarity.

"You are one crazy motherfucker," Tua said, and gave a thumbs up to the player's suite.

"You're an asshole," Derek said. "Go get checked out."

The world spun, and zings of pain sizzled throughout his entire body as he watched Tua and Watson run back onto the field, and two trainers flank his sides in their stead.

Though he knew football would be over for a few weeks, he put his helmet back on, to the frenzy of the fans. Giving a slight wave, he stepped onto the sideline and glanced over to see his coach. The man's jaw clenched as he walked up to within an inch of his player's face.

"Get your fucking ass to medical…Now!"

Colt took in as deep of breath as he could and moved toward the other end of the field. Trainers, doctors, and the home field director all chirped at him about his injury, the liability he subjected them all to, and his own stupidity. Once at the opposite end, he paused and looked back over at the player's suite. Chelsea and Travis now jumped and screamed at the rail, but Lilly sat in her seat, one hand supporting her head. He disappeared into the tunnel.

"Colt?" Twenty minutes later, her voice sounded like a gun blast in his head.

"Hey, babe." He raised a hand to his throbbing head. "I'm okay."

"I called my father and he's meeting us at the hospital."

"What? No."

"Colt, he's the most respected neurosurgeon in Seattle. We *are* seeing him."

"You're overreacting."

"Oh yeah?" she screeched, and he held the phone away from his ear. "So, you're saying you haven't just experienced a traumatic brain injury?"

"I have a concussion?" he whispered, hoping she'd do the same.

"Like I said," she responded with venom. "You lost consciousness! And then you got up and walked off the field, like an idiot! Without a board!"

"Yes, but…"

"I want to speak with your physician."

"No."

"You need an MRI scan, and…"

"Okay, Colt." The team's doctor came back to him with several papers.

"I gotta go," the player told Lilly.

"No, let me listen."

Irritated, Colt took a deep breath, then let it out with force. Astronomical pressure pounded in his head, and he didn't want the fight that would ensue if he refused. Placing the phone on speaker, he laid it on his stomach as the doctor spoke.

"Let me have it, Doc."

"Okay, Colt, like I told you earlier you suffered what I believe to be a grade three concussion. You have some abnormalities in your vision and some weakness that I'd like to see additional tests ordered." He said checking the player's eyes again with a small slit lamp. "I'd like you to go to Mercy-Haven General and get an MRI scan."

"Can't you just do that here?" Colt asked.

"We only have x-ray imaging here, and I'd like to see a clearer picture."

"Excuse me, doctor," Lilly interjected. "Excuse me for interrupting. My name is Dr. Lillian Morgan. I'm a pediatric cardiothoracic surgeon at Children's. My father is Dr. Theodore Lancaster, head of..."

"Yes, Dr. Morgan, I'm very familiar with your father's credentials. He's an excellent neurosurgeon."

"Thank you. He's willing to meet Colt and me at the hospital and look at his case."

"Oh, excellent," Lewis said, looking at Colt. "You can't do better than that. I'll email our findings to him right now. Just let me arrange transport."

"Lillian," Colt said through a clenched jaw, "if I have to do this, I'm not going in a fucking ambulance."

"You will. And you will do whatever I say from this point on. Do you understand me, Colton?" He didn't say a word, but a red flame fired on his neck and face. He closed his eyes, as Lilly asked, "Dr. Lewis, can you please have someone instruct me on where to meet up with you. I would appreciate it."

****

Colt arrived at the hospital strapped to a spinal board and spitting mad. The staff, informed ahead of time, carried him into an ER bay, where they cut him out of his uniform and dressed him into a gown. The couple remained silent as tests, bloodwork, scans, and monitoring occurred with organized precision. Once complete, Lilly watched them move Colt off the painful board and into a private room overlooking the greater Seattle skyline.

The tight end wondered aloud if he'd ever meet Lilly's father in the flesh. However, an hour after they'd arrived, the door opened and a tall, elegant man strode in. He looked neat as a pin, in a long, starched, white lab coat, shirt and tie, charcoal slacks, and jet-black hair swept neatly back from a strong, handsome face containing Lilly's eyes. Those eyes scanned Colt with an aloof detachment before turning to his daughter.

"Dr. Morgan." He nodded.

"Hello, Dr. Lancaster. Thank you so much for taking Colton's case," she said, nodding back.

Colt drew his brows together, watching the interaction, before turning to his girlfriend and muttering.

"I thought he was your dad?"

"You're correct, Mr. Stone, I am," the physician confirmed and extended a hand, which the player shook. "I am Dr. Theodore Lancaster. At work, Lillian and I agreed that we should treat each other with professional detachment." He eyed his daughter again. "Am I to understand that your relationship is that of a personal nature then?"

"Ah…yes, Mr. Stone and I are seeing each other personally."

"I see." Her father turned and snapped the MRI scans into place on an illuminated box. Now that the player's brain revealed itself on the screen, it ended the personal nature of the discussion. "Mr. Stone, your scan reveals multiple brain contusions. Here, here, and here." He pointed to three faded spots of various sizes on the right side of his brain. "There's a cautionary amount of brain swelling."

"How much swelling?" Lilly asked, concern filling her eyes as she gazed at the scan.

"Well, the intracranial pressure is being managed in the notations. However, if you continue in your current profession, Mr. Stone, I believe you're at a significant risk for chronic traumatic encephalopathy."

"CTE?" Colt said, heavy with sarcasm. "I'm a professional football athlete, Dr. Lancaster. I, like every other player, have been hit hundreds of times and never had a problem."

"Is that a fact?" Dr. Lancaster said, giving him a sardonic expression, and retorted without sympathy, "Well, Mr. Stone, *this* scan shows you've suffered multiple severe contusions and concussions over the years. It's my informed opinion that you should highly consider retirement."

Lilly looked at the scans, devastated that they confirmed her worst fears. Colt lay back on his pillow with a deep scowl etched on his face.

"Lillian, may I see you outside please?" Lancaster said.

"Ah," Lilly said, snapping back to attention. "Yes." She turned to Colt. "I'll be right back." Once in the hall, her father turned to her.

"How long have you been seeing this man?"

"We met about six months ago in Hawai'i but have only been dating for a few months now."

"Not your usual sort of companion."

"No."

"You realize you could be exposing yourself and the children to more heartache here? If, in fact, he continues doing what he's been doing. Do you want that for your life again?"

"What if he quit?"

"You're a physician and a surgeon, Lillian, you know the answer to that."

"I know, but I want to hear it from you."

"It's not unlike smoking. Some damage has occurred, but perhaps with time and an easier occupation, he'll lead a very satisfactory life. If he isn't too symptomatic. Nausea, vomiting, headache, memory loss, dizziness, fogginess…all indicators of severity based on how long they last, or how chronic the inciting events occur."

"Okay," Lilly responded and kissed his cheek. "Thank you for your time, Father. I appreciate you seeing him and on such short notice."

She turned to leave and was almost to the door when he called her name, and she turned. He walked to her with sedate precision and reached out two hands, clasping them on her shoulders.

"Be careful, dear. Your mother and I worry about you, and neither of us wish to see you and the children in that kind of pain again. Not for someone who doesn't seem to care if he lives or dies."

"He does care, Father," she commented loyally. "This sport has given him a lot, and his upbringing though different wasn't so foreign to my own." When he looked at her perplexed, she continued. "You taught me to be the best in my field. To work hard and transcend excellence. Correct?"

"Correct. However, your preeminence expands your mind, his consumes his."

Chapter Thirty-One

Lilly stayed with Colt that night, knowing her kids had fallen asleep on Que's sofa sleeper. Her father wanted the player to stay the night but he flat out refused. So, she stayed, observed his rest, and made sure he didn't slip into a coma during the wee hours of the morning. After an uneventful night, Lilly left, deciding to take the more scenic route home to think. Visions flashed in her mind. The collision. Colt unmoving on the ground. The devastation on her children's faces, wondering if another man they loved might be taken from them.

She wondered about her father's words and herself. Could she survive such an experience again? Thinking of David and what he would sacrifice to get another chance at life. She frowned. Colt seemed to like the fire he danced in and out of, without a casual thought to her, the kids, or his own well-being.

Analyzing her feelings, she tried to imagine a life without his large presence in it. They had come so far. Lilly knew she would have to make him choose and didn't know which way his conclusions would take him.

She showered early the next morning and went to work, did her rounds, and walked through the motions. Colt called, sometimes leaving a short message, other times just ending the call when she didn't pick up.

The kids waited for her outside their school and asked about Colt before they even stepped into the car. Each showed her drawings they'd done for him, asking if they could see him. Her heart sank knowing if he didn't choose them, her babies would suffer. The home phone rang, and Chelsea ran to pick it up.

"Hello?" She listened, then exclaimed, "Hi, Colt!"

"It's Colt?" Travis cried and ran to his sister. "Let me talk."

Lilly walked over to her children gearing up for a fight, took the phone and hit speaker.

"...so I wanted to see if you guys were okay, 'cause I know it looked scary."

"I was really scared," Chelsea informed him. "I even cried."

"I was scared too, but you're okay, right? Mom said you were."

"She's right, I'm good."

"When do you get to play again?" Travis asked.

"I don't know yet, bud. I have to wait and see how fast I heal up."

"Okay."

"Is your mom there?"

"Yes," Lilly replied. "I'm here." She took him off speaker and held the phone to her ear. "How are you feeling?"

"Sore, and one hell of a headache but I'm good. I tried to call you before...busy day?"

"Yeah."

"Well, I just wanted to say thanks...I know I was a dick, and I'm sorry I took it out on you. Thanks for staying last night."

"It's okay," she whispered, looking at the kids, who were chatting away as they set up their homework on the kitchen table. "I'm glad you're feeling better." Their conversation felt stilted, polite, and forced. She wondered if he felt it too. "Sleep well tonight."

Colt hesitated, then said, "You too."

Lilly looked back at the kids, heads bent to their work, and thought for a moment. She glanced down at the phone and punched in some digits.

"Hi, Hen, it's Lil."

"Lilly, we watched the game, is he okay?"

"Yes and no. Can I ask a favor?"

****

It started to rain by the time she reached his house and pushed in the code that opened Colt's security gate. He opened the door dressed in jeans, a hoody, and a dazzling smile.

"Hey, beautiful. What are you doing here?" He looked past her and into the driveway. "Where's the kids?

"They're home. Can we talk?"

His smile faltered a little at her tone, but he stepped aside and allowed her entrance. She set her purse and a folder in the foyer before she stepped into the living room.

"You want something to drink?"

"Ah, no. Thank you."

Lilly looked around the room and removed her jacket. A lively fire burned in the cozy fireplace, and an earthy smell of pine from his Christmas tree filled the room. Her eyes fell on the medieval and sinister looking helmet with crossed swords beneath it. It sent a chill sizzling up her spine. Colt popped the cap off a bottle of

351

beer and walked back to her. He appeared braced for what she wanted to say.

"So, what's up?" he asked, settling himself into the deep leather couch opposite of her and propped his feet on its matching ottoman.

"I've been doing a lot of thinking."

"Uh huh, and what have you come up with? Cut the mongrel loose?"

"No."

"Well, judging by your face, it doesn't look good."

"Do you…Have they explained what all these tests mean, Colton?"

"Now it's Colton," he mocked. "Well, yes…*Lillian,* they've explained it, so even a complete idiot, like myself, can understand it."

"I didn't mean it like that. I just wanted to know if you understood what the tests meant? To most people, it's confusing, to say the least, and I was just checking to make sure it made sense."

"I understand them."

"Okay, well, what do you understand?"

"I need to make sure I don't get tackled. The need for speed."

"Have you ever thought about retiring?"

"No."

"Never?" She looked puzzled. "But I thought you said…"

"Jesus." He stood and walked to the window, looking out at the water and taking a drink from his beer. "Yes, I've thought about retiring. But I'm going out on my terms, not because a couple of football doctors, and no offense, but your dad, gets overly cautious about a condition that's bullshit."

"It isn't bullshit, and I don't believe for one second that you believe that either," Lilly barked, as she stood up. "It's real, and it's serious. You could die, Colt, and even if you didn't die on the field from one more bad hit, you could die a slow and painful death, as your mind slowly disintegrates."

"Don't be so melodramatic. Your dad is looking at a brain and comparing it to a business man, who sits and does nothing all day. He isn't comparing it to other athletes. The docs told me I gotta take it easy and they would be extra cautious about my return, but that I could return."

"At what costs?"

"Lilly, this is what I do. It's who I am. You've known what I do from the second you met me." He glared at her, then walked back to the couch and sat down. "You're around disease, radiation, illness, and all kinds of shit at that hospital. Should I tell you to quit because of what it might expose you to or what you could bring home?"

"That isn't even the same thing!" Lilly yelled. "Not at all."

"Why not?" he yelled back, a flush rising up his neck, a clear indicator of his anger. "You could bring it home, infect the kids, infect me. Why don't you do something safer?"

"Colt, I know you're mad and I know this is a pride thing. You're digging your heels in because I'm challenging you," she accused. "But just because you stop playing doesn't mean you stop the sport. I'm sure there's a million jobs you could do."

Flashes of coaching offers and sports commentary popped into his mind, but he clenched his jaw.

"On the sidelines."

"Yeah, on the sidelines."

"Or what, Lilly?" He leaned forward on the couch. "What if I say that doesn't meet with what *I* want for my life?"

"Then you and I are so very far apart in what we want in a life together." She glanced down at her hands, then back at him. "Our lives are so different."

"You save lives, I'm just some dumb jock that likes to play football," he snapped, clenching his jaw.

"No." Tears welled up in her eyes.

"Oh, that's just great," he spat, gesturing to her tears. She swiped at them with impatience.

"Yes, I dedicate my life to healing people," she growled. "You're hell bent on destroying yourself. You've had major injuries...Multiple concussions, and I have kids to think about."

His eyes snapped up to hers and fired. "Just what the fuck does that mean?" He walked over to her and held her arms. "I love those kids, you know that."

"Yes, I do, and they love you, Colt. They really love you, and this will hurt them but they're starting to..." She stopped.

"Starting to what?"

"Starting to get the wrong idea."

"Wrong idea about what?"

"About us, okay!" she yelled

"Why does it have to be wrong?"

"Because, like I said, you're hell bent on destroying yourself, and fighting and just...drama."

"How does that affect my feelings for your..."

"Their father died!" Lilly yelled, shrugging off his hands, then turned to face off. "He died, Colt, and it destroyed my kids. Travis is over the moon for you. Chels has stars in her eyes. You're a hero to them. What happens when you get hurt worse, or die from an injury that is entirely preventable? What the hell do I tell my kids then, Colt? That's what Travis kept asking me, over and over again, if you were dead."

"Oh, hell Lilly, no one's dying. They have season ending injuries or maybe even career ending injuries but…"

"And CTE? Didn't you hear what he said? How many times have you been hit in the head?"

"Jesus." He started to walk away, but she held him in place.

"I'm serious, Colt. What happens to me and the kids if you just disappeared, by choice, because of a stupid game?"

"Stupid game!" he yelled at her. "Stupid game? That game gave me a life. It connected me to my father and made me who I am, Lilly."

"Is this about your dad, Colt?"

"No, it's about me, doing something I love and I'm good at. I'd have nothing without it."

"Maybe at one time, but not anymore." She grabbed his shoulders, but he shrugged them away. "You could do anything you want now. Retire, have a family, have a real life."

"Look"—he rounded on her—"I know I'm not the big brain that you are. My job isn't saving a bunch of little kids, but it's important to me. And you might not think so, but it's important to a lot of other people."

"Your fans?" She laughed.

"That's right, my fans, my teammates, my coaches, the city. I get paid a lot of money to be here and do what I do. I'm committed, and I'm not walking away from that. Not until *I* decide to and nothing and no one will decide that for me. Do you understand?"

"Yeah, I understand. Just know that in doing so you're making a choice to walk away from us then." She turned and hurried to leave.

"From where I stand, I'm looking at your back, not the other way around," he said and tried to grab her arm, but this time she shook him off and continued to walk to the front door. "Lilly, come on." She opened the door and without looking back walked out into the night.

****

Colt threw his beer bottle against the fireplace and watched it shatter against the stones. She asked him to give up the one thing that made him whole. The one and only commonality he had with his own father. Now the fucker was dust in a box.

Football gave him prestige and a livelihood. In the past, it gave him adventure, women, travel, and records. Lilly filled his mind. She gave him stability, love, and companionship. She gave him a family, with the possibility of a quiet, and stable life. Maybe even more children, fathered by him.

The dream he experienced months before formed in his mind. The dream of her family being his. Did he want that kind of commitment to something? The packaged deal, and that package had all kinds of strings attached, which he avoided like the plague. He looked down and saw a manila folder. He picked it up and opened it. Two drawings lay inside. Travis drew a large man, with red hair that filled the entire page, looking down at a boy, who held his hand. Both wore Colt's jersey with the number eighty-seven on it. Chelsea drew them as a family. A man and woman on the outside of a long chain, holding hands with two small children on the inside.

He walked back to his bedroom and entered the darkness without turning on a light. Approaching the window, he looked out at the inky black silk of the night shining off the water, then back at the two drawings.

Colt understood what she'd meant about her husband. He'd been polite and proper. He'd had the right job, said the right things, and behaved the right way. Beyond reproach...but also dead. Colt didn't have culture, the right job, and feared he'd never earn the approval of her mother or father. However, the fact he wasn't dead seemed like the bigger obstacle. That may be unforgivable. Could he ever live up to that?

Andrew and their last exchange filled his mind. The oddness of the whole thing baffled him, and sadness seeped around the edges. On an intellectual level, he knew his feelings toward his father should remain the same. A small, bitter man, trapped in his jealousy and anger. However, when his mind flamed in heat, he rarely thought, just felt...everything. His father's voice sounded in his head like cannon fire.

This sport made him special, and without it he had nothing. Lilly fought into his consciousness again, but he tried to clear her. Walking over to the bed, he sat and kicked off his shoes, then stripped down to his underwear. He stomped into the bathroom to brush his teeth. She wasn't even his usual type. Fragile, yet so headstrong and powerful, at the same time. A heady combination. Christ, she pissed him off. He spat into the sink then reached for some pain reliever. Shaking two tablets out, he popped them into his mouth and drank some water before using the commode. After washing his hands, he walked back to his bed and lay down, knowing the night would hold him captive and restless.

He heard a hissing sound and sat up. The sound vanished. He leaned back onto the bed and decided it must be his temper, on full boil.

Chapter Thirty-Two

Lilly felt as if on autopilot as she climbed into her car after dropping off Chelsea at ballet practice. It had been two weeks since she drove back to her house from Colt's. She remembered trying desperately to hold back tears as she'd taken a chance giving her heart to Colt, and he'd rejected it.

Even now, the physical pain in her gut radiated into her heart. Not only did it feel broken, but she knew she still had to break her children's hearts too. She'd put off the inquiries of why Colt hadn't been there for games, recitals, and even Christmas. Every time she told them he practiced, played, or needed to stay focused for a game. He'd sent presents and called them on the phone several times, to her relief, leaving her to question her actions and how hard she'd pushed him. Perhaps telling them and having their pain now when things still...still what? At this point she realized it didn't matter when the pain came. It would be just as hard whenever it came, and they deserved more than that. However, Travis, Chelsea, and she deserved someone to be there and love them too, not always worrying about one more hit, one more yard, one more touchdown.

She stared as the red light turned green and someone behind her tooted their horn. Cursing, she went through the intersection and pulled over to the side of the road. She needed someone to talk to. Lilly didn't feel she could burden Raven or Que with her relationship woes when they were ensconced in their own happiness. Thinking of her sister, her mother, and even Olivia, she knew those options weren't viable either. So, who could she talk to? Who would understand?

****

Danielle Morgan sat at her kitchen table placing mosaic tiles over its surface. Humming to herself, she selected a jagged cobalt blue piece and placed it on the adhesive. *Cobalt blue.* She smiled—David's favorite color. She looked over to the mantel at a picture of him and her celebrating Mother's Day. He'd given her a whimsical frog holding out a floral bouquet for her garden. Every time it rained, the metal flowers hit one another in a tinkling melody, as it did today.

She heard a car pull up the driveway, jolting her out of her memories, and watched Lilly jump out of the driver's side. She'd pulled the hood of her bright yellow slicker up over her head and ran up their path. Grinning at the timing, Danielle pulled open the door.

"Well, hello, honey. What are you doing here?" Lilly pulled off her coat and her mother-in-law saw the puffy, red-rimmed eyes. "Lilly, sweetheart, what's wrong? Are the kids okay?"

The younger woman just cried harder and collapsed into Danielle's arms. She rubbed her back and cooed. After several minutes, she led the distraught woman to a chair in the kitchen and made her sit. Reaching for a towel, she handed it to her, and Lilly sniffed, drying her face. Danielle helped her out of her jacket and swung it onto the back of another chair to dry, then walked into the kitchen and filled a kettle with water. She set it on the stove top and switched it on to boil before turning to her daughter-in-law.

"Okay, now, let's talk."

"I don't know why I came. I don't know how to tell you about it."

"Well, how about you start at the beginning? Does it have anything to do with the young man you're seeing?"

"Mom...I...?" Lilly dropped her head in despair.

Danielle placed her hands on either side of Lilly's face and tilted her head up to face her.

"Lillian Morgan, what is going on with you? You haven't been yourself at all. Where's your confidence? Where's your heart, darling?"

"I don't know," she laughed. "Not anymore."

"Did he do something? The football player?"

"Colt? No. Well, not exactly." She relayed the events as they had occurred, then she held her breath and was silent.

"So you gave a proud man an ultimatum?"

"Yes." Lilly burst out the breath she'd been holding, in a laugh. "Did I do the wrong thing? I did, didn't I?"

"You know I won't answer that."

"He could be seriously messed up, Mom. He could die..."

"We're all going to die."

"Yes, I'm aware of that, but I don't think we need to hurry it along, either."

"If you knew David would get sick and die from cancer before you married him, would you have still gone through with it?"

"Okay, what are you talking about? That's not the same thing, *and* it's not fair."

"Why? Because I'm his mother and you don't want to offend me?"

"No, because I loved him, and he gave me Travis and Chelsea."

"Do you love Colt?" When the look of panic swept into Lilly's eyes, Danielle softened. "Lilly, I know you loved David. I know you loved my son well. You knew him from the moment of your birth. Your love for Colt takes nothing away from your love of David."

"Yes," she admitted. "I love him, but at this point I have to think about the kids and whether or not I can be with someone that just disregards his safety and life. Someone that won't put us first, and we deserve to be first."

Danielle remained quiet.

"But," Lilly said, "Colt deserves his happiness too, and if it's football and the life he has from football, I can't take that away from him either."

"You know what, Lilly?"

"What?"

"I think you have your answer."

"No. I don't." She looked at her mother-in-law with tears in her eyes again.

"You can't live anyone's life but your own. Not even Travis and Chelsea's. You're guiding them, and protecting them, but their lives are also their own."

"I just want…"

"You just want things done your way."

"No, I…" Lilly started to reject the notion but looked at the way she'd been since meeting Colt.

"See"—Danielle squeezed her hands—"you

already have the answer."

However, when Lilly left her in-laws, she still didn't know if she did.

****

Colt threw himself into his recovery, every day working harder to regain his strength and concentration. Three weeks after the fateful game, he pushed down hard on the leg press, with a grunt, as he kept his body in athletic shape. Earlier that day he left the doctor's office, after reviewing his final CT scan. He'd reverted a physician recommended by the team doctor after seeing Lilly's father, and remained optimistic about his new diagnosis. Sitting in Mitchell's office he heard the good news he'd waited for.

"Doc said you're cleared for light practice," his coach said, throwing some papers on his desk.

"Fine. I'll start light but if I feel like more, I'll do more."

"Don't force me to bench you, Stone. This situation is…"

"This situation is bullshit. I got hit. It's football. I don't need a hug. Just let me get to it and get back out there."

"We'll take it one day at a time," Mitchell warned.

Four days later, Colt worked out at his normal pace, determined to play by the final playoff game the following week. He wanted to blow off the photo op at the hospital, but three weeks passed since he last saw Lilly and staying away from her left him itchy. Calling the kids and taking them out for ice cream relieved the sting somewhat, but he missed her. Somewhere along the line, he'd given the small surgeon a certain amount of control over his heart and life.

As Colt stood on the line for the opening drive of the semi-final game, he had a moment of pause. He'd never paused in a game before and cursed Lilly for putting the barrier there, whether warranted or not. In the first half, Derek threw to the other side of the field, or ran the ball, not because he didn't trust Colt, but circumstances forced him that direction. However, in the second quarter, the quarterback sought the tight end. Self-confidence waning, he dropped the ball twice and ran out of bounds before hitting the first down mark. Morale shifted, charging the tension already present.

He sat alone on the bench, trying desperately to get his head in the game. His teammates left him to his thoughts, but by halftime, down one touchdown, the players entered the locker room, throwing their helmets in frustration. Colt sat, perching his elbows on his knees, and cradled his head in his hands.

"What the fuck is wrong with you?" Eli challenged the moment he walked into the room. "Get in the fucking game, man. You dropped two."

"Fuck off, Williams."

"This is it, asshole. If we don't win this, we're done."

"Eli," Tua said, hands up, trying to soften the interaction. "You ain't helping, man. We all have to step it up."

"Fuck you, Tua," Eli screamed. "We're all doing our part, only your boy's playing like a fuckin' bitch."

Colt sprang to his feet and stood in challenge, chest to chest with his nemesis. Just then Coach Mitchell entered the room, glaring at the two men.

"Sit down and shut up, both of you." When they continued to stand in each other's space, Bill yelled,

"Tua, Watson, help these two little girls find their seats."

Heavy hands of several players moved the men to sit. Mitchell took off his ball cap with one hand containing a clipboard, while scrubbing at his damp hair with the other. He stopped and threw the clipboard down on a bench, then walked to a white board. He uncapped a pen and threw the cap in a corner.

"All right," he said, attacking the board with a vengeance, and scribbling plays, as the pen squeaked. "We're down by one TD. We will win by two by this game's end, do you understand me?"

As the coaches laid out their strategy, Colt watched in anger because he knew what Eli said was true. Failing his team, failing Lilly, and failing himself. As the team ran back out fired up, Colt took Mitchell's sleeve.

"Take me out."

"What?" The coach looked at him with incredulity that flamed into fury.

"Take me out," Colt repeated, not believing his own ears.

"Take you out? We've got a game to win, Stone. What the hell are you talking about?" Colt looked down at the ground and shifted his weight back and forth. "I need you to do your job right now. Do you understand me? Forget any shit you got going on in your personal life, Stone. Forget feeling sorry for yourself. Forget everything. There are people, money, your teammates, and a city, all depending on you to do your job. That's what we pay you for and that's what you *will* do...produce. You get me? Now, get your ass out on that field."

Colt looked up, glaring at him, then turned without a word and ran out onto the field. The team did not win by two TD's, but Colt redeemed himself when he caught a ball on tip toes in the corner of the end zone in the last twenty-eight seconds of the game. When the clock read zero, the Warriors won, but Colt's heart wasn't in it. They flew back to Seattle that night, and he left without saying a word to anyone or joining in any of the celebrations.

****

The weeks apart felt impossible for Lilly. No matter where she turned, Colt loomed there. His recovery and subsequent return to football for the playoff games touted from every news broadcast and water cooler discussion. His persona stared down at her on billboards, taxis, and ads in shopping malls. Travis and Chelsea spoke with animation about their phone conversations with him. They continued to ask when they could see him again, and Lilly knew she had to find a way to tell them. However, she hoped somehow things would shift back on course. Colt hadn't forgotten them, and relief flooded through her. His apparent total acceptance of blame made Lilly feel like a coward. She tried to keep Travis and Chelsea from watching the games but to no avail. Travis loved to tell her the play-by-play of every down, and each time they snapped the ball into motion, Lilly's gut tensed with dread, waiting for disaster.

After the Warriors had won the playoffs, revealing they would compete in the championship game in Florida, news about Colt and the team intensified even more. There seemed to be no place in the city she could hide and not hear about the accomplishment. If fans didn't talk about it, they wore it, in the form of jerseys, T-shirts, hats, hoodies, and beanies. A bright blue, iridescent spikey Mohawk adorned one of her little patients, and the face paint, banners, and car appliques moved things into overkill. Lilly realized the accuracy of Colt's words when he said people depended on him and the team. It didn't soften her on his own health, but comprehension about his predicament crystallized.

Aside from the turmoil of everything, Lilly missed him. She missed his presence, his cockiness, his confidence and kisses. Making love to him. Travis and Chelsea playing, wrestling, making them into a quirky little family. More than once, she wondered if she made a fatal mistake, then saw clips of a game, and the brutal violence of it, intensifying her resolve.

Que called and arranged for them to meet for drinks that evening. Lilly had seen little of Que since the new sitter and her engagement. As she walked in and saw Que sitting in a booth, all corkscrew curls and eclectic style, she experienced a pang of sadness. She missed her friend and the ease they once shared.

"Hi," Lilly said as she swung her purse into the booth and sat.

"Hey." Que smiled. "Long day?"

"No, pretty low-key today. It was nice." The waitress approached and Lilly looked at Que's glass of red wine. "I'll have what she's having. Thanks. So"—she looked at Que—"how are all the wedding preparations going?"

"You really want to know or are you just trying to be polite?"

"What? No, of course I want to know. Why would you say that?"

"'Cause you've not been exactly on board for this whole thing," Que challenged.

"Oh, honey, I'm sorry." Lilly took in a deep breath. "It's not that I don't like Aulelei, I do…very much. He's the sweetest man. I guess I've just been worried, it's all been too quick."

"And you don't trust that I know what I'm doing, and what's best for me and Ab."

When she said it like that, Lilly cast her eyes downward, realizing she *had* judged. She had judged everything. Looking back into Que's warm but penetrating stare, she blushed.

"I'm sorry, you're right. I did judge you, Que." She looked at her, her face pleading. "I promise it comes from a good place."

"Oh, hell, you think I don't know that? If I'd have thought any different, I'd have kicked your skinny ass by now." Que reached over and sipped her drink. "I know you have a whole lotta hurt and our situations are very different. Abby's father wasn't a great guy, and yes I left that situation, but it was hard. Making the choice to do things on my own and in my own way, you bet your ass it was hard. But, it's my opinion…and realize I'm not trying to judge on you either…but it's my opinion, planning everything out and waiting for all the perfection to shake out isn't always the best option either. You wanna know why?"

Lilly nodded.

"Because here's a news flash—there ain't nobody perfect, Lil. Abby's daddy was a rich man, and he wasn't perfect. Raven's husband, Donovan, was powerful, and he wasn't perfect. Wyatt and Finn, both fantastic men, aren't perfect. You came from two highly educated people and they aren't perfect either. Your husband, in hindsight, seems infallible, but he wasn't. Well, guess what? Aulelei and Colt aren't perfect either, and thank God." She grabbed Lilly's hands. "Thank God for that. You wanna know why?"

Lilly shrugged, let out a breath with acceptance, then nodded.

"Cause perfect is boring, Lillian. Being all crazy and out there...I'm sorry, but it's fun and exciting. Now, you don't have to be like me, but I'm willing to bet you've had yourself some fun times with Red."

"That isn't the point."

Que sipped her wine. "Then what's the point?"

"The point is Colt has a very dangerous job. So does Aulelei. As a physician, I can tell you, it's a sport that has long-term effects. Ramming your head into another person's head is..."

"Lilly, why did you become a doctor?"

"What does that have to do with it?"

"Just answer the question."

"I became a doctor because I wanted to help people, specifically children. If I can prevent a family from living the ultimate devastation, then I've done my job."

"Uh huh. Mom and Dad being in the field had no impact?"

"Of course it did, but..."

"How does it make you feel when you save someone's life?"

"I'm sure you know..." Que's irritated scowl, gave her pause. "It's rewarding, you feel on cloud nine."

"Why?"

"Why, what?"

"Why do you feel like you're on cloud nine?"

"Because I saved a life."

"What if I said you did nothing, and it was all divine intervention or something?"

"Well, yes, okay. God's will, but I guess I'm the instrument, right? They wouldn't live without me sometimes."

"So, god-like? Invincible?"

"What's your point, Que?"

"Aulelei told me once that being on the field is like the ultimate high. A genuine battle, where they get to play the game they love. They have thousands and thousands of people come to watch them. Whose happiness depends on their effort and ability." She gazed at her friend. "He's told me fans write him emails about how they want to be him. Some have used his picture to overcome an injury. Aulelei said Colt once told him about a high school football player, that got a spinal cord injury, and they said might never walk again. He used Colt's picture as an inspiration to walk, and eventually he did. He credits Colt."

"It's football," Lilly said.

"No, it's dreams, the stuff a good life's made up of."

"I don't want to lose him."

"Then don't."

Chapter Thirty-Three

Sitting in his living room a week before the championship, Colt stared into flames in the fireplace. The short days of winter gave way to night, and a light snow blanketed the city. He moved to take a sip of whiskey, but his hand brushed an empty glass. Reaching for the bottle on the end table, he heard his doorbell chime, and scowled. Deciding to ignore it, Colt poured two more fingers into his tumbler, and his cell phone buzzed next to the bottle he replaced on the table. He toasted the ringing phone without answering it, and sipped his drink. He'd already ignored calls from his agent, Aulelei, and even Travis. The phone stared back at him in accusation before ringing again. Growling, he reached for it and engaged the caller.

"What!" he spat.

"Jesus," Caprice said. "What's up your ass? Open the gate, honey, I'm freezing to death out here."

"Where are you?"

"I just told you! I'm outside your gate. Now let me in."

Cursing, he pushed the button to allow her entrance, then walked to the front door and opened it. She got out of her car and flipped up the hood of her jacket before running through the snow and up to his front porch. She flung her hood back as she approached him and gave him a weary smile. He waited, and when she said nothing after several seconds, he spoke.

"What are you doing here, Caprice?"

"What do you think I'm doing here, Colton?"

"I'm not in the mood for entertaining right now."

"Well, maybe you can just pretend for me. Are you going to ask me in or are we gonna build a snowman?"

He stepped aside, and she walked in, leaving a seductive scent in her wake. Taking off her coat, she set it on the back of one couch. She didn't dress for her fans today, wore no makeup, simple black leggings, an oversized pink cashmere sweater, and short snow boots, which she toed off, revealing pink fuzzy socks. Her strawberry-blonde hair, mussed from the jacket hood, laid in uncharacteristic natural curls. She padded to his sumptuous sofa and sank into it.

"You got any hot cocoa?"

"Cocoa?" he repeated, voice dripping with patronization.

"Yeah, with the little marshmallows?"

"No Cap, I don't have any cocoa. If you came all this way for that…"

"Never mind," she said, reaching into her purse and withdrawing the ingredients before throwing two packets to him. "I brought my own."

He eyed her in incredulity, and when he didn't move to prepare her drink, she sighed and stood, walking into his designer kitchen. Finding a kettle he didn't even know he had, Caprice walked to the sink and filled it with water. After she'd prepared the cocoa, she handed him a mug, but he shook his head and retreated into the living room. Caprice sighed deeply and, rolling her eyes to heaven, followed behind him, mugs in hand.

"Here."

"I don't want it."

"Drink it. Chocolate will make you feel better."

"Oh well, if that's all I have to do." He took the mug from her and set it on a coaster. When she just stared at him, he reached over, feeling like a child, and sipped. Damn, it *did* taste good. Caprice tucked her legs under her on the couch and wrapped both hands around her mug, sipping at intervals.

"Okay, so what's going on? How are you feeling?"

"I feel fine."

"You don't look fine, Colt."

"What are you, a shrink?"

"No, I'm better. I'm a friend that's known you for a decade and a half. Though I doubt neither of us would like to admit that." She laid a hand on his arm. "Come on, honey, we've shared time and I know you. Something's off and I want to know what it is."

"Why?"

"What do you mean why?" She laughed. "Because I love you, stupid jerk. Neither of us has many real friends, and I take care of my real friends. How's your head?"

"The headaches are gone."

"You looked like you were playing careful."

"I know."

She considered him. "Is it Lilly?" He looked at her with first supreme irritation, then softened into acceptance. "Trouble in paradise?"

"She gave me an ultimatum."

"Uh oh."

"Yeah."

"What's on the line?"

"She wants me to give up football."

"Why?"

"Because she's worried about the hits I've taken."

"Concussions?"

"Yeah."

"Well, I guess that's understandable."

"What?" He looked at her with venom. "No it isn't. She wants me to give up the one thing that defines me, Cap." He set down his mug, stood, and paced like a huge cat. "I don't knit and I don't like to garden or play tennis. I play professional football. Getting hurt is part of the deal I signed up for."

"Yeah, but she loves you, Colt."

"If she loved me, she wouldn't have asked me to do that."

"Okay, well, let me shift gears on you then." Caprice set down her mug, too, and leaned forward. "You've been telling me for a couple of years now that you wanted this to be your last run. And then when you got traded, you said you wanted to retire here. What's changed?"

"I can't let her think she has that kind of control over me."

"But, honey, look at yourself." He stopped and looked at her, confused. "She *does* have that kind of control over you. And judging by the thought daggers I get from her, you have the same kind of control over her."

"That's pretty sick if true."

"No, it's life. She's worried about you. She's worried about what an injury would do to you, to her, to her family. Maybe her ex hurt her and…"

"Her ex is dead. Cancer."

"Oh, Colt." Caprice slumped her shoulders, letting out a breath. The wood in the fireplace crackled and popped and they remained silent, watching it. "Okay," Caprice said after a full three minutes. "Be honest with me and be honest with yourself. What do you want?"

He sat back down and placed his elbows on his knees as he ran fingers through his thick copper hair. After a time, he interlaced his fingers and rested his chin on top of them. Caprice moved closer and wrapped an arm around his back, laying her head against his shoulder.

"Do you even want to play anymore, Colt?"

"I don't know. The network offered me a job doing commentary."

"Does that sound like fun to you?"

"No." His thoughts turned to Travis and throwing a football to him and the glow on his face. "I just don't want to go out this way."

"What way?"

"Playing with fear. I actually asked Mitchell to pull me, and I've never done that in my life. I've never been afraid of the game in my entire life."

"Maybe you aren't afraid of the game. Maybe you're afraid of what happens if you quit the game. You said yourself, you think football defines you, but it doesn't." She looked up at him. "It only defines one part of you."

"My father…"

"Was an asshole that never deserved you. You couldn't stand the man. The only thing he ever gave you was a complete set of instructions for what not to do."

"That's not true."

"No?"

"He just wanted it really bad, and someone stole his dream away. If I quit, what if I think Lilly did that to me?"

"Do you miss them? Lilly and the kids?"

Colt thought of Chelsea swirling around in her tutu, trying desperately to keep her toes pointed, and playing video games and football with Travis. Laughing with Lilly when they went to the open-air market one day and watched them famously throw the fish. Chelsea fell asleep with her head on his shoulder.

"Yeah."

"Don't you think you should tell her that?"

"No."

"No?"

"No, I just need to go out on my own terms, that's all. Playing for no one else but myself," he said, wondering if that idea held any possibility anymore.

****

Colt walked out into the open, empty stadium, yet heard the roar of the crowds. Horses whinnied in the distance, and the Warrior looked for their source. When he found nothing, the whinnies came closer, and he looked to the sky. A golden chariot, pulled by golden horses, manes made of fire, charged toward him. As the conveyance landed on the field, the back of the gleaming vehicle sparked with energy. Large, unlit torches secured on either side waited with quiet resolve. Colt expected heat, extreme heat, from the horses' manes but felt nothing. He turned away from the vision, rejecting it, when a scream in the middle of the field jerked his attention. He squinted, to see Lilly,

Travis, and Chelsea in its center, the earth falling away to leave them stranded. The small island they stood on rose above the rest of the field, propelling them upward toward the cloudless, bright blue sky. He could see Lilly struggle to hold on to both the kids so they wouldn't fall.

"Colt!" Chelsea cried. "Colt, help us!"

A dark cloaked figure emerged from the earth behind them, but they couldn't see it. Colt understood with innate fear—this being would kill his family without pause.

"Lilly," he called and pointed behind her, but she couldn't hear him or see it.

The player ran for the chariot, but his father materialized and stood in his way. Colt knew it to be his father, but it didn't look like the man either. The being had black soulless eyes, with no pupil, no iris, and no sclera, just like the day of his injury.

"Move," Colt commanded.

"I will not. You are mortal and weak." The man looked at the trio and the creature approaching them, then turned back to Colt with an evil smile. "You will not prevail."

Insatiable rage and untamed violence erupted from Colton's core as venom rose within him, disintegrating his clothes. Standing naked, he morphed into another being. The muscles of his body enlarged and hardened into a metal suit of armor. As he reached out toward the sun, the sphere turned into a disc that hardened at his side, creating a shield. He screamed out his anger and rage, igniting the torches on the chariot, as a helmet came down over his head, a plume of fire ignited on top of it. Pulling a spear from his body, he cut down the being that looked like his father.

His shield's glossy surface reflected a man with his eyes but more intense. His body muscular but somehow more hardened and chiseled. Strong in a way Colt knew he could never be. The warrior's hair, long and brown and kissed on the tips by the sun, peeked out under the helmet. He stepped onto the chariot, and after a sudden jerk, it and the horses flew. He drove them to the towering island where he sliced through the dark hooded creature, just as it lowered its scythe to cut down the three people he loved most in the world. Gathering them up, he still rode on his rage until the ground secured them once more. As Lilly stepped off the chariot, she turned to Colt and held out a hand. Colt, emerging from the man, looked at the gesture and scoffed.

"Come with me," she said.

"I cannot for my place is here," he replied, gesturing to the chariot and the man.

"Is it?" Lilly asked.

Colt woke to an avalanche of memories flooding through him. When he first picked up a football, winning his first game, his father's approval, playing in high school, his father's disapproval, signing his letter of intent, his mother's death, and playing in college. The day he became a first-round draft pick and playing in his first professional game. The money he spent on faceless women, cars, trips, fighting on the field and off. And a face, an old weathered male face he didn't know, loomed at him from the darkness. He looked at his suitcase packed in the corner waiting for his trip with destiny.

Chapter Thirty-Four

The day of the championship, Lilly spent the morning making rounds and charting on her patients. She'd promised the kids they would watch the game together and eat pizza in the living room while doing so. Over the past week she'd stopped herself a million times from going over to Colt's house to tell him she was wrong to make him choose.

By the time she got home, the kids already in their fan wear, had strung up homemade banners, and took turns doing cheers in the living room with Wyatt. She grinned at the trio for a moment, before calling out to them.

"It's game day!"

The kids, looking like someone had dipped them in glitter, rushed around her screaming. She winced at Wyatt, who just widened his eyes and kissed her on the cheek, grinning. The kids ran off again, and she raised an eyebrow at him.

"You're helping me get every speck of that up," she warned.

"If that makes you feel twitchy, you should see the kitchen," he quipped back.

She rolled her eyes, grinning. "Everything go okay?"

"Yeah, we had a great time, but they are ready."

"Okay. Well, let me go change and I'll be right there."

She walked to her room and stood in front of her closet. Colt's jersey turned toward her in hope, and she withdrew it from the rod. The weight of his jersey clung to her body as she put it on, and for a moment, she almost felt his arms around her. The children called out, and she smiled, running her hands down the numbers—eighty-seven—over her abdomen before going out to join them.

From the moment Colt stepped onto the field, the fans in the stadium and the Morgan living room, cheered as if electrified. Lilly couldn't help but admire him in his uniform. She had to admit, he looked good, healthy, and strong. However, after the first snap of the ball, the familiar tense feeling she experienced whenever he played settled into her gut.

The game would be one of Colt's greatest—his charges controlled, his hits methodical and measured. As he crossed the goal line into the end zone time after time, a look of pure adulation gleamed on his face. He played like his life depended on it.

When he ran the ball in for his third touchdown to end the game, he snapped off his helmet and threw it high into the air, as his teammates swarmed all around him, and confetti rained down from the rafters.

Lilly smiled, looking at the radiant joy on his face, and tears threatened. A well-known female sports reporter came up to him for an interview.

"Colt," she shouted above the noise. "Congratulations, another ring!"

"Yes," he confirmed, chest heaving. "Thanks a lot."

"Your play today was flawless." She looked down at her notepad. "Not only did you beat Shelly for most receiving yards in a single game, you shattered it at two hundred seventy-one. And the three touchdowns, just in case the folks at home missed it. You must be so excited right now."

"I'm just so glad we could bring it home for the fans. It's a great day to be a Warrior!" The crowd's reaction to the amplified statement reached a frenetic level. "My teammates are amazing," he continued, still breathless. "Aulelei with the blocking, Watson's throws, my God, so tight and perfect. He made everything look easy. Offense, defense. Everyone. Just a fantastic effort and I'm so proud of my team."

"It's been a stressful time for you this year, with the trade, losing your father and getting a late injury. Many people weren't sure if you'd make it back this season after that massive hit and concussion against the Cyclones. What would you say to those detractors after being so pivotal in today's success?"

He looked into the camera and into her soul.

"I love you, Lilly. Keep the light on."

****

Lilly sat on a throne of gold. A beautiful peacock with a large feathered diadem sitting upon its head stood at her feet. A bare chested, muscular man approached, kilted only in muslin. Her head jerked and maneuvered, like that of the peacock, as she glanced down at him. Though the man, backlit by the sun, appeared humble, Lilly believed him powerful. Too powerful. She feared if she looked at him too long she would give him everything and be lost forever.

Standing, she descended the steps and turned from

him. A magnificent tail she didn't know she possessed fanned out behind her, blocking his powerful, weighted desire. The man moved to her, but she turned again, denying him an audience.

"My petal," she heard him call, voice seductive and hypnotic, yet still she avoided his gaze. "Lower your barrier, for I will lay the world at your feet."

"I'm a peacock, my king," she said behind her tail. "You must let me fly."

The earth rumbled, and her feathers retracted. Turning into her mortal self, and also clad only in muslin, Lilly looked behind her, but the man disappeared. She turned a slow circle, looking back up at the throne, eyes full of wonder.

Upon it now sat the woman from her earlier dreams, statuesque and regal. Her back ramrod straight and her neck elongated and elegant. Her face beautiful and flawless, she looked down her nose at Lilly with appraisal. Standing, with the golden diadem twinkling in the sunlight, the woman stepped down the stairs with a haughty grace. She stopped mere inches from Lilly, who considered the unworldly eyes.

"Release me," the regal queen said. "For I, too, am a peacock who must learn to fly. I know that now."

Lilly woke with a start at the knock on her front door and looked up from the couch to the wall clock. Two a.m., but she knew who stood on the other side. She glanced down at the small box on the end table and picked it up.

After his statement, her eyes locked on Colt's image, then darted to Wyatt, who grinned at her. He'd left, and after a few hours Lilly settled the kids down into sleep. She paced the house not knowing what to do next, and after a while, lay down on the couch, and fell asleep. The knock sounded again, but with more insistence this time. Heart pounding, she moved to open it.

Colt stood on her front porch holding an armful of colorful lilies, looking like a suitor coming to ask her father for her hand. She looked at the flowers, wondering how he'd found them in the middle of winter, then at him, eyes stinging with tears.

"Colt, I'm so sorry…"

"I'm done."

"What?" Her eyes widened and mouth fell agape with incredulity. "I…"

"It's not because of you," he replied, considering, then laughed. "Well, okay, it's a little because of you, but it's also because of me. Can I come in?"

"Oh," she said forgetting herself and stepped back. "Yes, sorry." He walked in, filling up the small space. "Colt, I shouldn't have asked it of you. I'm just so scared for you, for us."

"I know, and you aren't wrong, but I needed to do this my way or it never would have been any good. I've told Coach Mitchell I'm not coming back. We're going to wait to announce anything to the media for a few days because I don't want to take anything away from the team right now…but I'm done."

A huge lump caught in Lilly's throat, but she managed, "Do the guys all know?"

"Only Tua and Watson, but that's it."

"Colt, are you sure?"

"What?" He laughed. "Am I sure? Now you don't want me to leave?"

"No, I do, but I also saw you tonight. That light…I

don't ever want you to have regrets or hate me."

"I won't have any regrets. I played a hell of a game today."

"Yes," she giggled, "you did."

"You guys watched?"

"Are you kidding? I even had my eyes open part of the time."

He cupped a hand around the back of her neck and drew her to him. "Do you really believe I could ever hate you, idiot?"

Her laugh muffled against his chest. "You're an idiot," she countered.

"So, did you hear what I said at the end?"

"Yes."

Colt placed the flowers on a chair and framed her face with his hands.

"I want you to marry me, Lil. I want you to be my wife, and I want those kids to be *my* kids. Maybe we could even have more, if you want." She grinned. "If I lose my mind, I want you to find it." She laughed and tried to lower her head, but he kept it in place. "Will you do it, Lil? Will you marry me?"

Lilly lifted the box in her hand and gave it to Colt. He looked at her with puzzlement, then opened the lid. Inside lay a thick platinum wedding band, with three small, thin bands underneath. Snapping his gaze to hers, he grinned.

"Wait," she warned. "I took David's ring, and mine, and another one that I picked out for you. I melted them all down together and created these." She gazed into his eyes. "I know it's not fair and weird, but I can't entirely let go of David. I loved him, and he's part of me...and part of the children." Tears shone in her eyes. "I'm hoping you can accept that...Accept all of us, because he's our protector now...yours too. And our life together can't be us forgetting about him."

"Lil..."

"Wait," she implored. "I'm not saying this to dwell on him or say you're a replacement, Colt. I love you...just for you. And I *do* want you to be Travis and Chelsea's dad...completely."

"I get it." He exhaled the breath he didn't know he'd been holding and leaned his forehead to hers. "I can be that man."

Epilogue

Kaua'i, Hawai'i

Several hours passed after the group waved goodbye to Que and Aulelei, as they departed for their honeymoon. The kids also left to go to the north side with Finn's friend Nate and his family, as the couples and Dee sat down for a celebratory drink. A knock resounded on the Taylors' door. Finn moved to open it and on the front porch stood a man he didn't recognize. He wore a tweed jacket with actual patches on the elbows and tan corduroy slacks. Finn looked at the thermostat attached to his house, next to the man's scarred head. It read ninety-two degrees.

"Good afternoon, I'm…"

"Dr. Raymond Butler?" Finn guessed.

"Ah, yes," the old man responded, looking as if he'd just woken up and found himself in an alternate reality.

"Come in." Finn stepped back and took in a deep breath while the man entered. As he closed the door, he murmured, "Here we go."

As Ray stood in the entry looking around at the unfamiliar faces, Finn wondered if he'd turn back around and leave the way he came in.

"Ray!" Dee exclaimed and ran up to give him a

hug. "You made it."

Ray let out a whoosh as the eccentric lady brought him in for a bear hug. He observed the woman in her electric blue and magenta muumuu. Some weird twig stuck out of her floppy hat, pricking him in the ear. As Dee introduced him to everyone, her multitude of shell bracelets clinked together in a cacophony. By the time she got to Wyatt, Ray looked overwhelmed and fearful by the lot of them.

"Anyway, so this here's Ray," Dee informed the group. "And he's a real smarty pants over in California, who specializes in history. Greek history. Here Finn, honey, take his coat."

Finn extended a hand and Ray began the laborious task of removing his jacket. Taking pity on him, Dee helped him and handed it to her grandson. Lilly, Colt, and Wyatt looked around as if a little perplexed at why the odd man was there, but accepted him with grace. Raven excused herself and went to the kitchen.

"So," Wyatt said, "you just over here visiting, Ray?"

"Ah, no. Ms. Taylor"—he looked at her and cleared his throat at the look of supreme irritation in her blueberry-colored eyes—"um, Dee, asked me to attend."

"Oh," sang Wyatt, drawing out the vowel. "So, you two are…together, then?"

"No!" both said in perfect unison.

Finn cleared his throat behind a fist to hide his smile, then looked around the room, at a loss for how to proceed. Raven re-entered carrying the drinks, and he rushed over to help her. Their eyes met, reflecting his discomfort. She handed a cocktail to each person and a lemonade to Ray, knowing from Dee that he didn't drink.

"Aw," Lilly said, "to the Tuas." Everyone clinked glasses.

"And to you guys," Wyatt said, as everyone clinked again. "I can't believe you did that."

"Well," Lilly said, grinning at Colt then looking down at the wedding band encircling his left ring finger. "We decided what the hell. We asked Que and Tua if we could commandeer their wedding day, and they were great about it."

"But why didn't you say anything?" Raven asked.

"We wanted to make it a surprise."

"I had to bribe the kids," Colt said, grinning. "I knew Travis wouldn't say anything but Chels..."

"And we wanted it to be simple; just on the beach, with all you guys there."

"Well, I think it's fantastic," Dee chirped, and rose her glass high in the air again, and everyone followed suit.

In the lull that followed, Lilly noticed Raven look at Finn, who looked at Dee, who looked back at Raven. She eyed them with cool interest before setting her drink down.

"Everything okay, guys?" she asked them.

"Ah, yeah," Finn said.

"You guys gonna say you're pregnant now?" Wyatt asked with suspicion but appearing receptive to such news.

"What? No," Raven answered a little too quickly. She glanced over at Finn, made a decision, and began. "Okay, so, we *do* have something we need to talk to you guys about. Um..."

"Yeah," Finn continued where she left off. "So a while ago, before Rave and I met...We, ah..." A long, silent pause ensued.

"All right," Dee said, commanding the room, as if tired by the whole situation. "The day Raven came onto the island; some weird stuff went down. I have a psychic thing...I don't know what you want to call it, but I knew something was coming. What I'm about to say to you is complete nuts. You aren't going to believe it, not a word, and you'll think we've all lost our minds because it isn't scientific and can't be explained."

"O-kay," Lilly said, elongating the vowels. "You guys are freaking me out."

"We should be," Raven confirmed, "but not because of us. But because...because..." She fell off and looked back at her grandmother-in-law. "Dee, just in front of everyone, again, I'm so sorry. I did *not* appreciate how hard it must have been for you when you told us."

Wyatt watched his sister and appeared to feel her distress.

"Why don't you guys just come out with it. Whatever it is."

"So, the wind started picking up," Dee said, taking up the tale again. "And I looked out to sea and saw this strange spout thing in the water. Those aren't uncommon here but I knew this one was different because it's happened many times before with me when something important was coming. The sun shot down through the center of the spout." She brought her hands down with a dramatic whooshing gesture to emphasize her point, then paused to test their readiness. "I felt...I don't know...called to my room." She looked at Finn, who reached for the chest on the kitchen table, where they'd set it earlier, and place it in front of her. "This old chest has been handed down in my family for generations. No one could open it before...it was completely sealed shut. Okay? And then somehow it just opened."

"How did it get opened?" Lilly asked.

"Well, I'm coming to that."

Lilly looked over at Colt, who eyed her back but remained silent.

"I touched the box," Dee continued, "and a lot of weird shit started to happen."

Finn's gaze darted to Ray, who watched the proceedings with interest. His eyes seemed to scan the room like a laser, watching the reactions of each person involved. The old man's gaze connected with Raven's before he looked away, perhaps feeling guilty at being caught.

"Long story short," Dee continued, "a woman appeared and started talking what I thought was nonsense."

"You had a hallucination?" Lilly asked, sitting forward concerned. "Or a lady actually came to your door?"

"No, she was real and she didn't come to the door. One minute she wasn't there and the next she appeared out of thin air. Now...before you say it, *no,* I didn't dream it. I didn't hit my head, and I didn't imagine it. This ghost like woman was really there."

Wyatt's eyes darted around the room, looking like he waited for the joke that didn't come. His eyes connected with his sister's, then flooded with concern.

"Rave?" he asked. "What is this?"

"I know, Wy. Believe me, I know how it sounds. When Dee first told us about it, we honestly thought she was crazy. But this is real, and we'll try to explain why. The only reason you're here is because we think somewhere down the line, you'll be involved too."

"Involved with what?" Wyatt asked.

"Okay, so this is the part that will sound super crazy," Finn said, picking up the thread of conversation.

"Oh, *this* is where it takes a turn?" Wyatt said, bemused. "Okay, let 'er rip."

"Wyatt," Raven chided. "Please, you aren't helping." He just stared at her and shook his head.

"Dee said this woman talked to her and started talking about a bunch of stuff she didn't understand. The basic gist was the woman...her name is Themis...said Dee was the descendent of Demeter," Finn told the group.

"Demeter?" Lilly queried. "Who's that?"

"Demeter, the Greek goddess of agriculture," Dee challenged.

Utter silence fell over the room. Colt stared at Dee, then Finn, and then Raven, as if now waiting for the joke too. Receiving nothing, he then exchanged covert glances with Lilly, Wyatt, and Ray, as if wondering if he heard them right. When no one said anything, he turned back to the storytellers.

"Um...what?" Colt asked.

"Themis told me I was the descendent of Demeter and that Cronus, Zeus's dad, unleashed a prophecy that began to fulfill itself the moment Raven stepped on the island."

"A prophecy?" Wyatt looked at his twin, dumbfounded, then a laugh rumbled in his chest. "Oh

God, you're fucking with us?"

"No," Raven said, flustered. "After Finn and I started dating, Dee told us all of this and again, we thought she was crazy too. She also told me I descended from Apollo and Finn was—is—the descendent of Poseidon."

Lilly's mouth opened and her brows drew together.

"We didn't believe her," Raven blurted.

"But then after we split up, we both started thinking on our own," Finn continued for his wife. "We both had been having dreams, very bizarre, crazy dreams, that seemed more real than actual life." He looked at Lilly and Colt. "I'd bet everything I have that you guys are having them too." Raven smiled at Finn before turning back to them.

"Maybe...peacocks or a crown. And thrones or jealousy." She looked at Colt. "For you, it might be some kind of battle or warrior and a lot of anger."

Lilly closed her mouth and looked away. Colt looked down, then under his lashes at Lilly. Neither said anything, but both stiffened, giving away the truth of it.

"We also saw some people in our dreams—each other, but also people we'd never seen before. No one that made any sense until later." Finn addressed Wyatt, "Do you remember the night Raven sang on Oahu, and we hooked up again?" Wyatt just nodded. "Well, the next day you, Que, and Abby went home, right? Raven, Dee, and I came here. By this time, we knew something beyond strange was going on, and we both kind of believed Dee. Well, maybe not all the way, but because I knew and trusted my grandmother, I gave her the benefit of the doubt."

"When we walked into the house," Raven picked up the story, "Dee brought in that box." She gestured to it, still sitting on Dee's lap. "When she touched it...I don't know how to describe it but her skin...her body, everything looked like something out of a science fiction film. Like, it went back in time, right before our eyes. Her skin was young, her hair had turned thick and blonde, just gorgeous, and it rounded her eyes and cheeks with, like youth. I swear she looked twenty years old. And I..."

"E-nough," Wyatt said, standing up. "I'm gonna go see what the kids are up to."

"No!" Raven barked. "You'll sit down and shut up, Wy, because you love me, and this is important. Trust me, in a few minutes you won't be able to speak at all."

"I doubt that. I've got a lot to say at the moment."

"Do you see this?" She ran a hand down a faint mark of her décolletage. "This was Mama's medallion, the one you think I lost. Finn and I touched that box at the same time, and it started to melt. It burned me ,Wy, and left Mom's lyre burned onto my skin. *That's* what happened to her necklace."

"I watched it, too," Dee said. "It fell onto the surface here." She pointed to what looked like an arrowhead on the top of the box."

"The box opened by itself," Finn said, looking at Colt. "It scared the absolute shit out of me. Then"—he laughed and shook his head a little—"Apollo kind of materialized. We knew it was Apollo because he was in Raven's dreams. He said nothing but kind of made peace with her or thanked her or something, then just disappeared. After that, my tattoo felt like hellfire." He turned and lifted his shirt to reveal the trident inked onto the surface of his entire back and shoulders. "Poseidon appeared and for some reason *he* could talk to us, but could only answer a few questions."

Finn caught Ray's eye, who watched the proceedings in utter fascination. The historian looked over at Dee, and she smiled back at him before reaching for her notes and taking up the story.

"We weren't prepared for that at all, but sure rallied quick and came up with questions on the fly, such as they were. Finn asked how to find the next people, and Poseidon told us Raven had already met one of them. He also said the next people would be the descendants of Hera and Ares, but we didn't know which one Raven had met. Then he said if we don't do this, don't finish this, the gods will get wiped out and Cronus, Poseidon's father, will unleash these, like, evil plagues on the world. In our real time."

"Poseidon said we had to be careful of these things called Primordials or personifications," Finn said, looking at Ray, who appeared to want to melt into his chair. "One was rage, the other was jealousy, but he called them Lyssa and Phthous. Raven and I think we figured out that they're trying to communicate with us in our dreams."

****

The hairs rose on the back of Colt's neck and Lilly trembled. Raven watched the couple, not without sympathy.

"Just think about it, Lilly," she said, "I know you said you've been feeling off."

Lilly jerked in her chair. "You actually think *I'm* involved with this?"

"Yes, I do," Raven breathed. "In fact, I'm sure of

it. I didn't know how to tell you before because I knew you wouldn't believe me. And we aren't sure if you have to believe it before touching the box. But in case you do, I want to tell you why I think you're the descendent of Hera." She reached her hand out and Dee gave her the pad of paper. "Hera is the goddess of marriage and childbirth," Raven read, then looked up. "First, I didn't know if it was you because you're a heart surgeon, but then I started thinking about it in the abstract. Husband and wife. Marriage. Children. They're matters of the heart, the core of the family. Her sacred objects are peacocks and lilies. Lilies." Raven looked up again. "When they describe Hera, they say she's super jealous because of Zeus's betrayals."

"Zeus was her husband," Finn offered, trying to be helpful, then smiled at his wife with encouragement. "He had a lot of affairs."

"Yeah, and she'd get furious about them and swear revenge. I know this is a stretch, but David died. Some people might look at that as a kind of betrayal. Maybe not a conscious one, but it's possible. You said you've been having weird dreams, and felt jealous, something you'd *never* dealt with before."

"So, what?" Wyatt said with venom. "So, you think Greek gods are reaching a hand into Lilly and making her do shit?"

"We don't know. Hera was all about perfection and being right." Raven looked at Colt. "We didn't understand who Ares would be. I thought I was right about Lilly, but I didn't know who you'd be."

"Me? I'm…what am I?"

"You're the distant grandson of Ares," Finn recited from memory. "Ares, the god of violent war. He was angry, like all the time, pure rage. He had a hard time with his father, Zeus, who never thought his son measured up but used him to do all kinds of shit. Ares' sacred objects are helmets, swords, and shields. His animal was a vulture."

Colt drew in a slight breath and remembered the dream again. Finn saw it.

"Football," Finn stated. "The modern-day gladiators…The Warriors. And uncontrolled rage. It's no secret you have some."

"And what? These two gods got it on, so you think that's why those two are together?" Wyatt retorted, gesturing at Lilly and Colt.

"No. Hera was Ares' mother. Apollo and Poseidon, both men, never had a relationship either. We don't think they paired back then, but we *do* think the pairings mean something. We just don't know what. Aside from Poseidon being Apollo's uncle, the only story that the two were involved in together was building the walls of the city of Troy."

"There's a lot to explain," Dee said, "but I don't think we should say anymore until you see it with your own eyes. Then we won't have to fight you so much." She eyed Wyatt, who had the decency to look uncomfortable under her gaze.

"Okay, but first"—Finn looked back at Lilly and Colt—"on a scale from one to ten, how much do you believe us? We don't know if you have to believe it for it to work or if you've conquered everything you need to and it will open on its own. Are you guys willing to try?"

Lilly looked at Colt, who raised his eyebrows. He turned back to the trio and nodded.

****

"Are we doing this?" Lilly whispered, glancing over at Colt in disbelief.

"Apparently," he whispered back. "But, as soon as this is over, we're outta here, okay?"

"Okay." She gave a nervous titter.

"So, we aren't sure what we're supposed to do," Raven announced to the group. "Before, Finn and I just held each side, and that's what started it all."

"Okay, but before you do that let's get our ducks in a row," Dee said, grabbing her pad of paper again. "So, we're gonna confirm we're right and they're talking to us in our dreams. We'll ask if, somehow, bad stuff's coming through, too, and manipulating the situation. Then we'll try to pinpoint our next couple a little better."

"Yeah, then if you guys can speak or think of anything, and we have time, go for it." Finn looked at everyone. "Okay, Colt and Lilly come over here. Wyatt, I don't think anything's going to happen with you or Dr. Butler, so maybe take notes or just be one more set of eyes and ears.

"Oh, you bet," Wyatt spouted with sarcasm. "We'll be right over here.

Ray sat on the couch next to Wyatt, looking intrigued. Raven and Finn stood on either side of Colt and Lilly, ready to help if needed. They nodded at the couple to grab the handles. First, they looked at each other, then indulged Finn with nervous smiles, before grasping the opposite handles of the chest.

"Holy fuck," Colt said, whipping his hand off the handle.

"What?" Lilly asked, concerned.

He shook his hand and looked at his fingers. The metal of his wedding band had softened, and he flexed his fingers at the heat of it, sucking air through his clenched teeth.

"You have to keep holding on, no matter what."

Colt let out a shaky gasp and held onto the handle again, with his right hand, laying the left one on the top of the chest. Wyatt stood, as did Ray, trying to see what the TE had reacted to. The ring began to melt quickly, and Colt gritted his teeth. The ring pooled on the chest's surface.

"What the hell is that?" Wyatt asked, sounding frightened.

"Wy, *please*, be quiet and just watch, okay," Raven called.

The melted ore formed, pooled, reshaped and moved down the chest, as unseen hands etched the wooden surface, creating a groove next to Raven's. The ore slid over the wood and settled into the groove.

Ray's hands jerked, and Colt noticed the blue veins in his hands scurry away. Ray shook them, as if not believing what he saw. The redhead looked over at Dee. Her appearance was changing, too. Her silver hair turned gold, and her old skin turned youthful once more. Feeling like a pinball machine, Colt's gaze bounced between the couple now, observing their transformation. Ray's hands cleared where only burns and webbing had lain moments before. His face softened and hair saturated in color and health. The burns vanished and his leg felt whole. The older couple eyed each other with awe. Colt looked around at the gob-smacked group and noticed everyone, though less visible, had changed into the best versions of themselves. Lilly cried out, and her free hand shot to her abdomen.

"Lilly?" Colt's entire attention shifted to the woman he loved, and once more almost removed his hand from the chest.

"No," said Finn, as at the same time Raven went to Lilly's side. "Make sure you leave it on. We don't know what'll happen if you take it off now."

Raven pulled up Lilly's shirt to reveal light strobing and tracing its way over the light stretch marks of her stomach, which illuminated from inside.

"Does it hurt?" Raven asked.

"No," the doctor replied. "It just surprised me. It feels like it did when I was pregnant, only even more fluttery." A bead of light pooled and traced the marks over and over, in rapid succession.

Without warning, the chest burst open, and a kind of purring emitted from inside it. Mist poured out, revealing a bright orb with no casing, just a solid ball of energy. The smoky mist soon consolidated, resembling a woman. Smoke thickened around her eyes, creating a blindfold, and her sash and robes billowed in an unseen wind. She raised her arms and spoke in a soft monotone voice.

"And now the quest and second sought; Have redeemed themselves and to the gods have taught." Her head inclined to Colt. "Son of Ares, your ire, your vengeance, your violence you've tamed; Acceptance of self and your gifts you can claim. To the head of Ares, victory was yours to possess; But now opens the Elysium for yours to access. The ore of this object like its owner was hard; His father's acceptance also blackened and charred. They cursed your father with my father's ire; Cronus took him from you, his powers lit the pyre. Selfishness and arrogance, once your only weapon; Until your sanctions of self, lifted, and the garden, you stepped in. Your father may now lay on the heavenly mound; In the Elysium and heart of the Underground."

Colt watched in terrified fascination, as the man of his dream in full gladiator regalia stood before him. His spirit looked spent, and faced ravaged, as the heavy shield and sword fell to the ground with a thunderous clatter. A heavy, soiled hand unstrapped the fire plumed helmet he wore. It followed its companions to the floor with a clang of uncertainty, metal on metal, as the flames extinguished. Only then did the battle warrior looked at Colt with acceptance and gratitude, leaving him to believe it was the first time the man had ever let go of his weapons. The Trojan landed hard on his knees and bowed his head before the metal, bone, sinew, and fibers turned to red talcum dust and blew away.

"Jesus," Colt managed, and felt a knot hard in his throat, for the man accepting his fate, of no more violence.

The sphere clouded and Themis turned to Lilly.

"Daughter of Hera, pain, anger, mortality was yours to behold; For your first man was too ill and too weak to grow old. Others loved, and were happy, each in one another; But you had your pride and self-pity, allowing none to discover. The children who once occupied your womb; Helped break you free from your gloomy tomb. Freeing the first, to draw in the second; indulges the fate of eternity to reckon. Opening your heart and accepting that fate; With the man by your side, brings us all to this place. Goddess Marriage cannot hold on to jealousy or rage; Because she too, desires release from her gilded cage. And now your mother, my queen, may lie on the heavenly mound; In the Elysium and heart of the underground."

The orb pulsed and radiated color until a beautiful and regal woman materialized. A golden diadem encircled her forehead and temples. The teals and blue of her eye color intensified until they turned black. Her skin, first dusky, striated and turned into the soft down of a peacock feather. At each tip an eye blinked back at Lilly. The bird dipped its head in a low bow, and the feathers exploded in every direction out from its body, leaving only one thready feather to remain. Themis returned but more translucent.

"And now we resume to third in our quest; For time shortens on me and this great chest. Darkness in one, desire in another; Darkness calls out from the ruler of the underworld, and second brother. Desire of Aphrodite both in beauty and passion; But also, these two things can reach you through Cronus' interaction. Yes, is the answer to your questions not yet spoken; Do not let revelations of the past leave you broken. Forgiveness lies in another key; for all must be revealed in order to see."

Themis faded, so Dee called out, "Is Aphrodite a woman or a man on this plane, and do we already know them?" The ghostly apparition turned in the old woman's direction.

"Ares and Apollo know *her* well, but Cronus already touches her shell."

"What about Hades?" Ray asked, surprising everyone. Themis turned and gave him a radiant smile.

"Hades will be a great challenge, as he is here; One

foot already in the underworld, his world with no fear. Beware of Nemesis, Oneiroi, Eros, and Thanatos, among others."

"Who's our greatest asset here, someone we can go to for help?" Dee called, panicked as Themis grew nearly invisible.

"He…" The goddess raised a hand and pointed to Ray, before fading away.

"Dee must dream with you, Oracle," Ray called out with the strength, tone, and veracity of a freight train, surprising everyone again.

The chest slammed shut, and power surged into the couple, igniting something within, then light shot down their veins igniting the shield and diadem on the chest. The pearl of light sparkled as it bounced through all the emblems and fired the thunderbolt before ebbing away. The room returned to normal. Dee and Ray cried out as they once more transformed, feeling their age return. The only difference in the room now…Where before there were three believers, now held seven. Lilly just blinked at everyone, in obvious shock. Colt kept opening his mouth, trying to think of something to say, and Finn looked at his grandmother, looking worried.

"Okay," Raven said, breathing out and encompassing the room with her hands. "Well, welcome to our world."

"I-I…" Wyatt stuttered.

"I don't even know what to say," Lilly replied. "How would anyone in their right mind believe *that* was possible?"

"Right?" Raven chuckled. She looked at her twin. "Wy? Ya doin' okay?" He blinked at her, speechless. "Okay," she giggled. "Well, assuming Ares and Apollo are you and me"—Raven gestured to Colt—"who do we know in common, that's an Aphrodite-esq kind of person?"

"Only one I know," Colt said on a laugh half strangled with shock.

"She *does* fit the bill, doesn't she?" Raven confirmed, then looked at the others. "It's got to be Caprice."

"Oh," Finn agreed. "Without a doubt. And what was that business about Cronus touching her? That didn't sound good."

"Yes," Ray said, snapping out of his stupor. "And she confirmed the questions you wanted to ask."

"But which one was the yes to?" Dee queried.

"She said questions. Questions plural, right?" Raven replied. "What were the questions you wanted to ask again, Dee?"

The old woman looked down at her notes, hands shaking with nerves.

"Whether we were right, that they talk to us in our dreams."

"Okay, and she said yes to that. And what was the next one?" Raven said.

"If bad stuff's coming through too and influencing people and situations."

"Well, she said the thing about Cronus doing just that," Finn replied.

"Caprice has some kind of weird stalker thing going on," Raven suggested, remembering. "But there's no way he can make things happen here, right?"

"After witnessing this, I wouldn't rule anything out," Ray said. "Remember, you said you weren't feeling right yourselves." He gestured to Colt and Lilly, then to Raven and Finn. "Did I understand that right?"

"I didn't always know what was going on with me, for sure," Lilly disclosed. "Some of those emotions were so off, they took me by surprise. But I'm not sure I could've controlled whether I'd known about them or not. Maybe."

Colt had an epiphany. "What did she mean about my dad?" The room fell silent. "She made it sounds like something happened to him, or controlled him or something. Did you guys catch that too?"

Ray nodded his head. "I did. We'll need to analyze that more." He reached into his pocket and withdrew a tiny recorder. Looking up, he said, "I'm sorry, I wanted ammunition should Dee come back begging for help, after I told her I wasn't interested in this project." His eyes found the old woman. "I'm sorry."

Dee waved a hand. "It's okay, Doc, I get it all the time."

"Okay," Raven said, "so we think Caprice might be Aphrodite, who do you suppose the guy is?"

"If he has a foot in the Underworld that can't be pleasant," Dee retorted.

"What did the...the..."

"Vapor Chick, is what I call her," Finn supplied.

"Yeah, perfect. What did the Vapor Chick say about us, last time?" Colt asked with curiosity and complete acceptance.

"Not much," Finn answered. "In fact, this time she was almost a gossip."

"Yes, a regular chatty catty," Dee confirmed.

"She just said I knew the next one, or I had already met the next one." Raven looked at Lilly. "And they're right, she answered more this time."

"Well, I'll be damned," Dee exclaimed and pointed down in her book. "You know what, we were so busy trying to figure things out, we never went back to what Themis said." Reading from her notes she took verbatim of that fateful evening, Dee's hand shook with nervous energy. "So, it was Poseidon that said Raven had met the next one. We have until the Immaculate Conjunction. After each god's done, they live in the Elysium and can no longer help." She flipped a page. "Cronus has power to unleash evil on the world, in both time zones."

"She means both worlds," Finn laughed, as he informed the new couples.

"Someone betrayed all of them, and we'll need them to win this thing." She squinted at the page before directing her next question to Ray. "Then there's Lyssa, Phthonus, and Oneiroi?"

"Who are they again?" Lilly asked.

"Lyssa is Rage, and Phthonus is Jealousy."

Lilly sat back in her chair and looked at Colt.

"That's what it is then, right?" Dee asked the group. "They told us those things would be the challenges, right?" She began ticking things off on her hand "Anger, Rage, Jealousy, Envy."

"What's the Oneiroi thing?" Finn asked.

"The Oneiros are dreams," Ray explained. "Kind of like a collective group. They are the offspring of Nyx, which is Night. Their siblings are Doom, Destiny, Death, Sleep, Blame, Pain, Retribution, and Discord, among others."

"Wow, their family game nights must be a helluva a lota fun," Dee quipped.

"How you doing there, brother?" Finn asked,

looking at Wyatt.

"I don't know how to respond to any of this," he said, eyes still a little shell shocked, "So, where do you think I am in all of this?"

"I'm not sure if you are," Raven replied. "Except Apollo and Artemis are twins, just like us. But Artemis was a virgin, so I don't know how she reproduced, unless immaculate conception, or something."

"So, you think I'm a chick?"

"I was a dude," Raven retorted, looking around the room at everyone. "So, now that we know you don't have to believe it..."

"Well, I don't know." Finn stopped her and turned to Lilly and Colt. "Did you guys believe us?"

"I'm not sure I believed it with my whole heart," Lilly admitted, "But I definitely couldn't argue the fact that some of that craziness applied to me. Colt?"

"The dream thing threw me for a loop," Colt said. "The anger, I don't know. I've always been competitive and played with anger or passion or whatever, but if that was this guy, Ares' thing, then who knows." He ran a hand through his hair. "I'm just trying to process what I saw."

"But you're in, right?" Dee asked. "You'll help too?"

Colt kissed the top of Lilly's head, then considered her eyes, "Are we in?" he asked Lilly on a laugh.

She looked back at him with love, then to the group, "Yeah, I guess we're in."

Glossary

Acheron River: The river of pain. The dead come via boat, into the underworld

Achlys: Personification; Misery, Sadness

Aether: Primordial; Upper Air

Anake: Personification; Inevitability, Compulsion, Necessity

Apate: Personification; Deceit

Aphrodite: Olympian goddess Love, Beauty, and Sexuality. Symbols include scalloped shell, mirror, girdle, dolphin, rose, myrtle, dove, sparrow, swan.

Apollo: Olympian god Music, Poetry, Oracles, Archery, Medicine, Sun, and Knowledge. Symbols include lyre, laurel wreath, python, raven, swan, bow and arrows

Ares: Olympian god Physical, Violent, and Untamed War. Symbols include helmet, spear, shield, flaming torch, sword, chariot, dog, boar, vulture.

Artemis: Olympian goddess Hunting, Moon, Forest, and Archery. Symbols include moon, bow, arrows, hunting dog, and stags.

Asphodel Meadows: The place in the underworld that ordinary people or souls go to. Those that are indifferent and didn't commit crimes nor do anything to warrant recognition.

Athena: Olympian goddess Wisdom, and Strategic War. Symbols include olive trees, owls, snakes, Aegis, armor, helmets, and spears.

Atropos: The eldest of the three sisters, known as the Moirai/Fates. She chose the method of death and used her shears to cut their thread and end their life.

Ceberus: The three-headed hound of Hades. Guards the gates of the underworld, to prevent the dead from leaving.

Chaos: The beginning. Birthed Gaia/Earth, Tartarus/Abyss, Eros/Desire, Erebus/Darkness, and Nyx/Night

Chronos: Personification; Time Often, Chronos, Time, and Cronus, Harvest, are used in reciprocity. Though Chronos is older, the two gods often switch places due to their similar names and similar appearance

Clotho: The youngest of the three sisters, known as the Moirai/Fates. She spun the thread of life and decided when one was born.

Cocytus River: The river of wailing in Tartarus

Coeus: Titan god Query, and the northern pillar

Crius: Titan god Heavenly Constellations.

Cronus: Titan god Harvest. The youngest of the Titans. He overthrew his father Uranus by cutting of his genitalia with a sickle and throwing them into the sea. He created the Titans and became ruler of the universe. He was overthrown by his own son and jailed in Tartarus. Symbols included sickle, scythe, grain, snake, and harp.

Cyclopes: A primordial race of giants that had only one eye in the middle of their forehead. The word Cyclops means round-eyed. Cyclopes, plural. Brothers to the Titans.

Demeter: Olympian goddess Agriculture, Fertility, and Harvest. Symbols include cornucopia, wheat, torch, and bread.

Deities: aka Primordials. The first gods and goddesses born from Chaos.

Dionysus: Olympian god Vine, Winemaking, Grape Harvest, Wine, Religious Ecstasy, Ritual Madness, and Theatre. Symbols include grapevine, leopard skin, thyrsus, and big cats.

Eos: Titan; Dawn

Elysium: Level in the underworld where only souls that are especially righteous, demigods, and heroes go to.

Erebus: Personification; Darkness

Erichthonius: King and early ruler of Athens, Greece. Born of Hephaestus and the soil, after he ejaculated on it, but raised by Athena

Erinyes: aka Furies. Three goddesses of crimes against natural order, vengeance

Eris: Personification; Discord and Strife.

Gaia: Primordial; Earth. Born of Chaos. Ancestral mother of all life.

Geras: Personification; Old Age

Great Conjunction: Occurs every eighteen to twenty years. It's the twelve-year orbital period of Jupiter around the sun and thirty-year orbital period of Saturn. Jupiter is associated with Zeus. Saturn is associated with Cronus

Hades: Olympian; Underworld, Dead, and Riches. Symbols include Cerberus, cornucopia, scepter, Cypress, Narcissus, and keys.

Hecatoncheires: Titans; Three giants with one hundred hands and fifty heads. Guard the gates of Tartarus.

Helios: Personification; Sun

Hemera: Personification; Day

Hephaestus: Olympian god Fire, Metalurgy, Stone Masonry, Forges, Sculpture, Artisans, Volcanoes, and Blacksmiths. Symbols include hammer, anvil, tongs, and volcanoes.

Hera: Olympian goddess Marriage, Women, Childbirth, and Family. Symbols include peacock, diadem, lily, cuckoo, scepter, throne, pomegranate, feather, cow, lotus, panther, lion.

Hermes: Olympian Messenger of the gods, god Trade, Travelers, Border Crossing, Guide of the dead souls to the underworld. Symbols include caduceus, Petasos (winged helmet), Talaria (winged sandals), and tortoise

Hestia: Olympian goddess Hearth Fire, Home, and State. Symbols include hearth and fire.

Hunter, Raven: Singer, songwriter, musician, and performer. Love interest of Finn Taylor. Descendant of Apollo

Hunter, Wyatt: Forest Ranger and brother to Raven Hunter

Hyperion: Titan; Heavenly Light

Hypnos: Personification; Sleep. One of the Oneiroi (dreams).

Iapetus: Titan god; Mortality.

Icelos: Personification; Presenter of Images, Beasts, and Serpents. One of the Oneiroi (dreams).

Isle of Blest: Island within the Elysium. If you achieve Elysium status, you could choose to stay in the Elysium or be reborn. If you achieved Elysium status three times, you're sent to the Isle of the Blest, to live in paradise.

Immaculate Conjunction: When the constellations of Cronus and each Olympian are aligned. It is the end. If the modern-day descendants have not completed their quest, or if one of the Olympians is captured, the original prophecy of Cronus will take place.

Jupiter: The fifth planet from the sun and largest in the solar system. Associated with Zeus. Aligns with Saturn for the Great Conjunction.

Lachesis: The middle of the three sisters known as the Moirai/Fates. She measures the thread after it's spun on Clotho's spindle.

Lethe River: The river of forgetfulness. Lethe is also the goddess of forgetfulness and oblivion.

Metis: Titan; Prudence, Wisdom, and Counsel. Impregnated by Zeus and because he feared the child, Athena, would overthrow him, he turned Metis into a fly and swallowed her.

Mnemosyne: Personification; Memory.

Moirai: Fates; The three incarnations of destiny and fate. Sisters, Clotho (spins the threads of light), Atropos (Cut the threads of life), Lachesis (measures the threads of life); Daughters of Nyx (night), they were adopted by Zeus and Themis.

Momus: Personification; Satire and Mockery

Morgan, Lilly: Pediatric cardiothoracic surgeon. Mother of Travis and Chelsea. Love interest of Colt Stone. Descendant of Hera.

Moros: Personification; Impending Doom

Morpheus: Personification; Presenter of human images. One of the Oneiroi (dreams).

Mourning Fields: Area in Underworld where souls who waste their time on unrequited love go

Nemesis: Personification; Retribution

Nike: Personification; Victory

Nyx: Primordial; Night

Oceanus: Titan; Oceans. It is also a river that encircles the world and marks the eastern edge of Tartarus

Oizys: Personification; Misery, Anxiety, and
    Depression.

Olympians: The conquerors of the Titans. Zeus, Hera,
    Poseidon, Demeter, Athena, Apollo, Artemis, Ares,
    Aphrodite, Hephaestus, Hermes, Hestia, and
    Dionysus.

Oneiroi: Dreams and nightmares. Hypnos, Icelos,
    Morpheus, Pasithea, and Phantos.

Oracle: A person or agency providing counsel and
    predictions of the future.

Ourea: Personification; Mountains.

Pandora: The first woman created by Hephaestus and
    Athena upon the direction of Zeus. Each god
    bestowed a unique gift onto the creation. Pandora
    was given to mankind and became the wife of
    Epimetheus. Instructed not to open the jar she came
    with, Pandora ignored the request. She released all
    the evils upon the earth, retaining only hope.

Pasithea: Personification; Presenter of Relaxation,
    Meditation, and Hallucination. One of the Oneiroi
    (dreams).

Phantasos: Personification; Presenter of Fantasy,
    Surrealism, and Apparition. One of the Oneiroi
    (dreams)., dreams.

Philotes: Personification; Affection.

Phlegethon River: The river of fire. It leads into the
    deepest depths of Tartarus.

Phoebe: Titan; Intellect and Prophecy

Poseidon: Olympian; Sea, Earthquakes, Storms, and
    Horses. Symbols include trident, fish, dolphin,
    horse, and bull.

Primordials: The first gods and goddesses.

Prophecy: Messages communicated by a prophet or

spirit to people. It comes in the form of revelations and inspiration. It's an interpretation of divine will of events that may come.

Religious Ecstasy: Expanded inward or internal spiritual and mental awareness. An altered state of consciousness. Usually paired with visions, physical and/or emotional euphoria, and short lived

Rhea: Titan; Female Fertility, Motherhood, and Generations. Wife of Cronus and mother of Zeus.

Ritual Madness: Things that elude human reason and are only attributed to a god's unforeseeable action.

Saturn: The sixth planet from the sun and the second largest in the solar system. Associated with Cronus. Aligns with Jupiter for the Great Conjunction. Aligns with the Olympians' constellations for the Immaculate Conjunction.

Stone, Colton: Tight end for the Seattle Warriors. Love interest of Lily Morgan. Descendant of Ares.

Styx: River in the underworld; The most widely known, centralized, and prominent river of the underworld. It circles the underworld seven times and is known as the river of hatred.

Tartarus: Primordial; Deep Abyss. A dungeon for torture and suffering. The Underworld lies directly above it.

Taylor, Dee: Master gardener and farmer. Grandmother to Finn Taylor. Descendant of Demeter. The prophecy is revealed to her by Themis.

Taylor, Finn: A marine biologist. Grandson of Dee Taylor. Love interest of Raven Hunter. Descendant of Poseidon.

Tethys: Titan; Fresh Water

Thanatos: Personification; Death

Theia: Titan; Brightness and Sight.

Themis: Titan; Divine Law and Order. An Oracle of Delphi. She intercepted Cronus' prophecy before it was complete and introduced several caveats to aid the Olympians.

Titanomachy: A ten-year battle between the Titans and the Olympians. The Olympians were victorious.

Titans: Members of the second generation of divine beings. The descendants of the primordial deities, predecessors of the Olympians. Mount Othrys was their home.

Underworld: The world below Earth, where the departed souls go. Contains Asphodel Meadows, the Elysium, and the Isle of the Blest. It's the afterlife and world of the dead. Tartarus lies beneath it.

Uranus: Primordial; Sky. Born of Gaia. Husband of Gaia. Father of the Titans. Uranus was overthrown by his son Cronus.

Zeus: Olympian; Sky, Thunder, Lightning, Law, Order, and Justice. Ruler of the Olympians. Symbols include thunderbolts, eagles, bulls, and oaks.

A word about the author...

Jeny Heckman is the award-winning author of the Paranormal-Romance series Heaven & Earth. Her debut novel, *The Sea Archer*, published in October 2018, won "Best in Category" at the Chanticleer International Book Awards.

Other works include *Dancing Through Tears*, as part of the Wild Rose Press anthology to benefit victims of the Australian Fires.

In her free time, Jeny likes to travel to the places she writes about, as well as volunteer with several charities, including Hospice.

She lives in the Pacific Northwest with her husband of twenty-eight years.

To learn more about Jeny and her novels, please visit:

www.jenyheckman.com.